The
INTERVIEW

The
INTERVIEW

a novel

KING HURLEY

PAANDAA
ENTERTAINMENT

Boulder, Colorado

THE INTERVIEW by King Hurley

Copyright © 2005 King Hurley

ISBN Number 10: 0-9774188-0-4
ISBN Number 13: 978-0-9774188-0-0

First Edition: December, 2006

Cover and interior design by NZ Graphics, www.nzgraphics.com

Printed in the United States of America

Published by Paandaa Entertainment, Boulder, Colorado

Visit our Web site at: www.paandaa.com

This book is dedicated to those who have love in their hearts.

1

THE CALL

"It was the best of times, it was the worst of times."

Long before my eyes opened, I heard Marvin Gaye singing 'What's Going On?' and knew without looking that the digital numbers on my alarm clock read 5:55 a.m.

I rolled to the edge of the bed and felt the waking mechanisms of another day slowly taking hold. What's going on? I guess not much, Marvin, other than a world going to hell at the hands of terrorists, a continent two thousand miles away dying of AIDS, a sixth of the planet's population in the throes of starvation, and a drug for every ailment known to man except a lack of common sense and a prevailing sense of doom. That, I had to admit, was the cynic in me talking. The other guy – the husband, father, and CEO – switched off the clock radio and turned his attention to more pressing matters. I automatically sought out the other side of the bed. The sheets were still warm from Lauren's exquisite body, but she had already migrated into Hanna's bedroom. This was their routine. Every morning at 5:30, give or take about 60 seconds, Hanna's small voice called out to her mommy, and I would hear Lauren's soft steps patting across the floor and out into the hall. The two would snuggle in Hanna's bed for the next two hours, a bonding ritual that had been going on since Hanna's premature birth five years before.

Some people would call it overindulgence, but they could call it whatever they chose to. Lauren and I didn't care. Hanna was our angel. She had been sent to us from above; that was one of the few things I was absolutely certain of. There was no greater magic in the entire world, and it was the kind of magic we would only experience once. Hanna had come to us late in life. Her mother and I were both 40 at the time. It had been a difficult and dangerous ordeal for Lauren, and her doctor had made it clear that she wouldn't tolerate another pregnancy. He had recommended in the most diplomatic of fashions that Lauren and I take pleasure in the blessings of this one beautiful and healthy baby, and we had accepted the news. This was my family. So when Marvin Gaye asked, 'What's Going On,' I pointed to Lauren and Hanna and gave thanks. Nothing was too good for them.

I got up and trudged into the bathroom. I switched on the light, and my mind automatically began the mental gymnastics of a Chief Executive Officer in charge of a precariously successful pharmaceutical company with yearly sales of 500 million dollars and a pack of demanding stockholders howling for more. Every quarter, I could hear the pack nipping at my heels, and every quarter they seemed a little hungrier.

I spent five minutes under a hot spray in the shower and then washed away whatever cobwebs were left with a 15-second-blast of icy cold water. I carried my towel back into the bedroom. I opened the drapes in time to see the rising sun peak above the horizon, a giant orb blinking away the fog of a long night's sleep. The eastern sky drank in the pinks and purples of a new day, and I let myself enjoy it for as long as it took to dry off.

I dressed with the expectations of the corporate business world in mind, not personal fashion: a gray Armani suit, blue shirt, and a tie with a splash of red in honor of the fading colors of another spectacular Rocky Mountain autumn. I had a full day on my calendar, but I didn't dare look beyond the quarterly analyst call that was scheduled for 10:00.

I knew there was a world out there where exceeding the expectations of stockholders was not a perpetual fact of life. They called that world the private sector, and, on days like today, it seemed like the pot of gold at the end of the rainbow. As I was tying the laces of my Cole Hahn shoes, I spent a fleeting moment wondering how I would react if the right offer came my way; maybe I could avoid another quarterly call altogether. Fat chance.

I stopped in front of the full-length mirror next to Lauren's dresser and straightened my tie. I had to admit that I wasn't unhappy with the reflection staring back at me. Twenty-three years after my last college football game, I still carried the same 202 pounds I had played with back then, and there was still a leanness to my face. This probably had as much to do with my addiction to long distance running as it did to the high protein diet that Lauren had discovered after Hanna was born. There was a sprinkling of gray showing around the temples of my sandy hair, but Lauren called it distinguished. I thought I was too damn young to look distinguished, thank you very much. However, if the years had taken a toll, it was in the eyes. Lauren likened them to the gray-blue of the sky after a hard rain. This morning, they just looked hard.

As I was about to leave the house, I stopped at Hanna's bedroom door and peeked into her room. Mother and daughter were curled up together on Hanna's bed, and there was a peacefulness about them that went straight to my heart. This was what made the headaches of a quarterly call and the inevitable assault of the short sellers worthwhile. I would have marched straight into a burning building for those two.

God, keep them well, I thought. I'd be lost without them.

I climbed behind the wheel of my Porsche Cayenne, an extravagance I had rationalized a dozen different ways, and headed for the office. The one undeniable pleasure on my morning agenda was a stop at the Starbucks on the corner of Clayton and Prince. I called it caffeine therapy. Starbucks called it the subliminal indoctrination of millions and millions of needy souls in the precise art of speaking the Starbucks' vernacular. Given the number of people awaiting their enlightened buzz at 6:40 in the morning, I figured Starbucks was well on their way to ruling the entire world. Well, there were worse ways to rule, I imagined.

You could tell I was a well-trained convert, because they already had my daily dose up and waiting when I walked in.

"A grande non-fat two-Equal latte," the girl behind the counter said with an enticing smile. She was 18 or 19 given the curves of her body, and every day I glanced down at the star tattoo on the back of her hand. Every day I gave her $4.00 for a $3.25 drink, a small price to pay for a great attitude and welcome jolt.

The corporate offices of Peak Pharmaceuticals were located in an office park off Highway 36. Stands of silver maples, pockets of quaking aspen, and rows of slender junipers surrounded the cream-colored four-story building on three sides. Gardens long past their summer prime curled along perfectly among manicured islands of bluegrass. A fountain out front would grace the entrance until the first snow; then, like everything else, it would sit dormant until the spring thaw.

Peak had a stretch of private parking, and I pulled into the public space next to the one reserved for Michael King, CEO. I didn't believe in the concept of assigned parking for upper management, but Peak's 'esteemed' Chairman of the Board, George Branden, thought otherwise. He called it a statement of power and presence, a way of letting the troops know who was in charge. I called it petty and self-serving and a great way to alienate the people I was trying to motivate. I may have been the company's CEO, but I didn't think about the title as I carried my briefcase into the lobby and hailed the private elevator accessing the fourth floor. Instead, I thought about the responsibilities the title brought with it and the authority. I tried to keep the two separated. The authority was a function of the responsibilities, nothing more. Leadership was about getting the best out of people, and you didn't get the best out of people by standing over them with a gun in your hand or a pink slip tucked in your shirt pocket.

The elevator doors opened onto our corporate suite. It was 6:59. I walked past the reception desk and into the conference room. Walter Dyer, Peak's VP of Investor Relations, and Carly Perisi, our irrepressible Director of Public Relations, were staring at a bank of computers and sorting through a neat stack of freshly printed quarterly reviews.

"Good morning," I said.

"So you say," Walter snarled. The room smelled of stale coffee and nervous tension, the latter mostly a product of Walter's unwavering intensity. Walter's eyes were shot with blood and the lines etching his 50-year-old face were stretched thin. His shirt had the wear-and-tear appearance of an all-night session spent revising, rewriting, and tightening today's formal presentation. Carly, a 33-year-old career woman with a Harvard MBA and more notches on her belt than most men her age, looked as if she had just spent a refreshing hour with an entourage of hairstylists, make-up artists, and a personal tailor – impeccable despite 24 straight hours at Walter's side.

"What's his problem?" I said to Carly with a wink and smile. "Sleep deprivation?"

"He's just a man who loves his job," she replied. "I can't keep up with him."

"None of us can. I quit trying."

"Easy for a man with a Starbucks non-fat latte in his hands to say," Walter said. He turned a glazed eye in the direction of the office coffeemaker, a drip machine with a long and sordid history. "We ever going to replace that thing with something from this century?"

"And part with a soon-to-be-invaluable piece of antiquity? Not on your life." I peeked at the computer screen. "How are we doing?"

"I'm happy," Carly said. "He's not."

It sounded like an easy job converting black and white data into an enticing sound bite that would have stockholders and traders falling all over themselves to get in our good graces, but it wasn't. Much like life itself, the trick was moderation, finding the balance, and using exactly the right number of words. Felix Kildare, my mentor from years gone by, used to say, "Never use five words when three will do."

I set aside the jocularity. "What's the problem, Walter? Too much hype or not enough?" I asked.

"We come across looking like the Stepford Wives of the drug industry, that's what. Everyone and their short-selling brother just know there has to be a flaw, and the Shorts are not about to stop looking until they find it. Even if they have to make something up."

Ironically, his analogy had an eschewed sort of logic to it. We were on the verge of celebrating 20 consecutive quarters with 20% or more bottom line growth. Impressive, right? I know I felt pretty good about it. It may not have been lights-out impressive by some people's standards, but it wasn't half bad in this post dot.com era. You would think the 'street' would be astute enough to spot a healthy company when they saw one coming. But it was the flaws Walter mentioned that shook the branches of these trees. A show of weakness was like the first blemish on a pretty woman's face; it was bound to get worse before it got better. Market analysts knew you couldn't go wrong with that kind of defensive posturing, and it was exactly that kind of thinking that got the 'Shorts' all pumped up. A show of weakness carried with it the scent of blood. I liked to think of it as a starving grizzly stumbling upon the likes of Bambi; let the carnage begin.

"It's a what-have-you-done-for-me-lately world out there, my friends," Walter said, stirring three sugars into a cup of coffee. "And it doesn't matter a hoot how sexy you looked the night before."

"I resent that," Carly said, as she deleted one sentence from the conclusion and replaced it with another.

Walter was right. Past performance didn't account for much with analysts looking into the future and betting their reputations on what was going to happen in an hour, or a day, or six months down the road. The analysts had expectations, but simply meeting those expectations wasn't worthy of applause or approbation. Exceeding expectations by exactly the right amount was the way to the analyst's heart – not too high and certainly not too low.

"They don't call them analysts for nothing, you know," Walter said, glancing at Carly's final edits and nodding his head.

"Uh-oh. Here it comes," Carly said. "I can't bear to listen."

"You know what they say. Disappoint the analysts, and they give it to you right where it all begins..."

"In the 'anal' canal," Carly said, smothering the words in well-deserved sarcasm. "If I only had your wit, Darlin'."

"If you had my wit, young lady, you'd have a weekly spot on the Comedy Channel."

I was looking over Carly's shoulder. I squeezed her arm. "Good work."

"We'll have it on the wire at 9:30 Eastern, Michael," she said. "Sharp."

At 9:50 Eastern, Steve Foley, our CFO and a man of little imagination, joined us in the conference room. Steve was the most boring man I knew. Like Otto Dreyfus, our head of Marketing, he was a holdover from Peak's previous management group. Unlike Otto, Steve pulled his weight. He had exactly one interest in life: numbers. Or, more accurately, the right numbers. This made him, if not a great friend or a kindred spirit, the perfect CFO. In all honesty, I knew deep down that I wouldn't miss Steve if I ever parted ways with Peak, but I would miss his dogged pursuit of stone-cold accuracy.

We had nearly 40 people on the line by 10:00, from traders and investors to business reporters and SEC lawyers. The quarterly call was typical of every quarterly call I could remember since joining Peak. The financial review and the PR presentation went off without a hitch simply because we controlled the rhetoric. Easy. The Q&A, on the other hand, was part dogfight, part bloodbath. Five years ago, I might have enjoyed sparring with the traders and placating the long-term crowd. Today, I was just glad to have it over and done with. I knew I would be hearing from George Branden, our Chairman of the Board, before the end of the day. I tried telling myself I would be disappointed if he didn't call and knew my rationale was more hype than truth. George would spend a half hour calling it another vanilla quarter, and I would spend a half hour defending it.

To my team, I said, "Thanks for another record-breaking quarter, gang. You did an outstanding job, every one of you. And I mean it. Congratulations. To all of us."

I spent only a certain amount of my time watching the market following the quarterly call, because there was a sense that I had lived this scene before and knew every line by heart.

I used the next hour to initiate a conference call with Pfizer's VP of Product Development and Harley Kilinger, our top research guy, and then sat back and listened to an update on the arthritis med we were researching together. We were in the first year of a three-year trial process, and my job was to keep the wheels greased, the financing in place, and the leaks to a minimum.

At 11:30, our stock price showed a nice point and three quarter bump from $52.00 to $53.75, and I resisted crossing my fingers. A voice in my head said, "Try keeping it professional, will you, Michael? CEOs don't cross their fingers." I wasn't so sure.

By 1:00, the price had trended down to $53.50, and I was willing to hope it would hold there until the market closed at 3:00. Walter Dyer stuck his head in the office five minutes later and gave me a thumb's down. "The 'Shorts' are on the hunt. They're trying to scare up some downside play by feeding the institutions a decline in scripts for one of our legacy products."

"The institutions aren't going to bite on a small decline in the number of prescriptions written for an old product we don't even promote anymore and that barely registers on our P&L statement," I argued.

"No way," Walter said with a twisted grin that told me how naïve he thought I was. "Those institution guys are a lot sharper than that."

Here I was hoping the market would focus on our hard work and a promising R&D pipeline. I was dreaming, of course. By 2:30, the ticker tape was showing Peak Pharmaceuticals down a half point from its opening price to $51.50. A half hour later, the stock closed at $51.00 even, a price drop that made no sense in light of a 20% quarterly rise to the company's bottom line. Thank you all for the kudos!

Walter peeked into my office for the second time that afternoon. This time he had his overcoat on and his tie off. "I'm going to get drunk," he announced. "Try and make some sense out of a little single malt Scotch."

"Better that than trying to make sense of corporate America."

"My thought exactly. See you on Monday."

To hell with the market, I thought. Let's get back to running a company. And that was exactly what I did. I countered frustration with aggression and flurries of what I considered to be positive acts. In this case, I placed five phone calls to our offices in San Diego, Austin, New York, Des Moines, and Chicago, sat in on follow-up meetings with Steve Foley in Finance and Carly Perisi in PR – hard to believe she could still look as good as she did at this time in the day – and arranged a brainstorming session with our in-house Sales and Marketing department. When these people worked their asses off all quarter only to see their company stock drop as a result, it was my job to prop them up again. Unfortunately, there was no one in the organization that could help prop up yours truly, and after five years of fighting the battle in the public market, I was mentally and physically exhausted.

∾

2

THE OFFER

"Rejoice! Rejoice! You have no other choice."

I pulled into the garage at home at 7:10, just slightly more wasted than usual. I glanced at myself in the rearview mirror and winced. "You look like shit," I said. Well, I don't know what I expected. Despite rumors to the contrary, the life of a CEO slugging it out in the public arena was neither glamorous nor fun, but you could count on it aging the hell out of you.

The reward was waiting for me at the door. She was 5-years-old, spectacularly beautiful, and still young enough to think I was pretty cool.

"Daddy!" She jumped, and I caught her. She wrapped her arms around my neck and squeezed.

"I've been needing a hug all day," I said: a true statement. Lauren joined us. "Two hugs actually."

"Long day?" She smelled terrific.

"You smell good." I ran my hand down her back.

"A compliment first thing out of the box," she said with a hint of flirtation. "Must be Friday night. Can I get you a glass of wine?"

We started toward the kitchen. Hanna was now on my shoulders. "You pour, and I'll cook," I said.

Friday was barbeque night. It was also the only night of the week my alcohol consumption ever exceeded a glass of wine or a cold beer, and tonight the chilled Australian Chardonnay I had discovered a month or so

back tasted particularly good. I carried the wine out onto the back deck –
with Hanna not far behind – and soaked in a last glimpse of the Flat Irons,
monolithic slabs of granite that formed a gauntlet along the Boulder
foothills. Then I fired up the grill and arranged two salmon steaks and a
dozen jumbo shrimp above the fire.

I heard footsteps, and Lauren was suddenly behind me. I felt her arms
drawing me near and absorbed the warmth of her body against my back.

"So, you didn't answer my question," she said. "Long day?"

"The 'Shorts' took a bite out of us, but we'll survive. And besides, it's
the weekend, and I'm home now." I turned, a spatula in one hand and a
wine glass in the other, and kissed her. "How was your day?"

"We went to the pool. You should see that daughter of yours swim.
She's a natural."

"Hey, there's a few athletic genes roaming around in that little thing,"
I reminded her.

"Well, now that you mention it," she whispered, "Want to get athletic
later tonight?"

"Damn right," I said.

We held each other until it was time to turn the shrimp. The scent
filled my nose and triggered a sensation that only food cooking over an
open fire can elicit. For a brief moment, I had this image in my head of
prehistoric man enjoying the same sensation, but the image evaporated
when the phone in the kitchen rang.

"I'll get it," Hanna shouted.

"Not if I get it first," her mom said, and the race was on. Thirty seconds
later, Lauren reappeared with the receiver in her hand. "It's George
Branden," she said, as if using the Chairman's whole name might make a
Friday night call a little easier to swallow.

I traded her the spatula for the phone and carried it over to the table
and chairs on the other side of the deck. I didn't sit. "George. How are
you?"

George wasn't the type to apologize for calling on a Friday night during the dinner hour. "I watched our stock price hit the skids this afternoon, so I guess I'm not as good as I could be," he said. "The Board is disappointed. We have to do something about it."

Translated: I want you to grow my wealth, Mr. CEO, not drag it through the dirt. How the hell else am I suppose to buy a bigger house and a faster boat and attach my name to another country club?

"We had a great quarter, Michael, but we're not getting the message out," he said.

"Apparently not," I said in an even voice.

"Let's do this," he said. "Let's plan on a little rendezvous at my Phoenix place on Monday. I'll send the company plane for you. Say 8:00 your time. We'll do a little brainstorming on how we can get some excitement behind our message and maybe give our stock price a boot in the ass."

A 20% increase in profits over a stretch of 20 quarters is pretty damn exciting if you ask me, I wanted to say. But, of course, I didn't. I said, "I look forward to it, George. I'll see you on Monday. Have a good weekend."

I was already pouring a second glass of White Tail by the time I hung up, and Lauren had the shrimp and salmon on a platter. My first thought was dinner on the deck, but Hanna talked us into watching *Shrek II* while we ate. Around our house, a heartfelt "Please, Daddy, please," will get you just about anything you want, and my daughter knew it by this time in her short life. We set up TV trays in front of the 60" plasma screen that nearly cost me a hernia trying to hoist it onto the wall mount.

When the shrimp and salmon had been consumed, Hanna curled up on my lap, and we settled in for what was probably the tenth or twelfth showing of her current favorite movie. What more could a dad ask for? The warmth of her little body, the innocence of her laughter, and love as yet untarnished by time or circumstance. I asked myself how it was that those feelings were so easily lost once the pains of adulthood reared their head and why it was so difficult to reclaim them. The real world had a cruel element to it, and the business world was unnecessarily ruthless.

People paid homage to titles and positions in an unholy way, and then took pleasure in seeing the holders of those titles crash and burn.

I pushed the thought aside and concentrated on the tiny hand resting in mine. Nothing else mattered. I might crash and burn out there in the real world, but I could always come home to this.

The phone rang a second time, just as Shrek and Donkey were drinking their magic potion and transforming into a handsome knight and a magnificent stallion. "Watch, Daddy. Watch!" Hanna cried with joy.

I was nearly as excited as she was when I saw Lauren appear at the family room door. She mouthed the word, "Phone" and then said, "Karin Baxter? Do you want it?"

Karin Baxter was the Managing Director of Executive Recruitment at Spencer Stuart, headhunters extraordinaire. Karin was the cream of the Spencer crop, and one of the two or three top recruiters in the drug and healthcare industry. We had known each other for a dozen years. Karin had been responsible for placing me at the helm of the Navarro Institute in the early 90s – my first shot at running a major player in the drug industry – and then again with my current gig at Peak five years later. On the other hand, it was 9:00 on a Friday night. What the hell?

I settled Hanna onto the couch and kissed her forehead. "I'll be right back, baby," I said. "Sorry," I said to Lauren. I took the phone and covered the mouthpiece. "But I think I'll see what this is about."

"I'm curious, too," Lauren said.

I put the phone to my ear. "Karin. How are you?"

"Sorry to call so late, Michael, but since I have no life at all, I thought I'd ruin your Friday night, too."

I laughed. If only George Branden had a fraction of Karin's people skills. "We were watching Shrek," I said. "High drama."

In truth, executive recruiters were generally a heartless breed who viewed both their client and the prospect they were pursuing the way a good butcher looked at a piece of meat: both were assets to be maximized as quickly as possible. The prospect's success or failure and the client's degree of happiness were far down the list from simply filling the requirements of the search and getting paid.

"Congratulations on a terrific quarter," she said. "Peak is on a roll."

"You heard. Thanks," I replied. I wanted to say, 'Why so nice, Karin,' but I already knew why. She had a position to fill, and I was the target.

"You know I wouldn't be calling if I didn't have something," she said.

Ah, finally. To business, I thought. "I've got a job, Karin."

"Not this job. Wanna hear?" She didn't wait for an answer. "You've heard of Panda Pharmaceuticals."

"Let me think? Panda who?" It was a joke, but it didn't come off very well because I was holding the phone so tight. Asking someone in the drug business if they had heard of Panda Pharmaceuticals was like asking someone in the computer business if they knew who Dell was. Except there was a difference: Panda was a private company. Private and hugely successful. Conservative reports estimated last year's sales at three billion at least, though no one knew for certain. "And?"

"And they have an opening."

"An opening," I said with a trace of sarcasm. Then I added, "Karin, it's Friday night. Make your pitch."

"Their President and Chief Executive Officer is one Philip Chatzwirth. He's been at the helm since co-founding the company 39 years ago. He's also their Chairman of the Board. You probably know that. The guy's 73-years-old. Evidently, he's made enough money to buy his own Caribbean island, so he's calling it quits."

"Poor guy."

"Life's a bitch, isn't it?" she deadpanned. "Chatzwirth is staying on as Board Chair and heading up the search for his replacement as President and CEO. And guess what? Panda wants you."

"How many candidates are there?" I said only because it was the first thing to pop in my head.

"Candidates? One. You. You're their candidate. Wanna hear their offer? You sitting down?" Karin was rolling. "Base salary, $5 million a year.

Against the puny $750,000 you're making now." That was another reason to despise the public sector; there were no secrets. She said, "A signing bonus of $5 mil, and $100 million guaranteed over 20 years."

"A job like that will kill me in 20 years," I said lightly.

"You'll have your own private jet. You'll have a $3 million dollar housing allowance. They'll make it $5 mil if you insist," Karin informed me. "And best of all, Michael, no more quarterly calls to the SEC and a bunch of shiftless traders."

"Good point."

I glanced back into the family room as Karin was reciting these almost unbelievable numbers – Hanna and her mother were laughing at one of Shrek's many antics – thinking how secure a job like that would make us. Our worries would be over. At that moment, Lauren looked my way and smiled. "Love you," she mouthed.

"Here's the catch," I heard Karin say.

"I was waiting for that."

"Panda wants you to fly down to their campus in Virginia next week. They want you to meet with their Board of Directors. Press some flesh. Get acquainted. Make an impression," she said. And then, with finality, "They want you for this job, Michael. It's the chance of a lifetime. Take it."

Only a fool could listen to an offer like that and not feel a rush of excitement. And a bigger man than me might have been able to keep his ego in total and complete check, but I had to admit that mine was swelling just a little. 'They want you. You're their only candidate.' No more Shorts, no more quarterly calls, no more bad dreams about spending the rest of my life behind bars because of some accounting error. Who wouldn't be excited? On the other hand, making Karin Baxter privy to my excitement was not in my best interest at the moment.

I said, "It's an honor to be considered, Karin. And I appreciate you calling me with the offer. I'll talk it over with Lauren tonight and give you a call tomorrow if that's convenient. We can get into the details."

"That works for me. Call me on my cell. You've got the number. Say ten o'clock."

"Ten o'clock."

"Jump on this one, Michael. You can't do better than Panda."

I waited until Hanna was asleep and Lauren and I were both propped up in bed before I got into the details of Karin's call. Lauren was as overwhelmed as I was.

"It's an amazing offer, Michael. I have to agree with Karin about that. What do you know about Panda Pharmaceuticals?"

"Three billion in sales last year. Probably a lot more no one ever hears about. Very private. They're obsessive about it, the way I understand it."

"Private means no more stockholders breathing down your neck. Think about it," Lauren said with a warm smile. She knew the pain and agony that went into managing the hopes and dreams of stockholders expecting the world out of their company. She knew, because I brought it home with me every night. "Virginia would be a huge change for us. Would I get a chance to visit?"

"We're not moving somewhere you're not comfortable with, Lauren. I don't care how good the offer is."

"You should go out there. Talk to them. See what you think," she said curling up next to me. "You've earned it."

I woke up Saturday morning with an air of expectation, but it wasn't Karin Baxter's offer that surfaced first; it was the smell and taste of Lauren's skin and the memory of her legs wrapped around me the night before that made me want to stay right where I was all morning. Instead, I kissed her cheek and rolled out of bed. I threw on my running gear. I plugged in the coffee and was outside just as the sun was cresting above the eastern horizon, a glitter of purple and pink tossed across a scrim of gray.

I crossed through the parkway east of the house and into a stretch of ponderosa pine and quaking aspen at the foot of the Flat Irons. A cool breeze brought the leaves alive. A chorus of robins and wrens filled the air with lively chatter. I had to ask myself if there was a better way to start the weekend and couldn't imagine what it might be.

The climb took me within shouting distance of the Flat Irons. Then I reversed my course and started back down. Shortening my stride and feeling the pressure ease in my chest, I turned my thoughts to the rather extraordinary conversation I'd had last night with Karin Baxter. I was a man of instinct. I trusted the gut feeling that every decision of impact seemed to arouse. Then, because trust in the business world seemed like the quintessential oxymoron, I would retreat into a place where balance ruled, a place of pros and cons, of pluses and minuses. There was so much right about this opportunity that I was overcome with the urge to exploit the downside. On the surface, it was a homerun, a no-brainer, a slam-dunk. That's what concerned me. It was too good to be true.

I went for the obvious. I would be uprooting my family from a place we had called home for nearly five years. I knew nothing about Virginia. Well, I knew that Thomas Jefferson had built his Monticello estate there two hundred years ago, but whether that was a sufficient endorsement for 21st century Virginia I wasn't sure. I knew nothing about the people or the culture or the lifestyle. What about the school system? What about friends and family? What about taking over a company five times as large as the one I was now running? I didn't really dig too deeply for the answers. I had moved before. Things worked out. People adjusted. We would find the right school. We would cultivate new friends and make damn sure we stayed in touch with old friends. I knew Panda Pharmaceuticals was huge compared to Peak, but size wasn't an issue. I knew the drug industry inside and out. I knew that running a successful business meant surrounding myself with good people, smart people, dedicated people. I also knew that if I didn't like what I saw when I went out to Virginia, I had the strength to pass on a $5 million dollar salary, a private plane, and a housing allowance that would make every executive I knew green with envy. Like I said: too good to be true.

I walked into the house drenched in sweat. I poured a cup of coffee, walked straight into my office, and called Karin Baxter.

I thought she sounded far too chipper for a woman working the weekend until I calculated her potential paycheck were this deal to go through. Then it occurred to me that anything less than chipper would be inappropriate.

"You're five minutes early. I take that as a good sign," she said. "Not that I'm surprised. A lack of smarts was never your shortcoming."

"Why don't you e-mail the Executive Profile to my home computer," I said. "I'll read it over this morning. I've got to be in Phoenix all day Monday, but the rest of the week looks like a possibility."

"I'll make the arrangements for Wednesday," she said. "I'll have Panda's private jet at Front Range airport at 8:00. You'll be sitting down with the Board by lunchtime."

"Wednesday," I said to Lauren after I hung up. "You sure you're ready for this?"

Lauren shrugged. "It's never easy changing jobs or packing up and moving to a strange place," she said, "but I'd be going if it were me."

3

THE BOARD

"To know one's self, one should assert one's self."

Panda Pharmaceuticals' twelve-seat Gulfstream made Peak's eight-seat Pilatus look like a throwback to the days of bi-planes and crop dusters.

The plane was forty-two minutes early. I knew this, because I was parking my car in the reserved parking garage at Front Range Airport south of Boulder at 7:18, and the Gulfstream was taxiing to a halt. This was my first executive test: if Panda's company plane wasn't fueled and ready for take-off a good twenty minutes before the scheduled arrival of its passengers, then I saw it as a direct reflection of the company's attention to details, or lack thereof. Call it petty or overly critical, but I was not going out to Virginia simply to put on a dog-and-pony show for my prospective employers. Panda was going to have to pass muster with me, as well, and they had done so this morning. Chalk up one for Michael King's suitors, I thought.

I made two phone calls from my car before heading for the terminal. The Gulfstream's co-pilot was waiting for me when I walked through the door. "Mr. King, Sir. I'm Dave Ridder." He extended his hand. "I'll be flying the right seat for your trip back east. Can I take your briefcase?"

"No, thanks."

"We'll be in the air by 8:00," he said as we walked onto the tarmac. "There's coffee and breakfast on board."

"Any other passengers?"

He looked surprised. "No Sir, Mr. King. Just me, your pilot, Captain Jeff Wize, and Karrie Lyn, your attendant."

Like Dave Ridder, the Gulfstream's pilot was clearly cut from a military mold, from the crease in his black pants to the pressure of his handshake. His shoes were spit-polished to a high gloss. His tie was narrow, uninspiring, and perfectly knotted. The Panda RX pin on his powder blue shirt glistened.

"How are you, Mr. King?" Captain Wize asked. He watched me with studious eyes.

"I'm well, Captain. How about you?"

"Excellent, Sir."

"Early morning for you guys," I said, knowing every person I came in contact with today would be expected to provide feedback to the interview committee. Did he make eye contact? How was his handshake? Did he make a pass at the attendant? Fine, I thought. Get your feedback. What you see is what you get. "What's our flight time?"

"Two hours and five minutes, Sir. I'll try and shave a couple of minutes, get you on the ground before noon." He led me up the steps to the cabin. "Let me introduce you to Karrie Lyn. She'll be taking care of you today."

I climbed aboard. The interior looked like an advertisement for the Fine Living Channel, all plush leathers and polished chrome. It smelled like a virgin Rolls Royce. Karrie Lyn was a Heidi Klum knockoff with a southern twang. She wore a sleeveless jumpsuit that turned every curve of her body into an adventure. Her skin was the color of winter wheat and the scent she wore was a subtle hint of lavender. She relieved me of my suit coat and said, "Welcome aboard, Mr. King." I'd seen that smile before: it was part invitation, part character test. It said, "We have two hours to kill, and we can spend it any way you want to."

Climbing the executive ladder had its advantages. I knew a dozen CEOs who would take Karrie Lyn up on her offer and chalk it up to the perks of their position. I had two problems with that: first, I'd have to step off this plane in Virginia and face Panda's Board of Directors knowing that they knew; second, I'd have to step off this plane when I got back home knowing that I knew.

I had been married to Lauren for 12 years. I had spent nearly as many years before meeting her trying to set a record for short-term relationships built upon a foundation of sex, alcohol, and indifference. I had since discovered a far more fulfilling foundation based upon love and mutual respect, and Lauren was the source of that discovery. That was not to say that I couldn't appreciate Karrie Lyn's jumpsuit or the lavender scent she wore; I could and did. But I was a one-woman man now and would be for as long as Lauren would have me.

I loosened my tie and fell into a seat that put first class flying to shame. Karrie Lyn offered me coffee once we were airborne, and I accepted. "Skim milk and two Equals, isn't that right?"

"I won't ask you how you knew," I said.

"Just a good guess," she said with that smile again. She held up a DVD. "The Board would like to welcome you. Would you mind?"

"I'm looking forward to it."

I opened my briefcase as Karrie Lyn cued up the DVD. I extracted my personal journal and found the notes I had been keeping over the past three days. Page one listed the three key points I wanted to emphasize during the course of my interviews: Michael King's personal take on leadership, motivation, and long-term strategic planning. First, a man didn't lead by putting himself on a pedestal; I believed that wholeheartedly. Second, he didn't motivate by putting the fear of God in the hearts and minds of his team, though a good butt-kicking was an occupational hazard that was inevitable from time to time. And third, without a viable long-term strategy, there could be no short-term goals with any meat on them.

Page two listed seven questions that the Panda hierarchy would have to answer to my satisfaction before any kind of a deal was struck. All seven dealt with commitment, freedom, and trust. Public companies invariably hedged on all three; if a private company like Panda came with the same baggage, I'd have to find out how much the baggage weighed.

I wasn't kidding myself though. I was in for a very long afternoon and evening. When Karin Baxter shared the profiles of the five men and one woman who comprised Panda Pharmaceuticals' Board, I was duly impressed. These were people with sufficient brain matter, business acumen, and political clout to know what they wanted and how to go about getting it.

I traded my journal for the profile sheet. Ten seconds later, Karrie Lyn dimmed the cabin lights, and the introductory DVD filled the screen. I listened with one ear to the history surrounding Panda Pharmaceuticals' remarkable emergence as one of the world's leading drug companies while reacquainting myself with my hosts of the day.

The company's co-founder and Chairman of the Board, Philip Chatzwirth, was a lean, wiry man with inquisitive eyes and hawkish features. Chatzwirth had been the company's one and only CEO and President. He had earned a Ph.D. in Chemistry from Washington University in St. Louis before taking Oxford by storm. I heard the voice on the DVD say that Panda had evolved from a two-man firm established in the mid-1960s into the behemoth it now was thanks to the "hard work and dedication of its founders." What the DVD didn't say was that when it came to the drug business, hard work and dedication more often than not translated into pure ruthlessness, a lust for risk, and imperviousness to failure. According to Karin Baxter, Chatzwirth had turned his 'hard work and dedication' into a passion for racehorses, women who loved racehorses, and an insatiable need to show off his wealth. Well, I thought, to each his own.

Board member #2 was Judith Susanne Claymore, the founder of Sirius Computers. Panda Pharmaceuticals had recruited Ms. Claymore to the Board after she sold her modest holdings in Sirius for 900 million dollars. A writer of fantasy fiction and children's books, Ms. Claymore was, according to Karin Baxter, the closest thing to a preying mantis that Panda had on their Board. "Watch out for Judy, Michael," she had said. "Her job is to find your most vulnerable point and see if she can break you over it."

I glanced up. The DVD was discussing Panda's state-of-the-art Virginia facilities, and the video screen filled with aerial shots of the surrounding countryside.

I flipped the page to the next profile. Patrick Truit, the newest member of the Board, was a former Director of the CIA, a close personal friend of President George Bush the First, and a one-time Navy Seal. In his spare time, Mr. Truit dabbled with his own international distribution company. What the company distributed, the profile didn't say, and Karin Baxter hadn't known; I tried not to speculate. Karin had mentioned a net worth in the area of 100 million dollars. I shook my head. Where did Panda find these people?

Willy Kellerman was a former two-term Governor of Virginia. Naturally, he had contacts up and down the Potomac, and Karin made it clear that not too many people could say 'No' to the Governor. "He's the diplomat of the group," she had said. "The kinder, gentler side of the Board." Right, I thought.

My last meeting of the trip was scheduled with Sir Adrian Glass, an Englishman hailing from Chelsea and a name familiar to anyone as involved in the drug industry as I had been over the last 20 years. Sir Glass was a noted molecular biologist with a knack for product development second to none in the business.

"The guy's got an ego the size of Jupiter," Karin had warned. "And he'll try and make you look like a fool if he can." Can't wait.

"If you pass muster with this bunch," Karin had told me, "you'll meet with Panda's other co-founder. His name is Dr. Chu Zhong Liu."

"I know the name."

"Absolutely brilliant. The good doctor developed Panda's powerhouse product. The one that put them on the map."

"Claraphine."

"Right," Karin said. "It's a non-addictive opium derivative, isn't that right? A pain reliever."

"Calling Claraphine a mere pain reliever is like calling Oeil de Perdrix a mere wine, but close enough," was how I had replied.

"Gotcha," Karin said. "Anyway, Chu is easily one of the wealthiest guys in Southeast Asia, and he doesn't travel. If things go well in Virginia – which they will – you'll have to make the trip to Thailand. Chu's blessing is the final one when it comes to Panda Pharmaceuticals' future. Keep that in mind."

"Piece of cake," I had said before hanging up.

I watched the rest of the video and examined the butterflies nesting in my stomach. We all have our ways of coping with anxiety – and it wouldn't be normal to look at the coming day without a twinge of nervousness – and the one that worked best for me was to look beyond the event to the return trip home and to remind myself that it would all be over in another 12 hours. I was good at interviewing. I didn't try to impress. I fell back on the age-old adage about being one's self. Hell, they were recruiting me, after all, not the other way around. On the other hand, Panda Pharmaceuticals had never been through this process before. Philip Chatzwirth and Dr. Chu Zhong Liu were handing over their baby for the first time in the company's history, and they weren't going to do it if the guy on the hot seat couldn't cut the mustard.

I was actually more paranoid over the prospect of George Branden, my current boss, finding out about my covert visit to Panda. Branden had more than his fair share of spies inside the industry. He was connected. He was also a procurer of favors. And though Panda was surely keeping a tight lid on their search for a new President and CEO, people like Karin Baxter, despite our relationship, were not known for their ability to keep their mouths closed. Hard to promote yourself if you don't promote yourself: I understood that. Hopefully, she and her colleagues would be smart enough to hold off until the deal was signed, sealed, and firmly delivered.

On the other hand, my Monday meeting at George Branden's Phoenix estate had resulted in a promotional strategy that he successfully leaked to the media that same afternoon. More glitz was how George saw the strategy; more fluff was how it struck me. Nonetheless, the leak proved effective. Peak Pharmaceuticals stock took a nice 5% bounce on Tuesday. We followed this with two lofty press releases. The first regarded our new R&D partnership with Merck. The second spelled out a new marketing package for C-Cap, a high-end arthritis medicine with an image problem. George called the releases revealing; I saw them as a word or two misleading. Still, our stock opened this morning with another bump.

Sure, aggressive PR could be a vehicle for short-term enthusiasm, but long-term optimism was the meat and potatoes of a healthy stock. As the company's CEO, I wanted to attract investors taking the long view. George's goal was to attract traders who could put a spike in his portfolio. He and I had been butting heads on issues exactly like this one for a very long time, and the contentiousness of our relationship gave me added incentive to make the most of today's interviews.

The DVD ended with a summary of Panda's product line, and this caused me to move to the edge of my seat. Within 30 seconds, I realized that the notes I had gotten from Karin Baxter were incomplete at best. The man delivering the product summary had curiously rectangular features for an Asian. He introduced himself as Dr. Xi Xianan, Assistant Director of Research and Development, Bangkok and Nankon, and strolled through a modernized laboratory where test tubes and Bunsen burners had been replaced by gas chromatographs and lasers. This was not a promotional tape. In fact, the doctor called me by name.

While Claraphine was still the Crown Jewel of the Panda line, the company had quietly introduced three derivatives, all opium based and all, according to Dr. Xi, non-addictive. Two of these – Trifil and Thorafil – were making steady inroads in advanced cancer treatment, which was odd because I had never heard of them. The third – Cielmeta – was slowly taking hold with patients suffering from rheumatoid arthritis. All three drugs were being produced in Asia under guidelines as yet unaccepted by the U.S. Food and Drug Administration. So there was my answer. The drugs were available in 120 countries worldwide, but not the U.S. Interesting. Was that a statement on the FDA's cautious approach on everything from Chilean-grown grapes to birth control or some hint as to the drugs' performance? A good question to ask of Sir Adrian Glass, I thought.

Panda had, according to Dr. Xi, also tapped into the ever-expanding market for cholesterol medicine. They had recently won approval for a blood pressure med called CDY-Norval. They were also testing fifteen in-development products, among them, a blood-clotting lozenge and an erectile dysfunction patch with a lifespan of 14 days. I could see their long-term strategy: stay with what got you there and tap the hot markets while they were hot. I did not disapprove.

The DVD ended. Karrie Lyn brought me a bottle of Virginia spring water. She asked me how she could make the next hour more pleasant and seemed disappointed when I assured her I had everything a man could possibly ask for.

Sixty minutes later, almost to the minute, the Gulfstream touched down on a private landing strip amidst the rolling hills east of Lake Anna and surrounded by thick groves of magnolia and cedar. I gazed out the window and found myself nodding at my first impression of the Commonwealth of Virginia. First impressions: Nietzsche called them the bane of intelligent men; Jung saw them as the fruit of synchronicity; I, Michael Alexander King, tucked them away for future reference having learned that life was a never-ending series of first impressions and therefore they were not to be dismissed.

We taxied for less than 60 seconds, pulling into a hangar housing three Lear jets, a second Gulfstream, and a matching pair of mint condition P-47 fighter planes straight out of World War II. I spent two minutes in the Gulfstream's lavatory knotting my tie and checking the fit of my suit coat. Before walking out, I stared at my reflection for ten seconds and fixed a look of confidence and calm on my face.

Karrie Lyn thanked me – for what I wasn't exactly sure – and assured me she was looking forward to our return flight later tonight. "Thank you," I said. "The video was informative."

"Hope we didn't knock you around too much back there, Mr. King," the pilot said as we descended the steps to the hanger floor. "More wind than we expected."

"Smooth as silk, Captain Wize. Thanks for the lift."

The pilot caught my eye and made a magnanimous gesture in the direction of a silver and gray Lear jet with a diamond emblem on the tail fin. "She's a beauty, isn't she? Brand spanking new."

"Looks it," I said.

"She's yours, boss," he said, as if I had just been formally introduced to my second child. "Twenty-four seven."

I suppressed a jocular comment that Wize would surely have taken the wrong way and said, "Very nice. I look forward to breaking her in."

"There's your ride, Sir." Dave Ridder, the co-pilot, walked me in the direction of a gleaming black Mercedes limousine and a driver with silver hair, a Cheshire cat grin, and a perfectly tailored suit.

"Mr. King. Welcome to Virginia, Sir. I'm Karlton Clay," he said. The door was already open, and I climbed in. The interior was immaculate, and the temperature inside was cool but not uncomfortably so. There was an unopened bottle of Perrier in the cup holder, a well-stocked bar, and three telephones. My driver settled into his seat and glanced over his shoulder. "I hope I've got the A/C right for you back there. Let me know if it's too cool. Can I fix you a cocktail for the drive?"

Another test. "No thanks, Karlton."

Karlton turned over the engine and eased out into a pleasant, if humid Virginia afternoon. "I'm an open book, Mr. King. Anything you need to know about Panda past or present, I'm the man to ask. I was 32 years in the HR department. Retired a VP, but couldn't stay away after the wife died. Panda's the best company in the industry, bar none. We're family, through and through."

"That's the way a company should be run, Karlton," I said. A former exec turned limo driver; I thought I'd heard it all. "Give me the tour."

He seemed delighted. "Campus is ten minutes away, but this is all Panda land. Mr. Chatzwirth thought you might like to see it," he said, a hand taking in patches of deciduous forests, stretches of chaparral and tall grass, and grazing horses. "Thirty-six hole golf course on your left. Stables on the right. Guest ranch. Corporate retreat and hot springs. Every square inch fully secured, both air and ground."

"Good to know," I said, as if anything less would have been disturbing, if not completely unacceptable.

"Here we are," he said, a hand again indicating an 8 foot high perimeter fence built of red brick and 42 enclosed acres that indeed looked like a sprawling college campus. The manned entry was a wrought iron design that framed the Panda Pharmaceuticals' logo: a black and white bear scaling a pyramid formed by the letters PPC.

The words stunning, opulent, and excessive passed through my brain as the limo wove among lotus ponds, Asian gardens, and well-concealed tennis courts. The corporate office, all granite and limestone, fit the Ivy League campus feel. Fifteen or so separate buildings were connected by tree-lined concourses, and the walks were busy. The dress code on 'campus' seemed to run the gamut from Armani and Ann Taylor to blue jeans and cutoffs. That appealed to me.

A macadam drive circled in front of a two-story complex with high glass windows and an impressive arched entryway. The car rolled to a stop, and the door was opened not a second later. My escorts were three in number. Two were junior executive types dressed like Wall Street MBAs: she blonde and very southern; he squeaky clean and eager. They both had firm handshakes, a good sign.

She said, "Welcome to Panda Pharmaceuticals, Sir," and he nodded as if the very words were on the tip of his tongue.

The man who stepped between them could only be Philip Chatzwirth. Tanned, dapper, raptorial. "Mr. King. I'm Phil Chatzwirth."

He took my hand. Another firm handshake, but this one had an aggressive edge to it that wasn't unexpected. I said, "I've been looking forward to meeting you, Mr. Chatzwirth. Thanks for having me out." Not too formal, not too casual.

"Do I call you Mike or Michael?" Of course, he already knew the answer.

"My mother was never happy with anything less than Michael," I replied. Gregarious, but not overbearing.

"Never contradict a mother, I always say," the outgoing CEO said. "And I'm comfortable with Phil, if you are."

"Very comfortable."

He placed a hand on my elbow and guided me toward the entrance. I couldn't help but notice the missing pinky finger on his left hand – Karin Baxter had failed to mention that – and I hoped he hadn't caught me staring. "It's been hard as hell keeping the Board in line," Chatzwirth was saying. "They can't wait to meet you. We thought we'd open things up in the Boardroom and then give you a chance to huddle with them one-on-one. You good with that, Michael?"

"I was thinking along those lines myself, Phil."

"Good, good."

The Junior Executives scrambled to get the doors, then hustled to get the elevator. I didn't have time to enjoy the portico, but it was hard to miss the gold and gray marble that seemed to cover every inch of the floor and walls.

The elevator opened onto a richly painted vestibule with wool carpets and a host of smiling faces. I shook hands with six department heads and traded smiles with six or seven lesser folks who had clearly been instructed to stay in the background and look positive. It was all very nicely orchestrated.

～

4

THE SHOW

"He not busy being born is busy dying."

The Boardroom was located behind a wall built of frosted glass and Brazilian Cherry wood, and Philip Chatzwirth nudged me in that direction. The remainder of the Board greeted me at the door. Judith Claymore – the preying mantis – was a rail-thin woman with carved features, diaphanous gray eyes, and the smile of a seductress. She took my hand in both of hers and squeezed. "You're better looking than I expected," she said coyly. "The question is, are you smarter?"

"Oh, for goodness sake, of course he is. Don't listen to a thing she says," former Governor Willy Kellerman, the diplomat, said, his handshake soft and damp. "I'm Willy Kellerman."

"Thank you for the advice, Governor. I'll remember that," I said, glancing from Judith to the Governor and sharing a genuinely warm smile. "It's good to meet you both."

"You'll be calling him Willy by the end of the day, and Judith, well, you'll just be happy you survived the experience," Patrick Truit intervened. He gripped my arm with powerful fingers and shook my hand for a good ten seconds. "You can call me Mr. Truit until we get to know each other a little better, Mr. King."

"Fair enough," I said. My eyes traveled next to a gangly man with a salt and pepper beard, tortoise shell eyeglasses, and surprisingly casual dress.

Even intentionally careless dress, now that I thought about it. This was Sir Adrian Glass, and he wasn't smiling. I nodded. "Sir Glass."

"Mr. King. Have a seat," he said with a brusque cadence. "You've come a long way."

"And we're thrilled to have you," the Governor said. He pulled out a chair at the near end of the table and made it clear the seat was reserved for me.

"We've been tracking your rather distinguished career for five years now," former CIA director Truit said when everyone was settled. The oval table, a burnished cherry wood inlaid with tiny granite tiles, had been tastefully arranged with canapés that no one had yet touched, tall water glasses, and stemware that an elegantly dressed and mute waiter was filling with iced tea. "You've done one helluva job at Peak, Mr. King, despite working in a fish bowl where every move you make turns into a media sound bite."

"Well, thank you for the compliment, Mr. Truit," I replied. "Such is life in the public sector."

"Patrick is completely accurate in his assessment of your record, Michael. And we all agree. A rare enough occurrence, but one which makes us that much more enthusiastic about your visit," Willy Kellerman said. He raised his iced tea in the air. "Welcome!"

His fellow Board members joined him, and I wondered briefly whether their solidarity was genuine or a front orchestrated for my benefit.

"Thank you. You're very kind," I said. "And I'm flattered by your invitation. The Panda campus is extraordinary. It obviously reflects the company's success, and I congratulate you all."

"That's very diplomatic of you, Mr. King," said Judith Claymore with a tantalizingly warm smile. Watch your step; I heard Karin Baxter's warning in the back of my mind. "Your first time in Virginia?"

"It is," I admitted. "Is the weather always this accommodating?"

"It's not altogether different from your Colorado climate, I imagine," Willy replied. "Not as cold in the winter, but a tad bit more humid in the summer."

"We look forward to a visit from your family. Lauren and Hanna? Do I have that right?" Mr. Truit asked.

I nodded. "My daughter's five."

"Would there by chance be any horse lovers in your brood, Sir?"

I had to compliment Truit for asking a question to which he already knew the answer. Then again, if they started asking questions they hadn't already researched in every detail, we would be in for a very short conversation. "My daughter got her love for horses from her mother. Lauren grew up with them in Northern California. She learned to ride a horse about the time I was learning to ride a bicycle."

I noticed Sir Glass watching me from behind hooded eyes. I also noticed Philip Chatzwirth watching Sir Glass. So, I thought, there was the bruise on this seemingly perfect piece of fruit. Okay then, explore it. "I reviewed the company's product mix, Sir Glass," I said directly. "I like the long-term model."

A moment of silence swirled around the table before Philip Chatzwirth, Panda Pharmaceuticals' co-founder and second most powerful man, chuckled. He said, "I think our guest has opened his first one-on-one interview, my friends. Throws our schedule off track before it ever got on track. I rather admire that. Perhaps we should give Michael and Adrian some privacy."

An awkward moment passed, and all but Sir Glass arose.

"However, before we take our leave, I will say this, Michael." Philip Chatzwirth took in his colleagues one after another. "What you called an invitation a moment ago is more of a courtship in our eyes. We wouldn't have asked you to come all this way if we didn't think you were right for the job."

"I take that as the highest order of compliment, Phil. But I'll also assume that my time with each of you is more than a formality," I replied.

Philip Chatzwirth chuckled again. "Judith will show you our corporate offices after you and Sir Glass are done, and then we'll all have some lunch on the 18th hole."

"Excellent." I shook hands with each of my hosts in turn and then sat across the table again from Sir Adrian Glass.

"We were talking long-term strategy," the Englishman from Chelsea said when we were alone. "You've either done your homework on me, or you and I have a common interest."

"You know what it takes to succeed in the drug business. So do I," I said conversationally. "You stay ahead of the curve, but you also take advantage of the curve."

Sir Glass sipped tea the way a man strokes his chin when he's planning his next chess move. "I couldn't have put it better myself."

"What's the prognosis on the patch?"

"Ah, dear me! Our answer to the Viagra-never-say-die craze. Quit smoking, cure male-pattern baldness, and get a hard-on all at the same time." Sir Glass grimaced. "Don't embarrass me, Mr. King. If it comes out of trial with a thumb's up, we'll make a bloody fortune. I just don't care much for wading in the other guy's pool, if you get my drift."

"It's not a market that's going away. That's the good news," I said. "Tell me more about the blood pressure med."

"CDY-Norval." Sir Glass drank his tea. "The goal is simple. We create a blood pressure drug that reacts to metabolism, blood type, and individual protein count, and it will be the last drug a cardiologist ever has to prescribe."

"Brilliant. Can it be done without bankrupting the company? That's the question," I said, as if an answer was neither required nor expected. "But let's talk about the new kids on the block."

Sir Adrian Glass pursed his lips. "So. To the heart of the matter. Trifil. Thorafil. And Cielmeta."

"What's holding up FDA approval? The production process or the side effect profile of the active formulation?" I asked. Sir Glass, of course, understood perfectly well what I was referring to. Did the Food and Drug Administration have a problem with the notoriously lackadaisical production standards in laboratories all over Asia or did the problem lie with the primary product source: opium. Probably a bit of both, I thought, but I shot for the latter nonetheless. "Where is the opium produced, if I may be so bold?"

"I'm counting on you being bold, Mr. King. This isn't a company that can be run by the meek and the mild," the Englishman assured me. He paused long enough to see that I wasn't biting on a slice of insincere flattery. "The opium is grown in the most glorious little poppy fields you'll ever lay your eyes on. Two hundred thousand acres of flowers so bright and inviting that you'll think the sun just gave birth on the side of a mountain. Of course, the mountain just happens to be guarded by misfits with M-1 rifles in their hands."

"Two hundred thousand acres. That's a lot of land," I said. "Located where exactly?"

"Thailand mostly. A swatch or two in Malaysia and Viet Nam. Oh, and I forgot to mention the fifty or so thousand acres in Myanmar."

Our eyes locked. Sir Glass was smiling. It was a prideful smile, not a humorous one. I said, "Ours?"

"Ours?" He raised an eyebrow, looking like a salesman who knew the deal was sealed even before he made his pitch. It was exactly the look I was hoping to see.

"My apologies," I said. "I didn't mean to get ahead of myself. I was speaking, shall we say, with the future in mind. What I meant was, owned by Panda Pharmaceuticals?"

"Down to the last acre."

I thought a moment. "Two hundred and fifty thousand acres. An acre produces, what? Ten pounds of viable crop per acre?"

"Fifteen," the man from Chelsea corrected, his tea momentarily forgotten.

"Four million pounds give or take." I drummed the tabletop with my fingertips. If 50% of that went into the production of Panda's four opium-based drugs, I would have been surprised. So what happened to the rest of it? But I was too slow. Sir Adrian Glass, by all accounts a scientific genius, had probably anticipated my question the day my name came up as a possible successor to their vacant CEO chair.

"Actually, it's more like two million pounds of production," he said. "You see, Mr. King, we only seed half of our acreage every year. Plant, rest, rotate. Quickest way on earth to ruin your topsoil if you don't. And we can't afford that."

"No, I guess not." I was relieved. I felt the tension go out of my shoulders.

We talked for ten more minutes, spending most of that time on Panda's Thailand-based research and development operation. Eventually, Sir Glass set aside his tea. He said, "I imagine Judith is waiting for you in the corporate center. She's dying to show you your new office. And she's not a lady you want to keep waiting."

"I got that impression," I said, following his lead and coming to my feet.

"I'll put together some reading material for you on the full product line. Also a couple of things on our Asian operations. You'll be impressed," Sir Adrian Glass said as we walked out of the boardroom toward the elevators. "I like your insight, Mr. King. We've got a well-oiled machine here at Panda, and we want to keep it that way. I think perhaps you're the man for the job."

Two minutes later, I was walking at Judith Claymore's side touring Panda Pharmaceuticals' well-appointed, if understated, corporate offices. "So how did your tête-à-tête go with our world famous biologist?" she asked.

"I'm a little concerned that we got along so well," I said with a smile.

"On the contrary. Sir Glass likes one in every fifty or so people he meets," she assured me. "I don't imagine it's happened since I've known him, so the odds were in your favor."

She smiled, and I laughed. "You're quite a writer, from what I've been able to gather," I said, as if the segue was perfectly natural. "Science fiction and children's books. Now that's something I know a thing or two about.

I'd love to read something you've done."

"You're trying to get on my good side, Mr. King. I'm always suspicious of that," she said, her eyes narrowing.

"Not at all. I have a five-year-old. She loves books. So do I," I said with a careful shrug.

"Then I'll send you home with something." Her mouth curled into a wicked smile, and I wondered how many men she had steamrolled in her day. Plenty, I thought.

"Inscribed, I hope."

"Naturally." Judith led me into an office the size of my backyard. It appeared as if some overambitious interior designer had thrown equal amounts of leather, mahogany, etched glass, and ivory into a huge vat, stirred it up, and tossed it carelessly about. Desk, furniture, lamps, bookshelves, armoire; somehow it actually worked, at least to my undisciplined eye. The walls were filled with tasteful reproductions of Degas, Chagall, and Camille-Corot, three of my favorites.

"Yours," the former computer magnate said of the office. "It's a bit much, but you'll have it looking like a well organized Congressional Library in no time."

"Obviously you've seen my office in Boulder."

"With apologies," Judith said. I could see that she was suitably embarrassed, knowing she knew everything there was to know about me, and knowing I knew. But that was just the way the game was played.

"No apologies necessary." I stopped in front of a desk the size of a queen bed, turned to face her, and caught just a faint hint of perfume. I expected her to fold her arms across her chest – the subtlest of defenses – but she didn't. I liked that.

I said, "Cielmeta hasn't been approved in this country, Judith. I'm wondering why?"

"A question I would have expected you to ask Sir Glass." She didn't move a muscle.

"I'm asking you."

"The government doesn't like anything that works too well, Michael. You know that. If Cielmeta gets on the market here, a whole bunch of doctors who make believe they have some idea of how to treat rheumatoid arthritis will be out of business. You think the AMA or the insurance industry is going to let that happen without a fight?"

"It works that well?"

A moment passed in which the preying mantis could either show her hand or pass. It was the kind of moment that made all the trivia and all the headaches of executive life worthwhile. Judith Claymore – a woman who had graced the cover of a dozen magazines during the late 80's and early 90's, had endured a Justice Department investigation over questionable distribution of proprietary software, and had successfully fought off a takeover bid by no less an adversary than Bill Gates – let her shoulders drop slightly, turned aside, and ran her fingers over the desk's pristine finish.

"Yes," she said. "It does."

I didn't know whether to be disappointed or ecstatic. I allowed my lungs to fill. "Then we should get it on the market," I said. "And fast."

She nodded, just briefly. Then a smile tugged at the corners of her mouth, and she made a magnanimous gesture toward the office. "So, how do you like it?"

"Big."

"Damn big. Maybe you could install an Olympic pool or a basketball court in one corner." We walked out. "I hope you're hungry. Lunch on the terrace, and Panda's kitchen staff has spared no expense."

We went outside. I looked across four or five holes of one of the most spectacular golf courses I had ever set foot on and didn't see one person with a club in their hand. Lunch was laid out on the terrace above the 18th hole. The Board was all there. So were the department heads I had been introduced to earlier, a couple of local politicians, and a five-piece chamber ensemble. I wasn't particularly interested in the food - caviar, crab cakes, and champagne at 1:00 in the afternoon might have been appealing if Lauren and I were dining on a deserted beach in Mexico – but I filled my plate as a matter of courtesy.

I could work a crowd when the chips were down, but I didn't need to in this situation. I was in demand. The department heads sought me out one after another, and I tried to get a glimpse into the company by asking each of them what they thought the company's most pressing need was. I thought, why not? See if you get a reaction.

The answers I received were the typical responses you found from business heads in virtually any company, but I was concerned by the way they answered as if they had been threatened not to waiver too far off the corporate path. The Regional Director of Sales said, "More men in the field. We're losing sales." The VP of Finance felt they needed to update some of their Oracle software, and the Director of Human Resources weakly proclaimed the need for more diversity in their workforce.

And when the VP of Research and Development, US Division, replied, "A little less reliance on Asian resources," I wondered if someone had put him up to it.

Raymond Leavitt, the head of Business Development, didn't want to talk business. He wanted to talk snow skiing. I took that as a sign his position was nominal and that his opinion didn't matter. But as I was about to excuse myself, he took my arm and whispered in my ear. "None of this matters, Mr. King. Dr. Chu Zhong Liu's opinion is the only one that counts. His is the final word. Philip and Willy might tell you it's a done deal, but nothing is a done deal until Chu puts his stamp on it." Mr. Leavitt released my arm when he saw former Governor Kellerman coming our way. "Just so you know."

"Thanks," I said, though I wasn't sure whether or not gratitude was in order.

"So, Raymond," Willy Kellerman said, his eyes narrowed slightly. "Are you filling Mr. King's head with meaningful tidbits about our fair enterprise?"

"Actually, we were talking black diamond slopes in Vail and the best restaurants in Aspen," I confessed. "It seems that Raymond and I would both trade 18 holes of golf for a run down the backside of the China Bowls in a minute."

"Don't blame you," Willy said. Then, as a way of separating me from the rest of the crowd and Raymond Leavitt in particular, he added, "But let me show you a view you won't see on the slopes of Vail, Michael."

"Ah, yes. Lake Anna. So true," Raymond said with a knowing tip of the head. He backed away. "I look forward to working with you, Michael."

"A good man, Raymond is. Knows the company line and walks it with the best of them," Willy said, leading me up a narrow slope behind the clubhouse.

I wanted to say that the head of Business Development may have been a tad bit more independent than Willy and his cohorts figured, but I thought I might do well to hold that card in reserve.

We climbed a set of steps to a circular gazebo. The view stretching beyond the Panda campus was indeed spectacular. Hills painted in shades of green, gold, and yellow so varied and vibrant that Pissarro and Cezanne would have had a field day were set against a swatch of silver and blue water that shimmered like fish scales.

Naturally, Willy Kellerman ignored the view totally. He didn't talk about Panda Pharmaceuticals. Rather, he settled into a floating monologue about his love affair with Virginia. He called it a land of a million trees, a place of unlocked doors, and a community of people with enough good sense to mind their own business.

"A good quality," I agreed.

"We're not as backward as West Virginia – who in the hell is – nor as opinionated as Maryland. We can attract the best and the brightest without alienating them from the politics of DC, which is an hour away. They want culture, Baltimore is another 30 minutes. It's a short shuttle to New York, and an even shorter one to Philly, though God knows why anyone would want to travel to Philly."

"Hear, hear!" I said, liking the former Governor just fine but wondering just how much I could trust him.

Fifteen minutes later, I was sitting with Patrick Truit in a small third floor office overflowing with books, clutter, and a sense of frustration.

"From Navy Seal to CIA Director to a seat on the Board of a major drug company," I mused, as Truit brewed espresso from a machine that any Starbucks in the world would have been proud to own. The aroma filled the room as he poured shots into two small mugs. "How does that happen?"

"Pretty damn boring, I have to admit. Steamed milk?" he said. I nodded, then smiled, thinking that Mr. Truit took his coffee consumption as seriously as I did. Score one for Panda's resident spy. When he was settled in his seat, he continued. "I'm a friend of a certain former President – you know that, of course – and he is a friend of a certain former Virginia Governor. You'd be surprised at just how well my credentials are received in some circles, Mr. King."

"I'm sure I wouldn't," I said. Truit's profile had referred to ownership in an international distribution company, but it failed to spell out exactly who, what, or where the company distributed. I wanted to assume that it had nothing to do with the kind of connections only someone associated with the intelligence community might have, but my curiosity wouldn't allow me to be so persuaded. It was a terrible flaw. But instead of broaching the subject head on, I strolled around it. I did this by making a show of my coffee cup and saying, "Excellent brew, Mr. Truit."

"Sorong."

"Sorong? That's a new one on me," I admitted.

"Indonesian."

"Available here in the States?"

"Hard to find, but I've been importing it for a couple of years. My own company." He looked at me with an appraising gaze, sipped his espresso without losing eye contact, and said, "Ask your question, Mr. King."

"Panda Pharmaceuticals does the majority of its manufacturing in Asia. The company produces product from opium and manages its own poppy fields, a quarter of a million acres worth. It would seem to present a control issue. Even a significant control issue."

Truit shrugged the way a man does when he hopes his words reflect the casualness of his body language. "Not really. Everything is internal. From the guy who plants the seed, to the soldier who stands watch over the fields, to the chemist who converts the opium. All of it."

"And, if I can be so bold, your former career plays into it how?"

"Meaning?"

"Meaning, Mr. Truit, your qualifications don't necessarily prepare you for a Board position with a major pharmaceutical company," I said.

"I see. But they do prepare me for…for what exactly, Mr. King?"

"To be the perfect sounding board. For a company with particularly tricky working relationships spanning half the globe," I said, as if nothing could be more obvious.

"That pretty much describes every company on the Fortune 500 list, Mr. King," Truit said. It was a protest of sorts, but not one with much teeth to it.

I amended my statement by saying, "A company with vital working relationships in the trickier parts of the globe – Southeast Asia and Indonesian – dealing with maybe the trickiest commodity on the planet."

"I'm not sure opium, or the by-products we are most concerned about, would rate as the trickiest commodity on the planet, but your point is well taken, Mr. King." Truit drained his espresso. He made a face, crunching his nose, mouth, and eyes into a tight ball. "A touch on the bitter side," he said, peering into his cup. "My apologies."

"I say if you're going to err when it comes to the fine art of coffee-making, Mr. Truit, better to err on the strong side, don't you think?"

"I think you're perhaps the most diplomatic interviewee I've ever sat down with, Mr. King," Truit said when the muscles in his face had relaxed again. "Though, now that I think about it, you might also be the best interviewer I've ever sat down with, as well. You are interviewing me, aren't you?"

I didn't bite. Instead, I set my cup aside and inched to the edge of my seat. "It's simple really. You're the one person on Panda's Board of Directors that has the answers to my questions, Sir."

"You mean the questions you haven't asked yet."

"Exactly."

"You're wondering who on the Panda Board has his or her own agenda," Truit suggested. "You're wondering if there are questionable aspects to the company you should know about. You're wondering if we're running amuck of the US government in general and the FDA in particular." He stared, his tarnished brown eyes calm and ubiquitous, and I stared back. "You're wondering if you're in over your head."

"No, actually, I'm not," I said plainly. "Believe me, I'll know all I need to know about the questionable aspects of the company before I leave today, Mr. Truit. And naturally, I already know that every member of your Board has his or her own agenda; they can make me feel as welcome as a spring day after a hard winter – and probably mean it – but that doesn't mean they don't view me as a tool to use for their own benefit. I wouldn't expect anything less."

"Very wise."

"And I've been dealing with government bureaucracy and the politics of the FDA for fifteen years now. I know they're not to be trifled with, but I also know they're not going to run rough shod over us either."

"Bravo, Mr. King. Bravo." Truit almost smiled. Even at that, he did not lose one ounce of his rather formidable concentration. "So then what are you wondering about?"

"I'm wondering who's in charge."

We were staring again. A good five seconds passed. Truit blinked, stood, and walked in a slow circle back to the espresso machine. He brought two shot glasses filled with thick black coffee back to the table, filled my cup, and then his own. He returned with a small pitcher of steamed milk and waited until my espresso was prepared. A true gentleman or a refined interrogator? I had to wonder.

Eventually, he said, "You're asking about Chu."

"Let's just say I'm not traveling all the way to Southeast Asia only to discover that I can't make a decision of any real significance about company policy without the blessing of a man 8000 miles away." It wasn't an aggressive statement; men like Truit tended to fold up their tents in the face of unnecessary truculence. It was just a statement of fact.

"That's not unreasonable," the former CIA Director and Navy Seal said. "It's also not a legitimate concern, believe me."

"Convince me," I said, raising my cup.

"You're going to like Dr. Chu Zhong Liu, Mr. King. He is the most refined man I know," he said.

"Refined is good," I agreed. "Insufficient as an answer, but good."

Truit made his second foray. "Nothing is more important to him than family, and Panda is his family."

"Dr. Chu's blessing is the final blessing when it comes to Panda Pharmaceuticals. True or false?" I asked.

"Dr. Chu is not an item of conversation within our organization, Mr. King. He is off limits to everyone except the Board." Truit's jaw tightened. "If someone here…"

"Don't be dramatic, Mr. Truit," I interrupted with a measured amount of force. He didn't flinch, and I gave him credit for that. But I wasn't going to let the members of the Board play unnecessary games at the company's expense if I did come onboard, and it was never too soon to deliver that message. "Do you honestly think that the woman who recruited me on your behalf…"

"Karin Baxter."

"Yes, Karin Baxter. Do you honestly think that a recruiter of her stature wouldn't mention exactly where Dr. Chu stood in your company? She also mentioned that Sir Adrian Glass would try to make me look like a fool, which he didn't. And that Judith Claymore would do whatever it took to expose my Achilles Heel. She didn't."

"And what did our high priced headhunter say about me, Mr. King?" Truit was curious, but hardly insistent.

"She told me you would shoot straight from the hip no matter how personal I got." Not exactly a quote, but something I had read between the lines. "Now, who's in charge? Is it Chu or the new CEO and President?"

Truit nodded. "If and when you pass muster with Dr. Chu Zhong Liu, he'll know you well enough and trust you implicitly enough to hand over the reins of our company – his company – without question. I'll say it again: if you pass muster with him, and that is a substantial if. Satisfied…? Michael."

"Satisfied, Patrick." I replaced my coffee cup in its saucer and stood up. "Oh, and I changed my mind. Clearly your qualifications did prepare you for a Board position with a major pharmaceutical company."

As I walked out, I could not say one way or another whether the Board interviews had met my expectations, but all in all I was, as Patrick Truit put it, satisfied. I was under no illusion; these were four men and one woman with the power to hire and fire, and the CEO job would not be immune to those prerogatives. They were also people who benefited in a very big way from Panda Pharmaceuticals' success, and much like the Board of a public company, they would be watching every move I made. I still had not had a substantial conversation with Philip Chatzwirth, the company Chairman, but I assumed that would take place during a scheduled stop at his estate.

Patrick Truit walked me back to the circular drive fronting the corporate offices, where the same limousine was waiting for me. Karlton Clay, with the Cheshire Cat grin and perfectly coiffed hair, stood by the open door patiently waiting.

∾

5

THE PERK

"It is our light, not our darkness, that most frightens us."

"Don't let Karlton talk your ear off, Michael," the former CIA Director instructed. "He knows more about the company than all of us put together, and I have rarely known him to be in anything less than fine fettle."

I had to admire Truit's subtleties. He was inviting me to pick Karlton Clay's brain with the kind of questions I might not have been comfortable posing to his fellow Board members or the various department heads I had met. I may have been naïve in many worldly matters, but I knew better than to give unnecessary fodder to the Board's favorite parrot. More than that, I would have been extremely surprised were the limo not miked and wired.

"How's your visit so far, Sir?" Karlton said once I was settled in back and the car was in motion.

"Very enlightening," I said for the benefit of anyone listening in. "As solid a group of people as I have ever encountered."

"I couldn't agree more, Mr. King. Any questions I can answer? Any concerns?" he said helpfully.

"Just the usual tour, Mr. Clay. Thank you." I watched the lush Virginia countryside roll past my window and imagined the changing of the colors come fall; I was probably two weeks too early. Well, if all continued to progress as smoothly as it seemed the morning had, I might be spending autumn here for the next twenty years of my life. It may not have been Colorado, but there was a certain charm to what I had seen so far.

"We're only a hop, skip, and a jump away," my driver informed me. "If you look off to your right, you'll see Mr. Chatzwirth's estate. The house up there on the hill is his. Quite spectacular."

From a distance, the estate appeared to be a generous mix of horse ranch and wilderness area. Acres of green-black forest formed a cincture around fields of wild grass and open prairie. Miles of white rail fencing turned the open space into perfectly symmetrical parcels of grazing land reserved for carefully bred herds of thoroughbreds, Arabians, and Morgans.

"Mr. Chatzwirth likes his horses," I said.

"Fanatical about his horses," Karlton Clay agreed.

"Beautiful house." My eyes traveled beyond the forests and the pastures to a rambling terra cotta-colored house that was part baroque, part Spanish, a clash of styles that some creative architectural mind had melded together into a modern day palace.

"Panda Farms," the chauffeur said, as if the name might somehow temper the opulence and the excess. "Mr. Chatzwirth has 150 acres here. Not huge."

Not huge. I got a kick out of that. I wanted to say by whose standards?

"You can just barely make out the horse stables and the riding arena in the valley below the house," he added, a right turn shuttling us off the county road.

The private road beyond followed a small stream that forked just before a pillared entrance gave access to the estate itself. Too bad the entrance required two armed guards and a four-wheel drive Land Rover to monitor the comings and goings of Panda Farms, but I imagined there was a whole garrison of similarly attired men roaming the grounds.

"You didn't mention the vineyards," I said to my driver, as the limo bisected several acres of perfectly aligned grapevines.

"Sorry about that, Mr. King. Yes, indeed. Panda Farms' very own label. A Pinot Noir. Quite flavorful."

"Pinot. My wife's favorite."

Karlton twisted his head around. "I'll make certain you leave today with a couple of bottles."

"That would make us both very happy, Karlton," I said.

Philip Chatzwirth, his wife, and daughter were waiting for me on the front porch of their house. At Karlton Clay's urging, I left my briefcase in the backseat of the limo, shed my suit coat, and walked toward the house with a comfortable smile on my face.

"Michael. Welcome to Panda Farms," the company's co-founder and Chairman called. "May I present my wife, Celia."

Celia Chatzwirth was nothing short of stunning. Tall, elegant, and at least 20 years younger than her husband. Eyes as pale as fine ash peered back at me. Behind them I could see a woman of power and influence. For all that, she was dressed in cotton pants and a casual knit sweater that only accentuated her composure.

"Mr. King." She extended her hand and her long fingers entwined with mine.

"I think you already know my daughter," Philip said with a smile.

My flight attendant from the Gulfstream stepped forward, a smile as dazzling as her mother's creased her face and then morphed into an innocent laugh.

"Karrie Lyn. How are you?"

"Fine, thank you," she said. "Surprised?"

"I had no idea," I said, a truer statement I could never have imagined.

"All in the family," her mother said. Karrie Lyn looked ten years younger in blue jeans and a silk blouse, and almost nothing like the sultry woman who had seemingly offered me more than just the run-of-the-mill in-flight services less than eight hours ago. Did her parents have any idea how easily their daughter could morph into a virtual sex kitten? Of course they did, Michael, I thought, giving myself a gentle tongue-lashing. All in the family: isn't that what Mom just said?

"This is an incredible place you have here, Philip. Horses and vineyards. Two of my favorite things," I said.

"Two of his, as well," Celia assured me.

"Next to my two best girls, that is." Philip wrapped an arm awkwardly around his wife and drew her close.

"I have to tell you that I was promised a couple of bottles of your special Pinot Noir," I said to Celia.

"The 2003 is fabulous." Celia slipped out from under Philip's arm and said, "Philip has something to show you, Michael…" Her eyes widened, almost innocently. "I can call you Michael, I hope? And your wife Lauren?"

"Of course."

"Good. But don't be too long. Because when you get back I get to put you under the light and ask you all the juicy questions the Board felt too squeamish to ask."

"That I'll look forward to," I said, as mother and daughter returned to the house.

"Don't be so sure," Philip said with a chuckle. He took me by the elbow and guided me down a cobblestone path lined with yellow and orange zinnias. The path meandered along the side of a hill thick with Magnolia and the sound of kingfishers chirping. "How'd the Board treat you, Michael? Not too rough, I hope. I heard you didn't shy away from the tough questions. Not surprising."

"I think I asked most of the tough questions, Philip," I admitted.

"Well, that's a hard bunch to intimidate. They can take it." The path fell in opposite a rambling brook and climbed even higher. "So what's your biggest concern? That an old man like me might not be able to keep his mouth closed?"

"I'm counting on it, Phil. I can't think of a better sounding board than the man who built the business from the ground up," I said. I could see that the Chairman took the words to heart. The truth was, I wasn't ready to share my biggest concern with Philip Chatzwirth, and that was Panda's reliance on a resource that half the world would have been happy to see eradicated, the wonderful byproducts the company had produced be damned. Instead, I went the diplomatic route and said, "My biggest concern is making sure everyone in the company knows how important they are to the Panda family, and that a change of leadership doesn't alter that."

"No, it doesn't," he agreed.

"You and Dr. Chu have built something special here, Phil."

"Ah! Speaking of building something special," he said excitedly.

We crested a small rise. A hillside flush with magnolia, oak, and pitch pine gave way to a meadow rich with purple blossoms and wild grass. The meadow curled at the feet of a well-manicured lawn. The bluegrass was framed by white rail-fencing and flower beds that rose in graduated steps to a rambling two-story house – with southwestern tones and Gothic curves – that almost seemed a natural extension of the fields and forests that surrounded it.

"Brand new," Philip Chatzwirth said proudly. We continued to hike, but our pace was perfect for taking in the sights and listening to the Panda Chairman's selling pitch. "What do you think of the landscaping?"

"It doesn't look landscaped, if you know what I mean."

"Indeed I do. Well put." He raised a hand in the direction of an enclosed swimming pool. "We argued over whether or not the pool belonged next to the tennis courts – my wife's suggestion, and I use the word 'suggestion' lightly – or up above – my thought."

"She won," I noticed.

"Not an unusual occurrence in the Chatzwirth household, I might add."

I was impressed with the understated rows of slender birch trees that formed a protective screen around the tennis courts, both shade and windbreak, but the horse stables that nestled in the trees a hundred or so yards below the house drew my attention as we circled the house. Two horses grazed in the fenced corral next to the stables. One, a dappled palomino, looked like an exact replica of the one pictured on the poster covering Hanna's bedroom wall back home. The other was a chocolate-colored Arabian with a white blaze running along its nose and the posture of a champion. Magnificent.

"What do you think?" Chatzwirth said. He used a sweeping gesture to indicate the whole works: house; pool; stables; grounds.

"Nice," I said.

"I built it for the company's new CEO," he said in case there was any misunderstanding on my part.

"Well, Phil, I can't imagine a CEO with half a brain being anything less than ecstatic with a house like that," I offered.

"I think I'll take that as a compliment," the Chairman said with a wry smile.

"Now it does come with the horses, I assume," I said with a pointed nod in the direction of the stables and the corral. I was only half-kidding. "That Palomino can't be a coincidence."

"You'll have to pardon my research staff, Michael," Chatzwirth said with a well-calculated mixture of pride and embarrassment. He gave me a friendly pat on the back and led me around to the far side of the house and the enclosed patio. "But when I say, 'Be thorough,' they take me at my word, I'm afraid."

"Thorough is good," I said, though I was thinking, 'Except when thorough becomes intrusive,' and knowing the wall décor of a little girl's bedroom was getting pretty darn close to intrusive.

"Well, the good news is that you'll have access to the same research staff if this all works out," he added. Then he asked, "So, what do you think Lauren would say about the place? Too much? Not enough? Is this all there is? You did say she was a California girl after all."

Chatzwirth chuckled at his own joke. I chuckled to give myself time to recall when I might have mentioned anything about Lauren's California roots. "I think we can rule out 'Is this all there is?'" I said and hoped I was on safe ground.

"What if we get her out this way while you're in Thailand talking things over with my partner? Give her the red carpet treatment. Let that daughter of yours take the Palomino for a spin around the property," Phil suggested.

"I'm sure Lauren would enjoy it."

"You've heard our offer?"

"Offer?" I said. "Karin Baxter said something about a housing allowance. Is there more?"

"If the house here isn't what Lauren wants – and I know how women are," Chatzwirth said. Then he backtracked. "The house is yours, Michael, free and clear, plus the land: $15 million worth. But if it's not what you're looking for, we'll give you the housing allowance Ms. Baxter mentioned."

"Very generous. I appreciate the option."

"Good." Philip Chatzwirth clapped his hands together. "Now, for the coup de grace. The workout room. You're going to love this hummer. Not that you'll ever have time to use the damn thing."

We both laughed.

Celia Chatzwirth greeted us at the front door with an offer of dark Virginia lager, Panda Farm Pinot Noir, and fresh squeezed lemonade. I chose the lemonade and hoped I wasn't bringing shame upon the winery's vintner. "What took you so long?" she asked with a wink that told me she knew already.

"Guy talk," her husband said.

"In other words, he gave you a tour of the workout room."

"We had to do a couple of reps on the bench press," I informed her.

"Showing off, was he?"

"Not me." The Chairman took his wine and closed the study doors behind him.

His wife used her eyes to indicate a room off the back of the house and said to me, "Join me in the solarium?"

"Sure. Thanks."

We were suddenly and conspicuously alone. She invited me to a couch looking out on a well-tended rose garden. "Long day?"

I shook my head. "Interesting day," I said truthfully.

"I'm looking forward to meeting Lauren," the Chairman's wife said. She kicked off her shoes and curled her feet underneath her legs. "Is she a full-time mother?"

I nodded. "We're lucky that way," I said. I wouldn't have presumed even for a second that Celia Chatzwirth was unaware of Lauren's legal background, so I didn't preface my next remark. "Whether she'll practice again once Hanna's in school is something she hasn't decided yet."

"Virginia is desperate for women lawyers," she said, and I could tell from her tone that the state of women in the world was a serious interest. I liked that. So would Lauren. "Not to mention women in politics. We're about a century behind the rest of the country and the rest of the country isn't in all that great of shape either."

Celia Chatzwirth, I had to admit, was nothing short of brilliant; the techniques she displayed in leading me through the 'ultra-sensitive' minefields so carefully avoided by Panda's Board members – issues like religious affiliation and political leanings – was almost as adroit as her forays into family values and morality. I tried not to frustrate her with my less-than-forthcoming attitude, but she seemed to be hearing what she wanted to hear. Or, if she wasn't, she didn't show it.

"Not that any of this has anything to do with the job," she tried telling me after I gave her my unabashed views on Canadian prescription drugs and my disdain for fresh Rocky Mountain oysters.

"What does it have to do with, Mrs. Chatzwirth?" I asked.

"Just a nosy woman interrogating a potential next door neighbor," she said rather spiritedly.

"Because I respect a man who seeks out the opinion of the woman he shares a bed with," I admitted with complete sincerity.

"Well, Philip and I don't actually share a bed, Michael," she said with an expression that could only be described as candid, "but I think I know what you mean. And I'll take that as a compliment. I should, shouldn't I?"

If I hesitated a beat, it was only because I was trying to decide if I'd been thrown a hanging curve ball or an un-hittable slider. But I recovered nicely when I realized she wasn't playing detective on behalf of her husband at all; she was gathering information for the man in Thailand. Interesting. Very interesting. Now, how to exploit that on my own behalf? As my old mentor used to say: hit it right back into the other guy's court, or hers, as the case may be; answer a question with a question; and personalize it. "May I ask some advice, Celia?"

"Please." She seemed receptive the way a cobra was receptive to the overtures of a mongoose.

"Do the Thai people expect a gift from one accepting their hospitality?" I asked.

"Your host may live in Bangkok, but he is not Thai. Do not mistake him as such," Celia Chatzwirth warned me. "He is Taiwanese. And a gift in hand is considered a slight to the Taiwanese. As if their hospitality is somehow more than it should be: a humble offering. Does that make sense? Your gift is the acceptance of their hospitality."

"Yes. Absolutely," I said, as if I had been steered from an irreparable error in judgment. "I'm looking forward to meeting your husband's partner. I should acquaint myself with some of the more basic Taiwanese traditions, I imagine."

"You can not learn in a week what the Chinese have known for ten thousand years, Michael. Don't embarrass yourself. Let Zhong…I should say, Dr. Chu. Let Dr. Chu and his people show you things from their point-of-view. You'll learn more."

Zhong, I thought. Well, at least I know they're on a first name basis.

Celia came to her feet. She was halfway into her shoes when she stopped. "Oh, and I might not use the word 'partner' when I'm talking to Dr. Chu, Michael."

"No?"

"There are no partners in Thailand. Partnership implies equality. No, two people, in their view, are equals. For every strength, there is a weakness."

"One defines the other," I suggested. I also rose.

"Not necessarily," Celia Chatzwirth said in return. I waited. If she was making a reference to the relationship between her husband and Chu, she didn't say so.

Well then, I thought, go fishing. "Is that your philosophy or Dr. Chu's?" I asked.

"That is a discussion for another day," she said, her eyes signaling a willingness for just such a conversation. She touched my arm, inviting me once again toward the main part of the house. "I believe your plane is waiting for you, and I have monopolized far too much of your time."

"I've enjoyed it," I said. Then I smiled. "Though I'm not letting you off the hook quite so easily the next time."

"Ah! And all this time I thought it was I who had let you off the hook, Michael. I must be losing my touch." There were two beautifully wrapped presents sitting on the waiting table next to the front door, and Celia threw up her hands the way a child does after discovering a long lost toy. "Good, good, good. They're ready. Very good! This one," she said, placing the larger of the two – the one adorned with pink and purple paper and two suckers - in my hands, "is for little Hanna. I've heard how much she likes horses."

"A fanatic," I said with a smile.

"And this is for your wife." The narrowness of the box suggested jewelry, as did the weight. "I can't wait for her to open it."

"Thank you. You didn't have to do this," I said.

"On the contrary." She gave me a warm hug and guided me outside. "Your car is waiting. And I believe Philip would like to go along for the ride."

"Until next time."

"Soon. I hope."

Philip Chatzwirth used the ride back to the airport to inform me that the Board – those on US soil, as he put it – had given me their most hardy approval – also his words. He extended an invitation for me to fly to

Bangkok in ten days time to meet with his partner. Beware of that word, I thought.

He called my interview with Dr. Chu a necessary formality, but I wasn't accepting the explanation at face value. I said I would talk over the situation with Lauren, but, yes, I would expect to make the trip, thank you very much.

The major difference between the plane ride out this morning and the ride home tonight was the evolution of Karrie Lyn Chatzwirth. The seductress who had transformed into an innocent teenage girl at Panda Farms this afternoon was now a young professional with copious amounts of respect for the man who might well be her next boss: me. There were several ways I could have reacted to this. Amusement came to mind, but this was more complicated than that. Amazement might not have been totally out of line, but I had seen plenty of people go a lot further than a show of multiple personalities when issues of money and influence were involved. Here was a young woman – this afternoon she looked like a high school senior; this evening, she could have passed for 25 – already well-versed in the art of manipulation, and with her parents approval and, I was sure, their guidance. This told me just how intertwined business and life had become in the world of Panda Pharmaceuticals' upper echelon. It made me take pause for a moment and examine my own existence. I was the CEO of a major drug company, and I had called it a 24-hour occupation on more than one occasion. You could leave the office, but you couldn't turn off the mental machinery; it ran even when you ordered it not to. I had an office at home. Lauren was my sounding board, my consultant, my confidante. Gratefully, she didn't back away from those roles. I could only hope she didn't feel obligated to live those roles every hour of the day.

I watched Karrie Lyn moving around the cabin, available but unobtrusive. I could have dropped my guard, shed my coat and tie, and kicked off my shoes, but I didn't. Instead, I accepted her offer of a light meal – fresh fruit, poached halibut, grilled asparagus, and chocolate mousse – light by

Virginia standards, I suppose. I wasn't sure why I said no to wine – St. Supery, one of Lauren and my favorites – but I wasn't dropping my role of CEO and highly coveted recruit until I was on the ground in Boulder and behind the wheel of my Cayenne. Rules were rules. Panda had theirs. I had mine.

"Can I impose a very short video on you while you eat, Mr. King?" Karrie Lyn asked after filling my glass with Perrier and lime.

"Let's do the DVD before dinner, Karrie Lyn, why don't we?" I said, eager for the flight to be over and already thinking about how good a particularly beautiful woman's body was going to feel next to mine.

"It's a personal message from the Board, so I'll disappear up front until it's over," she said, sliding the disc into the machine.

"We'd like to take a moment away from your flight, Michael, to say how much we enjoyed your visit," Willy Kellerman said on behalf of the Board of Directors. "I know Philip already shared the Board's overwhelming enthusiasm. But just to prove it, I've been authorized to add a touch of an incentive to our package. Up the ante, as it were. I think Phil and Celia are particularly eager to have you, Lauren, and Hanna in the neighborhood, so we thought we'd toss in the $5 million housing allowance along with the house. A gesture of good faith, you might say. With Lauren's approval naturally," Willy added with a nod and a chuckle.

"You will be receiving some details tomorrow via Karin Baxter about the trip to Thailand and your visit with Dr. Chu Zhong Liu. Do make certain it fits into your schedule. The visit is a formality, to be sure, but still one Dr. Chu's position in the company requires. I'm sure you understand that.

"It might be a bit premature to welcome you to the Panda team, Michael, but I will do so nonetheless. We're at your disposal night and day. Enjoy your flight."

The video ended with the Panda logo fading to black, but I stared at the screen for a full 30 seconds. "A formality, to be sure." There was that word again. Why was everyone so eager to convince me that the interview with the renowned Dr. Chu Zhong Liu was hardly worth the time? A point of etiquette; good form; ceremony? That his approval was more a compulsory exercise than anything? In that case, a round of video conferencing should have sufficed. An hour on the phone. Heads of State did it all the time. I did some of my best work with people 3,000 miles away and faceless. That was the beauty of technology, right? To make the world a smaller, more accessible place? No, this was more than a formality. If not for the Board or Philip Chatzwirth or his beautiful wife, then for me. More importantly, I would have bet my $5 million housing allowance that it was more than a formality for one Dr. Chu Zhong Liu, co-founder of Panda Pharmaceuticals and guardian of 250,000 acres of invaluable poppy fields.

I had my eyes closed and my head back against the seat rest when the jet's cabin phone rang. Karrie Lyn answered it. "It's for you, Mr. King," she said with a hand over the mouthpiece. "Karin Baxter. She wants to congratulate you, Sir."

I shook my head. "Tell Ms. Baxter that I'm sound asleep and not to be disturbed, will you, Karrie Lyn?" I listened to Karrie Lyn turn my lie into an indisputable order, and then closed my eyes again.

"She's expecting a call the minute your eyes open," Karrie Lyn whispered even as the lights dimmed.

"You're a lifesaver. Thanks."

❧

6

THE OFFER

"If you try sometimes, you might find you get what you need."

It was well after 8:00 when I pulled into the drive at home. I had already called Lauren on the cell phone, and Hanna was waiting for me at the front door.

"Daddy! You're home."

I swept her into my arms and listened to a peel of laughter. I had to admit that I had been through one helluva day, but this was the highlight. "You're up late, young lady," I said, nuzzling her cheek. "And I'm sure as heck glad you are. Have you had a bedtime story yet?"

"Two of them," Lauren said.

"Goodnight Gorilla. Goodnight Gorilla. Please Daddy!?"

"Goodnight Gorilla it is." That got me another hug.

Lauren relieved me of my briefcase, which allowed me to wrap an arm around her waist; the highlights were mounting up. "How'd it go?"

"Quite a day."

"Quite a day? Hmm. I'm dying to know what that means," Lauren said, as if 'quite a day' was a secret code.

"Presents first," I said holding up the bag Celia Chatzwirth had instructed me to deliver. "Gifts from my host. Or at least from his wife."

"For me? For me?" Hanna wanted to know.

"One for you. One for Mommy," I said as we made our way through the house and into Hanna's bedroom. The three of us sprawled on the bed, and I made my offerings. "This is from a very nice woman back in Virginia. That's where Daddy was today," I said for my daughter's benefit. "Her name is Celia."

Hanna tore into the paper and let the pieces fall where they might. The rectangular box inside was made of sweet-smelling cedar. Inlaid across the face of the lid was a horse made from slivers of abalone. "Oh, Mommy, look," Hanna said dramatically.

"Pretty! Open the lid."

Hanna did, and Brahm's Lullaby filled the air. "It's a music box!" Hanna exclaimed, as if the music boxes lining her bookshelf didn't exist. We listened until the music ran out, and then Hanna called, "Now you, Mommy! Now you!"

"I think I'll save the card for later." She gave me a wink and peeled away the wrapping paper. "Pretty paper," she said.

Hanna yawned and rubbed her eyes. "I don't care about the paper, Mommy. What's inside?" She yawned again.

"Why don't you crawl under your covers first," Lauren suggested, and Hanna didn't argue. When her head was on the pillow and there was a stuffed rabbit in her arms, Lauren opened the box.

Inside was a silk scarf, very sheer and subtle enough to fit any style, and not something I would have ever bought Lauren. "My goodness. It's beautiful." When she wrapped it around her neck and shoulders, I had to admit that it suited her well. "I love it. What do you think Hanna Banana? Do you…?"

Hanna's eyes were closed, and her breathing was already deep and rhythmic. I drew the blanket up over her shoulders and kissed her forehead. Lauren and I tiptoed out. We went into our own bedroom. I shed my shirt and tie and kicked off my shoes. Lauren folded her scarf and opened the envelope that Celia Chatzwirth had attached to her gift. I watched her expression as she read the note. I saw one raised eyebrow and a brief, hint of smile, but Lauren wasn't reading the card as if it had been attached to a welcome-to-the-neighborhood gift. This was her this-is-my-future-we're-talking-about-here face. I was glad to see it. She glanced up, closed the card, and then opened it again.

"Wow! That's quite the sales pitch," she said with equal amounts of awe and caution. I had always been able to rely on Lauren for perspective, but it was clear that Celia Chatzwirth was doing her best to sway the vote.

"That seems to be the Panda way. No holds barred. Full steam ahead," I said. "What does she say?" I didn't really expect Lauren to read the note out loud, but she did.

"It says, 'Dear Lauren:

'I wanted to let you know how important I think your input is into this process your husband is going through. Your life will be greatly impacted if you and Michael elect to move to Virginia, and I understand that. Panda has had only one Chief Executive Officer over the course of its wonderful history and only one Chairman, roles my husband Philip has filled since the company was founded. As you know, we have been searching for a successor to the role of CEO, a leader with enough passion, vision, and positive energy to lead Panda into the 21st century. Michael is more than just the ideal candidate, Lauren. We believe he is the only man for the job. It may be premature to welcome you to the family, but I want you to know that we're all looking forward to meeting you.

'I know Michael will be sharing the details of the company's offer with you. I wanted to let you know, however, that the house we have built for you at Panda Farms, if you chose to accept that part of the offer, is yours to decorate and furnish any way you chose. At the company's expense, of course. It's 20,000 square feet and surrounded by some of the most beautiful acreage in the country.

'I also know how hard it can be to leave family and friends behind, so there will be a private Lear jet available to you seven days a week.

'As far as your daughter's education goes, there is an exceptional private school less than a half hour away from Panda Farms, and I have *arranged for you and Hanna to tour the facility when you come out for your visit. Her enrollment has already been assured if you like what you see.*

'I've included a picture of a pony from our stables that I would like Hanna to have as a welcome gift. Her pedigree is exceptional. She's already becoming accustomed to the new stables we built on your property. Her name is Princess, but we want Hanna to choose any name she wants, of course.

'I look forward to meeting you while Michael is traveling to Thailand. I hope you're as excited about your visit as I am.

'Your neighbor, Celia Chatzwirth.'

Lauren looked up from the letter, her eyes fixed on me. "Obviously, you passed with flying colors."

"Well, I don't know if flying colors describes it, but it seemed to go well," I admitted.

"Tell me about the Board."

"It's not the kind of group you'd want to get on the bad side of, I'll tell you that much," I said.

"Heavy hitters?"

"One and all."

"That's a good thing, right?" Lauren was still watching me.

"As long as the CEO doesn't end up tap dancing around their inflated egos and spending half his time babysitting." I took off my pants and socks and stretched out on the bed.

"Is that a possibility with this group?" Lauren slipped out of her sweats, let down her hair, and joined me.

"Their agendas worry me some, but that's to be expected."

I went down the list, giving her mini-bios of former CIA Director Patrick Truit, Sir Adrian Glass, former Governor Willy Kellerman, Judith Claymore, and Philip Chatzwirth. Lauren stopped me when I got to the missing pinky finger on the Chairman's left hand. "Who knows," I said with a shrug. "He didn't offer, and I didn't ask."

"Good thinking," Lauren said. Then she asked, "What about the company? Will you have the authority you need to get the job done?"

"I won't be there five minutes if I don't," I assured her "But I have a feeling the real power lies in Thailand."

"This Doctor Chu?" Lauren ran her hand over my chest. I had never had much luck resisting her touch, but then I couldn't remember an occasion when I had tried very hard.

"Everyone kept using the word 'formality,' like it was a slam dunk with this guy," I told her.

"There's no such thing."

"Not in my experience," I agreed. I told Lauren about the reference Celia Chatzwirth had made about Chu's relationship with her husband and about the warning I had received from Raymond Leavitt, the head of Business Development. "He said, 'Nothing is a done deal until Chu puts his stamp on it.'"

"Sour grapes?" Lauren wondered. She let her hand wander more freely.

"Don't know." I shook my head. I took the hand and drew her near. I kissed her neck and shoulder and inhaled the scent of her hair. "Enough talk about corporate intrigue. I haven't made love to you in 48 hours."

Lauren laughed. "Damn. Forty-eight hours. We'd better do something about that."

∽

7

THE FINAL STEP

"Granted that I must die, how should I live?"

"Y ou ready for this, Mr. King?" Karin Baxter said with a teasing air that filled my cell phone. "From the frying pan into the fire?"

"It's still just an interview," I said into the phone. It was Thursday morning. I'd been the first person in line at Starbuck's, and the clock on the Cayenne's console read 6:02. Karin was, of course, referring to a day's worth of conversation in Virginia versus a five-day stint in Bangkok, Thailand. "I've been through them before, and I'll..."

"Don't say, 'And I'll go through them again.' Not if you say 'yes' to this one. You say 'yes' to this one, and it'll be the last interview you'll ever do. And if you don't say 'yes' to this one, my friend, I'll strangle you with my bare hands," Karin informed me.

I looked out the window of the car and caught the outline of Peak Pharmaceuticals four-story headquarters looming a block away and wondered how many more times I would be parking next to the space reserved for the company's top dog. I was already going down the list of staff members I might want to approach about a potential move to Virginia – my Executive Assistant, Peg Fuller, was at the top of that list, and I would probably try and drag Carly Perisi, our PR Director, away from her beloved Boulder – but I knew I was getting way ahead of myself.

"So, what's my schedule?" I asked Karin.

"It's a five-day jaunt," she said, jocularities at least momentarily aside. "You'll fly out on Sunday, the 15th."

"That's absolutely peak time for the changing of the aspen trees here in Colorado, Karin. Can't miss that." I was kidding, of course, though in fact Lauren and I always paid a yearly visit to the high country when the aspens were showing off their fall colors. It was a family tradition, and I didn't like giving up family traditions.

"You can buy your own aspen grove with the signing bonus Panda is offering you, Bub. You and Lauren can run naked through the trees for the rest of your days if that's what gets your motor running. But this fall you'll be in Thailand putting on the performance of your life." Leave it to Karin to cut through the subtleties, I thought. "So, like I was saying, you'll fly out on the 15th. You'll take the corporate jet into LAX. From there, you'll fly first class commercial to Bangkok, arriving at 6:00 that evening. Panda will have a limo waiting for you, and you'll have until noon the next day to get your beauty sleep."

"You obviously have never spent much time in Bangkok, Ms. Baxter," I said, speaking from the rousing two-month experience I'd had there – it had to be 16 years ago if it was a day – when business and partying were essentially one and the same animal. "No one ever stops long enough to sleep."

"That's the old Michael King talking," Karin Baxter assured me. "My money says you'll be tucked in bed and dead to the world by 8:00."

"You're probably right," I admitted.

"Can you clear your schedule with Peak?" Karin wanted to know. "It's probably not the best idea in the world to broadcast your plans."

Karin was right about that, and I appreciated her concern. But, on the other hand, the drug industry had an incestuous side to it, and there was every chance in the world that word of my visit to Thailand would leak out somewhere along the line. Trying to conceal it would only stir the rumor mill. "I'm going to Thailand to visit with Panda's upper management. It's a business trip. I'm not going to lie about where I'm going or who

I'm meeting with. If I lie about the reason, it will be a lie of omission."

"A guy with principles. How heroic," Karin chided.

"It's not a matter of principles as much as it is practicality," I said without an overabundance of conviction. I parked the car, grabbed my briefcase, and locked the Cayenne behind me. "And besides, I've already informed Tom Palmer that I'm coming, and we're meeting the day I arrive. Strictly business."

"Palmer? Tom Palmer?" There was hardly a soul in upper management that Karin didn't know either personally or by reputation, and I could sense the wheels turning. "You mean the American Financial guy?"

"That's him. He's an old college buddy. Graduate school actually. We roomed together for a while at Thunderbird in Arizona." Tom and I had chased some of the same women, earned our black belts in karate together, and cultivated a love of fly-fishing in the blue waters of the Verde River. Tom was one helluva businessman. He ran American Financial's Southeast Asia branch, which meant he had a finger on the pulse of the region's entire business community.

"And you think he'll have the lowdown on the good Dr. Chu. Is that it?" Karin suggested.

"I'm not looking for the lowdown, Karin. I'm looking for insight," I said using the private entrance off the rear of the building.

"Right! Uh-huh. Sure thing," Karin cracked. "In the meantime, have a look at the FedEx package I had sent over to the house. It's the full scoop on Dr. Chu. At least as full as I was able to get without opening myself up to a lawsuit."

"Good."

"And I'll fax over your itinerary to the home office. Let me know when you get it."

We hung up. I took the stairs two at a time to the fourth floor. The night staff was just closing down. Peg Fuller was already at her desk. A bowl of whole bran granola and peach yogurt was half eaten and her coffee cup was empty. It was 6:15 in the morning. By my estimate, my Executive

Assistant – perhaps the most pedestrian, inaccurate, and unappreciated title a woman of Peg's experience and responsibility could ever wear – had been on the job since 5:30.

"Good morning," I said. Way too upbeat for 6:00.

Peg peeked over a pair of half-cut reading glasses. "What's with the good cheer? You get laid last night, boss?"

"Hey, watch your mouth, Ms. Fuller."

"Meaning, yes, you did." Peg was 55, a widow of 18 years, and a grandmother of eight. She worked 60 hours a week here at the office and volunteered at least another 20 at a local treatment center. Peg had been behind the wheel when her husband was killed in a head-on collision with a flatbed truck loaded with fencing materials. The police had tested her blood alcohol level at .21. "Halfway between dead drunk and losing consciousness," was how Peg described it in the one and only conversation we had ever had about the accident. "The only good piece of news was that my husband was drunker than me at the time and never knew what hit us. Wish that helped me sleep at night, but it doesn't."

Peg was more than my right hand; she was a great friend. Lauren loved her. Hanna was like her ninth grandchild. Peg came to work for me three years after the accident. I was in my second week at the helm of the Navarro Institute. She started as a temp assigned to reorganize the filing system of the outgoing CEO's staff. After a month, she had created a communications pipeline between the Institute's department heads and my office that made it seem like every call was getting my personal attention – which they were – but all of a sudden I was spending less time on the minutia and more on the details. Peg started working after hours. When she began arriving at the office long before my then-Executive Assistant, a woman I had inherited from the outgoing CEO, I took her on permanently. Back then, she was called a clerical liaison. No one knew what that meant, but it didn't threaten my EA's position even though Peg was doing twice the work. When I took over at Peak Pharmaceuticals, Peg finally got the promotion she deserved.

I went into my office and settled behind my desk. Peg followed with a fresh cup of coffee. She set it on a coaster next to Hanna's picture. "You've got a full day," she informed me. "Let me get my book."

"Why don't you warm up your coffee and bring it in here instead," I said.

Peg didn't like it when I changed our routine, so a raised eyebrow wasn't surprising. She went out and returned with her cup. "Close the door, will you, Peg?"

A closed door only happened when the shit was about to hit the fan, and Peg loved it when that happened. I could see the beginnings of a crooked grin as she closed the door and took a seat. "What's up, boss?"

"I'm going to Thailand next week to talk to Panda Pharmaceuticals," I said between sips of coffee.

That was not what Peg was expecting. No heads rolling, no reprimands in the making, no ultimatums to be issued. "I didn't know we had anything going with Panda."

"We don't," I told her. "I do."

"Oh?" I held her eye. A trace of uncertainty evolved from an initial wave of confusion, and then I saw the first traces of discovery touch her face. "Oh!"

"This is one of those conversations, Peg. Know what I'm saying?"

"You're saying you don't want me to get on the phone with CNN as soon as I get back to my desk."

"Right," I said.

"Gotcha."

"Panda is looking for a new CEO and President." Peg's eyes widened involuntarily when I said this. "I was in Virginia yesterday meeting with their Board. I've got one more guy to see."

"In Thailand." Peg was gripping her coffee cup in two hands.

"Their co-founder. Dr. Chu Zhong Liu." I said with a nod. "It's a good offer, Peg."

"Goodness." That was the highest form of exclamation in Peg Fuller's vocabulary.

"I want you to think about coming along if I accept," I said. "Panda will double your salary and double your retirement benefits. Housing, transportation, everything. On them."

"If, you said."

"Well, a few things would have to go wrong for me not to think about it pretty hard," I admitted. "Lauren is going out to Virginia to check out the housing situation and Hanna's school, so we're at least that far along."

Now Peg lifted her coffee to her lips. "Sounds serious, boss. How do I play it while you're gone?"

"I'm in Thailand talking to some people at Panda and American Financial. Everyone knows how private Panda is about their operations. All you know is I'll be back on Friday or Saturday," I said.

The phone was ringing in the outer office, and Peg jumped up. She stopped at the door and glanced back. "Thanks for being straight with me, Mr. King. I appreciate your confidence."

I heard Peg answer the phone, but none of her conversation. A moment later, she was back at my door saying, "It's Lauren. There's a FedEx package at the house. The sender is K. Baxter. Should I send a courier over to pick it up?"

I nodded. "Thank you."

The package containing Dr. Chu Zhong Liu's personal profile was in my hands 30 minutes later, and I had to admit that it made for compelling reading. Chu was born in 1930 in the city of Taipei, in northern Taiwan. Four years later, the profile had Chu and his family living in Sattahip, Thailand, 40 miles south of Bangkok and due west of the Bay of Thailand. His father apparently held a position at the Taiwanese Embassy in Sattahip, but what the position was the profile didn't say. His mother was a translator. She spoke six languages fluently. According to the profile, she had taught herself English in the 5th Grade when she was struck by the urge to read Charles Dickens' *Tale of Two Cities* and found there was no such thing as a Taiwanese translation. Impressive, I thought.

Chu was home-schooled until the 9th grade when his father used his influence to gain admission for his son at the Science Academy of Bangkok. Chu had clearly inherited his mother's thirst for learning and devoured the curriculum at SAB in two years. His record gained him a special exemption from the Thai government and a recommendation to attend Harvard in the United States.

The profile spent a full page noting a flock of honors earned while at Harvard and a Ph.D. in chemistry netted over two years at MIT, but I found myself skimming.

Once MIT was behind him, Chu spent six years at Eli Lilly as an Associate Scientist doing research at the molecular level. There was no mention of specific projects or products that might have come out of his work, but the very mention of this type of work put Chu far ahead of his contemporaries.

In 1958, Chu finally stepped out from Eli Lilly's shadow and established his own research company – Panda Services – selling his extraordinary intellect to the highest bidder and making enough money to fund his own private projects. The profile hinted that his own private projects focused on a Thailand staple: the poppy plant.

In 1959, Chu suddenly and unexpectedly returned to Thailand, and, as the profile put it, 'by all indications, never set foot in the United States again.' There was a handwritten memo scribbled in the margins of the profile next to this notation, and it read: *It was also in 1959 that Chu's father was apparently held in house arrest for nearly two months in the Taiwanese embassy. I couldn't find anything to connect the two incidences, but his father was released without facing any formal charges. From what I can tell, he and his wife returned to Taiwan shortly thereafter, but Chu remained in Thailand. Don't know why I mention it, but something told me you'd want to know. I know how cynical you are.* Karin Baxter had scribbled her initials next to the note: *KB.*

The profile then jumped 12 years to 1971 when Chu won a Nobel Prize based upon the development of a non-addictive, opium-based pain reliever called Claraphine. Interestingly, he chose not to travel to

Stockholm to accept his prize in person, and no reason was given. Chu apparently used his award money to open his own lab in partnership with Philip Chatzwirth, whom he had met during his years at Eli Lilly. They called the new company Panda Pharmaceuticals. Company headquarters were established in the US while their research and development facilities were housed in Thailand. Close to the source, I thought. Sure, that made sense.

Unfortunately, my mind was still back in 1959. I buzzed Peg Fuller and asked her to come into the office.

Peg was a marvelous EA, but computer research – at least the kind of research I was thinking about – was not her forte. "Boss?"

"See if you can track down Emily Reimer for me, will you Peg?" I asked.

Peg's face knotted into a tight ball. This was her I-don't-like-it look, and her I-don't-like-it look usually called for an explanation. Not this time. Peg already knew that Emily Reimer was one of two or three independent contractors who I only called when the business at hand was to be handled with complete confidence and absolutely no ties back to either the company or me. "Get a number that I can call her on." I didn't look up. "Thanks."

"It's not something I can handle?" she asked, though it didn't really have the sound of a bona fide question. Now I looked up. I raised an eyebrow. "Fine."

She turned on her heels and stomped out, bringing a momentary grin to my face. I used the rest of the profile to keep my mind off the wait, and it made for interesting reading. Over the years, Dr. Chu adopted a polygamist view of the world and acquired exactly 11 wives; best guess had him fathering 35 children over the years. And I thought one was a handful.

Karin Baxter's profile characterized Chu as a deep thinker, a people person, and a student of the human condition. This guy, I began to think, was too good to be true. Which meant that it would not do well to underestimate him, and I didn't plan to.

Now 75 years old and worth a billion dollars by conservative estimates, Chu housed his entire family in a well-guarded estate on the outskirts of Bangkok. Karin had scribbled a second note in the margin that said: *From what I've been able to gather, better to use the word 'castle' than 'estate,' but I guess you'll find out soon enough.*

"Guess I will," I whispered.

Peg appeared at my door, knocked briefly, and entered. She passed me a slip of paper with a phone number on it. "She'll be there for an hour."

"Thanks," I said. When I was alone again, I reached for my cell phone.

Emily Reimer answered after the first ring. "I'm not optimistic," I told her, "and it's probably not a big deal anyway, but…"

"But you figured if there was one person on the planet…"

"Right," I said and explained in detail what I was looking for. "No hurry. I'm leaving town on Sunday."

"If this takes until Sunday," Emily Reimer said, "please fire my ass, all right?"

"Will do. You've got my number." We hung up. I put the profile aside and turned my attention to the company that still employed me.

I didn't have to leak word of my trip to Thailand to anyone. That happened quite naturally when Peg began fielding requests for meetings, phone calls, and such for the following week. Her basic response was, "He'll be in Thailand next week. Can we put something down for the week after?"

More and more, it began sounding like an exploratory meeting for potential partnering projects with the highly regarded Panda Pharmaceuticals, and that was fine with me. Mid-week, I met with our VP of Research and Development, Harley Kilinger, over coffee. However, before bringing up the subject of Panda's latest entries into the world of opium-based pain relievers – those being Trifil and Thonefil, the cancer-related drugs, and Cielmeta, the rheumatoid arthritis med that was making a dent in every world market except the United States – I deemed the meeting confidential. Harley understood.

"This have anything to do with your Thailand trip?" he wanted to know.

"We'll find out," I said. "But if it does, I'm wondering why the FDA has been so slow in approving the drugs here in the States."

Harley shrugged. "Probably because the FDA isn't as convinced as everyone else that there are no addictive properties in Trifil, Thonefil, or Cielmeta."

"Everything has an addictive property, Harley," I replied. "Could be cheeseburgers. Could be sex."

"Make mine sex," Harley said, rising to leave. "I'll make a couple of discreet inquiries. If I hear anything before you leave on Saturday, I'll let you know."

When Carly Perisi was seated across from my desk later that afternoon, I said, "I don't want the press or anyone else making hay out of my trip to Thailand, Carly. Can you keep a lid on it?"

Carly shrugged; I was getting a lot of that today. "When there's something newsworthy, I'll get the word out. Until then, I'd be wasting their time. And we sure don't want to waste the media's time."

"Good. Thanks." Carly didn't get up right away. I glanced up. "Anything else?"

Our eyes met. Hers did the quizzical you're-not-being-straight-with-me thing that women do with their eyes. Mine did the there's-nothing-to-tell thing that men do with theirs. This was hard. Carly was part of the management team I had handpicked when I took the Peak job. They were loyal to me, and I would have called myself loyal to them. Yes, they would be more or less devastated if I left and not necessarily because Michael King was such a great guy; a change at the top guaranteed changes in their lives. It could be good, or it could be bad. I was about to rock the boat, and no one wanted that.

By intent, I did not make friends with my employees. Not that I wasn't friendly; I was. But I tried very hard not to become personally attached. Carly was an exception. We shared a chemistry that made it possible to drop our professional roles, to talk about things like politics, family, and religion, and to do so as equals. I could seek Carly out for a moment of levity during a rough day, and she could do the same with me. I had introduced her to Lauren, and the two of them had gone to lunch numerous times. She bought Hanna gifts at Christmas and birthdays. If I were observing a similar relationship in another CEO, I would have said, "Bad policy." Screw that. I didn't know one person with too many friends, and I was not giving up this one because it was bad policy.

She still had me captured with those eyes of hers. I said, "Ever been to Virginia?"

Now the eyes narrowed. Then she shook her head. "I drove across the Mississippi River once. Does that count?"

A warm smile tugged at the corners of my mouth. "Let's get some lunch when I get back from Thailand."

Carly's nod had a deliberate feel to it. "Lunch sounds good," she said after a moment. When she was at the door, she looked over her shoulder and said, "Stay away from those Thai women. They'll change your view of sex forever."

"I'll keep that in mind," I answered, knowing that everything was again on the up-and-up between us, or at least as much as it could be until my interview was over.

I was not good at letting things slide at work, even with Panda Pharmaceuticals' offer staring me in the face. I knew Peak had recorded a strong quarter, and I knew we were ramped up for a banner year. The sales were there. The team was focused. Research was ahead of the game on new products. Our stock price had popped up nearly two points since our numbers had come out three weeks ago. I knew I could probably drop my guard for the next four or five days, gear up for the Thailand trip, and speculate over what might be ahead. That wasn't me. I dug my claws into every issue that crossed my desk over the next couple of days, explored a half-dozen potential projects, and made sure my department heads were doing the same.

At night, I used my personal computer to research the life and times of Dr. Chu Zhong Liu. He was clearly not a man who sought the spotlight. Still, his name surfaced in articles touching on matters of politics, industry, social change, and, in particular, philanthropy. I looked for blemishes, controversy, or even a hint of impropriety; there was none. A guy with 11 wives, 35 kids, and 250,000 acres of flourishing poppy fields. Give him credit. If there were black marks to be found, Chu had the machinery in place to hide them.

And then my cell phone rang as I was pulling into the drive at home on Thursday night. It was Emily Reimer. She didn't waste time on pleasantries. "Here's what I've got," she said. "Chu's father, Chu Sun Yat-sen, was an attaché at the Taiwan embassy in Bangkok back in the 1950s. He was arrested by the Taiwanese police for running secrets to the Chinese, a crime punishable by death in that part of the world. Our Dr. Chu was ordered home from the States. He crafted some type of a deal with the Taiwanese government. Don't know the details, but whatever it was it got his dad out of jail and on a boat back home to Taipei. If Chu paid someone off, I can't find out who. You know he never leaves Thailand, and I'd be very surprised if it isn't related. Does that mean someone's holding him hostage? Hard to say."

The next night, I stumbled upon a photograph of the man I would be meeting in three days. It was the first I had seen. Karin Baxter's profile had not included Chu's picture, and Panda Pharmaceuticals had not been inclined to make one available either. This one appeared in a recent edition of the *Economist* magazine and had been captured at a charity event in Surat Thani, a city on the Thai peninsula. It showed a man slight of build and very erect, handsome, and looking far younger than his 75 years.

"He looks 50," Lauren agreed.

Lauren had been the beneficiary of rather lavish flower arrangements delivered daily to the house in the name of Panda's Board of Directors. Hanna had received a stuffed horse two mornings ago that was now standing watch over her bed at night. Yesterday, a FedEx envelope arrived with a photograph of the horse I had seen in the stables at Panda Farms. The photo was accompanied by a handwritten note from Celia Chatzwirth inviting Hanna to take the horse for a ride the following week. Needless to say, we had one very excited girl on our hands.

My wife and daughter were not the only ones on the receiving end of our Virginia suitors' constant attention. I had come home two nights ago and found myself looking at a private guide to the company's private golf course. The brochure was laid out as if each hole was a holiday experience. And then there was the eight-page glossy listing the many choices I had available to me in the way of a company car. There were Jaguars, Mercedes, a couple of very nice Beemers, and a Cadillac Escalade that could have passed for a school bus had it been painted yellow. No Porsches. No Cayennes. Well, maybe they took special requests.

"The Mercedes works for me," Lauren joked. "I'm assuming it comes with a driver."

"What fun would that be?" I wondered.

"Good point. Especially if I wanted to drag you away from the office some afternoon, so we could spend a couple of hours in the backseat doing who knows what," she said, batting her eyelashes at me.

"No driver. Definitely no driver," I said.

The golf guide and the company cars were good for a laugh, but it was not all fun and games. Philip Chatzwirth also forwarded the company's five-year-strategic plan for, as he put it, 'my perusal.' He wanted me to know that every aspect of the plan was subject to my approval and that the Board was anxious for any feedback.

Panda wasn't leaving any stone unturned. It was ironic in one sense, because the heightened attention was really more of a distraction than an enticement. The offer itself was the important point. Their interest in my skills and expertise was the motivating factor, not the extras, not the sweeteners.

In some ways, the excessive attention made me wonder if the trip to

Thailand didn't carry more weight than the Panda Board and Philip Chatzwirth were letting on. Maybe, I thought, the issue was not whether or not Dr. Chu Zhong Liu would approve of me, but whether or not I would approve of him.

I posed the question to Lauren once Hanna was in bed and the house was quiet. Too quiet, in fact. Before she could answer, I put Coldplay on the bedroom sound system and listened to the opening chords of Clocks. If I could play piano like that, I thought, I probably wouldn't be contemplating a CEO job with a Virginia drug company.

"What do you think?" I asked her again. I put my back against the headboard and stretched my legs out across the bed. "You think they're afraid we might say 'no?'"

"They're trying awfully hard to impress us, aren't they?" Lauren agreed.

"I'd like to think I was the crème de la crème of candidates, but..."

"Who says you're not!" I looked at her and grimaced. She said, "I'm serious. Every indication is that Philip Chatzwirth and his Board think that highly of you."

"Right. And they're sending you flowers every day. If you ask me, that's odd."

"I think it's nice."

I turned my attention to the music for a moment. The chorus always got to me. *Nothing else compares. Nothing else compares.* Compares to what? Now that I wasn't sure about. Maybe life. Maybe love. Maybe just being wanted.

"You can always say no, you know," Lauren reminded me.

"Why? Because the company keeps sending my wife flowers?" I said. "There's probably going to have to be a better reason than that."

"Glad to hear it." The phone on my nightstand rang, and Lauren jumped. "Who the hell can that be?"

"Tom Palmer. Calling from Bangkok. He's 14 hours ahead. Or behind. I'm not sure which." I picked up the phone. It was Tom. And yes, he was calling from Bangkok, and it was tomorrow there. We kept it short. I had already e-mailed him about breakfast on Monday, and he had already done some preliminary research on Dr. Chu Zhong Liu.

"Eleven wives and all gorgeous," he said.

"You have been busy," I said with a touch of sarcasm. "Thanks a lot."

"You been in the gym lately?" Tom was checking up on the current status of my karate workouts.

"Not as much as I should," I admitted.

"Good. Cause I'm kicking your butt while you're here, and if you're out of shape, so much the better."

"Who says I'm out of shape?"

"Running is not fighting, brother." He laughed. "See you Monday."

∽

8

THE JOURNEY

"I may not have gone where I intended to go,
but I think I have ended up where I needed to be."

Call me old-fashioned. I just didn't like putting my wife and daughter on a private plane with two highly experienced pilots, one doting flight attendant, and the prospect of spending a couple of days in the lap of luxury without me. It wasn't the pilots or the attendant; I knew they could not be in better hands. There was a little part of me that saw them stepping into a lion's den not of their own choosing, soon to be consumed by a group of very nice people whose only interest was their own. Panda Pharmaceuticals' Board of Directors wanted me, and I was flattered. But to get me, they would woo my family with every possible entrapment.

It was probably a ridiculous point of view – something only an egotistical male would dream up – but I couldn't help myself. No, I would never have shared such a banal notion with Lauren. She would have laughed. She may also have been slightly insulted. That wasn't the idea. I knew Lauren could take care of herself. That gift of independence and self-sufficiency was one of the things that had attracted me to her in the first place. That she was taking time away from her own career to raise Hanna full-time only emphasized her lack of interest in playing by the rules set out by society for the 'modern woman.'

There were two private planes waiting for us on the tarmac of Front

Range Airport. The Lear jet with the intertwining P's on the tail would shortly carry Lauren and Hanna off for three days in Virginia and a taste of what Panda Pharmaceuticals had to offer. The Gulfstream – the very plane that had transported me to Virginia ten days ago – would connect me with a Thailand-bound commercial plane in Los Angeles and a first-class ticket to Bangkok.

"I wish you were coming with us," Lauren said when the hatch to the Lear opened.

I was surprised, also pleased. "Me, too."

"This is all happening so fast."

"You don't have to make a decision while you're out there," I said. "We have plenty of time to decide."

"I know. But a place feels different when we're together. You see things I don't, and I see things you don't. We're a team."

"Yeah, Daddy," Hanna chimed in. "We're a team."

"You better believe it, kiddo." I gave her a hug and several kisses. "You look after your mom, okay?"

"I will." She gave me a thumb's up.

"I'll see you in five days. Be careful on that horse," I said.

"Her name's Princess."

"You be careful on Princess. Make sure she knows who's boss."

The flight attendant was standing at the foot of the jet ramp. "Whenever you're ready, Mrs. King," she called.

Lauren nodded. She kissed me. "Knock 'em dead."

"You, too." I held her a moment. "Call me."

"Don't forget my doll, Daddy. You promised," Hanna called from the landing.

"No way," I said. "Have fun."

When the hatch was sealed behind them, I boarded the Gulfstream. Same crew, just as formal, just as professional. Karrie Lyn, the chameleon, looked magnificent. Today, she had the air of a young executive assistant, eager to serve but also ready to consult.

"Anything you need," she said when we were airborne and two hours from L.A. She had used the same phrase on the flight to Virginia, but the connotations were purely business today. "My father gave me a DVD with your agenda. We can play it whenever you're ready."

Here was an opportunity, I thought, to test the level of Karrie Lyn's place in the company and to see if my assessment of the situation was any-where near accurate. "We won't need the DVD, Karrie Lyn." I used an open hand to indicate the seat across from me. "Talk me through it."

"Yes, Sir. My pleasure." She sat. I studied her posture and then her face. The first was erect and dignified; the second was relaxed and focused. "You'll arrive in Bangkok at approximately 5:15 in the afternoon, slight-ly ahead of schedule. Panda will have appropriate escorts for you, and they'll see you through the red tape of customs. From there, you'll be taken to the Pearl Magnolia in downtown Bangkok. The Pearl is a five-star hotel owned by Dr. Chu. You'll be staying in the Presidential Suite. President Clinton spent two nights in the suite last month, so you can imagine the amenities."

"Well, if it's good enough for Bill, it's good enough for me," I said, a demonstration of my quick wit that Karrie Lyn clearly missed. "Just kidding," I assured her.

"Oh!" She smiled, a little embarrassed, and pushed a strand of blond hair behind her ear. Then she pressed on. "You'll have Sunday night and Monday morning to shake off any jet lag, though you're being encouraged to stay close to the hotel. Is that a problem?"

I didn't suppose that it was, though I found it a curious request. "You can assure my host that I'll barricade myself in my room until someone comes for me."

"Right." This time she suppressed a smile. "Representatives from Panda will pick you up at your suite at 1:00 Monday afternoon. The plan is to give you a tour of the area and get you acquainted with the city. It might be a good time for questions," Karrie Lyn suggested.

"Good thought," I said.

"Thailand is considered a US ally, but I think they're a little suspicious of Americans," she added helpfully.

"They probably have a right to be."

"Yes, Sir." She cleared her throat. "That night, at 5:30, promptly, you will be taken to the home of Dr. Chu for dinner and some private time."

"Private time? Your words?"

"No, Sir. That's how the agenda reads."

The interview, I thought. "And then?"

"The next morning, your escorts will take you on a tour of the company's Research and Development facilities near Nakhon. The tour will include lab facilities, their development plant, and several of their more prominent properties," Karrie Lyn said.

Properties. Meaning the poppy fields. Excellent. "The following morning, you'll be driven back to the airport for your flight home." Karrie Lyn smiled.

Three days in Thailand and twenty hours on an airplane. All for a dinner date and some small talk with a man who might well hold the key to my future. A long way to come for a short conversation.

I spent the remainder of the L.A. leg of my journey reviewing Panda Pharmaceuticals' five-year strategic plan, even though I knew it by heart already. The pros were obvious. A projected billion dollars in yearly profits was not only feasible, it appeared conservative given their track record. Long term debt – my pet peeve – was negligible, because every foreseeable project was to be internally funded, and the company had the wherewithal to do just that. Their product pipeline focused on pain relievers, antibiotics, and cellular development. These were all areas with substantial growth potential and all areas able to support outlandish mark-ups. The one con was the company's over-reliance, as I saw it, on opium-based drug development. It wasn't a matter of ethics or legality; it was a matter of resources.

I didn't know as much about Thailand as I would have liked, but I was learning. And not everything about the country thrilled me. Thailand was the one and only country in Southeast Asia that had avoided occupation or colonization by a European power. Why I found that noteworthy, I wasn't sure. The country was not democratic, but their economy was freewheeling and on the upswing. Apparently, the more foreign investment they could attract, the better. They loved Japanese money, and the Chinese weren't far behind. Pros and cons, I thought.

Americans loved Thailand. They loved the weather, the beaches, the shopping, and the sexual freedom. The Thai government was doing everything in its power to keep a lid on the alarming rise in the AIDS virus, but word was finally getting out. Tourism, the country's number one industry, was bound to take a hit, though I couldn't foresee how that would impact Panda Pharmaceuticals' business.

I was more concerned about the escalating violence in the country's Muslim-dominated provinces in the south. If I had my geography right, Panda's poppy fields were within spitting distance of the turmoil. The fields were also a short plane ride from the borders of Burma and Cambodia, and there was no love lost between those two and the Thai. Border disputes, ethnic rebels, and international drug running. Thailand had it all; they just pretended they didn't.

The changeover in LAX was no more painful than any ridiculously busy airport trying to cope with the rules governing the new security game and creating as many problems as they were solving. I was seated in first class on Asian Air flight # 312 at 10:05 Pacific time and out over the Pacific 20 minutes later. I had a window seat. I watched two naval cruisers, a container ship, and a fleet of fishing boats making their separate ways out across the water. The minute they were out of sight, I closed my eyes.

We were halfway to Thailand when they opened again. I spent a few meditative moments watching swells of slate gray traveling across the surface of water 31,000 feet below us. Then I opened my briefcase and removed a blank legal pad. I spent an hour scribbling my impressions of my Panda experience to date, most positive. Then I flipped to a clean page and printed my expectations for the trip ahead. First on the list was: Figure out who the real Dr. Chu Zhong Liu is. Last on the list was: Learn something new about yourself. I didn't know which would be more difficult.

When I heard the pilot informing us of our impending descent, I put the pad aside and closed my briefcase. I saw land for the first time in seven hours when the 747 swept over the Philippine Islands. Viet Nam was a solid mass of green broken by bands of blue water and hills dotted with farms and rice paddies. The jungles of Laos bled across the borders into Thailand, and then the sprawl of Bangkok – from shacks built with barrel staves and sheet metal to skyscrapers reflecting smoked glass and gray steel – stretched out before me.

I was on the ground ten minutes later. Out of habit, I turned on my cell phone and was greeted with a brief version of Pop Goes the Weasel that Hanna had helped program into the phone. I realized that her first day in Virginia was probably over by now. She was probably sleeping next to her mother right about now and dreaming of a horse named Princess. Lauren was probably chalking up her first impressions of Virginia, Panda Farms, and our potential neighbors: Philip and Celia Chatzwirth.

We deplaned. Once I was inside the terminal, I expected a chauffeur with a sign reading: Mr. Michael King. There was none. Instead, there were two Asians the size of middle linebackers wearing black suits, perfectly knotted ties, and solemn expressions reserved for bouncers and bodyguards. The heftiest of the pair studied the bustling concourse with all the attention of a Secret Service agent. The other watched me. When our eyes crossed, he raised a hand and stepped forward. In heavily accented English, he called, "Mr. Michael King."

When I saw the Panda Pharmaceuticals pin displayed on the breast pocket of his jacket, I said, "Yes. I'm Michael King."

"Welcome to Thailand, Sir. Dr. Chu sends his greetings. I'm Teng Juewen. I am your personal driver. This is my associate, Ji Xiong." His tiny eyes traveled for a split second to his partner, a bulldog of a man whose eyes never left the growing throng. Given their names, they were both

Taiwanese, and if not Taiwanese, Chinese. I found that interesting. Teng Juewen motioned to my carry-on. "May I take your bag?"

"Thank you." I relinquished my suitcase but not my briefcase. It wasn't paranoia, just habit. Well, maybe a little paranoia.

"Right this way, Mr. King." They walked on either side of me, and I didn't know whether to feel silly or exalted. When we neared the extraordinary lines forming in front of four Thai Customs Agents, we veered in the direction of the diplomatic entry. Here there were no lines and few impediments. I could feel the envious glances of those less fortunate travelers and could almost hear their inquiring minds trying to identify this guy worthy of such preferential treatment. No one special, ladies and gentleman. Just a lowly CEO with a dinner engagement in the company of one of Southeast Asia's most influential men.

We stepped up to the diplomatic entry. Two men dressed in uniforms that looked in part military and in part police rose to their feet. My bag, briefcase, and credentials were scrutinized and the purpose of my visit was documented. I suspected that Dr. Chu Zhong Liu's name and Panda Pharmaceuticals reputation carried a certain weight in diplomatic circles, but I was still expecting an exchange of money. When it didn't happen, I ordered myself to put aside the movie stereotypes and the Western expectations and to look at every aspect of the trip with an open mind from now on. For a brief moment, I thought about the last thing on my list – learning something new about myself – and hoped to hell I hadn't discovered a man trapped in a world governed by television, sound bites, and the need to believe the worst in people.

"This way, Mr. King." Teng Juewen used an open palm to direct me down a private escalator labeled 'Gold Club Members Only.' He flashed a laminated card at the woman posted at the head of the escalator. The sentinel had apparently seen my escorts before, because she waved us through without examining the card. The escalator descended one floor. A moving walkway led to a set of card-operated doors, a well-lit garage, and several limousines-in-waiting. At the head of the line stood a black

Special Edition Hummer with a mirrored finish worthy of a glacial lake. Bodyguard #2, the silent bulldog, opened the back door and graciously allowed me to climb in under my own power. I was surprised to find the seat opposite mine already occupied.

"Ah! Mr. King. Welcome! Welcome!" This effervescent greeting was delivered by a whisper of a man garishly dressed in silk from head to foot. He smiled and bowed simultaneously. After I was settled in, he extended a hand with long, reedy fingers and a grip worthy of a Sumo wrestler. "I am Yuehan San, Dr. Chu's nephew and humble servant. And yours, as well."

"Mr. Yuehan," I said, recognizing the Chinese origins of his name. I took his hand. "It's a pleasure."

"Call me San, Mr. King." My bodyguards took their places in the front seat, and Mr. Yuehan called to them. "To the hotel, if you please, gentleman."

"Yuehen San doesn't sound Thai to me," I said to Dr. Chu's nephew as a conversation starter.

San laughed. "Hardly, Mr. King. Hardly. The Thai people have these long, exaggerated names like Sirindhorn and Suphamongkhau." He spread his arms out at his sides to emphasize the point. "You can't mistake them for Taiwanese or Chinese or any other sane language. Of course, then they give themselves tiny little nicknames like Fon and Mot. Every native born Thai has one. They never use their given names or their surnames. And most of them will call you Mr. Michael, so don't be offended."

"Good lesson. I'll remember that," I said. "Then you're Taiwanese, I assume."

"I was born in Taiwan. I took my Thai citizenship eight years ago. It makes it easier to do business according to my uncle."

I nodded; the gesture gave me a moment to think. I knew from my research that Dr. Chu had himself taken a similar route regarding his citizenship, but I wondered where his true allegiance lay. "Your English is very good, San," I said. In fact, I could hardly detect an accent.

"I studied in the US at Dr. Chu's urging. Bristol Mark Academy. Harvard." San dropped his eyes, as if taking advantage of a US education was not the most honorable thing an Asian man could do. We exited the airport parking garage and fell into the inexorable and unforgiving grasp of Bangkok's notorious traffic. "The ride will not be swift, Mr. King, but I will try my best to make it interesting."

"And I will try my best to stay interested, San," I said.

"A long flight, Sir?"

"A very long flight."

"We'll have you settled in your hotel room as quickly as possible, I assure you," he said. "As for Thailand…"

As my host's nephew rambled on – I heard bits and pieces about October's temperate weather, umbrellas, plastic shoes, and $5.00 massages – I couldn't help but notice the heightened diligence of our two bodyguards. Their heads swiveled from one side of the road to the other, taking in every passing car, every driver, and every pedestrian, man, woman, and child. If an emotion could be attached to their expressionless faces, it was an emotion produced from equal doses of heedfulness, mistrust, and paranoia. Was there a threat I wasn't aware of? Or, was caution just the better part of valor in the world of Dr. Chu Zhong Liu?

I was not really interested in the fact that Thailand was twice the size of Wyoming, though that surprised me, or that tin and gypsum were its most abundant natural resources, but when San mentioned that the country's population was over 20% Chinese, my interest level jumped.

"Is that so?" I said.

"Indeed. Sixty percent of those are from Taiwan. And it makes the Thai very nervous. Mostly we stay to ourselves, I will say. Except when it comes to business. Then everyone is fair game." San laughed again. The Hummer inched forward, circling onto a main thoroughfare called Thanon Charoen Krung. When San was satisfied as to our progress, he said, "A couple of small pointers. Ice."

"Ice?" The walks were packed. Jostling seemed to be the way of life in the streets of Bangkok. "What about ice?"

"Stay away from it. Ice isn't made from drinking water, but then, you should avoid Bangkok's 'drinking' water, too, now that we're on the subject." San pointed to a long line of street vendors. Most of them appeared to specialize in jewelry and gemstones. "Ignore them like the plague. Most of it's fake, and all of it's a rip-off."

"I promised my daughter a genuine Thai doll," I mentioned. "Any suggestions?"

"You'll have it before you leave. The genuine article," San assured me.

"Your escorts will get you acquainted with the local merchants. You can spend a few minutes bartering."

"Thank you."

"Oh, and remember. No tipping; it's not the Thai way." San perked up. "Oh, we're here. A victory for modern transportation."

The Hummer exited Thanon Charoen Krung for a crowded side street called Soi 34, turned toward the riverfront, and swept around a tree-lined roundabout fronting the extravagant Pearl Magnolia Hotel. Our vehicle was descended upon by three bellmen dressed in red and black, but my newfound bodyguards would have none of it.

Ji grunted, Teng scowled, and San said something in Thai that sounded like, "Thank you anyway. We'll take care of it." He handed each of them 100 baht, which I estimated to be around $2.50. They escorted me past a bank of tall Colonial-looking doors with beveled windows and colored fanlights. The lobby was a showstopper. It rose up in vaulted ceilings painted in shades of rose and paneled with hand painted murals that looked more Japanese than Thai to my eyes. Gold leaf accented every wall, and pinpoints of gold and white light formed a filigree overhead that suggested a mini constellation or a spray of fine fairy dust. Flowers of every color and variety, lively fountains, and perfectly placed settees had turned the lobby into a living entity where guests could linger all day if the mood struck them.

We did not stop at the front desk, but there was suddenly a very

official looking man and primly dressed woman walking at our sides
and leading us in the direction of a private elevator. "Mr. Michael," the
man called, as if we had known each other for decades. "Welcome to the
Pearl Magnolia. I am Somporn Devakulu. The hotel's general manager.
And this," he said gesturing to the woman, "is Ms. Tirini Arhamohareon.
Your personal concierge."

"How are you?" I said, nodding from one to the other. We boarded the
elevator.

"What did I tell you?" San whispered. He gestured with outstretched
arms. "Names a mile long."

The hotel manager vouchsafed San a burning look, then returned a
slightly more pleasant look my way. "Please call me Mhu."

"What did I tell you?" San said again. "Tiny little nicknames."

"You're to be complimented," I said, glancing from the man called
Mhu to my private concierge. "Your hotel is exceptional."

"Thank you, Sir. I'll pass your kind words onto Dr. Chu." Mhu bowed.
The elevator doors opened. The bodyguards stepped out first. The
Presidential Suite was directly ahead of us, and the hotel manager
unlocked the door. The bodyguards entered first.

I was expected to enter next, but I held the door for Tirini
Arhamohareon. As she walked passed, I said, "And how do I address
you, Miss...?"

"Tir. Tir is fine." She bowed.

"I'm Michael."

"Yes, Sir." I had a feeling she was going to say that, but at least I tried.
Tir followed Teng and my luggage into the bedroom. As it turned out, it
was her job to unpack my luggage, and she did it with speed and grace.

I had stayed in a few very nice hotel rooms over the years – CEO perks
and the occasional romantic getaway; I always liked to splurge on Lauren
– but the Presidential Suite in Dr. Chu's Pearl Magnolia put them all to
shame. In fact, it put most of the houses I had ever been in to shame and
was bigger than most; my mind calculated 5,000 square feet, and that was
probably on the conservative side.

The hotel manager stepped forward to make sure I knew where everything was: a living room, dining room, parlor, three bedrooms, five bathrooms, video room, office, kitchen, private bar, two enclosed balconies, and two or three other rooms that had no use as far as I could tell. Voice control for music, television, video, atmosphere control, ambient light, and hotel amenities; yes, the suite had been programmed to my voice, and every command, option, and response was highlighted on big screens in the living room, bedrooms, and master bath.

It was extravagant to be sure, but every extravagance had a purpose. Was this one intended to sell me or to distract me? Or, was this just the Panda way? In any case, I was ready to dispense with the company and enjoy the room. When I saw Tir returning from my bedroom, I turned to San and said, "I understand my tour of the city begins at 1:00 tomorrow afternoon." I sidled toward the door.

"Yes. Though 1:00 means 12:45 for my uncle's people. Be aware." San handed me his card. "My number. Call any time, day or night." A brief nod took in Teng and Ji. "Your drivers will be downstairs, as well. They are at your service 24 hours a day."

"Dinner will be served at your leisure," the hotel manager informed me. "May I advise the kitchen?"

"Seven will be fine," I said.

"And if I may have Tir do the honor of selecting your menu?"

I glanced in the direction of my private concierge. "Thank you. I look forward to it."

She beamed. Or at least beamed as much as a Thai woman could given the circumstances. And then they were gone. I kicked off my shoes, unbuttoned my shirt, and let my eyes wander around 5,000 square feet of prime real estate.

"I could get use to this," I said. I looked at the big screen in the living room. "Voice controls."

A woman's voice, as fluid and pure as a light rain, said, "Yes, Mr. Michael. Controls on. How may I help?"

"Nice. Music."

"On screen." The television illuminated, and a list appeared on the screen: classical, opera, jazz, light jazz, alternative, rock, new age, seascapes; you name it.

"Jazz," I said.

"Artist?"

"Let's see. Why not go for broke. Keith Jarrett." No way, I thought. "His concert at the Fillmore. 1978."

Three seconds later, Keith Jarrett's distinctive piano filled the room. "Now that's cool. Very cool."

"Volume, Mr. Michael?"

"Lower." The volume dropped one level. "Lower. Thank you. But don't go too far."

"I'm right here," the voice said.

I stepped out onto one of the room's two glass-enclosed balconies, heard a low hum, and felt a subtle draft of cool air. The balcony was just slightly smaller than my bedroom back home. Pale gray marble graced two walls. Plush carpet gave way beneath my feet. A brass and glass dining table and four chairs were arranged beneath a crystal chandelier that illuminated slightly when I entered. Orchids bloomed in planters set among sculptures made from rough bronze. "And this is the balcony."

The exterior glass was spotless, and the view gazing down on the Chao Phraya River from the 25th Floor – glittered with golden lanterns and the white lance of a full moon – made me long for Lauren at my side. This was no fun without female companionship. Lauren would have loved the sight of the river merchants parading up and down the water with their long-poled propellers, asymmetrical flotillas that suggested a pace of life that had not been a part of my world since childhood. Sad, I suppose. But we all chose a course and take what comes. We all make the most of the good and slug our way through the bad. That was life.

Still, we all fantasize. I had a romantic image of myself in pursuit of a simpler life. Homesteading a small cabin along the banks of the Snake

River, perfecting my fly-fishing skills, and opening a backcountry guide service. It wasn't just my fantasy; Lauren and I had talked about similar scenarios who knew how many times. We had even scouted potential home sites around Telluride and Jackson Hole. We had imagined ourselves starting a vineyard in Palisade or opening a gallery in Crested Butte. Well, that was what couples did; they dreamed. But even river merchants and fly-fishermen have their own set of challenges: personal, professional, and otherwise. The trick was turning the challenges into opportunities and new adventures. That, I suppose, was why I was here in Thailand entertaining an offer that would make me a very powerful and very wealthy man. It was interesting to me, however, that my fantasies did not hinge on wealth or power. Figure that out.

I heard a knock on the door. "Lights," I said, as I worked my way from the sitting room through the living room to the entry. The lights came up, and I had to smile. "I could get used to this," I said for the second time.

I opened the door onto a small entourage led by my private concierge, Tir. Her colleagues were dressed in the bleached white smocks of a professional kitchen staff. They were pushing a silver service cart stacked with covered dishes and, I hoped, hidden Thai delicacies.

"Mr. Michael. I hope we're not interrupting," Tir said, her hands clasped before her. "You requested dinner at 7:00, Sir."

It was hard for me to believe that an hour had passed, but I also imagined that looking at my watch would be construed as an insult. "Perfect timing," I said. "Come in. I think I'll take dinner on the balcony."

"Very good, Sir." Tir and I followed the cart onto the balcony, and she expounded upon the menu dish by dish, raising the lid briefly on each plate as she went. "Here we have a leaf-wrapped miang kam. Next is hot-and-sour shrimp salad with roasted chili sauce, lemon grass, and mint. We call it plah neung."

"Magnificent."

She raised another lid. "Chicken and roasted eggplant in red curry sauce. Delicious. And your main course is salted black olive fried rice. Kao pad nahm liap. And for dessert, grilled coconut cakes."

"Grilled coconut cakes! It looks delicious."

"It's my very favorite."

"Huh!" I gave her a conspiratorial wink. "In that case, I might have to start with the dessert."

It wasn't much of a joke, so I wasn't surprised at the lack of response. "I'd be glad to serve you," Tir said instead.

"No, thank you. You've outdone yourself already."

"Then do call if there's anything else." Tir left her card on the table. Another card; I was collecting them like bad habits.

When she and her coterie were gone, I settled in with a view of the city. I removed the cover on the grilled coconut cakes and scooped a healthy spoonful into my mouth. Pure heaven! I closed my eyes and groaned. Never one to short sell pure heaven, I had another.

By 8:00, I had sampled each dish. I had declared the plah neung the most flavorful dish I had ever eaten in my life until I tasted the red curry sauce. I used the word incomparable knowing full well there was no one in the room to debate the issue. Too bad: this was a meal worth sharing. Even at that, I only ate a bite or two of each entrée. I knew my private concierge would be disappointed, but I hoped she wouldn't take offense. I was really more interested in a hot shower, a bed with clean sheets, and a couple of hours of uninterrupted sleep. It wasn't jet lag as much as it was overkill. I had seen enough of the spotlight for one day.

I managed the shower – 30 minutes of it, in fact – and was parading around my home away from home in a pair of drawstring pants when the doorbell rang. I stared at the door for a moment and shook my head. "Don't these people ever give up?"

A light tapping followed the ringing bell. I thought for a moment about throwing on a t-shirt, but decided it was probably my two body-guards and what difference would it make to them. I opened the door and found myself staring at two young Thai women so sensually dressed that I used the first ten seconds of our encounter just to drink in the sight of them. The perfumed air emanating from them was so intoxicating and sexual that it would have been impolite not to allow my eyes to travel over their bodies. The one with her hand on her hip wore a red silk dress the cut and sheerness of a Victoria Secret nightie. The silk clung to breasts so perfectly formed that the only aberration were nipples that brought the material to a delicate point. Her hips and legs were muscular in a way that drove the imagination to new heights of erotic thought. Her skin was a rich, satin brown, like virgin mahogany or milk chocolate.

Her friend was tall and lean by Thai standards. She was perfectly proportioned under a pale cotton tank top that revealed adolescent breasts. Her shorts were hardly more than panties, and her legs were the kind of legs normally reserved for runway models and volleyball players. The top button on her shorts was conveniently opened, and a yellow and orange butterfly had been tattooed at the hemline of a yellow thong.

"Ladies," I said, though 'girls' might have been just as appropriate.

"Good evening, Mr. Michael," the one in red said in broken English that did absolutely nothing to diminish her sensuality. On the contrary. "I hope it's not too late."

"It depends on what continent you're on," I said. "Did my good friend Yuehan San send you?"

They both smiled, which I took to mean, 'Yes, who else in Thailand could afford two women who look as good as we look.' The tall one laughed. "Mr. Michael, you are the hotel's most honored guest."

"And its most handsome one, too," her friend said shyly.

"And to help you recover from your long journey and to welcome you to Bangkok…" A hand reached leisurely out and grazed my arm. "…Gina and I would like to offer you a special massage."

"Special," I said. I was alone in Bangkok, Thailand, and two of the sexiest women on the planet were offering me a 'special' massage. My imagination didn't need to work particularly hard to see down the many roads we might travel in making this a night to remember. Nope, not too hard. I would not have expected any significant internal debate on the matter, and none materialized. "Thank you, ladies. But I have my own personal massage therapist, and I think I'll just have to wait for her to give me that 'special' massage. Tell San thank you though."

It was not disappointment I saw on their faces. It was more genuine astonishment. But then, I didn't imagine these two often heard a negative reply. I wondered briefly if they'd had any better luck with President Clinton. "Goodnight, Ladies."

A test? Was that what that was? I was briefly disappointed with Dr. Chu Zhong Liu for tendering such an offer, but then it dawned on me that Thailand was not the United States. The sexual mores were different. My host kept eleven wives, and there may have been an upside to that arrangement that we didn't fully appreciate in America. Just because I was satisfied with a monogamous relationship did not mean it was the only way to go. For all I knew, a sexual offering here may even have been considered good manners. Well, good manners or not, I was not trading in one set of principles just to meet the needs of my host. Dr. Chu might view me as crazy – I may have even viewed myself as a little crazy – but I doubted his job endorsement hinged upon it.

Speaking of monogamy, I glanced at the wall clock in the sitting room and realized it was too early in Virginia to be calling my one and only wife. Too bad. Instead, I went into the bedroom and climbed between the sheets. "Lights out," I called, and the lights slowly dimmed. I was getting the hang of this.

Sleep may have come in bits and pieces, but for the most part, I was barraged by images of circumspect bodyguards and doting hotel employees, the clashing sounds of bumper-to-bumper traffic and soft piano, and the incongruous smells of sex and spices. In one dream, I was standing on the shore of a raging torrent holding a fishing pole; in the next, I was tittering on the edge of a jagged escarpment with sweat burning my eyes.

My eyes snapped open. The clock on the nightstand read 1:05 a.m. I swung my legs off the edge of the bed and rubbed my eyes.

"Lights." They came up slowly. "Stop. Thank you." I shook my head. "You just said thank you to a machine."

I picked up the phone, dialed the international operator, and gave her Lauren's direct number. She answered after the second ring. "Michael?"

"Hey."

"Hey. How are you? Shouldn't you be sleeping?" she asked.

"Too much stimulation," I replied. "How about you? How's Virginia?"

"In no way, shape, or form related to the real world," Lauren said with a giggle. God, it was good to hear her voice. "Not that our daughter sees it that way."

"They spoiling you guys?"

"That would be an understatement, baby. Not that I don't like to be spoiled, mind you." We both laughed. "We're visiting the school today, and Celia Chatzwirth is going to give me the grand tour. I think she had her eye on you."

"Had her eye on me? What's that mean?"

"It means you made quite an impression, buddy boy. And I think she's kind of bored despite having it all," Lauren said.

"Well, you can tell Mrs. Chatzwirth that I have it all, too. And I'm not bored in the least. Just lonely," I replied.

"Does that mean you miss me?"

"You could safely say that, yes," I assured her.

"Good. Me, too. Hope it goes well with Dr. Chu tomorrow. Get some sleep."

"Tell a certain young lady that I love her," I said.

"It was love at first sight with that pony. Just so you know," Lauren said. "So if this thing with Panda doesn't work out, we may have to trade in her stuffed horse for the real thing."

I smiled at that. "Talk to you tomorrow. Love you."

"You, too."

I hung up and realized I had two choices: I could fantasize or I could read. Opting for the latter, I reached into my briefcase for the profile on

Dr. Chu. I opened it to the first page, lay back, and didn't remember another thing until the phone on the nightstand delivered my 7:00 wake-up call. Five and a half hours of dreamless sleep. I shouldn't have felt refreshed, but I did.

A creature of enduring habit, I threw on my running gear, splashed water on my face, and stretched for ten minutes in front of the local news. Then I rode the elevator to the lobby. I took it on faith that one or both of my faithful bodyguards were lingering close, so I exited the hotel from a side door. I headed for the waterfront and a beehive of activity that rivaled New York City's harbor in terms of sheer energy and noise. The Chao Phraya River was a huge body of slow moving water. Cargo boats and cruisers coexisted next to flatboats and gondolas. The shouts of roustabouts and river merchants melded with the crack of gas-powered motors, the wail of horns and whistles, and the slap of water against metal and wood.

It was more humid than hot, and I was dripping with sweat five minutes after I started. It felt good. I could feel yesterday's jet lag breaking up. As I ran, I let my mind play out the best and worst case scenarios for the coming day, while my eyes feasted upon the people, places, and uniqueness of a remarkably diverse city. I was the one and only person doing what I was doing. I was fair-haired, light-skinned, tall, and conspicuous. Most of the glances were friendly and curious. But not all. In thirty minutes, it occurred to me that Bangkok could probably be as forbidding as it was enticing, as cruel as it was inviting, and as cold as it was friendly. My first impression was of a place where nothing was free; a place where buying and selling drew no distinction between people and things; and a place where survival came first and profit a close second.

My bodyguards were waiting by the elevator when I returned. They were not happy.

"We were worried, Mr. King," Teng said. "Dr. Chu would prefer that you don't go out without someone who knows the city."

"I appreciate your concern, Teng. I didn't mean to worry anyone," I said, as the elevator doors opened. I stepped in and smiled. "Tomorrow morning. 7:00 sharp. Don't forget your running shoes."

The doors closed. I could see by their expressions that my sense of humor was lost on them. I was getting that a lot here in Thailand. I could also see Teng reaching for his cell phone and wondered to which of his many masters he was reporting.

I was seated at a table with Tom Palmer in one of the Pearl Magnolia's five restaurants at 8:30. Three years had passed since our last face-to-face rendezvous, and it was like we had never been apart. Tom was nearly my height, wiry and strong, and every bit the athlete I was. His first words were, "You're out of shape, brother. I could see it from the door."

Mine were, "And you're looking like an old man. Where'd that gray hair come from?"

"Too much work and not near enough sexual activity."

"That'll do it," I said, and we both laughed. "You look great."

"You, too. You look fit," he said, this time nodding with the appraising eye of an older brother. Tom was, in fact, older than me by all of two days. And I never let him forget it. "I've missed you, bro."

This was almost too good to be true. Three thousand miles from home and having breakfast with one of my best friends in the world. We talked about everything: politics, family, sports, mutual friends, and business. Well, I talked business. Tom waved me off when I asked about his American Financial gig. Head of Southeast Asian operations for a company like AmFin was a heady position, and I expected him to do more than shrug his shoulders.

"Same old, same old," he said. "I'm halfway around the world from my kids and scratching out a living kowtowing to a bunch of slants."

This didn't sound much like Tom – neither the complaining, the ethnic slur, nor the distracted look in his eye – and I was about to call him on it when he said, "But you're knocking on the door of the Golden Goose with Panda Pharmaceuticals, my friend. Very big time."

"Good or bad?" I asked.

"From all I know, you're looking at a company that will open whatever the hell doors you want to go through, Michael. Money, politics, social reform. You name it. They've got the clout. And you're about to get your hands on the stick that controls the clout. I'm proud of you."

"Will we be doing business together?" I asked.

"Little brother, I'm expecting you to play the palimony card every chance you get. Understand me?"

This sounded more like the old Tom, but I still couldn't shake the character glitch from a moment ago. I decided not to probe. I would suggest a drink later that night and let a glass of wine loosen his tongue.

"Keep your wits about you when you meet with this Chu character, Michael," Tom said, as we were walking out of the restaurant a half hour later. "In all my time here in Asia, I've never met a Thai without a hidden agenda, and the Chinese are even worse."

"I'll remember that." We shook hands. His grip wasn't the same. What the hell? "I'll see you tonight for that drink."

"We'll do it up," he said and headed for the door. I watched him for a moment. When he was out of sight, I started toward the elevator.

9

THE ESCORTS

"If it is thought that men are made by nature unequal,
then where do we turn for understanding?"

There was something different about the two women standing at my door at ten minutes to 1:00 that afternoon. I wouldn't have thought in my wildest dreams that Dr. Chu or San or whoever was charged with recruitment of female escorts could possibly do better than my two visitors last night, but these two were special. Pure beauty. They made no attempt at selling their sexuality with revealing tank tops or low-cut silk dresses. They were twins. Identical in what looked to be a rare meld of Asian radiance and Polynesian elegance. I had never seen such finely sculptured cheekbones next to full, wide lips, and eyes the color of flecked emeralds. Flawless was such an insignificant word to use in describing their complexions. Hair that would have been midnight black had it not been for a subtle maroon sheen that almost seemed like a figment of my imagination.

They distinguished themselves with the cut of their hair - the one standing with her arms crossed and her legs anchored just slightly apart wore hers shorter and tied in a loose ponytail; her sister's pose was more formal and her hair tumbled in rich waves to the middle of her back – and by their dress – cotton pants and a sleeveless blouse the color of ripe peaches versus a tailored, yellow and white business suit. The one similarity in their dress was the matching opals that hung around their necks.

They must have seen the look of admiration on my face, because the one with the shorter hair said, "No, I'm sorry, Mr. King. We're not here for that. You had your chance last night."

"Then I was just about to make a fool of myself," I said.

"Please excuse my sister. She rarely minces words," the more formal of the two women said. "I am Chu Kym Dasao. This is my sister, Chu Lyn Sangsu. Though we would be very comfortable if you were to call us Kym and Lyn."

"Indeed we would." Lyn offered her hand first. It was not a man's handshake – aggressive and grappling – but her grip was firm and purposeful, and I could tell that she had been taught the value of making this first impression count. She also smiled with just a hint of sarcasm and said, "I don't suppose you'd like to invite us in."

"We'll be seeing quite a bit of each other over the course of the next couple of days," Kym noted. Her handshake had a touch more of the executive businesswoman in it. "We're Dr. Chu Zhong Liu's daughters."

"We're your escorts, Mr. King," Lyn said in case it had not registered.

"I was hoping you might be." I stepped aside and used an open palm to invite them in. A subtle jasmine scent filled my nose as Kym walked past me. As Lyn entered, I caught sight of the Bengal Tiger tattooed on her shoulder.

She said, "On behalf of Panda Pharmaceuticals here in Southeast Asia and our father, welcome to Thailand."

"We trust the room has been satisfactory," Kym said with a slight bow.

"I'm particularly impressed with the entertainment center. Have a listen," I said turning toward the big screen in the sitting room. "Music, please. Classical. Bach's Flute Concerto in C Major."

Three seconds later, the lilting sound of a flute with full orchestral accompaniment was drifting down from the speakers. The girls were smiling. "I think our guest likes the room just fine, Sister," Lyn said.

"And he has exceptional taste, as well," Kym added.

"A touch on the arcane side, but very pretty."

Kym raised an eyebrow in my direction. "She's more the Coldplay and Dave Matthews kind."

"Excellent choices," I admitted. "And you?"

"Give me Pink Floyd and Mozart any day," Kym said. "Are you ready to see Bangkok from the Panda point of view, Mr. King?"

I thought for one moment to say, 'Call me Michael,' but I didn't. A few minutes of light bantering was a nice way to break the ice, but I intended to stay on the business side of this relationship, and Mr. King was a good start.

"I'm all yours," I said.

"May I say before we set out, Mr. King," Kym said, with considerably more gravity, "how honored we are to meet the future President and CEO of our company. The 'family' welcomes you."

She bowed, as did her sister.

"And I'm honored to be a candidate for the position," I assured them, dropping my head slightly in return.

"Not just a candidate, Mr. King," Lyn corrected. "You see, Panda is more than just a company. It is family. Like our father, we are dedicated completely to the family. And from the family's view, you are the chosen one."

"Our father has only one interview to conduct," Kym assured me. "And that is the one he will attend to at dinner tonight."

"Then I am that much more honored," I said, letting the CEO surface.

"And with that, I think we should go."

"Yes, Sir. Our boat is waiting."

"Tell me about yourselves," I said, as we walked from Charoen Krung Road through a shop-lined alley toward the waterfront. A cacophony of city noises, modern and old world, echoed down the cobbled walks. The scent was universal: cars, crowds, and commerce.

Kym led. "We're 29 years old. Born in the year of the tiger. Taurus according to your American astronomy."

"Ah! As is my daughter," I said. "Sign of the bull, and just as hard-headed as her father."

"Hard-headed. That would be Kym," Lyn assured me with a smile.

"Your English is impeccable," I said, looking from one to the other. "Have you spent time in America?"

"Our father insisted upon it. He doesn't entirely trust the Thai educational system."

"We both followed in his footsteps to Harvard," Kym said almost mechanically. Ah, good old Harvard. Where would we be without it, I thought with perhaps more sarcasm than the twins would have appreciated. "My sister went onto Stanford for her MBA. I chose MIT for their Chemical Engineering department."

"Great schools, both of them," I said, wondering if Kym's mechanical response suggested a lack of pride in their accomplishments or simply an attitude of high expectations fulfilled.

As we approached the waterfront, the river coiled like an indefatigable serpent that no amount of cars, crowds, or commerce could inhibit. The high-powered riverboat awaiting us at the Soi 34 docks was drawing the envious glances of tourists and waterfront workers all along the peer. White and spotless, it was part yacht, part speedboat, and manned by a crew of seven, bodyguards all despite their seafaring duties; it did not take a genius to make that observation. Fine, I thought, make the world safe for an aspiring Panda Pharmaceuticals employee. I knew I should feel honored instead of doubtful, but that wasn't me. What were they protecting us from? Drug lords? Muslim separatists? Or, I thought, potential kidnappers? True, I might eventually want to put the question to Kym and Lyn, but I knew I would be far more interested in Dr. Chu's explanation.

When we were underway, I returned to our previous conversation. "So you both came back to Thailand and joined the company," I said to the sisters.

"To do otherwise would have been to waste the education we'd been blessed with," Kym said with unabashed solemnity. "It was our family duty."

"Please understand, Mr. King. It is a privilege serving the family," Lyn added, and by family I assumed she meant the Panda family. "Kym is the head of Research and Development at the Panda Thai laboratories. I am the Director of Product Marketing for Southeast Asia. Both positions that answer directly to the President." Lyn stopped. She pressed her lips together, and quickly retraced her steps. "I should say, as the company is currently organized. No disrespect intended."

"Research and marketing." I wanted to say that 29 was a trifle young to be holding down two positions of such importance in a company with almost three billion in yearly sales, but then these were clearly not your run-of-the-mill 29-year-olds. "It sounds like we have a lot to talk about." Lyn beamed. Kym bowed her head. Score one for the CEO-in-waiting.

The boat settled into the middle of the river and picked up speed. The Chao Phraya's water was the color of chocolate milk. "We planned a light lunch at the Wat Phra Kaew and the Grand Palace Shrine, Mr. King," Kym told me. "The Shrine is, I suppose, the heart of Bangkok for many Thai people. If you look around, you can see how strongly Buddhist the country is."

"95%," Lyn said. I followed her hand toward a series of elaborate stone temples gracing the banks of the river and heard her say, "Wat Thong Nopphakhum, there. And there, the Temple of the Golden Buddha. And on the water, Wat Pathuma Kongkha."

I nodded, confining my remarks to, "Beautiful setting."

Whether anyone wanted to admit it or not, religion and business – much like church and state – were not separate islands unaffected by one another, and there were certain countries where it just didn't pay to try and make a buck. Unless I was mistaken, Thailand did not fit that mold, and I was glad I didn't have to deal with it.

The river bent to the left, and the sun peaked out from behind a stream of feathery nimbus clouds. "Chinatown," Kim said, gesturing to a sprawling section of the city on our left.

"Ah!" Lyn called. "And the Talad Kao Market."

"If we stop now, we'll never get her out of there," Kym assured me. We shared a smile, and hers was filled with genuine love, as if all parts of them were equal despite obvious differences.

"Do you mind a personal question?" I asked them.

"Not at all," Kym replied even as Lyn said, "Sure."

"You speak of Panda the company also as Panda the family. And I respect that," I said.

"And you're wondering if there is a life outside the family," Kym said. "I don't mean to be presumptuous."

"You're both attractive, intelligent women. And there is more to life than just work," I said.

"Of course there is a life outside the family," Lyn said. "We just haven't found the right partners, Mr. King."

In other words, I thought, not only a partner your father approves of, but a partner the family endorses, as well. I said, "I appreciate your candor," and waited to see Kym's reaction.

"Not at all," she said quickly. "You have every right to know the level of our commitment."

I was beginning to get the picture. The question that begged to be asked was this: when does commitment end and obsession take over? I was probably the most committed guy I knew. Family and work were at the top of my list, no question, but family and work were not one and the same. I had to admit that I was excited about the hours I would be spending with Dr. Chu tonight. I also had to admit that listening to Lyn and Kym and watching the wide range of emotions that played upon their faces only fueled my enthusiasm.

The river swelled with activity, commerce that stretched from one bank to the other – the sights, sounds, and smells of an overheated waterfront – but what impressed me was the obvious role that religion played in the country: for every Catholic Church and Hindu shrine, I saw ten Buddhist temples. And if I wanted an exclamation point to the phenomena, the Royal Grand Palace and the Emerald Buddha were it. Regal, opulent, and excessive were the words that came to mind as we docked, but I took it in the way any avid tourist would and allowed the twins to lead me to a neatly appointed outdoor café across from the Phra Kaeo museum. Hot tea and spring rolls were served, and the girls used the moment to segue into a formal explanation of the hours I could expect in the company of their father tonight.

"He is, most of all, a respectful man," Kym said, and I could tell that her words were heartfelt. "And we want you to feel completely at ease in his company."

"I'm sure I will," I said encouraging them with my eyes.

"Our father is extremely warm and kind," Lyn said, as if that might be a difficult concept, "though oftentimes people can't see that."

"Why is that?"

"They see a man who wields enormous power, but they don't see the man who puts his family first and who has done more to feed the hungry children of Thailand than perhaps anyone. They see a man who lives in a large house, but they don't see how much Panda Thai has contributed to the economy here, and, for that matter, in the States."

I leaned forward, cradling my tea cup in two hands, and took in every word. "Our father is the type of man who looks deep into your eyes when he speaks to you, Mr. King," Kym added. "He is not being rude. He is looking for the man inside. Does that make sense?"

"There's nothing rude about looking someone in the eye, Kym," I assured her. I didn't like calculating every word, but something told me that the rules of engagement called for it over the course of the next few days. "Quite the contrary."

"We want you to feel like you can be yourself tonight. I think that's Kym's point," Lyn explained.

"But also inquisitive," Kym said. "There are no off-limit subjects."

"That's good to know," I said evenly.

"If our father seems overly inquisitive in return," Kym wanted me to know, "please understand that you represent a historical change for our company."

"Well, hopefully I can give him enough information to convince him of my sincerity," I said diplomatically.

"Absolutely," Lyn said, as the food arrived. It was a light meal. Morsels of thinly sliced beef spiced with peppers and curry; three vegetables doused in red pepper sauce; and a small serving of Pad Thai and shrimp.

"How about a lesson in Thai Etiquette 101 while we eat," I said to my escorts. "I would like your father to know that I respect the finer points of his country's table manners."

The twins were pleased by my thoughtfulness. I did not let on that I was eager to change the subject or that I preferred to make my own assessment of their father less the pre-prepared lionization.

When I was certain I knew where to sit and when to eat and how to propose a toast Asian style, I turned the conversation toward the subject of Panda Pharmaceuticals. "What is the most promising research the Panda R&D department is pursuing at the moment, Kym? I know about Trifil and Thorafil, and I know about Cielmeta, the rheumatoid arthritis med."

"Tell him about the ED patch," Lyn suggested.

"I know about that, too. Promising. Also the blood pressure med. Even more promising." I held Kym's eye. "What else are you working on currently?"

"A molecular pain killer derived from the cells of the lion fish and the fugu fish," Kym replied simply.

"Revolutionary," her sister added.

"I'd like to see Panda look beyond opium-based products just a little more."

"So would I," her boss-in-waiting offered. Then I said, "Maybe we can find that balance together."

Then my eyes fell on Lyn, a picture of poise and confidence. Up to now, she and her sister had made certain that my cup was filled with tea each time they filled their own. This time, I did the honors, topping her cup first, Kym's next, and then warming my own. I gazed over the rim of my cup. "And how does the Director of Product Marketing respond to that?"

"Balance is important in the marketplace. Over reliance on one product can be dangerous. But I don't concern myself with new research per se, only that our current lines are generating sufficient revenue to fund that new research. I look for holes in the market, and I gauge whether Panda should attempt to fill those holes. In my eyes, a molecular painkiller is only worth pursuing if it trumps what is currently on the market in terms of effectiveness and that an acceptable percentage of the population will be able to afford it."

"Say it takes ten years to develop," I said.

"As long as we're bringing a balanced approach to our internal R&D projects and applying a defined long-term strategy. That's what I'm focused on, and that's what the entire Panda family is focused on."

"And if the R&D fails?"

"We only need one in ten products to make it, Mr. King," Lyn said with a blitheful grin.

"And our average is one in seven," Kym noted.

"Let's shoot for one in five, ladies, and turn the industry upside down," I said. "Doable?"

"Doable," Kym said without hesitation.

"Good." I held up my teacup, inviting them to do the same. "Now tell me more about your father." Nice transition, Michael. Very nice, I thought.

"How does he spend his free time?"

The twins were delighted by the question and seeing them delighted was as refreshing as standing beneath a cool waterfall. "He hikes nearly every day in the estate's wild flower gardens. If not there, then in the woods behind our house," Kym began. "And tends his precious orchids as it they were the source of all beauty."

"If you want to get on his good side, Mr. King, ask him for a tour of his greenhouse," Lyn suggested.

"He practices his martial arts one hour a day. Karate and kendo."

"Hope you've been practicing, too, Mr. King," Lyn added with a quick smile.

"I'm a little rusty," I had to admit. And then, "But not that rusty."

"Good thing." The smile broadened. What does that mean? I wondered.

"He also spends considerable time working with his foundation," Kym said. "The Housing is Hope Foundation. You may have heard of it."

"Yes. I've read about it. Very impressive," I said, wondering when my host found time to work and sleep and father 31 kids. "I'll be sure to ask him about it."

Our plates were cleared. It was 2:30, and a cool breeze carried us to our feet. "Can we invite you to visit the temple, Mr. King?" Kym asked. "It's customary to say a prayer toward the success of a coming event. In this case, your evening with our father."

"Of course. I'm moved. Thank you," I said and meant it, despite my lack of faith in what I called the rituals of request. Expressing gratitude, yes. Asking for intercession, maybe not.

A perfectly tended hedgerow led to the temple entrance. Inside, the temple was a monument to simplicity, strength, and devotion. All stone walls, silk adornments, and candlelight. Bronze statues looked out with dour eyes and probing smiles, and I wondered what exactly they were thinking, these representatives of Buddha and his curious lack of regard for ritual and formality. I noticed the quiet hum that seemed to float down from the ceiling seconds after a waft of sandalwood enlivened the olfactory senses of my nose. An air of peace pushed whatever tension I may have been toting around into a distant place. The three of us stopped at a side altar near the front of the temple. Kym struck a match to a small square of incense. Lyn invited me to light one of the hundreds of votive candles flanking either side of the altar, and I accepted with a silent nod. As scented smoke spiraled above the burning incense, the twins lit two candles opposite mine.

"Thank you," I said again.

"As the Thai are fond of saying, Mr. King, 'May the stars land on your shoulders tonight,'" Lyn said.

"And," Kym added, "May they not weigh you down."

We left the temple under the watchful eye of two monks and several kindly Buddha statues, all with the same amused expressions.

The girls used our boat ride back to the hotel to add historical spice to the stew that was Thailand – I heard mention of tungsten and tin, King Phumiphon and Prime Minister Thaksin something or other – but I couldn't shake the image of the Wat Phra Kaeo monks, their eyes like hooded veils of secrecy measuring our passage through the temple. They had not been there when we arrived, I realized. Which, I further realized, almost certainly meant nothing at all.

When the riverboat tied off at the Soi 34 pier a few minutes later, I gave the pilot a grateful nod, and the three of us jumped ashore. As we wove our way among the river merchants and the fishing boats, I glanced over my shoulder and found we were still under the vigilant eye of the riverboat crew. When I looked back, Kym was watching me. "So tell me, Kym," I said before she could look away, "Why the bodyguards?"

"Kidnapping, Mr. King," she answered plainly.

"It's big business in Thailand," Lyn said.

"And the children and guests of a man like our father are ideal targets."

"We don't intend to let that happen to them or to you."

I nodded like a man listening to an unsatisfactory script. "So then all your brothers and sisters are protected."

"Day and night," Lyn said.

"And the two of you?"

"We can take care of ourselves."

"Mr. King. If I may add," Kym said.

"Yes, please," I said, knowing there was more and wondering how much information the girls had been instructed to share.

"Panda Pharmaceuticals, you should know..."

"Or may already know," her sister interjected.

"…is the single largest grower of poppies in the world."

"Legal grower," Lyn emphasized. "One licensed to extract opium from those poppies with the intent of producing medically accepted drugs."

The sidewalks were jammed as we approached Thanon Charoen Krung; traffic funneled onto the thoroughfare like feeder streams into a rushing river. We waited for the light to change. Kym leaned close to my ear and said, "Naturally, our raw materials would prove to be a boon to anyone wanting to convert them into an illegal substance."

"Heroin being at the top of that list," Lyn said with less regard for the people around us.

"Naturally," I said as we crossed the street and turned in the direction of the hotel. "And every self-respecting drug lord on the planet would pay handsomely to gain access to our fields or our processing centers. Am I right?" There I was using the 'our' word again.

"Indeed," Kym said, a cryptic tone still shielding her voice. "It's true that our fields are guarded 24 hours a day, seven days a week, and the only way we can do this is by employing a considerable number of highly trained people."

Her sister sighed. "What she means, Mr. King, is that it takes employing one of the largest independent armies in the world."

"Essentially," Kym agreed. "And you can imagine the street value of even one harvested crop."

"Has it ever happened?" I asked. "Has anyone ever tried?'

"No one has ever been foolish enough to try," Kym said with measured assurance.

I fell silent as we marched toward the hotel entrance. This was getting complicated. Bodyguards and soldiers-of-fortune. But I suspected it was even more complicated than that. The responsibilities of these so-called bodyguards almost certainly ran deeper than just protection. After all, how better to keep track of the people you employ than with the people you hire to protect them. Complicated, I thought once again.

A rush of cool air hit me as we entered the hotel lobby. Then the entourage converged: Tir, my personal concierge, and Teng and Ji Xiong, my personal bodyguards. "Good afternoon, Mr. Michael," Tir called. "Are you finding the Thailand weather agreeable?"

"We couldn't have ordered a better day, Tir," I said magnanimously.

"Your new clothes are laid out for you, Sir," she announced, as if she couldn't keep the news to herself for another moment.

"New clothes? I didn't know I was in the market."

Lyn touched my shoulder. "It was supposed to be a surprise, Mr. King."

Kym raked Tir with her eyes. "Silly woman."

"Oh, my. I am so ashamed," Tir was mortified. "My sincere apologizes, Mr. Michael. I was not told."

While the twins scowled, I suppressed an urge to chuckle in favor of an overriding desire to rescue the poor lady from her distress. "It's not a problem, Tir. All you've done is pique my interest. Believe me."

"Mr. King will call if he needs anything," Lyn said when the concierge stepped up to the elevator. When the elevator doors opened, the twins made eye contact with my bodyguards, and Lyn told them, "We'll be down shortly. And we'll be picking Mr. King up again at 5:30. Have the car ready please."

"Very good," Teng said.

"The clothes are a tradition," Kym was quick to explain as the elevator delivered us to my suite. "A Taiwanese tradition."

"Consider it a gift," Lyn said, as we passed through the sitting room into my bedroom. On the bed lay a pair of perfectly pressed khaki pants with pleats and a fitted waist. Overlaying the pants was a gold and white short-sleeved shirt exquisitely embroidered in stitching so intricate that it must have taken a seamstress many painstaking hours. "A gift from us to you. We would be honored if you wore it tonight."

I held the shirt up in front of the mirror. Hardly my style, but nice. "Beautiful," I said. I peeked at the label. It was my size exactly. As were the pants. They had done their research, obsessively so. And that I found more bothersome than the implication that I might not have had the good sense to know how to dress for dinner with a prospective employer.

"Thank you," I said, bowing shortly to each of the twins. "Very thoughtful."

When Kym and Lyn were gone, I resisted the urge to pick up the phone and check in with the two girls in my life. By my watch, it was midnight in Virginia. I could imagine Hanna curled up in her mother's arms, sound asleep and dreaming of horses and endless green pastures. That was not a picture I was willing to disturb. Instead, I stretched out on the bed, instructed my electronic hostess to dim the lights and bring up a soft rendition of Vivaldi's Four Seasons, and played back the events of the day.

~

10

THE ESTATE

"The wild geese do not intend to cast their reflection;
the water has no mind to receive their image."

The twins returned at 5:41. When I opened the door, I was greeted with a new formality emphasized by matching bows. Though they did little more than tip their heads and lower their shoulders, both formed steeples with their hands to emphasize the gesture.

Their dress was similarly formal. They both wore perfectly tailored silk dresses, Kym's in traditional golds and whites, and Lyn's touched with shades of rose and pink. Even Lyn's cosmopolitan haircut had been styled for the occasion.

Except for their opal necklaces, they wore no jewelry.

I bowed in return. If lacking their grace, I wanted to be conscious of their traditions without looking foolish. I greeted them by their full names: Kym Dasao and Lyn Sangsu. They seemed pleased.

"You look lovely," I said.

"Thank you," Kym replied. Her eyes traveled over my new shirt and pants. "Very nice."

"Very handsome indeed," Lyn agreed.

"Shall we go?" I suggested.

"Your car is downstairs," Kym said. "I hope you find it comfortable. We have an hour's drive ahead of us."

I was suitably surprised. "Your father doesn't live in Bangkok."

"No," Kym replied. "The city has no appeal to him."

"It's the congestion more than anything," Lyn said, but neither explanation, I thought, rang with absolute truth.

The Hummer was the very one that had transported me from the airport, and the men in the front seat were the very same as well: Teng behind the wheel and Ji Xiong riding shotgun.

Teng's greeting was polite and monosyllabic – very different in the presence of the twins – and Ji Xiong, naturally, said nothing at all. Why mess with a good thing, I thought.

The girls sat opposite me. Kym exchanged a quick word of Taiwanese with Teng, and we set out. "Music, Mr. King?" Lyn asked.

I shook my head. "If you don't mind a bit of silence," I said simply.

A quick turn on Thanon Charoen Krung led to an overpass connecting with Thanon Rama IV, a stretch of highway that drew a northern swatch through the heart of the city. A sprawl of endless buildings grew increasingly shabby and ever more rural until the city abdicated into fields of newly planted rice, sugarcane, and rubber trees.

I treated the journey like a business meeting, drawing as much information as I could from the twins about product research and marketing to be sure, but even more so about the personalities involved in the running of the Southeast Asian arm of Panda Thai. As the saying went: Know the people. Give them place and time, and their efforts will multiply.

In the end, what I discovered was that Dr. Chu Zhong Liu, whose sole title within the company was that of Honorary Board member, had the last word on all major decisions regarding the company's southeastern operations. Interestingly, the interplay between the twins gave me more insight into this dynamic than either of them surely intended, and the net result was that operations were suffering under this 'last word' arrangement. An arrangement, I thought, that will have to change pretty darn quick if and when yours truly comes on board. I hope Dr. Chu is as open-minded as his daughters would lead me to believe.

Acre after acre of rubber trees eventually gave way to rolling hills and forests of palms, cypress, and teak.

"We're here," Kym said, though it was another thirty seconds before a ten-foot-high stone wall suddenly rose up alongside the road and another ten seconds before I was convinced that someone or something other than trolls was responsible for the intricacy of the work and its natural fit into the surrounding countryside.

The wall was broken eventually by a massive set of iron gates set off at the heart by intertwining Ps and silhouettes of huge iron Panda bears. The bears looked downright playful compared to the armed guards stationed at the entrance. No, I thought, guards they may have been, but soldiers – and highly trained soldiers – were what they looked like. I counted six of them, all conspicuously armed, two Land Rovers, and several saddled horses. This was serious business. And make no mistake about it, I told myself.

Kym must have seen the introspective look on my face, because she was quick to say, "It's only precautionary, Mr. King."

"Better safe than sorry. Sure," I said. "The trouble is, I don't know whether to feel safe knowing they're here or concerned knowing they have to be here."

"We have a lot to protect," Lyn said casually. "And with you here now, we have that much more to protect."

"That's a compliment, right?" I said, smiling out of the side of my mouth.

The girls rolled down their windows as the Hummer came to a halt inside the gates, and guards peered in on either side of the vehicle.

"Miss Chu. Dr. Chu," the guard on my side said to Lyn and Kym respectfully. "Good evening. Hope you had a safe trip."

"Wang Dawei. How are you?" Lyn said. "This is Mr. King. Our special guest."

The guard bowed. "It's an honor, Mr. King. We've been expecting you, Sir."

"Nice to meet you," I said, as the gates closed behind us. The Hummer glided down a tree-lined path lit with rows of gas lanterns. "Very professional," I said of the guards.

"We use only Taiwanese personnel," Kym said, and I wondered if she knew that was the information I was seeking.

With the sun casting its last rays over the estate, the grounds were bathed in a soft yellow hue that accented the vibrancy of sweeping gardens and tastefully arranged fountains. I caught sight of a yellow and blue bird that was either a Macaw or a very large parrot and two others with white wings and gold crowns. "Golden Eyes," Lyn said with unabashed pride. "Nearly extinct."

"Not if father has anything to say about it," Kym added.

"Beautiful," I said.

"Legend has it that anyone fortunate enough to see a Golden Eye in person is destined for greatness."

"Imagine the many ways that greatness can be defined," I said, "and the legend is no doubt true."

The path opened onto an expansive courtyard encapsulated by low hedges and manicured lawns. It was quite a sight to see a dozen children dressed in white linen and practicing Tai Chi, their movements choreographed to perfection and a look of gravity etched across their youthful faces. I was about to compliment the twins on the magnificent Tudor mansion that rose among the trees at the far end of the courtyard when Kym informed me that the house served as a school, theater, exercise complex, and study retreat for 22 of Dr. Chu's younger children and, as she put it, "A select number of special kids from neighboring communities. We even have three kids enrolled from the tenements in Bangkok. Forty-two students in all. High school age and under by US standards."

"Most without a chance in hell of a university education otherwise," Lyn chimed in.

"We have a full-time staff of six, two music teachers, an art teacher, a martial arts instructor, and a teacher of sports and sports competition."

"Kym and I were the school's first graduates. With honors, I will have you know." Lyn's smile was electric, but I was determined not to notice.

I glanced toward the school. "Your family's interest in children is commendable," I said.

"Our father deserves the credit. He doesn't believe in a life without education."

"And he's followed the work that you and Peak Pharmaceuticals have done for the schools back in Colorado, Mr. King," Kym assured me. "The tutoring programs and the scholarship funds. Very impressive."

"It's not much more than scratching the surface, to be honest, but every little bit helps," I said, as the Hummer circled the school and crested a small hill blanketed with King's Crown and tulip trees. I rolled down my window. What looked like a meadow filled with rainbow-colored flowers turned out to be a three-acre garden tended by three men and two women who stopped long enough to wave at us. Lyn waved back, but I was too busy staring at the palatial structure rising from the crown of the next hill, a sprawl of white stone and rambling rooftops that may have been smaller than Westminster Abbey, but only just.

I noticed the fountains first. There were three dozen of them at least, and they were flowing over marble structures that matched in design the pillars that formed the entrance to the house. Then a delicate breath of color took shape around the fountains. The shapes became orchids of every conceivable variety. Their scent wafted across the grounds and perfumed the inside of the car. The birds flitting among the flowers were doves, so white that the first snow of winter came to mind.

What I liked best about the house, I decided, were the open-air porches that fronted every room. Looking at them, I wondered briefly why Dr. Chu had not chosen to put me up here at the house. How much easier that would have made everything. Well, I wasn't part of the family yet. Maybe next time, I thought.

"Are those what I think they are?" I said suddenly. I was pointing to a pair of orange and black cats romping across the courtyard with two men in hot pursuit.

"If you're thinking they're tigers, you're right. Bengal tigers. Babies. They're another of our father's quests to save a dying species," Kym said.

"Now that is not something you see everyday," I said, as the Hummer followed a circular drive to the front of the house. We drew to a stop before two men and two women dressed head-to-foot in white and yet another man in a black tuxedo. Our reception committee.

We were ushered out of the car with a flurry of bows and well wishes that made me realize how much of my trip had been spent on ceremony, protocol, and preparation. I was tired of it. I was ready to talk business with the man I had traveled 20 hours and 3,000 miles to see.

Despite my dwindling patience, I still could not help but notice the delicate hand paintings and scroll work decorating the columns and panels leading to the door. "It tells the history of Siam dating back 10,000 years," Kym said, as we entered the portico. "And the story continues here in the entry."

The servants multiplied as we moved through a series of rooms dedicated to Queen Anne furniture and Chinese art in media as varied as pottery and paper, watercolor and lacquer, and bronze and blown glass.

"Our mothers spend a good deal of their time filling these rooms with their growing collections," Kym explained.

"You will only meet nine of them tonight, I'm afraid," Lyn said. "Yi Min and Sufen Wei are hosting an exhibit in Hong Kong this week."

"Next time perhaps," I said because nothing else seemed appropriate.

A hallway with high arching ceilings led past a series of closed doors to an expansive room that clearly served as a dining hall, one worthy of thirty guests, not just a high-minded CEO candidate in his embroidered shirt and starched Khakis. Chandeliers dangled above four individual seating areas. At the heart of a room was a central dining table carved of zebrawood and black cherry. Instead of place settings, the table served as a pedestal for a hundred flickering candles.

"You will be patient with our customs, I am sure, Mr. King," Kym said.

"Conversation without proper ceremony is not considered good form either by the Thai or by the Taiwanese," Lyn added.

"Of course not. Only in America," I said.

"It's all a bit much sometimes," Kym admitted unexpectedly. "But a good host never wavers."

"And when you see the girls in the dance ensemble, you'll be glad we didn't waver," Lyn told me with a playful smile.

The man in the tuxedo directed me toward a high-backed chair that rose like a throne on a dais between two others. I felt a little foolish until the girls joined me. A moment later, a woman in white appeared with a tray of ginger tea. The tea was served in tiny porcelain cups.

"With honey," Lyn said. "For luck."

"For good fortune, Sister," Kym corrected.

"For luck and good fortune," I said. "We can all use a little more of both."

The melodious tinkling of a bell filtered through the hall. The man in the tuxedo clapped his hands, and the twins both jumped to their feet. Lyn reached out with her hand and invited me to rise, as well.

"Mr. King. It would honor us if we could introduce you to our mothers," she said excitedly. "Well, nine of them anyway."

"Yes, thank you," I said, as a curtain fell away at the far end of the room and a petite, highly energized woman with an engaging smile entered the room, a black silk gown brushing across the tops of her bare feet. Her graying hair was trimmed neatly at the neck. And while the lines in her handsome face suggested a woman in her mid-sixties, there was no mistaking her beauty.

"Our mother. Mae Song," Kym said. She reached out and touched the woman's shoulder. Mae Song looked nothing like the twins, but I took Kym at her word. "Mother, this is Mr. Michael King."

"Honored guest," Mae Song said, her English thickly accented. She inclined her head a millimeter, her rich brown eyes holding mine.

"It's a pleasure, Mrs. Chu," I replied, taking her hand momentarily.

"You can call my sisters Mrs. Chu if you like. I'm a little old for that, Mr. King. Mae Song will do fine."

"Thank you. And I would appreciate it if you called me Michael."

"A gift." She laid a tin of rich smelling herbs in my hand. "Thyme. That you may live long."

Mae Song stepped aside, taking her place next to the dais, even as another Mrs. Chu moved forward. Younger by several years, taller and more graceful, her hair untouched by gray, and very serious. Even the sensual curve of her mouth reminded me of the twins. Lyn called her, "Our mother. Jiang Li."

The introduction was the same from woman to woman. "Our mother," Kym and Lyn called each of them, even as their ages decreased and their bodies became more defined beneath their silk gowns. Mae Song's lava black silk was never duplicated. Jiang Li wore midnight blue. Others wore sienna, Prussian red, and apricot, all delicately embroidered. There were, I realized, no Thai women among them. Their names were all Taiwanese and Chinese. Fen Suen, Xue Fang, and An Xiang. They all carried small gifts of similar size and meaning. Ginseng, for energy. Yin, yang, huo, for sexual enhancement. Caramel kisses, for exotic dreams.

When Dr. Chu's wives – numbers nine and ten – could no longer be viewed as senior in age to Kym and Lyn, they introduced them as sisters. "My sister, Meihua Zi," and "My sister, Park Rong." All were elegant, if not as beautiful as Mae Song. All were respectful, if not as watchful as Jiang Li.

I was curious which of this fascinatingly diverse group of women was the one, true mother of Lyn and Kym. The twins shared Mae Song's openness, Fen Suen's green eyes, and Li Ming's long, athletic gait. But it was the dominate presence of Jiang Li, despite her reserve, that the girls seemed to have come to naturally. I wondered if I would ever know for certain.

Finally, the curtain parted to reveal the last of Dr. Chu's many wives. The girl striding toward me – and girl was truly the only description that fit, because she could not have been more than 15 or 16 – looked less

Asian than any of the others. Her narrow face hinted of a European influence, but the russet tone of her skin suggested something Mediterranean, I thought. Her hair was cut as short as a boy's and was raven black in color. A layer of golden silk accented her lean, still developing body. But it was the flash in her eyes in the moment that she took my hand and the demure tip of her head that separated her from the rest.

Kym used neither the word sister nor mother to describe her, merely, "Ting-Ting," yet there was clearly affection in her tone.

Ting-Ting's tin was small and decorated with glitter. When I cracked the lid, I caught sight of a glistening, intricately faceted red stone that could only be a ruby. "A gift from us all," she said in a voice that was at once small and yet confident.

"I'm overwhelmed," I said, although a part of me wanted to shout, 'Are you crazy!?' Ginseng and thyme were nice; those I could handle. But a ruby? That was going a little overboard, I thought. Nonetheless, I looked from one woman to the next and said, "My thanks to you all."

∾

11

THE PALACE DINNER

"In the great future, you cannot forget your past."

Ting-Ting took her place next to her shared wives even as Kym was gesturing in the direction of the open curtain. "Our father, Mr. King," she said, as a man appareled much as I was entered the room. Surprisingly, he was nearly my height, slender, lean, and strikingly handsome. He was surely Chinese, but his face was narrower than most Asians, his eyes were fierce slits of concentration, and his small mouth was curved in a pleasing, unassuming smile. "Dr. Chu Zhong Liu."

"Mr. King. At long last." A hand with exceptionally long and graceful fingers reached out to me. I took his hand, noticing both the vice-like grip of his right hand and the missing pinky finger on the left, like Philip Chatzwirth. What the hell? Coincidence? Uh-uh, I thought. Coincidence be damned.

Chu's mien exuded an unmistakable warmth, while filling the room with the kind of energy that was more uplifting than overpowering and more inspiring than temerarious. I could understand the women in his life holding him in awe. I also imagined him having a similar magnetic grip on most men.

"Dr. Chu. It's a pleasure. Thank you for your hospitality."

"When a host is as pleased as I am at sharing a piece of his life with as honored a guest as you, hospitality is merely a byproduct of genuine enthusiasm," Chu assured me. His English was flawless. He did not release my hand before saying, "Welcome to our family."

"And those that I have met," I said, nodding first at his wives and then with affection at the twins, "are as genuine as they are generous."

"There is music in the next room, Mr. King, and refreshments. Let us talk before dinner, as wine will lessen our perspective." He touched my arm, inviting me to step beyond the dining room into a larger-than-life parlor with pillows arranged in a sitting area lit by a hundred candles. In the background, a five-piece chamber ensemble played Bach as if it had been written just for them. I was pleased to see that Chu drew the curtain aside and allowed his nine wives and two daughters to enter ahead of us. He said, "I've been told by reliable sources that Bach has a special place in your heart. I hope I wasn't misinformed."

I glanced briefly at the twins; Kym smiled demurely and Lyn winked. "I've been called old-fashioned in some circles, Dr. Chu, but if an appreciation of Johann Sebastian Bach dates me, I think I can take it."

We settled ourselves on the pillows. His wives took their respective places to Chu's left. The twins sat to the right of me.

"Do you, by chance, know the music of Huang Yat-sen?" he asked me. All eyes watched as if a single word or an unexpected movement might tip the scales of an unfolding stage play or street performance.

"I'm afraid not," I said.

"Flute and cello melded together like fresh fruit and dry wine," he said, as another round of ginger tea was served. "I'm sure I can convince our players to find a piece or two in their repertoire."

"I would enjoy that." I watched as the 'order' traveled in subtle gestures of heads and hands to the chamber orchestra and found Jiang Li, Chu's second wife, clearly at the center of this communication chain. Interesting.

"When I was a boy in Taiwan," Chu began rather unexpectedly, "we played a game very reminiscent of your own hide-and-seek. A game you know, Mr. King?"

"Knew and enjoyed," I said, sensing a shift in the conversation and realizing the interview was already well underway. Focus, I told myself, matching the seemingly casual eye contact of my host with the engaging attentiveness that was my own trademark. If you can make a person feel as if he or she is only person in the room, my long-departed mentor Felix Kildare used to say, then the battle is half won. Of course, Felix was talking about his uncanny success with women at the time, but I had managed to bastardize the rule to fit the business world, as well.

"I always preferred to be the seeker," Chu said. "The boy who could ferret out the best hiding places in the shortest amount of time."

To this I said, "He who seeks finds. Even if the discovery isn't exactly what we expected it to be."

"But then expectations are a dangerous business, are they not," Chu replied. His eyes closed for a moment. "I often wondered if it was discovery I was seeking or acceptance, Mr. King. My father was a government official. We were never in one place for long. Making friends was difficult. It helped if you were willing to be the one who looked instead of hid."

He paused, held my eye, and left plenty of space for me to comment. I didn't. Time to listen, I thought.

"I loved my mother," he said after the violins in the background gave way to the euphonious notes of a single cello. I experienced a moment when all I wanted to do was listen, and I expected that Chu felt very much the same. When the moment passed, he continued. "She had a lust for life and learning and laughter. I often pondered exactly what it was she saw in my father. I respected him, because he was my elder and because he provided for my mother, but I had no grounds for admiration, therefore little grounds for love. Yet the person I most admired and loved had married this man, so what did that say? I have spent much of my life seeking an answer."

His eyes left me for the first time. They traveled over the breadth of his family here present and paused only twice. First, they settled on Jiang Li and next upon the newest of his brood, Ting-Ting. Never shy about interpreting where interpretation probably was not warranted, I saw in the first a source of strength, and in the second an acknowledgement of time's inevitable passing.

"Moving to Thailand was difficult," Chu began after a time. "I was eight. I blamed my father for uprooting us from our home in Taiwan. I suppose that was natural, don't you think, Mr. King?"

"Moving is difficult enough under normal circumstances. Moving to a foreign country could not have been easy," I replied.

"You know what the most difficult thing was when all was said and done? Finding out that it wasn't his fault at all." I waited for an explanation. "Life is what it is, Mr. King. Life is what we make it. I was home-schooled. You know that, of course, from your research. My father did not trust the Thai educational system, and who better to teach me than my own mother. He wanted me to pursue political science. But I was never interested in anything but pure science. I had few friends, but I could break down the properties of aspirin and dissect the organs of a frog by the time I was 13 and speak five languages. Friends are nice, but family is vital, Mr. King. Don't you agree?"

An actual question. Until now, I could see him searching for character nuances that might give him pause or telltale signs of weakness, indifference, or aloofness. I could see him looking for the slightest aberration in my posture, gauging the momentary changes in my expression, and judging the tension I applied to my teacup. I told myself to let him search. What you see is what you get, Dr. Chu, I thought. But now I was looking down the barrel at a question cinctured with trapdoors and potential pitfalls. The solution? Absolute honesty, what else?

"My friends are important to me, Dr. Chu. Don't get me wrong. I would go to the ends of the earth for my closest friends," I said. "But I would jump off the edge for my family. That's not commitment. That's a reality."

I did not study my host for a reaction the way he had been examining me. The cue that suggested a certain appreciation for my answer was the

smile I saw out of the corner of my eye; it lit Lyn's face like the unexpected deliverance of good news.

Dr. Chu's itinerant discourse went on this way for twenty more minutes. He looked at his life as a series of building blocks that culminated in
his current station without ever mentioning his parents again. He referred
to his marriage to Mae Song and the birth of their first child, a son named
Long Sying, as the beginning of his inner family and the founding of
Panda Pharmaceuticals as the birth of his extended family.

"I hope I haven't bored you, Mr. King," he said, as the chamber orchestra traveled beyond Bach to a haunting duet of cello and flute that must
certainly have been my introduction to the composer Huang Yat-sen.

"No. Not bored. Appreciative, Dr. Chu. I take your candor as a compliment," I assured him.

"But a man cannot come away from a display of candor without one
pertinent question, however," Chu suggested in return. "What is your one
pertinent question, Mr. King?"

The rustling I heard was Jiang Li pressing forward slightly in her seat,
her interest suddenly heightened by this very interesting inquiry. Even in
a moment of tension her posture reflected poise and elegance, and I
found this fascinating.

Instead of plunging ahead, I allowed my eyes to travel to the five
musicians in the background and then to settle briefly on Jiang Li. "The
music is beautiful. Thank you," I said to her with a nod. If my gesture
caught Dr. Chu's second wife unaware, she gave nothing away, bowing her
head slightly, and bringing her fingertips together momentarily.

This carried me back to my host. I said, "One question. I'm honored
that you asked." My expression did not change, nor did I hesitate. "You
were born in Taiwan. Your lovely wives, unless I am mistaken, are all
Taiwanese. Your employees are, for the most part, Taiwanese. The art in
your house is Chinese. The embroidering on my shirt and yours is
Taiwanese. And yet you gave up your Taiwanese citizenship in 1971 in
favor of a permanent residency here and became a Thai citizen. Your

THE INTERVIEW   ∾   133

nephew San described the decision as purely business. I have my doubts."

"And your question?" Chu said, his face a blank page.

I resisted the urge to shrug. "Should I have my doubts?"

A wide smile suddenly eclipsed my host's otherwise serene face. "I appreciate your style, Mr. King. You are a guest in another man's house, and you show your respect with a display of well-honed diplomacy. For that, I thank you. And while your doubts are well-founded, I can assure you that the change in citizenship opened considerable doors for Panda Thai." He paused. "Fair enough?"

"Fair enough," I replied. A part of me may have wanted to push for more details, but Chu may have given me more than he intended. I went back momentarily to the information I had received about Chu's father, the Taiwanese attaché who had long ago been arrested for running secrets to the Chinese, a crime presumably punishable by death. Dr. Chu had struck a deal with the Taiwanese government that had gotten his father safe passage back home. Shortly thereafter, Chu changed his citizenship. And, according to my sources, he had not ventured beyond the borders of Thailand since.

Chu reclined on his pillow. And while eight wives and two daughters took this as a positive cue, I noticed out of the corner of my eye that Jiang Li had yet to take a breath. I naturally read something telling into that and prepared myself for a question of some importance. It came even before I could glance in her direction.

"And you, Mr. King?" Chu said. "Tell us something of your life."

Murmurs of assent sounded from around the circle, and while a part of me wanted to study the ever-expressive faces of Dr. Chu's twin daughters, I instead held fast to the probing eyes of my host. The request, I reminded myself, had been delivered by the most powerful of Panda Pharmaceuticals Board members and my last hurdle toward a lifetime position that I still found myself coveting. How to answer? Where to start? How to know what was behind the question? I took my cue from Chu's own life analogy.

"My favorite game when I was growing up was football. American football. Though hide-and-seek was a close second," I said with a conspiratorial nod that Dr. Chu acknowledged. "Football is a team sport. Eleven players. When the game works, it looks as if all eleven players are one cohesive unit, each with a task, and each with a responsibility."

"Ah!" Chu said. "An interesting analogy."

"But there is only one true leader on a football team, and that is the man who calls the plays and handles the ball on every down."

"The quarterback. Yes, I have observed my share of your American football."

"That, however, is not what makes him a leader. What makes him a leader is his ability to inspire the best performance from his team without overshadowing them. So when a play works, each member of the team takes ownership of that success."

"Which, I might suggest, gives them an inflated view of their importance," Chu said, his eyes narrowed almost to the point of closing.

"Which makes them work that much harder on the next play," I corrected. "People with inflated egos lack confidence. They have created their own ceilings. A man who is allowed to feel confident because he has proven his worth is a man with no ceiling, only the boundaries of his own abilities. It is the quarterback's job to recognize those boundaries."

"Very enlightened." Chu gestured with an infinitesimal movement of his hand.

"My father was a professor of economics at the University of Kansas in Lawrence."

"Good school."

"He provided well for four kids and my mother. I was the youngest. My father was a man of few words and few feelings. When he talked, he talked about the world from the perspective of dollars and cents, supply and demand. I don't remember him ever saying, 'Good job,' or 'What do you think?' or 'I love you.' Even to my mother. I would have traded any one of his economic insights for a pat on the back. But, like you say, that is life.

"My mother was a cautious woman who loved to laugh. But she only did so when my father wasn't around, as if he wouldn't approve. She wrote poetry that she never formally showed to anyone. For years, I begged her to share even one stanza. But she was too shy, too proud, or too self-conscious. Too bad, too, because they were exceptional."

"You saw them."

"She called me into her room a week before she died and handed me a box filled with her writing. For the next five days, we read to each other, line after line, page after page. And when we were done, I realized I finally knew who my mother really was, inside and out. And a remarkable woman she was, Dr. Chu."

I paused long enough to hear a sigh from one of his nine wives and then said, "My family lived in the same house my entire life and never wanted for anything. I didn't really get it at the time, but I was learning what it meant to be part of a family and part of a community. Imperfect, but all the more real because of its imperfections. And when I went away to school, I had that to fall back on."

"Indeed," Chu whispered.

"And when my father died, I was surprised how much I missed him."

"Isn't that often the way it is, Mr. King."

"And when I thought back on his life, I realized he had taken his responsibilities seriously and had done what a father in his generation was supposed to do. When I got out in the business world – my first job after earning my MBA was with Sandoz, a Swiss pharmaceutical company – I realized just how many managers there were out there without a clue as to how to motivate their workers or how to get a good day's work out of them. We spend the majority of our waking hours with the people we work with. I didn't intend to be miserable during those hours. And I knew the best way to create the kind of environment I wanted was from the top."

"Very sensible."

"You get to the top by making the most of the people around you, not by steamrolling them. And you stay at the top by letting those people know that the world won't come to an end if they push the limits a little bit."

I used this philosophical treatise as a platform to discuss life on a broader scale. Tending, as I put it, to my physical needs through a love of karate, skiing, and running. Interweaving my relationship with Lauren into a picture of spiritual and mental well-being. Touching on my forays into politics and religion without giving them more credence than they deserved. All without calling up details that Chu and his research juggernaut probably already knew inside and out.

I ended by saying, "The challenge is balancing what the past has given me with what I have today, while still having expectations for the future."

The smile that tugged at the corners of Chu's mouth was gentle and sympathetic without being maudlin. "Thank you for that, Mr. King. You honor me – honor all of us – with your openness, yes, but with your modesty as well. I sense genuine humility without the sacrifice of duty."

"I hope I didn't put anyone to sleep," I said, glancing momentarily at the twins and seeing their warm expressions.

"I think you held our interest, Mr. King," Chu said. "And I am wondering now if we can entice you with a genuine Panda Thai meal?"

"I think you can, Dr. Chu," I said, though neither he nor I made any move that suggested an end to the immediate discussion, and my sense was correct.

"Very good. However…" He gestured with his index finger. "…Before we break bread together, let me ask one last question."

"Certainly." Ask away, I wanted to say.

He leaned forward slightly. "This job with Panda Pharmaceuticals. This position in our family. A rather significant responsibility. What causes a man like you to seek it? Why do you want it, Mr. King? Why do you really want it?"

A logical question, of course, and one that any good interviewer would ask. I was just slightly surprised that he would ask it here among his wives, though I was also surprised at the lack of direct questions that had been asked at all. This time I allowed my gaze to travel around the room, scrutinizing each woman with CEO eyes. Ironic to have their full attention in return. Quiet and self-composed as if my answer was not only relevant but also significant to them. Mae Song was not smiling. Jiang Li was perched as she had been moments before, well forward in her seat. The 15-year-old Ting-Ting sat with hands folded in her lap, eyes bright and unblinking. Kym and Lyn observed the situation with a level of detachment matched only by their father. Among the others was a stillness that had either been well coached or was a product of mates chosen with extreme care and not simply at the whim of a man in need of sexual gratification or female adoration.

"Mr. King, you must see that these women here are more than mere trophies or possessions. Like your wife Lauren, they are my sounding board and my confidantes," Chu said, as if my thoughts were printed in big letters across the back of the room. "I wish them to hear your answer, because they will provide points of view I may miss or wish to ignore. Just as you will discuss your visit here in earnest with Lauren when next you meet, I will have the ear of my wives and daughters and they will have mine. They do, after all, have a vested interest in the man who will replace me."

I began by saying, "It would be too obvious and too specious to say that I view the leadership position at Panda Pharmaceuticals as a challenge. I would not consider it if it were anything less than a challenge, but neither would I consider it for that reason alone." Keep it short, I reminded myself. Three points. No more, no less. Direct and businesslike. "Three reasons. All of equal importance. All indivisible.

"First, I have developed a passion, Dr. Chu. I have a passion for building and growing a world-class, research-driven pharmaceutical company whose focus is the development of products on the cutting edge of technology, created with the intent of truly helping people. There is no other reason to be in the business.

"Second, and I admit this freely, I want to pursue this passion free from the interference and intervention of outside investors with zero interest in the long-term future of the company or any real love for the company beyond the enhancement of their own portfolios.

"And third, I want to make a commitment, Dr. Chu. I want to be committed to building a legacy that reflects in the best and most positive light upon you and your family, upon me and my family, and upon the Panda family as a whole."

I ended there. The room was quiet. Somewhere along the line, the orchestra had paused as well, which was enough of a coincidence that I had to stop myself from smiling. Dr. Chu was nodding the way a man nods when his expectations have been realized. I took this as a good sign. Who wouldn't?

"Excellent answer. Excellent answer, Michael," he said, emphasizing the use of my first name. I would wait for him to invite such informality in return, I decided. "Genuine unless my instincts deceive me."

"Very genuine, Dr. Chu," I assured him.

"Welcome to the family," he said in a voice that was almost a whisper. I was struck by his sincerity, also the underlying gravity in his tone, though I reminded myself that a deal was not officially a deal until the fine print had been successfully navigated, and fine print, I knew, came in many forms. Stay on task, I heard a voice in the forefront of my mind saying. Even at that, however, I could not deny the ingratiating smile I saw on Lyn's face nor the warmth of Kym's very respectful bow. In truth, I knew very little about the twins, and they were likely to be subordinates within a very short time, but their reactions touched me in a special place nonetheless. I gave them both a slight nod of thanks, and even Kym smiled.

Dr. Chu invited his wives and daughters to their feet. Suddenly, the man in the tuxedo was distributing goblets filled with champagne, and everyone – even Ting-Ting – was accepting one. I took the last goblet from the tray and felt the chilled glass against my skin.

"Come. Come close everyone," Dr. Chu was saying. He raised his glass and his wives and daughters joined him. "Let us formally welcome Michael King as the newest member of the family."

A cheer mixed with Thai and Taiwanese versions of 'Hear, hear,' rose from the circle of women, and I had to admit I was moved. The sound of glasses clinking filled the room, and everyone drank, I, sparingly.

"Shall we return to the dining room, my husband?" Jiang Li asked, though it was more directive than question. "I imagine our guest is famished."

"I have that affect on people, don't I, my love?" Chu said. Jiang Li took one arm and Ting-Ting took the other. "You don't think I was too hard on him do you?"

"Brutal." She smiled with exceeding charm, and I was struck by this unexpected interplay. A well-rehearsed script, I wondered, or the natural improvisation of a man and woman many years married? Some of both, I decided as Kym and Lyn stepped up beside me. They escorted me back to the dining room and a meal fit for, well, the new CEO and President of a three-billion-dollar company and the man who made it possible.

The seating arrangements were well planned. Chu sat at one end of the table and invited me into the seat next to his. Mae Song and Lyn sat opposite me. Kym settled in on my right. Jiang Li, I noticed, sat opposite her husband. "I hope you don't mind several dishes from the old country, Michael," Chu said.

"He means Taiwan," Lyn said lightly. "Not to be mistaken for Chinese. And definitely not to be mistaken for Thai."

"Not that we frown on either," Kym added. "Properly prepared, that is."

"And the difference?" I asked with interest.

"Adaptability and creativity, my friend," Chu said. "When you have little, you make do."

"Taiwan is tiny to begin with, Mr. King, and very crowded," Kym said.

"And the amount of land where you can actually grow something is about the size of your Boulder," Lyn added.

"Our father can remember a time when rice was in such short supply that they used sweet potatoes and taro roots just to get by."

"We call it congee," Chu said. "Made with root vegetables of all kinds. I still crave it."

"The bottom line is that most of what the Taiwanese eat comes from the sea, Mr. King," Kym said. "As you'll see tonight."

"But the key, Michael, is creativity. Flavor, my friend," Chu said. "It's a matter of spices, yes, but also the order in which the spices are added. Tell him, Fen Suen." Chu smiled at wife number seven and then gestured at the appetizer that had been set before him: steamed mussels served in a smoky sauce so pungent that it tickled the inside of my nostrils. "Fen Suen comes from Taipei and a long line of master chefs, Michael."

Fen Suen's green eyes were nearly as magnetic as the swell of her cheeks when she smiled. "First taste," she said, speaking directly to me.

I did, and the flavor was indescribable: hints of onion, almond, and ginger crashed over my taste buds, but all I could say was, "Wow!"

This made everyone at the table laugh. "Wow? That's good, yes?" Fen Suen asked.

"Good. Yes. Very," I replied.

"We begin with crushed green onions in hot sesame oil. Add just a dash of soy. When you hear the…the…" she paused, looking embarrassed and clearly searching for the right word.

"Sizzle," I said and made the sound.

"Sizzle! Yes, sizzle!" she nearly shouted. Everyone at the table made the 'sizzle' sound except Chu and Jiang Li, who both watched over the table with pleased expressions.

By the time Fen Suen had described the delicate art of melding tomato paste with ginger, almonds, shallots, red pepper, and mussels, a soup made of pork bones, pineapple, and bitter melon had been served and greedily consumed.

As the meal progressed, Dr. Chu invited Li Ming to talk about the estate school where she was a science teacher, Park Rong to discuss the art of kendo, her expertise, An Xiang to gush about the orchid garden that was her passion as well as Chu's, and Xue Fang to list the endangered species they were trying to repopulate on the estate grounds. Except for Jiang Li, each of the nine wives present that night spoke, if only in brief, but with pride and dignity. I had to credit Chu for the respect he showed them. But the truth was, it was an object lesson, and I was the subject. Did I listen? Was I truly interested in what they were saying? Did I have questions?

You were right, I said to the voice in my head: the interview is not over. Still, it did not take an effort for me to listen to the women at the table nor to be genuinely interested. Listening was a skill I had long cultivated. It was a selfish thing. Listen and learn. In my entire CEO arsenal, I had no more basic rule. Knowledge, I knew, was the first step toward insight. Insight was leverage. Leverage was priceless.

Dinner was served in company with a plum wine that had the freshness of fruit juice and the tang of something considerably stronger. The dishes kept coming: meat pies with bamboo shoots; oysters with vermicelli; tiny buns stuffed with clams; and almond tofu with squid. And for dessert, steamed turnip cake, a dish I would never in my life have imagined could taste so good.

THE DANCE

*"Do not dwell in the past, do not dream of the future,
concentrate the mind on the present moment."*

Halfway through dinner, I was surprised and disenchanted to feel the effects of the plum wine I had written off as a drink with less punch than Gatorade. I had broken one of my cardinal rules that essentially prohibited, barred, and banned mixing alcohol with any business-related activity. I defined business-related activities as any event in which a man, woman, or child with even the slightest intent of engaging me or my firm was in attendance. A board meeting or a company picnic, it did not matter. I had been lured into breaking that rule based solely upon the casual, informal nature of this gathering, knowing perfectly well it was neither casual nor informal.

Fix it, I told myself as if sobriety was a switch-operated affliction.

The first step in this process was to refuse the plum wine carafe the next time the man in the tuxedo made the rounds and to hope he understood my request for Thai coffee. He may not have, but someone at the table did, and not two minutes later, I was the grateful recipient of a slender glass mug spilling over with thick black coffee topped with heavy cream. I looked around the table, and Jiang Li, who also had a cup in front of her, was signaling her approval.

"It is not meant to be stirred, Mr. King," she called to me. "The coffee will rise through the cream as you drink it. Like this."

She demonstrated, and I followed. "If the Thai have perfected anything," Kym interjected, "It is their coffee."

I tasted it. Well, it wasn't a grande non-fat, two-Equal latte from my favorite Starbucks, but it wasn't bad. "Exceptional," I said, realizing that Webster defined 'exceptional' with enough latitude to spare me the burden of outright lying.

The plates were cleared, and Kym leaned across the table. The subtle hint of her perfume drifted my way though there was absolutely nothing alluring in her expression. I was expecting a history lesson on coffee as a source of early morning addiction or an introduction to the night's evolving entertainment, not a business question so open-ended that even a blind man could see the pitfalls.

She said, "My impression is that you would frown upon any research project that required this or any company to enlist the monetary support of either a financial institution or capital funding groups, Mr. King."

"You've been reading my profile," I replied.

"I'm wondering if that approach hasn't inhibited your current company's long-term growth," she said. In other words, I thought, your father is wondering if that approach hasn't inhibited Peak's long-term growth.

"That's a good question," I said, though the answer seemed obvious to me. "However, I…"

Kym interrupted me, and did so rather abrasively, saying, "But if a company wants to improve its standing in the marketplace or take the lead in advancing new technology…"

This was fascinating to me. Kym would have been the last person I would have expected to act with such aggression. It just did not fit her personality. Which meant the aggression was planned, which explained the sudden interest of everyone at the table. Kym was saying something about risk and reward, but I was not listening now. I was watching and waiting; I was studying body language and looking for nervous tics.

"…and I think, at the very least, it needs to be on the table," Kym ended with a quick and telling rise in her voice.

The tension at the table was not something I shared. Employee outbursts were a reason for calm, not aggression, and surely not in the company of non-employees, which was exactly how I viewed Dr. Chu's many wives. I held Kym's eye. Then I pushed my coffee cup away, leaned forward slightly, and intertwined my fingers.

"I have a rule," I said. I glanced at Dr. Chu and added, "If you will excuse me?"

"Naturally," he said with an infinitesimal shrug.

"I have a rule," I said, looking from Kym to Lyn and back once more. "A question asked is a question that deserves an answer. Uninterrupted." I gave a little added emphasis to the word. "Whether you ask the question or I ask the question. Whether a member of my staff asks the question or the janitor on the night shift asks it. No exceptions. We all deserve that respect, I think." I paused, but just for a beat. "Don't you?"

"Of course." Kym bowed her head. "And I apologize."

"It's a very good rule," Lyn said, the relaxed tenor of her voice suggesting the exercise was over.

"Wait till you hear the rest of them," I said lightly, but knowing the exercise was far from over.

"Are there many?"

"Not more than you can count on one hand," I replied, "But mutual respect is pretty close to the top."

"I suppose I am still slightly curious about Kym's question, however," Jiang Li said from the far end of the table. "If I may."

Well, well, well, I thought. Relentless, aren't they? I decided in this case to speak to the entire table and let my eyes move from one woman to the other, saying, "I won't poison any company I lead with unnecessary long-term debt and all long-term debt is poisonous, especially in the health and drug industry. And if a research department can't carry its own weight without dragging the company into a long-term debt position," I said, my gaze settling momentarily on Kym before coming to rest on the man at the head of the table, "then we make changes in the department until it can."

Chu let the words sink in. Then he pursed his lips and nodded. "An exemplary policy. Quite so." He pushed away from the table. "Join me, Michael. Mae Song has arranged some entertainment for us in the ballroom, and no one has ever been disappointed with my lovely wife's dance troupe."

"Thank you. Sounds wonderful." I nodded at Mae Song as she scampered ahead.

Chu clutched my arm and shoulder as we walked through the house, saying in a perpetually casual voice, "My daughters have been invaluable to Panda since joining the firm full-time, Michael, but sometimes their father still asks of them duties as my children in light of their position with the company. It's not always comfortable for them. You will forgive me for using them like that, I hope."

"Employees are sometimes asked to represent themselves in ways that serve the company, while forcing them to act out of character," I said. "But we would never ask them to do what we ourselves would not do, would we?"

Chu thought about that for a moment. "On the other hand," he said eventually, "position does have its privileges, doesn't it?"

He laughed, and I smiled.

"What are you two chuckling about?" It was Jiang Li. She was walking with Xue Fang and An Xiang, their arms locked together like three playmates heading for the playground. "No secrets."

"I was just about to lecture Michael on the four keys to a great Chief Executive Office according to an old fool who still thinks he has something worthwhile to share."

An Xiang said four words in Taiwanese that her shared wives acknowledged with sincere nods. "They're trying to get on my good side, I'm afraid, Michael," Chu said.

"I wish my Taiwanese was better," I said.

"My lovely Xiang said, 'That's because you do.'"

"Well, then, I suppose you should accept her tribute and honor me with your words. The four keys to a great CEO! I'm very interested," I said and indeed I was.

"They are these. Agility. Strength. Empathy. Evolution," he said succinctly. "A man of leadership has to demonstrate agility, Michael. He has to have the unequivocal ability to respond quickly and calmly to unforeseen problems."

Chu paused long enough for me to offer an opinion, but this, I decided, was a moment better spent listening. Unless I was mistaken, this was clearly part of the script, and my host seemed pleased with my silence. He continued on, saying, "A man of leadership must have the temperament and willingness to show unwavering strength of character and resolve every day, in good times as well as in bad, and he must know that his employees will be looking to him as a source for their own personal strength. A serious responsibility.

"He must be empathetic enough to know that a company is only as good as the health and well-being of its employees and that caring begins at the top. This does not lessen expectations for performance. It promotes excellence.

"And lastly, a leader is not a leader unless he has the ability to change rapidly in rapidly changing environments while, at the same time, maintaining integrity." Chu's hold on my shoulder tightened just slightly. "Does our candidate for CEO think he has those personality traits?" he asked without hesitation.

I thought a moment. Would an affirmative answer be viewed as arrogant? Would a display of humility be viewed as a sign of weakness or diffidence?

"Interesting just how intertwined the four traits are," I said eventually. "Much like our mutual love for karate and kendo, an agile man is also a man who anticipates the unexpected and the unforeseen, because agility cannot counter a lack of preparedness, either physically or mentally."

Unlike Chu, I didn't allow for an interjection or a comment. "Strength is also a state of mind that reflects a state of preparedness," I said. "A strong man is not a boastful man, because a boastful man will eventually lose face in the eyes of his employees. But when they see a man who does not need to explain his actions or to brag about his achievements, they see a man who allows his hard work to speak for him.

"When a man leads by example, it shows his employees that actions speak louder than words. It shows them that what they put into their work means more than trying to impress for impression's sake. It shows he cares about the effort and the people making the effort.

"And when everyone is concerned more about effort than appearances, the ability to change and change rapidly becomes second nature to the entire organization." I was rolling. I figured I might as well stir the pot a little further and said, "The CEO who presents himself from a pedestal has two problems. One, you're alone. And two, once you've looked down at people from a pedestal, they don't entirely believe you once you try and come down from the pedestal."

We traveled through a circular courtyard with a domed roof, an island fountain, and sculptured groundcover gardens.

"You express yourself well, Mr. King," Chu said. A broad archway funneled us to a short stairway and a large chamber that was part ballroom, part bird aviary. The room was oval shaped and the domed ceiling was built from thick timbers and panels of clear glass. A hardwood floor the size of a small basketball court was bordered with slender trees with white, papery bark. Vines coursed along the roof and spilled over the treetops. I saw golden eyes moving from branch to branch, rounded and graceful doves, and a pair of very active Kingfishers. "Like a man who talks from experience."

"The best CEOs I know are men and women on a mission to learn new things and explore new horizons," I replied. "They are risk takers who abhor recklessness. They respect the past without getting stuck there. They enjoy success, but they don't entirely trust it, which means they always have an eye on what's up ahead."

The orchestra had relocated from the parlor, and a concave

arrangement of comfortable chairs looked out on the ballroom floor. Chu allowed his wives and daughters to be seated first. Before taking our seats, he stopped and looked me directly in the eyes. "Are you describing yourself then despite your use of the third person presentation?" he asked pointedly.

Ah, what the hell! Go for broke, I told myself. Even a display of modesty starts to sound a little tired after a while. I said, "My performance over the last 20 years has exceeded the results of every other CEO in the healthcare industry, Dr. Chu. That's not a boast. It's a fact. The achievements recorded by the organizations I have represented during those years are as good or better than any other pharmaceutical company I can think of. So am I describing myself despite my use of the third person? I guess I must be since I'm the best CEO I know."

"Finally," Chu said, as if he had been waiting for me to proclaim my place in the world of top CEOs. He reached out and gripped my shoulder again, this time the way comrades-in-arms might. "I think some entertainment is in order, Michael. Sit with me. Let's see what the troupe has in store for us."

There were two empty chairs at the center of the seating arrangement, clearly reserved for the host and his honored guest.

Chu called out something to the man in the tuxedo. Given his tone and body language, I interpreted it as a politely delivered order.

Whatever it was, the man in the tuxedo must have already anticipated the request, because two bottles of wine materialized within seconds, a Peruvian white and an Australian Chardonnay. Instead of refusing the wine this time around, I accepted a glass of the Australian, came to my feet, and faced my host and his rather remarkable party. I raised my glass.

"To my host and hostesses and your generosity."

Wine glasses were raised, and the women nodded their appreciation. "We're honored by your presence in our home, Mr. King," Jiang Li assured me, her very careful smile mirroring that of one twin and her striking posture that of the other.

I took a small sip. On another occasion, the chardonnay would have been a fine compliment to a perfectly grilled piece of halibut, but tonight it was just another distraction. Like all the others – the women, the gifts, the meal, the bantering – it was a calculated distraction, one Dr. Chu would use to exploit my weaknesses and test my strengths. I had disappointed myself in misjudging the plum wine's potency; I would not do so again. As I was returning to my seat in the wake of a well-received toast, I caught the eye of the man in the tuxedo. He patted over, bowed shortly, and said, "Yes, Sir?"

Ah, so he does speak English. I whispered in his ear. "May I trouble you for another cup of that very delicious coffee, please?"

He bowed again. "Yes, yes. Right away."

"Thank you," I said, noticing that Jiang Li even more so than Dr. Chu had taken note of my actions.

"Is there a problem with the wine, Mr. King?" she said. "We can offer you any variety of drink you might otherwise desire."

"Actually, I was just thinking how perfectly the Australian Chardonnay would go with grilled Sea Bass or a nice cut of Ahi. We call it barbequing back home, and I confess to being a bit of a fanatic about it, Jiang Li," I replied. "However, I am also a bit of a coffee aficionado and couldn't resist another cup of the Thai. I hope I wasn't being too bold."

"We're very glad you like it," Mae Song said to me suddenly, though what she was really offering was a slight rebuke to her shared wife and a message that the entertainment was about to begin. And indeed, the moment my coffee was served, a pair of spotlights illuminated the heart of the ballroom floor, the chamber ensemble struck up a traditional Chinese folksong, and two dozen brightly attired dancers – an equal number of men and women – swept into the room. Young, talented, and provocative in an exotic, sensual way, their energy seemed to grow with each new number, each more modern than the one previous.

"Extremely talented," I whispered to Dr. Chu. "Mae Song should be proud."

"Magnetic, aren't they?"

"A good choice of word," I agreed.

"Especially the women."

"That I can't deny," I admitted.

"Choose," he said.

"I'm sorry?"

He must have seen the momentary surprise that touched my face, because he laid a hand on my arm and smiled an avuncular, almost paternal smile. "Don't be embarrassed, Michael. It is our way. Our tradition. You would bring honor to any member of the troupe, believe me. So choose."

"I already have chosen, Dr. Chu."

"Excellent. Tell me." I measured his tone. The hint of excitement I heard had nothing to do with the members of the troupe.

I said, "She's back in Virginia enjoying the hospitality of your partner and the other Panda Board members."

"Ah, yes. Lauren," he replied. I listened for a thread of disappointment, but heard instead a hint of admiration. "Fealty. Loyalty."

"Yes. Two of my traditions," I said.

"And mine," he said with total sincerity, his eyes taking in the nine women who were among his eleven wives. His face did not reflect a sense of ownership. More like partnership, I thought. "A relationship is hard pressed to exist without loyalty and fidelity."

"Actually, a relationship is pretty much dead without them," I intoned. "Personal or professional."

Chu leaned close and touched his glass to mine in a silent toast that suggested the interviewee had slugged his way through another line of inquiry. Interesting, because the interviewer had also scored some points with the exchange. Maybe Chu knew that.

The exchange did something else as well. It made me realize that Lauren and Hanna may not have been at the forefront of my mind over the last 14 or 15 hours, but they were a part of every question I answered and every statement I made. Our relationships were built on fealty and loyalty to be sure, but they were also fed with strength and assurance, and I would have been a ship adrift without them.

The last dance number was a modern piece infusing percussive instruments wielded by the troupe's own members with Bob Fosse-like choreography that was as professional as it was energetic. It would have been a smash hit on Broadway, and here it was being performed for an audience of thirteen. When the number was over and the music fell silent, I had the urge to come to my feet and clap loudly with genuine enthusiasm but told myself to follow the lead of Dr. Chu. When Dr. Chu finally stood and clapped, I joined him, his wives and daughters did as well, though I could see they were eager to do so the moment the piece ended.

Still, I could not resist a nod of approval in the direction of Mae Song. "Wonderful. Thank you," I said to her.

She bowed her head silently in return, but I could see the appreciative smile stretching her face. "Yes, my dear," Dr. Chu added, as well. "A delight."

"The troupe will be touring Taiwan next month," Chu told me in a voice they could all hear. "And we're all very proud of Mae Song."

"Congratulations," I said.

Mae Song responded to this by looking with great expectation at her husband and saying, "May we bring out the children, my husband?"

"Most assuredly," Chu replied enthusiastically. And then to me, he said, "Several of the children have prepared a song or two for you, Michael. They are very excited, and I have a feeling you'll enjoy it."

"I have a feeling I will, too. What a nice surprise," I said. I wanted to look upon the entertainment as a compliment to me in my role as an invited guest and as a display of Panda Pharmaceuticals' desire to show me all sides of their far-reaching 'family.' I wanted to see the presentation by Dr. Chu's children as the genuine article – songs sung for the simple sake of lifting the spirit and such – but I reminded myself that not one event, incident, or encounter since my arrival in Bangkok had transpired for its own sake.

Twenty-one children, all clad in flowing royal blue robes decorated with golden embroidery, filed in like a well-prepared drill team, except half of them were smiling broadly. "It's not the entire brood," Dr. Chu said with obvious pride, "but it's not a bad showing. With two still in diapers and eight making their mark out in the world, we'll have to be happy with those here at hand."

"You have a beautiful family," I told him.

"They are my progeny. My legacy," he replied, as they formed two lines based upon height and age. The oldest, I judged, was in his late teens, while the youngest was probably three or four and a spitting image of Fen Suen, the young chef from Taipei. I was surprised and, for some reason, pleased when Ting-Ting excused herself from the circle of shared wives and placed herself in front of the group. Every eye in the choir, from the youngest to the oldest, was glued to her. I was even more surprised when Ting-Ting used her long and graceful hands to give cues to the orchestra. "Not a girl to be underestimated," Chu whispered in my ear, as if perhaps I had done so.

"Apparently not," I replied, as the orchestra followed Ting-Ting's directions and the room filled with a choral arrangement I could not identify.

"Mozart. An early work, the way I understand it," Chu said.

"You read my mind," I whispered.

Voices as pure as newly fallen snow carried to the lofty heights of the room, and I found myself smiling when Ting-Ting's own voice rose above them all, a perfect compliment to the varied talents of her charges.

"I found her singing in one of our fields in the Khorat Plateau," Chu explained between numbers. "I thought, a poppy field is no place for a girl of her skills and beauty and introduced myself. She returned home with me the next day. And I assure you, she is far more woman than her years, Michael," he said, a comment I determined required neither a response nor encouragement, and I was saved from doing so by the opening bars of a lilting Oriental piece by a composer named Ts'ao.

When the song was over and the cheering had died down, the children filed up to their father, hugging him fiercely. Each then bowed to me in response to their individual introductions. Chu would say, "Mr. King. My son, Chu Lok Long." "Mr. King. My daughter, Chu Zhi Zhang." And so on down the entire line of 21.

When the introductions were complete, they marched from the room much as they had entered. Their mothers followed, each bowing as they departed. Only Jiang Li spoke. "You have endured enough of nine curious women, Mr. King, and we appreciate sharing your story. May our paths cross again."

"I look forward to that, Jiang Li," I said, trying unsuccessfully to read anything into her words.

13

THE DOJO

"Remember, we all stumble, every one of us.
That's why it's a comfort to go hand in hand."

I t had been a surprisingly long evening already, and my legs were on the wobbly side as Chu and I came to our feet. It was, I decided, part wine, part meal, part inertia.

"If I may suggest a short walk to my dojo, Michael," my host said. "A meal like that deserves a few minutes of relaxation before you return to your hotel, and what better place than a man's private retreat. What do you say?"

"I say an invitation to a man's private dojo is an honor of the highest degree," I replied politely.

"I might ask my lovely daughters to accompany us, if you don't mind," Chu said, nodding stoically at the twins.

"I would enjoy the company."

The dojo was hidden toward the back of the estate in a forest of bamboo and juniper. A path made of red stone and lined by pencil-thin torches followed a rambling stream in and among the trees. It was haunting and beautiful beneath a waxing moon. In time, the stream forked at the base of a rounded drum bridge. We passed over the bridge and into a Japanese-styled garden with neatly raked sand the color of spring wheat, stone edifices standing like proud sentinels, and bonsai trees that reminded me of the windswept Monterey pines populating the Northern California coast. The garden formed a gateway to the dojo; it was built on low stilts, and the stream curled beneath it. A covered porch encapsulated a simple structure framed by tall bamboos and enclosed by hand painted paper walls.

"It's magnificent," I said of the setting and felt, even at that, that I was at a loss for an appropriate adjective.

Sliding screens opened onto a rounded room with octagonal walls. The walls were adorned with ancient swords, bejeweled daggers of every conceivable design, shields made from brass and accented with gold and silver, and a display of fierce-looking fighting chains that no man of right mind would want to face in close combat.

Thick beams and sheets of tan canvas formed a circus tent ceiling that moved like the main mast of a tall ship in a calm sea. The floor of the room was broken into islands exposing the stream below. Two small foot-bridges carried over the stream to the center fighting ring and a spotless white mat. The aura of the room was far more meditative than combative though I suspected a good deal of both had gone on here.

"You're to be congratulated, Dr. Chu," I said, my voice reflecting the atmosphere. "You've created a very special space here."

"A man needs a place to meditate, Michael. Don't you think? A place to search within himself. And a place to push himself physically, as well as mentally," Chu replied. "I prefer karate for its purity of form and kendo for its artistry."

"Very well put. Purity of form and artistry," I said. "I've always felt that karate allowed me to express myself from the inside out, while kendo did just the opposite. A nice balance."

"Then you will honor me with a light workout," he said in a casual tone that alerted me to a pre-arranged course of action.

I was hardly prepared for such a request, though, by now, I was less than surprised. I allowed myself a glance in the direction of the twins and a quick study of their faces. I appreciated the serenity they exuded, but it was just enough out of character to support my instincts. I knew that refusing Chu's request was not an option, but presenting a false front was not a wise course either.

I said, "I appreciate the use of the word 'light,' Dr. Chu, because I'm sure that's all I will be able to offer you in my rusty condition."

"You're too modest, Michael," Chu said. "And I appreciate a man showing respect for his elders."

I wanted to assure him that it had nothing to do with modesty or respect but rather a healthy dose of reality. Instead, I went for the middle ground and said the obvious. "And I am honored by the invitation."

"My daughters will help you find the appropriate workout gear," he replied. "I only hope we have your size."

A touch of the cynic flashed in me when I heard this last comment, because I knew perfectly well that they would have an outfit measured to my exact size awaiting me. The changing room was located off the back of the dojo next to a natural hot spring and a cedar-enclosed sauna. The twins escorted me in. Kym made a beeline for the closet, and Lyn invited me to disrobe.

"I think I can manage on my own, ladies. Thank you," I said, aware even as I did that I was promoting a lost cause. Sure enough, neither budged.

"Out of respect for our father's wishes, please allow us to stay," Kym said with exceeding courtesy.

"Then we won't have to insist." Lyn smiled.

This actually had another dimension to it that was probably a product of America's deep-seated Puritanical history or at the very least could be attributed to the fallout of my Midwest upbringing. But these women, I realized, would soon be working for me – I really didn't think I was getting too far ahead of myself given the tenor of the interview so far – and I was particularly sensitive to the employer/employee relationship. Undressing in front of my employees did not fit my vision of that relationship, but, by the time I had finished this interplay in my head, I was already knotting the drawstring on my pants and belting my robe.

The belt was black, which showed respect for my training but also reflected just how well my prospective employer knew me. Once again, I viewed the depth of their research with ambivalence. I may have found it intrusive, but I also admired their thoroughness. The crest sewn onto the back of my robe also intrigued me. It was a rounded design featuring a Bengal tiger and a bright orange sun pushing through a traditional Yin and Yang motif. Three Chinese symbols ran vertically along the side of the design, and I assumed the initials identified the dojo as belonging to Dr. Chu.

"Your father's crest?" I said.

"Yes," Lyn said.

"You have the same tiger on your shoulder."

"A Bengal, yes, but different," Lyn said. "Female."

"The male tiger stands for virility," Kym explained. "The female represents longevity."

"I noticed you don't share the same tattoo," I said.

"But I do," Kym said, her eyes gleaming.

When I realized she wasn't inclined to elaborate, I changed the subject and said, "You know already that I have a black belt in karate."

"And a brown belt in kung fu," Kym replied.

"But I don't want your father to think I've done any serious sparring for fifteen years. Maybe longer now that I think about it."

"Are you suggesting our 75-year-old father go easy on you, Mr. King?" Lyn said with a quick wink.

"Not exactly," I said, refusing to share her jocular mood. "This is his dojo. A visitor honors the rules of another man's dojo. Perhaps as his daughters and my future associates, you can give me some insight into his rules."

"His rules are simple," Kym said. "Regard not the age of your opponent. He will give no quarter to you, and he will expect none in return."

"Translated: he may look old, but don't let that fool you," Lyn said.

"Respect your opponent at all times, both in the level of his skill and depth of his commitment," Kym continued.

I looked to Lyn for the street version. "In other words, you have entered enemy territory. The rust accumulated from your apparent lack of commitment to your disciplines does not mean a thing here," she said frankly.

"Point taken," I said.

"And lastly," Kym said. "The dojo is first and foremost a spiritual place serving spiritual needs."

"That's very esoteric," I said. "Meaning what?"

Lyn looked at her sister and grinned. Kym said, "It's not over until your host says it's over, Mr. King."

"Glad I asked," I said, as we exited the changing room for the dojo. The girls were right about two things. For one, age, size, and speed were secondary to focus, commitment, and confidence once a man crossed the bridge to the fighting ring. And for another, this was not a game; it was an extension of life and living fully, and living fully was about respecting yourself first and your fellow man second. Or, in the words of noted deep thinker, Michael King: Bring it on, Dr. Chu.

The dojo, the combat dress, even the swords on the wall had produced an unexpected effect on me. They brought back memories. They triggered a rush of adrenaline. They made me realize how much I had missed the arts. And what I missed the most about them were the many layers that went into the discipline: physical, mental, and, as Dr. Chu's third rule suggested, spiritual. One without the other made for an empty cup. A man who was only interested in a means of inflicting pain on his opponent would never have the self-assurance or the depth of character to rise to the level of the true disciple, and only the true disciple could feel the pull of the arts in every fabric of his being. I had touched that plane a few times, and the only thing close was making love to an extraordinary woman. On the other hand, I reminded myself, it did not do to take it too seriously, because then you missed out on the fun.

As I paused at the foot of my bridge, I wondered just how much fun this was going to be given the fact that the man stepping up to the bridge on the other side of the ring was supposedly interviewing me for a job.

Dr. Chu wore an orange robe with a black belt. The crest decorating the back was a black and white version of the tiger and sun motif on my robe. Very striking.

We crossed our respective bridges simultaneously, while the twins retreated to a bamboo bench opposite the fighting ring. Chu and I met at the center of the ring and bowed. He then struck a classic fighting pose and moved in a counterclockwise motion that told me two things: his training was Chinese in origin whereas mine was traditional Okinawan; and his age had done nothing to reduce his flexibility or his mobility.

He struck quickly, turning my hesitation against me, and catching me by the front of my robe. He dropped to his back foot and threw me easily to the ground.

"The strength and agility of a tiger," he said in a playful voice that belied the aggressiveness of the move. I knew it, but maybe the twins didn't, because I heard them giggling in the background.

I rolled quickly to my feet. Now the adrenaline was pumping. I was pleased with the swiftness with which I recognized the subtle way my host had blended the frontal attack of karate with a classically lateral Kung Fu application. Unfortunately, my physical responses had not quite come to life yet, and I was forced to fend off a series of spin kicks by backpedaling to the edge of the fighting ring and retreating.

"You move well, Michael," Chu said lightly.

The comment, for better or worse, only served to bring a wave of anger to the surface. I realized, of course, that the anger was self-directed. I was ill prepared, and there was no excuse for that.

We circled the ring. Chu was no longer smiling. There was a predatory glint in his eyes that I was not able to match. I tried pressing the attack, using my size to cut off the ring, and launching a salvo of waist-high leg kicks. Chu parried one after another and countered with an open palm to my chin – a stinging blow – and effortlessly delivered an elbow to my nose. A jolt of pain sent me reeling. A spray of blood colored the front of my robe and spilled out over the dojo floor.

I instinctively raised my sleeve to my face, pressing it momentarily to my upper lip, but knew it would take a lot more than that to stem the flow. I was no longer pissed, and that was good news. I was now in that state of mind that wove together the core of my survival instincts, an animal aggressiveness, and an icy streak that reflected in my eyes, the calmness of my position, and the slow-motion quickness of my step.

Chu moved in for the kill. The man was ruthless. A part of me admired such a mindset, but a part of me also saw the flaw in it. I had one chance. My first instructor back in Arizona had called it his 'foxhole' move. I understood him to mean a life-threatening last resort, and it felt very much like that to me at this moment. Interesting that even as Chu was preparing to attack again I was struck by the silence in the room. There was no more giggling and no cheering. It was the silence of anticipation, and it only served to confirm my predicament.

The 'foxhole' move was part feign, part attack. The feign energized Chu and told him I was beaten; he overplayed his hand and gave me the very small opening I was looking for. The attack came from his blindside. It was a left hand that caught my host squarely on the side of the head and dazed him long enough for me to follow up with an abbreviated hip throw. Chu hit the mat at the same moment my palm found the base of his chin. His eyes rolled to the back of his head. His body fell limp. In a fight to the death, I would have finished the move by snapping his neck. That seemed a little extreme given the circumstances.

Behind me, I heard the girls gasp. They were across the bridge and next to their father an instant later. I expected them to be furious with me, but they weren't. Kym raised her father's head. Lyn scooped water from the rolling stream beneath the floor. She dabbed his face. The chill of the water brought my host back to life. His eyes opened like the slow rising of a stage curtain; the stage lights coming up was a state of consciousness returning to his face. When my face came into focus, he actually smiled.

"Excellent job, Michael. Well fought." Kym and I helped him to his feet. When the delirium passed, he and I bowed. It occurred to me for one fleeting moment to apologize for my aggression, though I was not in the least sorry – not when the bottom line was survival – and in the end, I realized an apology would be viewed as an insult.

"I thought for a moment I had you," Chu was saying. He put his arm around me. "You have to teach me that move. It caught me off guard, and I don't like being caught off guard."

I was lucky. I knew it, and he may have known it, as well. But then, luck was oftentimes a manufactured asset, and I was just industrious enough to come away with an appropriate dosage. Chu may well have known that, too.

I said, "You fought well," knowing it was not a compliment he was about to accept, and his response confirmed it.

"Well enough to lose," he said, but there was no venom in the words. In fact, I sensed a hint of admiration.

When the girls stepped up beside me, it was not as the man who had inflicted pain upon their father, it was as witness to something special, something honorable. It was not, however, until we were back in my changing room that they actually congratulated me.

"Well done, Mr. King." Kym bowed to me.

Lyn did as well. "You are the first of our family to defeat my father, and nothing could be more appropriate."

"I'm not sure how appropriate it is when the opponent is nearly twice my age. Not that he fights like it," I said. "Are you sure he's all right?"

"He wishes to be alone," Kym assured me.

"You fought by his rules," Lyn said. "You showed respect for our father. Now sit still. I have to tend to your nose before you bleed to death."

She was right. I had broken my nose before, and the pain told me I had done so again. Not surprisingly, the Chu household had its fair share of potent painkillers, and Lyn had me swallow two pills with water.

"What did I just take?" I inquired after the fact.

"The official name is Tri-X-410," Lyn said, stabilizing my nose with gauze packing, ice, and a level of effectiveness that came as no surprise to me. "It's not on the market yet, but it will be one of our first projects once you're on board. If you find it appropriate, of course."

"That could be our new marketing slogan. All experimental drugs personally tested by our President and CEO. Just in case," I quipped.

"I'm taking notes," Lyn said, finding in her tone a nice balance between jocularity and empathy. In another life, I thought, watching a smile spread across her rather remarkable face. In another life!

I took a long, hot shower and spent a few minutes alone in the sauna. Predictably, my thoughts traveled back to the fighting ring and the sparring match with my host. I did not analyze the bout with regard to the implications it might have on my interview or the status of my CEO candidacy, which, of course, would have made perfect sense. No. Instead, I replayed the match second-by-second, move-by-move. Where did I excel? Where did I stumble? I chastised myself for entering the ring ill prepared. How could I have so underestimated my opponent? Was there a sin more unforgivable than that? How could I have stepped into another man's dojo and taken a 'friendly' workout anything less than completely seriously? Cardinal sin Number two: I had been slow in my movements and slow in my reactions. I had wasted energy and miscalculated Chu's efforts. "Well done, Michael," I said with utter cynicism.

Then I went through the list of positives. It was a short list. I had survived. Okay then. That's something to hang your hat on, I thought, disguising the cynicism if not dispensing with it altogether.

"Sometimes hanging on by a thread makes it easier the next time around," I said to myself. "Sometimes survival is the only club you have left in your bag."

A guy who despises golf using a golf analogy to pump up his bruised ego, I thought. Wow! This made me smile and propelled me out of the sauna and back to my changing room. The twins had shown their own understanding of the situation by giving me my privacy. I changed back into my embroidered shirt and khaki pants. The pain in my nose had begun to subside.

I wended my way back through the dojo, stopped long enough to offer a respectful bow to the crest of my host, and exited onto the covered porch and the soothing sound of moving water. Dr. Chu occupied a straight-back chair with a view of the garden. He was conspicuously alone. His eyes were closed, but my footfalls brought him to life.

"How is your nose, Michael?" he asked. His gaze showed a complete lack of fatigue. The gleam in his eyes reflected the energy of our encounter, not the deflation of defeat. "I am sorry about that. My aim was off by three centimeters. It's a matter of age, I suspect."

"My nose is fine, Dr. Chu. As is your aim," I said, refusing to enter an arena of half-truths and recognizing our ongoing interview.

"I suppose you're right," he said, arising in one graceful movement and taking hold of my elbow. "It's just that some aspects of the interview process require less subtlety than others."

And don't you forget it, I reminded myself. We strolled back through the garden, over the drum bridge, and followed the path back toward the house. "If I may be so bold, Michael?"

He phrased it like a question, and I replied in kind. "Bold is good, Dr. Chu. Especially here and now."

"Alone at last. Yes. I completely agree. The evening had needed a moment like this. If only because it allows me to tell you how much I've enjoyed our time together. I've had more than my fair share of business meetings, but this one tonight stands head and shoulders above the rest. I don't say that to be polite."

"That's very kind of you, Dr. Chu." We skirted the house by way of a cobblestone path that coursed among lavender hedges. "And the best part of it for me was the ease of our interaction. I never felt it was anything less than genuine. When I see the fabric of a friendship emerge from the usual constraints of a business meeting, that says a lot."

"Well put," Chu said. "And hopefully you know that my house is open to you at any time."

I knew from some gut instinct that this was as close as we were going to get tonight to an affirmation of my job status. A contract, if and when it was offered, would be issued by the Virginia office of Panda Pharmaceuticals. I understood this. And Dr. Chu had already welcomed me into his family. Okay. Then why did my gut also tell me there was unfinished business still on the table?

The Hummer was waiting out front. Kym – her pose formal and hands locked in front of her – and Lyn – her arms folded across her chest and legs spread just slightly – were stationed by the back door. Dr. Chu stopped halfway to the car. "The girls will see you back to town, Michael. I thank you for indulging an old man and traveling all this way to see me. I assume your interest in our little company has not abated."

Well, well, I thought. A nibble. "My interest in Panda Pharmaceuticals has done anything but abate, Dr. Chu," I assured him.

"Good. Good." We both watched as Jiang Li emerged from the front door of the house and started our way. Elegant. Each step a piece of choreography.

"Mr. King," she called, holding out a hand to me and bowing. When our hands met, she said, "Michael."

"Jiang Li."

"I wanted to say thank you for honoring us with your presence. From all of us," she said.

"On the contrary. The gratitude is mine." I waited. Choreographed, I reminded myself.

"I heard you emerged victorious from the dojo," she said.

I thought before replying. "Victorious in that I left the dojo renewed. For that, I have your husband to thank."

She nodded, a single dip of the head. "May your journey return you to our house soon, Michael." A handshake turned into a warm hug. Her lavender scent, I noticed, was the same as Kym's.

Dr. Chu punctuated his handshake with a broad smile. "A safe journey to you," he said simply.

I turned before climbing into the Hummer and exchanged a departing wave. I sank into the backseat of the Hummer. Kym and Lyn joined me. Colliding emotions bombarded me from all sides. I felt numb, energized, and confident. I was awash in as many questions as answers. My senses burned. But for now, I decided to bask in the exhilaration of a remarkable evening.

∾

14

THE PATPONG

*"Do not wait for the last judgment.
It takes place every day."*

The twins were aglow, almost giddy. Lyn took the seat next to me, and her presence was like a brush of cool air and the warmth of a familiar room, a dichotomy made that much more profound by the opiate she had given me for my nose. Kym sat in the facing seat, more composed than her sister, but exuding a similar air of approval and success. I had tried to fit her into the mold of her mother, Jiang Li, and there were certainly elements of her character and her mien that fit, but Kym was also in many ways a reflection of her father and his ability to control a situation simply by his presence. I could imagine her as an effective business associate.

"So? How did we do?" I said to her.

"Well," Kym said.

"Well? Certainly I think you could say that," Lyn said with a wide berth of good-natured exasperation. "Try very well. Try smashing. Try a home run."

"All thanks to our expert advice and counsel, of course," Kym added.

"Oh, without question, sister. Without question."

We all laughed, and the laughter led Kym to say, "I don't think I've ever seen our father quite so comfortable quite so quickly."

"Nor our mothers. Did you see them?" Lyn said to her sister. They could have been two small children burning through a stack of presents on Christmas morning. Then Lyn nudged me good-naturedly with her elbow. "They loved you. You won their hearts. And that's not easy to do with that bunch."

"I'm glad. They're a remarkable group. You're lucky," I said, and then went out on a limb. "I enjoyed meeting Jiang Li. Her presence is…" I thought a moment. "…commanding and warm and genuine all at the same time."

Kym eventually filled a lingering silence. "We're proud of her. And we try to make her proud."

"She's proud of you," I assured them. "I could see it a mile away."

"How did you know she was the one?" Lyn asked, and I could tell that she was happy that I did know.

"You have her best qualities," I said honestly. "Poise. Leadership. A sense of humor. High expectations."

"You honor us," Kym said. "But we rarely look at it that way, to be truthful. We have many role models."

"It can be confusing to someone new to the family," Lyn admitted.

"And not a subject we want to burden you with when we should be celebrating a successful evening," Kym said, putting the subject to rest.

"To the PatPong," Lyn shouted.

"We know you'd probably like to buy your wife and daughter souvenirs of your trip, and we're probably not going to have a chance tomorrow."

"And we would like to share a celebratory drink with you, if you would do us the honor," Lyn said suggestively.

"And we can do both at the PatPong."

"How can I refuse such an invitation," I said, though every fiber of my being was calling out for sleep.

"Excellent," Lyn proclaimed.

"To the PatPong," Kym called to our driver.

I had spent a very entertaining night at the PatPong in my one previous sojourn to the city of Bangkok. That, however, was in another lifetime when entertainment was directly related to any libation I could get my hands on and the pursuit of female companionship without much regard for anything other than sexual gratification.

But the girls were right. The PatPong was as famous for its shopping as it was its red light district, and its red light district had no rival, not even the world famous 'window shopping' along the canal in Amsterdam. It was as if some magician of extraordinary power and robust sense of humor had taken the best of Las Vegas, mixed in the mystery of San Francisco's Chinatown, seasoned it with the energy of Rio and the sounds and scents of an Istanbul bizarre, and spun out six blocks that only got more rambunctious as the night wore on.

An hour after departing the tranquility of Dr. Chu's palatial retreat, the Hummer entered the PatPong and parked in the one and only space not overrun with cars, taxis, motorcycles, bicycles, and hand carts. A sign said reserved, but no one seemed to dispute that it was reserved for us.

We clamored out. Vendors, visitors, street performers, and nightwalkers alike stared at the oversized Hummer, as if a spaceship had just fallen from the sky. Not surprising, I thought, since it probably cost more than any house in the city.

Teng Juewen, our driver, stayed with the Hummer. His silent partner, Ji Xiong, followed us into the melee of shops, open-air booths, and street vendors. I was as impressed by the reverberating din of men and machines, shouting and singing, ringing bells and slamming doors, and sirens and barking dogs as I was the mixture of scents as powerful as a Thai kitchen and as subtle as a woman's powder room.

"So what are we looking for?" Kym had to shout.

"If I can't find it here, it probably doesn't exist," I said, running my hands over a silk scarf, clinking the brass tubes of a wind chime, and peeking into the lens of a gold-plated kaleidoscope.

"No 'probably' about it," Lyn said. She held up a stuffed octopus with one hand and pointed with the other to an aquarium housing a boa constrictor as big around as my bicep. "How about that for the little lady?"

"The little lady would lock me out of the house," I said.

"That would not be good," Kym said.

I spied a cart decorated with handbags and purses that looked as if they belonged in a Gucci catalogue.

"There," I said.

"Nice." Lyn saw it too. "The man has taste."

We stopped in front of the cart and speared three bags from the display. Lyn went for the one with a metallic veneer that reminded me of fish scales or titanium. Radical. Mine was brushed leather the color of milk chocolate and typically conservative. Kym held up a shoulder bag that was more maroon than red and had traceries of black running like symmetrical spider webs across the surface. Elegant.

"This is for Lauren, right?" Lyn said. She pointed at mine. "Too dull." Then at her own. "A bit much." Then she eyed the one her sister had chosen. "Perfect."

I had to agree. "It's a deal," I said and almost wished I hadn't.

A woman descended upon us from behind the cart, her chest puffed out and her eyes gleaming with the scent of the kill. I was almost afraid to ask how much, but Kym did not give me time.

Within seconds, she and Lyn were engaged in a heated exchange with the woman, unintelligible Thai phrases flying through the air like daggers. I would not have been a bit surprised if it had come to blows.

Finally, the woman slammed her palm down on the lid of the cart, hard enough to make it shake, and Kym did the same. "Done," she said to me with a triumphant smile.

The woman looked miserable as I passed her the money, but she did not impress me as the kind who came out on the short end of the stick very often, and I doubted seriously if she had this time either. I also did not stop to question the twins about the deal I had gotten, because their excitement alone was worth the price I had paid.

"What's next?" Lyn said, taking my arm. I decided against protesting. It was too late and I was too tired to worry about the finer details of employer/employee protocol.

"Miss Hanna King," Kym said with enthusiasm. She latched onto my other arm, and this somehow made me feel better about Lyn. Now we were just three lost souls making our way through the PatPong jungle. "She's five, right? What's on a five-year-old's shopping list, Mr. King?"

"A doll, naturally," her sister chimed in.

"Actually, a Hello Kitty doll," I said. "My daughter can be very specific."

I knew the chances of finding a Hello Kitty doll in Bangkok's most decadent neighborhood were almost none, but the girls were not so pessimistic. They posed the question to a dozen merchants, and each answer led us to a different booth. Antiques, jewelry, handmade birdhouses, paraphernalia, music boxes, toy trains, imported dolls.

"You're kidding," I said when I saw the full compliment of Hello Kitty dolls staring out at us from behind the glass of an expensive children's store.

The girls cooed over the assortment of dolls, while I was left to bargain. A man with a fistful of bhat in his hand and not two words of Thai in his vocabulary negotiating with a five-foot-tall man with pop-bottle eyeglasses, yellow teeth, and a mean streak.

I held out 50 bhat, and he shook his head like I was suffering from delusion. He opened and closed his hand five times, which I took to mean 50 bhat times five. I waved 100 bhat in front of his nose and said, "Last offer." Last offer, hell. I wasn't leaving without the doll, and he probably sensed that.

This time, he opened and closed both hands five times; if he meant 10 x 100, I was in trouble. "Forget it," I said.

"Okay, forget it," he spat in guttural English that made me glad that in real life I only negotiated deals with six or seven zeroes behind them.

Suddenly, Kym walked up, slapped 300 bhat on the counter from her own pocket and shook her finger in front of the man's nose as if to say the negotiations were about to put his life in jeopardy.

"Deal?" she said, but the doll was already tucked under her arm, and she was guiding me toward the door.

"Deal!" the man called. At the door, I glanced over my shoulder, and he was smiling like a Cheshire cat. "Thank you very, very much."

When we were on the street again, I said, "He got me, didn't he?"

"You were brilliant, Mr. King," Lyn said, beaming.

"Your sister was just a little more brilliant was all," I replied.

"Sometimes she has absolutely no patience," she whispered, but just loud enough for Kym to hear.

Here I was walking down the street with the two most beautiful women in the entire PatPong – hell, maybe the whole city – and all I wanted to do was give my baby girl her Hello Kitty doll and watch a replay of Shrek. I was either getting really old, really sentimental, or on the verge of really figuring it all out. How did Coldplay put it? *Nothing else compares.*

"Now that you're all set on the shopping front, Mr. Michael King," Kym said after depositing my purchases in the Hummer, "I think we need to share the other side of the famous PatPong with you."

"Shabu's," Lyn cried. "Lead on, Sister. Decadence and perversion call."

I knew about Shabu's, or at least I thought I knew about it. Shabu's was a world-renowned bar featuring the roughest, toughest boxing ring in Southeast Asia, the youngest, most erotic, and most willing prostitutes in all of Bangkok – a bold statement – and side bar shows without peer. I didn't know what that meant, but I was about to meet decadence and perversion, as Lyn hailed it, head on.

Shabu's was like a magnet for travelers from every corner of the globe, and it looked like every one of them was trying to get through the front door, mostly without success. Kym and Lyn were undaunted. Lyn sidled up to the extremely large bouncer monitoring the entrance and making certain the only people allowed inside met Shabu's 'high' client standards. I didn't see an exchange of money, only a quick word and a nod of the head, and a moment later we were slipping past the barricade. The bouncer paid no heed to the grumbling of would-be customers overlooked in favor of more worthy clientele – meaning the three of us – and suddenly we were inside.

A firestorm of music and clashing voices nearly brought me to a halt, and then there were two young girls – and girls they surely were – latching onto my legs. A third one literally jumped on my back, and I could feel her tongue exploring my ear. I had no idea what such a greeting would have led to had the twins not come to my rescue. It was almost as if they were talking to stray dogs the way they shooed the girls away, but the three took their dismissal in stride and went searching for other prey.

"What was that all about?" I said naïvely.

"Pretty much all about sex, Mr. King," Lyn said.

"I probably would have figured that out," I said in return.

Lyn winked. "Yep," she answered, sounding very American and very West Coast. The twins were holding my arms again, but I realized now it was their way of setting boundaries for the entire bar. I was not available and neither were they.

As my eyes adjusted to the dim light, the decadence and perversion Lyn had spoken about reached out and slapped me in the face.

Two small stages, lit with colored spots and distorted with moving strobes, had been set up on either side of the hall. A third, larger stage occupied a space behind the bar. These were not the kinds of stages that featured banjo players, magicians, or stand-up comics. Like Lyn had said. This was all about sex. Sex at its most base. On stage left, two men were having sex with a young Thai woman who may have been over-acting in my eyes, but you could not tell it by the rousing reaction the trio was receiving. On stage right, two lesbian women, covered from head to foot in oil, were eagerly pleasuring each other. Center stage, a naked woman was inserting all types of phallic-shaped objects into her body, groaning with each insertion, and then passing the objects to the eager men crowded around her.

As the twins and I moved up to the bar, I was at least as interested in the crowd's reaction to these 'performances' as I was the 'performances' themselves. Beyond those enthralled souls nearest the stages, most of the patrons sat with drinks in their hands, either oblivious to the acts or watching them with the bored expressions of couch potatoes enduring a re-run of Little House on the Prairie.

When the song filling Shabu's ended, the trio on stage one was replaced by another, this with a twist: two women, one man, and a baseball bat. I couldn't watch. The lesbian couple gave way to a straight pair who went at it like two dogs in the wild, and their enthusiasm seemed to earn them a receptive audience. To each his own, I thought. Those of us closest to the bar and center stage were treated to another woman who was part stripper, part contortionist.

The bartender had to shout to be heard. It sounded like 'What will it be?' in Thai, and Kym held up three fingers and said something in return. I was fairly sure she hadn't ordered a Bud Light, but that was as far as I was willing to go.

The drinks were the color of grapefruit juice and topped with a layer of froth like a cappuccino. "What is it?" I asked, deferring to my conservative side.

"The list of highly toxic ingredients is just too long to recite," Kym explained. "It's called an Atomic Bomb."

"Sounds dangerous."

"You'll like it. Take my word for it," Kym said. She held up her glass. "To a day and a night that could hardly have gone better."

"Hear, hear," Lyn said, our glasses clinking.

"Thank you," I said, sampling the Atomic Bomb. I would not have guessed that a drink thusly named would have tasted sweet, but this one did. Also very strong, which made better sense to me.

"And if I may," Lyn said, her glass again raised. "To a working relationship with long life and the bearing of much fruit."

"I couldn't agree more," I said, a second sip bringing out the cranberry flavor in the drink.

"What do you think?" Lyn nodded at my glass.

"Dangerous. Like I said before."

The contortionist was amusing her audience by inflating a balloon with a device protruding from between her legs. A moment later, the bartender was coming our way with the very same balloon in his hand. He presented it to me with a broad, rather amused smile and a command I couldn't understand.

"He says to hold it steady," Kym interpreted. "And to keep your eyes on the woman."

I was not particularly keen on either suggestion, but it was hard not to wonder what was coming when the woman inserted something that looked a lot like a small dart into her vagina. The crowd was getting excited, and I had to ask myself how the rise in their voices and the balloon in my hand were related. Suddenly, the contortionist propelled herself to the edge of the stage and struck an erotic pose. She threw her arms back, rolled her shoulders, and thrust her spread legs in my direction. She pumped her hips and grunted. The dart burst out of her vagina, flew across the twenty or so feet that separated us, and impaled the balloon dead center. It exploded. The crowd roared. I dropped the balloon and wondered whether the look on my face expressed amusement or just pure shock.

The twins were laughing. The bartender, who was also laughing, snatched up the dart and offered it to me as a reward for…for what? For being such a good sport? Or such a naïve victim? In either case, I declined his offer, took a long pull on my drink, and let my eyes settle on the violent boxing match taking place in the caged ring beyond the bar. The crowd cheering the boxers on was mostly Australian if I had their accents right. A very drunk, very formidable bunch of Australians.

"That looks a little less dangerous than sitting here with a balloon in my hand," I said in hopes of recapturing my self-respect.

"You're a good sport, Mr. King," Kym said. "We should have warned you about the balloon."

"Can't wait to tell my daughter about her dad's big adventure in the Bangkok night scene," I said facetiously.

"You know what they say about Las Vegas, Mr. King? What happens there, stays there?" Lyn said, sipping the drink in her hand. "That applies doubly to Shabu's."

"You've got my vote."

Kym's gaze had followed mine to the boxing ring. "I've seen 10,000 American dollars change hands in there," she said.

"Which means you're either a damn good boxer, a guy with too much loose cash, or a damn fool with four or five of these Atomic Bombs under your belt," I said.

"Yes, and a serious overdose of testosterone," Lyn suggested.

The man taking the beating was a U.S. Marine if the tattoo on his arm was any indication, and he didn't look like the kind of guy who generally came out on the short end of these sorts of encounters. The man standing triumphantly over the Marine was an Aussie giant given his brutish size, the knotted brow, and the crimped eyes.

He tossed back a beer as the Marine was helped out of the ring. As the beer rolled down his chin and chest, he panned the room for his next victim. He challenged two or three potential candidates and had no takers. His eyes ticked off the patrons lining the bar and settled on me. I had no desire for a staring contest and gave my attention back to the twins. "I think one drink in Shabu's might be enough, ladies. Shall we…"

I didn't get a chance to finish the thought, because the Aussie troll was shouting at me. "You! You at the bar!" I looked up. Sure enough, he was pinning the guy in the embroidered shirt and the stunning women on each arm with his bloodshot gaze: Me. "Yeah, you! Another blue-blooded American pussy! Right?"

The smart side of my brain told me to ignore the guy. Unfortunately, I couldn't quite resist the impulse to hold his eye another moment and let him know this blue-blooded American pussy wasn't quite ready to concede the game before it even started. He shouted, "A thousand bucks says I can whip your candy ass, Yank."

Now he had an audience, and this wasn't the kind of guy who let an audience get away before playing it for all it was worth. I had seen it a hundred times. He threw back the rest of his beer and pointed. "I just called you a candy-ass Yankee. What are you going to do about it?"

"I think I'll just finish my drink," I said, aware that the bar shows had come to a screeching halt and that all eyes were on us. "Though I take the Yankee comment as a compliment."

"Check it out, Lou," one of my new best friend's buddies called out. "The bloke's already taken a beating tonight by the looks of his snout."

Another shouted, "Maybe the lad's hearing's not so good, Lou. It's my bet he's got shit in his ears."

Predictably, the rest of Lou's fan base laughed and jeered, and I tried to placate them. "Why don't I buy you and your friends a round, and we'll call it a night," I said. Bad move. The Aussie named Lou stormed out of the ring and onto the barroom floor. I was hoping the music might start up again or that one of the bouncers might intercede, but it didn't happen. A sparring match with a martial arts devotee like Dr. Chu was one thing, but a brawl with an intoxicated Sherman tank was not on my agenda. I hoped he wasn't going to be too disappointed.

Lou pushed his way through the crowd and planted himself in front of me. "I don't need some candy-ass American buying me and me mates a drink."

"Another time perhaps."

The man was awash in sweat and the stench of what smelled like three-day-old beer. I was tempted to point this out to him, but Lyn beat me to the punch. "Try a shower, a bar of soap, and some mouthwash why don't you? We're having a drink. Go away."

Lou scowled. Not at Lyn, at me. "I call you out and one of your tarts speaks up for you. The bet's a thousand dollars. In the ring or right here. It makes no difference to me."

"Thanks, Lou. You're a true gentleman," I said with more sarcasm than I intended. "But I think I'll decline your very thoughtful invitation."

"Declining ain't no option, mate. I'm on a roll. I made mincemeat of one of your kiss-ass Marines, and you're next on the plate."

"Son of a bitch!" Lyn snapped. She slid off her stool. "The bet's $5,000. And I'm your opponent. If you've got the guts. The Yank here is my guest, and I'm not fond of your ill manners toward him. Mate!"

The Aussie burst out laughing. He shouted back to his buddies. "The tart wants to have a go for five thousand bucks, lads. Don't know if I can resist."

"And $5,000 more," Kym said. I could feel her hand on my arm, and her grip was telling me not to intercede. "But I imagine ten thousand is out of your price range, isn't it? Especially when it comes to fighting a tart."

The Aussie's face turned a bright shade of crimson, and the shocked silence running through the bar seemed to frame Kym's challenging tone.

"Ten thousand," he shouted. "Fight accepted."

"Let's see the money," the fight referee shouted. "On the table."

"No way, ladies." I finally spoke. It was probably the sight of all that cash materializing like water from wallets all around the bar. "I'm not letting you go up there, Lyn. No way."

"You're not going to deprive a girl of a little fun, are you, Mr. King?" she said. And then more seriously, "You are a guest of our family. You are also our friend. It would be dishonoring to myself and my sister to let such an insult pass."

"I'm not insulted. And…"

"Trust in my sister," Kym said softly. "This is important to us."

The crowd parted as Lyn bounded toward the stage in a gown that probably cost $2,000. I noticed that both Teng Juewen and Ji Xiong, my personal bodyguards and the girls' ever-present shadows, had entered Shabu's and were wending their way through the crowd. Teng, who had apparently abandoned the Hummer, was headed our way. Ji had his sights on Lyn.

Before Lyn entered the ring, she kicked off her shoes. Then she pulled her dress over her head, exposing peach-colored panties, a sheer bra, and the body of a swimsuit model. The crowd exploded. As exquisite as she might have been, I couldn't appreciate it at that moment, because the Aussie named Lou was himself clamoring back onto the caged stage.

Before he stepped into the ring, he accepted a mug of beer from one of his countrymen and chugged it down. He tossed the empty mug aside and roared. "I'm going to knock the living shit out of this Thai bitch." Then he thrust a finger at me. "Then I'm coming after you, mate."

The ring man fitted Lyn with a pair of red boxing gloves that dwarfed her hands and made her sinewy arms look like toothpicks. On her opponent, the gloves looked like padded extensions of hands already fat and swollen from a life of aggression.

The frenzy surrounding what I saw as a complete and total debacle had captured every person in Shabu's attention, patrons and employees alike. The sideshows had been momentarily suspended. The music may still have been blaring, but I couldn't hear it over the rising din. Fistfuls of money were being exchanged even as the lights surrounding the stage dimmed.

"This is ridiculous," I said to Kym. "I can fight my own fight."

I felt Kym's fingernails dig into my arms. "Please, Mr. King. Of course you can. That is not what this is about." The eyes staring back at me now, calm and forceful, mirrored her father's completely. "This is Lyn showing her loyalty."

"To what? To the family? To the…?"

"No! To you."

The fight bell rang. The Aussie came at Lyn with a slow, deliberate gait, an animal fury in his eyes, and a mocking grin on his face. It was a sobering, ironic contrast to the fluid, easy step that propelled Lyn in a circular motion around the ring.

Lou, a man clearly consumed with violence, stalked her. He had boxed before. I could see that in his footwork and the angle of his shoulders. He jabbed twice, missing Lyn's face by a foot. He set his feet and launched an upper cut with his right hand. Lyn stepped inside the blow, planted her back foot, and brought her other foot with speed unlike anything I had ever seen into the Aussie's groin. Even before he could double over, she twisted her body into a flying scissor kick and caught Lou with two stunning blows on either side of his huge head. His eyes rolled to the back of his head, his knees dropped out from under him, and he hit the floor like a cow in a slaughterhouse.

The crowd was nearly as astounded as her opponent's cohorts, and the sweetest hush I had ever heard prefaced an eruption of cheering, jeering, and shouting. Utter turmoil. Lyn raised her arms in triumph. Kym burst out laughing. I could only breath a sigh of relief and accept the fact that I was no longer cut out for the kind of nightlife places like Shabu's provided, an understatement if I had ever uttered one.

Three things happened in the next fifteen seconds.

First, Ji Xiong materialized inside the ring and placed his rather formidable girth at Lyn's side. If the big Chinese man had an exasperated look in his limited repertoire of facial expressions, I was seeing it right now. He helped her off with her boxing gloves and on with her dress. Then he hustled her out of the ring and off the stage almost before she could collect her winnings.

Second, Teng Juewen, tight-lipped and dead serious, moved up next to Kym and me, his eyes studying every living thing within ten feet of us and expecting the worst. I didn't know if the situation was quite that serious, but, now that I thought about it, I guess that was what a bodyguard was supposed to do.

Third, the boxing ring filled with drunken Aussies who were more pissed off about the money they had lost than they were the condition of their unconscious mate. One of them put the toe of his boot into Lou's ribcage and snarled, "Get your fat arse up."

Lyn was flushed from her victory and hugging everyone in sight, her future boss included, and receiving a congratulatory high-five from her sister. "Kick ass, girl," Kym shouted.

"You better believe it," Lyn replied. She held up a huge wad of money. "Spending money, sister."

"The PatPong beckons." Kym was feeling her oats.

"If I may make a suggestion, Dr. Chu," Teng Juewen said to Kym politely.

"I think he's about to say that we've worn out our welcome," Kym replied.

"I think he is," I said with a certain amount of emphasis. "And I agree. If I may assert my as yet unconfirmed CEO powers. I say we call it a night, ladies."

"Mr. King is right," Teng said, bolstered by my intervention. He nodded at Ji Xiong, who used his considerable bulk to forge a path to the exit.

A blast of fresh air hit my face as we stepped outside. I was glad to have Shabu's behind me. I could safely scratch it off my list of recommended places to visit in Bangkok.

"Glad to see you two," I said to Teng and his silent partner.

"Not me," Lyn said, still aglow from the thrashing she had inflicted on the Australian and maybe a little high from the Atomic Bomb. She waved a finger at Teng and Ji. "Killjoys."

"Don't mind her," I said, grateful to see that our Hummer was still in one piece. "You earned your keep tonight."

"Thank you, Sir," Teng said. He could not usher us into the back of the Hummer fast enough.

I didn't wait for Kym to issue driving instructions. "To the hotel, Teng," I said. "Your American guest has seen enough for one night."

"Killjoy," Lyn said in a voice that hinted at a night well spent, but also suggested a certain pleasure in seeing her future boss act like one.

"How'd you do that?" I said to her.

She and her sister both knew what I meant, but Lyn said, "You mean kicking some serious Aussie tail?"

"He means showing the Aussie gentleman the error of his ways," Kym corrected. Then her calm eyes settled on me. "My sister proudly represented our country in the 1994 summer Olympic Games, Mr. King. She returned home with a silver medal in the open competition in the under-20 karate competition. I personally thought she was robbed of the gold, but that's a subject for another time."

The pride in Kym's voice impressed me nearly as much as her sister's accomplishment did. I was tempted to remind Lyn that displaying her skills in a Bangkok pleasure bar was probably beneath her, but instead I said, "That's a remarkable achievement. You should be proud."

"Kym was an alternate on the same team," Lyn said, taking her sister's hand. "But that was a long time ago. Our father encourages us to live in the present and to plan for the future. That's what we try to do."

I watched the bright lights of the PatPong fade in the distance and said, "Yes. But I'm sure your father would also remind you that planning for the future is often best served by an examination of the past. And that the fabric of the present is a reflection of where we've been and what we've done, also the relationships we've created."

The twins held my eye. Kym spoke for them both. "Thank you for that, Mr. King."

We rode the rest of the way to my hotel in silence. It was a good silence, a comfortable one. As the Hummer pulled up to the entrance, I took the girls' hands. "Thank you for a great day. I couldn't have done it without you."

"We'll walk you up," Lyn said.

I smiled and shook my head. "No. I have Mr. Ji. I'll see you tomorrow."

Kym squeezed my hand and said, "Ten o'clock. We'll pay a visit on our R&D labs and tour a couple of our poppy fields."

"Until then," I said, closing the door behind me and walking with Ji Xiong toward the entrance. I could not remember ever feeling so physically drained and mentally exhausted. Tomorrow, I imagined, would be a breeze in comparison.

∽

15

A FRIEND IN NEED

"Adversity introduces a man to himself."

"**P**earl Man! Yo, Pearl Man!" The booming voice trailed out to me from the hotel bar as I walked through the lobby. Ji Xiong was immediately on his guard. His eyes flashed, and he created a shield in front of me with his body.

"It's okay," I said quickly. Only one person I knew still referred to me as Pearl Man, and that was Tom Palmer. The voice matched, but the drink in his hand seemed a little out of place at this time of night. I also didn't imagine it was his first given the boisterous greeting.

"I won't be long," I told my bodyguard and started toward the bar.

"Pearl Man!" Tom shouted again. Every eye in the bar was watching him, and they were even more taken aback when Tom threw his arms around me in a roaring bear hug. "Mi caro amico. Buonanotte."

I held a finger up to my lips. "You've been practicing your Italian. I'm proud of you."

"I hold it in reserve for my closest friends. Especially the ones who stand me up for a drink," he crowed.

"Sorry about that. Long, long meeting. I just got back." The truth was I had completely forgotten our planned rendezvous. "Is it too late to make amends?"

"It's never too late to make amends." Tom turned back to the bartender and called out, "Barkeep. One more for me, and..."

"Whoa! Whoa! Tom," I said quickly. I took him by the arm and guided him away from the bar. "This place doesn't have much atmosphere. Why don't we go upstairs? I'll show you my digs. The Presidential Suite."

"The fucking President..." I put a finger up to Tom's lips.

"Shhh. It's not something I want to broadcast, Tom."

"Don't blame you. No goddamn way," Tom said drunkenly. "Lead the way, oh grand Pearl Man! Lead the way!"

"So, what's the occasion, good buddy?" I said to Tom, as we headed for my private elevator. I glanced over my shoulder, caught Ji Xiong's watchful eye, and gave him a wave and a nod to indicate that Tom was not to be taken for the enemy. "You get a raise or something?"

The elevator doors closed us in, and we rose to the top floor. I kept talking. "The last time you called me Pearl Man I was about to get my butt kicked by that 250-pound linebacker from Arizona State. He didn't know much karate, but he didn't need to, if I recall."

We exited the elevator. I unlocked the door to my suite and watched Tom's eyes widen at the unfettered opulence. "Goddamn, dude. You and Dr. Chu Man Fu must be thick as thieves. Look at this place."

"I'll call room service for some coffee," I said. "We can sit out on the balcony and toast the great city of Bangkok."

"Forget the coffee," Tom said, as if he had been insulted. "It's Dewars time, my friend. On the rocks."

"One Dewars on the rocks and one coffee," I said magnanimously. Something was definitely wrong. Tom was hardly a tea totaller, but I could not remember the last time I'd seen him drunk like this. Tom was maybe the most health-conscious guy I knew, and he took pride in not polluting his body, as he put it, with the various poisons of the world. "What kind of music are we listening to?" I said after calling down to room service for a pot of coffee and filling a cocktail glass with ice.

"Opera, my friend. This is a night for opera," Tom proclaimed.

Opera! Right, I thought. I don't care how drunk you are, good buddy.

"It may be a night for opera," I said, handing him his drink and showing him the way to the balcony. "But you're going to have to settle for Coldplay."

"I say opera and you say fucking Coldplay. Goddamn killjoy."

"Coldplay," I said in the direction of the entertainment center. "Any album. Volume, low."

Tom's eyes turned to saucers when the music suddenly drifted down from the balcony speakers, but all he said was, "Candy-ass music."

I laughed, but stopped dead in my tracks when I saw Tom kill half his drink in one swallow. "You want to tell me what in the hell is going on, Tom?"

"Ever heard the saying, 'Up the creek without a paddle?' 'Between the devil and the deep blue sea?' That's me, good buddy. As fucked as a man can be. Ruined." Tom drank again. He was dead serious.

"We've been friends for twenty-plus years, Tom. Tell me what's going on," I said. "Maybe I can help."

Tom finished his drink and stared at the Bangkok night. I didn't push. The door was open; he would either walk through it or turn away. A shove would not help.

"The Federal Banking Authorities raided our offices this afternoon," he said dully.

"What? Raided your American Financial offices? What the hell? Why? What happened?" A lot of questions.

"Last year, corporate headquarters stateside introduced a very questionable investment program designed to maximize returns by emphasizing high risk portfolio add-ons. They wanted to introduce the idea here in Asia. It was a crooked deal from the beginning. Not illegal, but shady. I fought it, but they refused to budge. It went south fast, Michael. The Feds targeted my offices when a group of investors sued. We're being held liable for individual losses well over 500 million."

"Jesus, Tom. How could that happen? You seemed fine this morning."

"It happened so damn fast. Everything was hunky dory until just a couple of days ago." Tom started talking. He went into details. I didn't understand exactly how the investment scheme worked, but I could see how Tom ended up holding the bag. The company had focused on the Southeast Asian market, and Tom's offices controlled that investment pool. The high-risk funds that were at the heart of the case were factored into every local advisors portfolio. They were doomed to fail, and Tom knew it.

"I should have walked. I should have gotten out while the getting was good. I'm going to lose every fucking thing I've worked for over the last 20 years, Pearl Man."

"Have you talked to an attorney?"

"Oh, yeah. Oh, you bet your ass." Tom tried to laugh, but it came out like a deep-throated groan. "Know what the motherfucker advised me? He advised me to cop a plea. You know what copping a plea means? It means ten years in some Thai jail. It means a lifetime ban from the securities industry. I might work again in East Timor, but that's about it."

"You told Nancy?" Nancy Palmer was Boston society through and through. Blonde, thanks to her hairdresser; beautiful, thanks to a world-renowned plastic surgeon; rich, thanks to a long line of family money. For all that, I liked her. She had raised their three kids while Tom barn-stormed the American Financial corporate ladder. He could take his career anywhere he wanted, as long as she didn't have to abandon her world of private parties and society gossip.

"I called her first thing this morning." I saw tears rolling down Tom's face. Nancy obviously hadn't taken it well.

"What did she say?"

"She said if the Boston papers got a hold of it, she was filing for divorce."

"She doesn't mean that."

"She means it all right." Tom wiped his face with the sleeve of his shirt. The tears kept coming.

The doorbell rang. "Room service," I said, as if Tom might not be capable of figuring that out on his own. "I'll be right back."

I unlocked the door. The woman from room service wasn't alone. Ji Xiong stood over her like a bulldog on a leash, watching every move she made. She delivered the coffee tray to the porch. As they were leaving, I said, "Thanks for coming up" to my bodyguard. I didn't expect a reply, a nod, or a twitch and didn't get one. I was still grateful.

I didn't ask Tom if he wanted coffee. I just poured two cups and put one in his hand.

He took a small sip and said, "The motherfucking Thai government has frozen all our assets, and American-fucking-Financial is cooperating with them. I'm screwed big time, Michael. I'm worth more dead than alive. No kidding."

"Yeah, well, we're not going there, Tom. The 'I'm worth more dead than alive' talk ends right now. Hear me?" I delivered this rather melodramatic line with my CEO voice. I had never used it on Tom, but the nod I received told me it had worked. At least for now. "We'll work this out. No one is going to jail, and no one is copping a plea. We'll find the right lawyer for the job and use every connection we have. You're not going down for this, Tom."

I sure as hell didn't have enough facts to make such a bold statement, but I had to engage Tom's warrior side; I had to get him fighting back. We drank coffee. Tom lasted another 30 minutes before his eyes began closing.

I said, "You're sleeping here tonight. There's a spare bedroom and the cleanest sheets in all Asia."

"All right. Thanks, man. You're a good friend."

"Tomorrow, you can ride along with me on my tour of the Panda poppy fields. We'll talk more then." I helped him to his feet. We treaded through the suite to the guest bedroom. "Maybe Dr. Chu can lend a hand. Tap a couple of his political contacts."

"You think?" Tom sprawled on the bed.

I helped him off with his shoes. By the time I threw a sheet over his shoulders, he was snoring. I looked down at the man I had called a friend for 23 years. He twisted onto his side, groaned, and turned back again. Hardball was not really Tom's style, despite the semi-truculent persona he tried to superimpose upon his rather unruly business world. The truth was, Tom liked order and organization far more than he did conflict and chaos, the bywords of a CEO's world. Tom even imposed those characteristics on his martial arts regimen. Not that he wasn't aggressive and confrontational in the fighting ring, he was. But it was always according to a plan. A well-executed plan. Tom was most susceptible in the ring when the plan went awry. Improvisation was not his strength.

Work was much the same. He scheduled office meetings on the same day at the same time every week. His employees knew exactly what was expected of them, and they could predict Tom's behavior down to the color of the tie he would be wearing on casual Fridays: blue with dashes of red or, caution to the wind, splashes of orange. That was pushing the envelope in Tom's world.

He was an exceptional investment guy for those very reasons. He calculated every move. First, he made certain the risk factors of every investment had been minimized. Then, and only then, did he focus on profits. I had probably heard Tom say, 'Never get greedy' a hundred times. 'Take what the market gives you.' Tom never worried about leaving a little money on the table. Better that, he would insist, than the alternative.

All the more reason for him to have revolted against overly aggressive investment policies created at the corporate level. On the one hand, it didn't make any sense that he would get caught in the bind he was in. The problem, on the other hand, was that Tom was not a revolutionary. He had scrambled up the corporate ladder on the strength of an exceptional financial mind, but he also understood the 'I'll scratch your back if you scratch mine' school of thought.

Hell, who in the business world hadn't done that at one time or another, I thought.

I navigated the hallway back to my own bedroom. I kicked off my shoes and stretched out on the bed. Even for a guy who tallied up 12 and

15 hour works days on a fairly regular basis, this had been one hell of an interesting day.

I reached for the telephone. When I got the operator, I placed a credit card call to Charlottesville, Virginia hoping to hear a friendly voice. When Lauren answered on the fourth ring, just the sound of her voice washed away some of the day's fatigue and made me realize why I had made the journey to Bangkok in the first place.

"Hey," she said.

"Hey."

"How are you? It has to be 2:30 in the morning there," she said with that subtle mixture of concern and curiosity that I had learned to recognize over the years. "Are you all right?"

"No fair," I replied. "You first. How's Virginia?"

"Well, to say it's been a roller coaster of a day would be a considerable understatement," Lauren informed me.

"I can definitely relate," I told her. "Give me the highs and lows."

"Low number one? Your daughter fell off her horse."

"Oh, shit! Any damage?"

"A broken wrist, scrapes and cuts all up and down her legs, and a serious case of the spooks. I tried getting her back out to the stables after we got back from the infirmary, but she didn't want anything to do with horses after that," Lauren said.

"A broken wrist. Poor kid." Three thousand miles away and all I can think to say is 'poor kid.' "Where is my baby?"

"Napping before dinner. They're giving her the royal treatment here at Panda Farms, but I think she misses the man of our house. So do I."

"I wish I could be there," I said. "How are you holding up?"

"Celia Chatzwirth gave us the grand tour this morning," Lauren answered. "I wish you could have seen the school. I don't think we could do better. It's first rate. Everyone from the kids to the teachers made Hanna feel at home. And I think it was genuine."

I listened to the sound of her voice and thought I detected just a hint of discomfort, maybe an edge of impatience. Probably fallout from Hanna's accident, but I threw out a lure just in case she had something more on her mind. "So, what do you think of your hosts?" I said.

"Nice people. Trying awfully hard," Lauren said with an intake of breath. "Celia made it clear that there was no shortage of benefits in the Panda world for us girls. Just in case I ever felt the need."

Sounded like the nibble I was looking for; now I just needed to bring her closer. "I have a feeling you're using the word 'benefits' loosely," I said.

"What else? Pills and men."

I waited. All I heard was a sigh. "Pills? What are you talking about?"

"Remember that Rolling Stones' song, 'Mother's Little Helpers?' Those kinds of pills!"

"What did you tell her?"

"I told her to set me up." There was a pause. "What do you think I told her, Michael?"

"Sorry. Dumb question."

"The men are in case I ever get really lonely waiting for you to come home. I guess she's had that problem on more than one occasion. I told her if that ever happens…" Lauren paused. "Sorry, I was just about to make a really stupid joke." There was another pause. "I told Celia that you weren't Philip, and that I wasn't her, but thank you very much anyway." Now she laughed. "Aren't you glad you asked?"

"I miss you," I said after a moment.

"You, too." She laughed again. "What about the interview? I want to hear all about it."

"It's the most remarkable interview I've ever been through, let's put it that way." I found myself taking her through it and realized even as I was doing so how much I valued her as a sounding board and confidant. I didn't leave anything out. Well, the sideshows at Shabu's, but who needed to hear about that? I even called Dr. Chu's many wives by their names and referred to the Australian troll at Shabu's as Lou.

"It was one test after another," I said. "An inference here. A suggestion there. Every gesture was calculated. Every interaction had a purpose. I have to give Chu credit."

"It sounds a lot like your interview style, to be honest," Lauren said, but I could almost hear her thinking ahead. "This Jiang Li sounds similar in a lot of respects to Celia Chatzwirth. I've wondered more than once who the real power is here at Panda Farms. Philip or her? There is something calculated about everything she does, Michael."

"How so?" I had an idea, but I asked anyway.

"I know she didn't plan for Hanna to fall off that horse and break her wrist, not anymore than Dr. Chu planned your confrontation with that Australian at the PatPong, but she was sure watching how I responded to the situation."

"Don't try to impress anyone, Lauren. That's not why you went out there. You went out there to see if you and Hanna…if you, me, and Hanna could make the kind of life we want for ourselves in that kind of situation," I said, but I was still holding onto something she had just said: Not anymore than Dr. Chu planned your confrontation with that Australian at the PatPong.

"I'm not trying to impress anyone," Lauren was saying. "You be yourself, too, Michael. If that's not good enough for them, then we don't need this job."

"Thanks for that. You're right," I said. "Have a safe flight home tomorrow, okay? I love you. Tell Hanna I can't wait for a hug."

"Kisses from both of us."

The phone went dead in my ear. I laid the receiver slowly back down in the cradle. "Lights out," I said to the automated system in my room. My eyes were already closing as the lights dimmed, but Lauren was whispering: Not anymore than Dr. Chu planned your confrontation with that Australian at the PatPong.

The pounding noise was real; I just didn't know it yet.

I flew off the bed, but I was sure it was still part of a bad dream, something about Hanna's broken wrist and…

The pounding had an urgent sting to it, and it was the urgency that made me realize someone was at the door of the suite, knocking and calling my name. I stumbled through the dark to the door and peered through the peephole. It was Ji Xiong, my bodyguard, and Tirini Arhamohareon, my personal concierge.

I opened the door, hoping the pounding hadn't awakened Tom. That was the last thing I needed. "This had better be good," I said, though the tension tugging at Tir's eyes and mouth was hard to misinterpret. "What is it?"

"A fax from your home office. If it hadn't been labeled 'Urgent-Immediate Attention,' I would never have disturbed you." Tir handed me the fax. I read it without moving. A sexual harassment lawsuit had apparently been filed less than two hours ago against Peak Pharmaceuticals' Vice President of Marketing by five female sales reps.

"Fucking Dreyfus." I looked up from the fax.

"Is everything alright, Sir? I surely did not want to wake you," Tir was saying again.

"No. You did the right thing." I nodded to them both, closed the door, and stood there shaking my head. "Fucking Otto Dreyfus. I should have fired your butt a long time ago."

By the time I had marched back into my bedroom, the fax was a crumpled ball in my hand. I picked up the phone again and used my credit card to call Peak's Boulder office. The switchboard patched me through to Conrad Marshall, my Director of Human Resources.

"Marshall," he said, and I could hear the strain in his voice.

"Fucking Dreyfus," I said for the third time.

"Michael! You got my fax. Thank God! Sorry about the timing, but this just broke," Marshall said.

"Let's hear it, Con," I said. "The gory details. Every one of them."

"We're screwed if we can't cut this thing off at the pass." Conrad Marshall must have grown up watching Audie Murphy movies, because his speech was peppered with Western clichés that had a way of cutting through the minutia. He would say things like, 'Circle the wagons,' or

'Smile when you say that, partner,' and you'd know exactly what he was talking about. "Otto is being accused of trading sexual favors for preferential territory budgets."

"What woman in the world would be that desperate?"

"That's another question," Marshall admitted. I had asked for the gory details, and he proceeded to lay it all out for me. When he was done, he said, "I'd like to put Dreyfus on paid leave until we can complete our own formal investigation, if you're in agreement."

"Do it. Like 60 seconds after we hang up, Con. You got that?" I said. I looked up and saw Tom Palmer staggering out of the guest bedroom. What the hell? I figured he was trying to make it to the bathroom before he threw up. "Make sure the paperwork is letter perfect, Con. Alright? Everything by the numbers. Copy Peg Fuller, my Exec Assistant, on everything. Get Bill Walberg from Legal on this immediately. Bill and no one else."

"Bill's on it. He's already preparing a response, and..."

"Hold on, Con."

Tom Palmer had not stopped at the bathroom to throw up. The son-of-a-bitch was headed for the balcony. I was sure of it. I dropped the phone and raced into the sitting room. Tom had gone out onto the balcony. He had opened the exterior window and was climbing onto the ledge. I burst through the balcony doors shouting, "Tom!"

He was teetering on the edge of the railing when my outstretched hand latched onto his waistband. His momentum had already started forward, and I had to use every ounce of my strength to prevent him from tumbling 25 floors to his death.

We sprawled on the balcony floor, me on top and gasping for air. All I could manage to say was, "That was close. Too damn close, Tom! What the fuck are you thinking?"

A flood of tears spilled from Tom's bloodshot eyes and gushed over his cheeks and chin and onto this shirt. He shook. I could see the hysteria gripping him and resorted to a hard slap in the face.

The blow shook him from his stupor and almost caused him to retaliate, but he had neither the strength nor the will. "Get up, Tom. You're not killing yourself tonight, my friend. You hear that? Not on my watch. Let's go lie down."

I dragged him back to bed. I pulled. He stumbled. But at least he did not fight me. I lowered him onto the bed for the second time that night. Then I hurried back to the sitting room, used the security key to lock the balcony doors, and then made a quick stop in my bedroom. The phone was dead. "Shit!" I went through the process of getting Conrad Marshall back on the phone and was informed that Otto Dreyfus was missing.

"We've got the police looking," Marshall said, "But he's nowhere to be found at the moment, Michael."

"You and Legal concentrate on the paperwork, Con. With any luck at all, Otto will walk in front of a freight train and save us the trouble."

"Our luck's not that good, boss," Marshall said.

"Don't I know it," I replied and hung up.

The coffee Room Service had delivered well over an hour ago was lukewarm. But this was the Presidential Suite. It didn't have just one microwave oven; it had three. I used the one in the pantry to warm the coffee, pulled a chair and an ottoman up in front of Tom's bed, and collapsed.

"No more suicide attempts tonight, Tom," I whispered. "No way, my friend."

I sipped the coffee and stared at the rise and fall of Tom's chest. I thought about Otto Dreyfus and the sexual harassment lawsuit his behavior had garnered. Odd that what angered me even more than the blatant disrespect he must have shown his accusers – all five of them – was the fact that I hadn't foreseen his potential for such behavior.

"You should have seen it," the self-deprecating part of my brain said, as if seeing into the hearts and minds of every person who worked for you was part of the CEO job description. The problem was, the organized, pragmatic part of my brain believed it, too. I should have seen it coming. Just like Tom should have seen this Federal probe coming. His excuse was that it had happened so damn fast. Those were his words. But things like that don't just happen overnight, I reminded myself. And things like Otto Dreyfus don't just happen over night either.

I did not feel my eyes close. I did hear music, however. "Oh, no! Now what?"

My eyes opened in slow motion, because my brain was still lost in a dream. Sunlight filtered through the curtains of the guest room. How had that happened? I felt something cold to the touch and realized I was still gripping my coffee cup. I was coherent enough by then to peek at my wristwatch. 7:00 a.m. Was that possible?

Tom had not budged. He was snoring, so I knew he was alive. I dropped my feet down from the ottoman, rolled out of the chair, and stumbled toward the bathroom. If Tom wanted to kill himself while I was peeing, I would just have to risk it.

I turned on the bathroom light and was stunned by what I saw in the mirror. The damage to my nose had spread to my eyes. I looked like a light heavyweight after a bruising 15 rounds with Sonny Liston. "It's not as bad as it looks, my friend," I said to the reflection without much conviction.

My bigger problem was sleep deprivation. I reassured myself that no one had ever died from a lack of sleep and turned on the shower. I looked in on Tom before stepping under the water and found him as comatose as he had been moments ago. I decided to risk it.

Had it not been for the fact that I was nursing a broken nose and two black eyes and that my very good friend in the next room was a suicide risk, it would have rated as one of the best showers of my life. When I got out, I toured the suite in my towel.

I checked on Tom, ordered coffee – a rush order – from Room Service, and then went back into my room and threw on clothes appropriate for a visit to Panda's R&D facilities, but comfortable enough to tour their opium fields.

16

THE LAB

""Everything has beauty, but not everyone sees it."

I drank three cups of coffee and made three phone calls between 7:30 and 8:00. If the phones were wired, so be it. I was not going to try and hide the fact that a sexual harassment suit was pending against my current company or that my college roommate was up to his nose in trouble.

It was midnight or thereabouts in Boulder, so I left messages for Conrad Marshall, my HR Director, and Peg Fuller, my Executive Assistant. They both said essentially the same thing. Keep the ball rolling on the Otto Dreyfus suspension, make certain Legal was conducting their due diligence on the suit, and dot every 'I' and cross every 'T'.

Then I called the American Financial office here in Bangkok and spent ten minutes on the phone with Tom Palmer's secretary. I told her that Tom was taking the day to get a few things in order. She, in return, got me the information I was after about any life insurance policies he might have in his name.

At 8:00, I put in a fourth call to Kym's cell phone.

"I'm bringing along a guest for our tour," I said. I gave her Tom's name and company affiliation to give it an official ring. "I hope that won't put a damper on the day."

"Not at all. I will make sure we do a thorough background check on Tom, per the Panda corporate protocol, and get his approval from our

Head of Security this morning if there are no issues, which obviously I do not anticipate. I'll make sure we pack an extra lunch," Kym replied in a voice that so nded a lot more rested than mine did. "Have you recovered from last night's extracurricular activities?"

I almost said 'Which ones?' but thought better of it. "I'm looking forward to the day," was how I crafted my response. Not very inspired, but then it was still early.

"See you at 10:00 on the dot." Which, by now, I realized meant 9:45.

I called for some rock 'n roll from the entertainment center. Something upbeat. "Dave Matthews," I said. "His first album. You know, before he started taking himself too seriously. Volume, medium."

I marched into the guest bedroom and shook Tom awake. It took nearly two minutes before he could rouse himself into a sitting position. The first thing out of his mouth was, "You shoulda let me do it."

My level of patience was not at an all-time high, but I had to remind myself that I was dealing with Tom Palmer, a man I had long respected and loved, not Otto Dreyfus, a man I hoped would throw himself in front of a freight train. Big difference. I knew I was risking my potential offer from Panda by bringing a suicidal and hungover executive with me today but our friendship meant more to me than any offer they could put on the table, and I was not comfortable leaving Tom on his own after last night's adventure. I brought Tom a cup of coffee, worked it into his reluctant fingers, and drew a chair up next to him.

"Drink," I said. He did. After he had taken two sips, I leaned forward. "Your 10 million dollar life insurance policy doesn't cover suicide, Tom." His head came up, eyes narrowed. "What? How…?"

"You're not worth more dead than alive, Tom. I had your secretary at the office do some checking. She's very thorough. Jumping out a 25-story window isn't going to help anyone. Your wife and kids need you alive. They need you fighting back."

Tom drank coffee for 30 seconds, one slow sip after another. "Sorry I put you through that last night. I was scared."

"Scared isn't such a bad thing, my friend. You've told me that yourself. Mad is even better. Sound familiar? Get mad, Tom! Focus. Focus on getting through this thing."

Tom managed a nod. "Yeah."

"Finish your coffee. Take a shower. You've got some time. My people won't be here for another hour and a half. We'll lay out a plan of action while we drive. Deal?"

"Deal."

I was not convinced. I actually considered removing the disposable razor blade from my sundry bag before giving it to him, but that would have meant taking the shoelaces out of his shoes and requisitioning his belt. I thought Tom deserved more credit than that.

I still wasn't disappointed, however, when the twins arrived at our door at 9:45, exactly 15 minutes ahead of schedule. They didn't break out laughing when they saw the condition of my face, but I thought I saw Lyn suppressing a smile. "You look...how should I put it? Ruggedly handsome," she said.

"He looks like shit," Tom called out. He entered the room wearing day-old clothes and a businessman's pre-prepared smile. "Honesty is always the best policy in these cases."

He held out his hand to Kym. "Tom Palmer."

I said, "These are Dr. Chu's daughters and two of Panda Pharmaceuticals' department heads. Dr. Chu Kym Dasao."

"Please call me Kym," she said.

"And Ms. Chu Lyn Sangsu."

Lyn also shook his hand, but her first words were, "Do we know each other, Mr. Palmer? You look familiar."

Tom shook his head. "You're not someone I would forget, Ms. Chu. And I mean that as a compliment."

"Speaking of compliments," Kym said, turning to me. "Our father could not have been more impressed with your meeting last night, Mr. King. Assuming you like what you see today, he will be calling the rest of the Panda Board to add his approval and recommendation toward your candidacy as the company's new CEO and President. Congratulations."

Both Kym and Lyn bowed, but the bows turned into warm hugs. "You're going to do a great job," Lyn said. "We're looking forward to working with you."

"You're damn right he'll do a great job," Tom said, grasping my hand and wrapping an arm around my shoulder. "I'm proud of you."

"Thanks." It felt good. I couldn't deny it. I was glad the girls had been the ones to deliver the news, and I was pleased Tom had been here to hear it. I was also realistic enough to know that their father's approval, delivered secondhand as it had been, was a far cry from a signed contract with a retainer check attached.

What's more, we still had a full day of interaction that was sure as hell not designed simply for Michael King's edification and entertainment. The minute you start thinking the interview process is over and done with, I thought, is the minute you make an unfavorable impression on an engineer at the R&D lab or raise the suspicions of a Site Manager at one of the poppy fields. Relax when you're back home in Boulder sipping a dry white wine on your back porch.

"Let's take a ride," I said, moving everyone toward the elevator.

We were exiting the hotel lobby when Lyn drew up in front of a newsstand selling newspapers from London to Singapore and magazines as diverse as the Smithsonian and Asian Outrage. She reached across the counter for a copy of the morning's Bangkok Press Review.

She glanced at Tom and said, "I knew I'd seen your face before. I just didn't have a chance to read the story." She hoisted the paper for Kym, Tom, and I to see. There was Tom's face staring back at us from the front page. The caption read: Financial Scandal.

"Oh, shit!" Tom uttered. "I'm toast."

I could see the color draining from his face. I think I said something like 'Oh, shit' too.

"What's going on?" Kym asked.

"Let's talk in the car," I said, guiding everyone toward the waiting Hummer.

Teng Juewen was sitting behind the wheel. We exchanged a brief nod. Ji Xiong held the back door open for the four of us. "Good to see you," I said and realized I was getting used to his blank face.

Lyn fell in next to me. Tom and Kym sat opposite us. I could have eased Tom's burden, I supposed, by filling in the girls myself, but the look on his face told me he was slipping back into the black hole that had nearly consumed him last night. "Tell them, Tom. From start to finish," I said to him. "If there is anyone in Thailand that can help, it's their father."

The Hummer nudged away from the hotel roundabout, into and out of bumper-to-bumper traffic on Soi 34, and merged onto the Thanon Charoen Krung overpass. Tom spelled out his dilemma. The twins listened politely, but without emotion. They asked no questions. If I read anything at all on their calm faces, it was a look that said, "If you play with fire, odds are you're going to get burned at some point."

It was not an altogether unreasonable point of view, I had to admit, but it was not likely to help my longtime friend. When Tom was done with his story, I said, "Do you think your father might be willing to look into the matter?"

"It's a huge favor, I know," Tom added. "But I honestly don't think I could last ten years in a Thai jail."

Lyn's expression didn't change a bit when she said, "I think that's a safe assumption."

"We can take the matter to our father." Kym was looking at me when she said this, and I understood that only the bond that had been created over the last 24 hours made such a thing even remotely possible. Then she turned to Tom. "Assuming you're not able to beat the charges facing you..."

"And it sounds as if they're lining up against you," Lyn interjected.

"...There is one possibility I can see."

We had exchanged the Thanon Charoen Krung for Thanon Rama IV, and I recognized it as the same highway that had delivered us to Dr. Chu's estate last night. I said, "And the one possibility?"

Kym was looking at me again. "That the Federal authority and the Thai government might possibly agree to an exchange. Ten years in a Thai prison – or whatever penalty befalls your friend – for a work program of like duration under my father's supervision."

"In what capacity?" Tom asked, as if there might be something worse than looking back at the world through the bars of a prison.

"Does it matter?" I said with an edge of irony and irritation in my voice.

Tom must have heard the irritation if not the irony. "No. No, it doesn't." And then to the girls he said, "Anything. Any help. I couldn't begin to thank you."

Kym responded by pointing to the passing factories outside our window, then to the interchange. The Hummer was leaving the Rama IV highway and veering north and east onto Thanon Oriental. I saw a road sign that read: Nakhon Ratchasima – 175 km. "It's 90 minutes yet, but we have a lot to talk about."

I nodded, grateful that the subject of Tom and his financial woes was, at least for the moment, pushed to the back burner. The business of Panda Pharmaceuticals was now front and center, and I opened the conversation by asking Lyn how the company viewed Thailand as an economic partner. Interestingly, she fielded the question by talking about the Thai people as opposed to the Thai government. "The literacy rate here is 93%. Not bad. The fertility rate is 1.80. Even better. The Thai are smart, funny people and industrious as hell."

"When they want to be," Kym interjected.

"On the other hand, they have a horrendous mortality rate due to AIDS and other infectious diseases like hepatitis A, dengue fever, and encephalitis that may not be out of control yet, but pretty close. Their infant mortality rate is sky high, and they have a drug problem that makes the US look tame."

"The point is that we have restricted our dealings with the Thai infra-structure while maintaining a robust working relationship with the Thai government," Kym explained. "We try to contribute to the country in socio-economic ways that may not translate into Thai jobs. What we have given back to the country in terms of trade and taxes is enormous. I hope you don't disapprove."

"Very diplomatically put," I said. "It does sound like Panda Thai has pumped considerable money and energy into the Thai school system and into its poverty programs. I'd like to know more about that. I don't have a problem using foreign workers – Chinese and Taiwanese I assume we're talking about here…"

"You'll be amazed at how diverse our research and manufacturing per-sonnel are," Kym said hurriedly.

"…as long as we're doing our part for the Thai economy and giving something back to the community."

"I agree. Absolutely," Kym said.

We crossed an unnamed river that would have made the rivers back in Colorado look like babbling brooks. Riverboats and fishing boats followed the current downstream. The road narrowed. Concrete turned to asphalt. Passage to the north soon fell under the dominating presence of a tropical jungle thick with towering trees and lush underbrush.

"If you look close," Lyn said, "you might just see monkeys."

"Not to mention the occasional boar or antelope," Kym said. "Though not much else at this time of day unless you want to get out and walk."

I was not inclined for small talk or banter after the night I'd just sur-vived and gave Kym a short nod. "Give me a preview of your R&D lab before we arrive, Kym. I assume the facilities are first rate."

"I'd stack them up against any in the world. Merck, Pfizer, Lilly. Any of them," she said. It didn't come across as a boast, just fact. "Our equipment is imported from La Forge in Paris and Straub in Frankfort."

"Top flight. Good," I said, noticing the omission of Peak from her list and wondering if it was intentional. Little, if anything, had been discussed over the last two days about my current employers and my success there. I attributed that to the intense research Panda had done on my background. They knew what I had accomplished. On the other hand, how I had accomplished it was something only I could tell them, and Dr. Chu had chosen his own method of extracting that information. Was choosing, I reminded myself, not had chosen. The process was ongoing. Don't forget it.

"Tell me about your senior staff," I said, as drops of rain tinseled the Hummer's windows and the jungle darkened.

"I recently hired Dr. Fritz Sanabria away from the Berkeley Institute in Oakland," Kym began. "This was before we started looking for someone to replace Philip Chatzwirth. I would have waited had I known."

"I know Fritz. He certainly has the credentials," I said. "We'll see if he has the temperament for the corporate world."

"That, and life in the jungle," Lyn said with a wry smile.

"Who else?"

"Dr. Liang Liang. I doubt you know him," Kym said. "He trained in England, Berlin, and Shanghi. He is the head of my first research team. My father hired him nearly twenty-two years ago. He's first rate."

"He's recalcitrant, hardheaded, and inflexible," Lyn said with her usual bluntness. "Liang was not happy when the Board passed him over for the Department head in favor of Kym. It wasn't easy for him to admit that a 29-year-old woman could run circles around him in science, applied science, and research at every level, and he's still fuming."

"Ah, yes. Some good old-fashioned internal turmoil." Tom rubbed his hands together. "Nothing like it."

"Dr. Liang will get over it," I said, watching Kym closely. "Has he made waves?"

"Let's just say that diversity is not a word Dr. Liang is comfortable with, Mr. King," Lyn answered before her sister could respond.

Kym came to Liang's defense. "He recognizes our opium-based meds as the heart and soul of our product line is all. Most of our diversified research is under the auspices of our second team."

"Your second team," I said curiously. "And who do you have running that?"

"Dr. Amed Amezuca."

"Outstanding," I said with a fervent nod of the head. You could not pick up a reputable health-oriented journal without seeing Amezuca's name; he was known as much for his innovation as he was for his realistic, and sometime harsh, assessment of the healthcare industry. "Not half bad for a second teamer. What about processing and manufacturing?"

"The facilities are run by John Caden, a former exec at Shimmer-Blaze in Holland. He's good," Kym said. "Our Director of Processing is P.K. Ton. MIT educated and trained for the position by my father. Unsociable as hell, but a fanatic for detail and the most organized man I know."

"That's because you haven't seen me in action yet, Dr. Chu," I said with a wink.

"Tell him about Paul," Lyn said excitedly.

"Paul? Paul who?"

"Paul Kapulka. He's our head administrator," Kym said with an uncontainable smile.

"You're kidding! Paul Kapulka? He was the COO at the Navarro Institute when I was there. He left about the time I took over at Peak. He said he was going on sabbatical in Taiwan…"

"Yeah, well, he kind of lied about that, Mr. King." Lyn laughed.

"He's excited to see you," Kym assured me. The jungle opened suddenly onto a broad valley and the specter of a fully-banded rainbow. Spectacular. "We're almost there."

What my eyes saw first were the helicopters. Two of them, their rotors blinking in the sun and their sleek bodies banking through the air the way the most impervious birds of prey do before launching their attack. These were not traffic helicopters ruining an evening commute with news of a stalled vehicle or an accident. These were attack choppers with battlefield written all over them.

When they took up positions on either side of us, Tom said in amazement, "What is this place? Fort Knox?"

"Not Fort Knox, but nearly as secure," Kym said. "If there was trouble out here, we could expect no help from the Royal Thai Army. Not for at least two hours."

"Trouble from whom? UFOs?"

I told myself to get the whole picture before leveling judgment. I told myself the same thing when the guard towers edged above the horizon. We were a half-mile from the perimeter fence when Lyn punched a code on her cell phone. I heard her say, "We're five minutes early. And we're now a party of four. Thank you."

We now had a two-car escort. Up ahead, a clear-cut staging area fronted a 15-foot-high steel gate. The gate was under the protection of a dozen soldiers clad from head to foot in combat gear and toting automatic weapons. One of them waved us forward. Ironically, I was not thinking overkill as I had at Dr. Chu's estate. I was thinking about the protection of Panda Pharmaceuticals' future product lines. I was thinking better-safe-than-sorry. I was thinking how easy it was for me to start thinking like a CEO instead of a man evaluating a prospective employer. Then I heard a voice in my head suggesting rather strongly that I take off the rose-colored glasses and get back to the business of observing and asking questions. There was, after all, very little that was normal about the last 24 hours.

The gate did not open until one of the guards eyed each and every one of us, reserving his sternest evaluation for Tom and me. I had no problem with that. We were the new guys on the block. When he was satisfied, he waved us inside.

The transformation beyond the fence was like something out of an Isaac Asimov science fiction novel. We were suddenly swept up in a futuristic community planned down to the cobblestone drives and the beach resort condominiums.

"All of our workers in the R&D facilities, the processing center, and the poppy fields are given a place to live, rent free," Kym was saying. "It's a self-contained community."

"What she means is that you can buy a six-pack of beer, lawn furniture, and your gas grill all at the same shopping complex," Lyn explained. "We have a clinic with an OBGYN, a shrink, and a dentist. We have a movie theater with two screens and a bar with Karaoke."

I saw a park, a volleyball court, a tennis court, and a baseball diamond. The recreation center was built from cinder block. The temple looked as if it had been transported here from the heart of Bangkok. "It's a full-fledged city."

"That's exactly what we call it," Kym said. "Panda City."

"I'd be interested to see a cost breakdown," I told her.

"It's not cheap. But we think it pays for itself. I'll have an analysis printed up for you," she promised.

"How big?" I asked.

"Seventy-six acres, including the lab and manufacturing facilities."

"And the opium fields?"

"There are three fields in this location. 120,000 acres in all."

Tom whistled. "I could get comfortable here," he said. "No problem."

"You said it yourself last night, Mr. King. The difference between a happy, productive work force and a disgruntled one is the difference between success and stagnation," Kym reminded me. "Our workers commit to a two-year contract, but most of our people have renewed their deals two or three times over. Our research people have four-year deals. You'll want the specifics of those deals at some point, but we feel they are more than fair."

I nodded. "And how often do they get into Bangkok? Or, wherever they go to get away from here?" The question was not planned, but it seemed logical.

Lyn had an answer. "Four days every eight weeks."

I could not make up my mind whether I was seeing a slice of utopia or a futuristic prison. The Hummer exited the workers' side of the residential city and entered a parkway that looked a lot like Golden Gate Park. Gardens, lily ponds, groves of eucalyptus, and walking paths. I saw a man on a bicycle and two joggers. Very normal.

The parkway, however, ended as abruptly as it had started. The collection of buildings that took its place reminded me of the business center where Peak Pharmaceuticals had their offices. Rising up on either side of the road were two long rectangular buildings, each two stories high, and encased in brass and glass and pre-stressed concrete the color of red sandstone. Not my style, but then it was the activity inside that most interested me. The walks were bustling with people carrying boxed lunches and looking for a spot of shade to enjoy the October afternoon.

"Our manufacturing facilities," Kym said. "The poppies are shipped directly here after the harvest. Once they arrive, the opium is synthesized and converted according to specifications developed by our father nearly twenty years ago and perfected over the last decade. Very precise. Unfortunately, we won't have time for a full tour, Mr. King. Our father wanted you to meet the R&D staff and visit the lab facilities instead."

"That's fine. I'd rather get the full tour the next time out rather than a brief glimpse today," I said. "How many people does the manufacturing plant employ?"

"Three shifts of thirty in each building," Kym answered.

"It sounds like a skeleton crew, but it's highly automated," Lyn added.

"Very impressive."

"Let's put Quality Control on the agenda for today if you don't mind, Kym," I said, though it did not come across as a request.

The Research and Development laboratories stood in the shadows of the manufacturing complex and directly across the road from the administration building. All white stone and dark glass, the entrance reminded me of the Delphi in Greece. The fountain out front sent ripples across a circular pond that was home to lotus flowers and lily pads. A coterie of a dozen people was lined up to meet us. Three of the men sported tailored suits and shoes polished to a high gloss. I recognized Paul Kapulka as the senior member of the three. The rest of the group wore lab coats, aprons, and white smocks and looked as if they had come straight from the job.

There were smiles aplenty, but the smiles were tinged with anxiety. I couldn't blame them. There was a new sheriff in town, and his name was Michael King. Change was inevitable. How much change was anyone's guess?

"Looks like you're a popular man, Michael," Tom said.

"Everyone's looking forward to meeting you," Kym assured me.

"Hah! Everyone's nervous as hell," Lyn sagely corrected.

"Actually, I'm honored they would think enough of the occasion to meet us," I said, glancing at Kym and knowing she would have had it no other way. She bowed in return.

The Hummer came to a halt next to the fountain. The bodyguards were first out, no less vigilant than they had been in Bangkok. They surveyed the grounds for ten seconds before opening the passenger doors. "I'll skip the tour if you don't mind, Michael," Tom said as we exited the car. "I'll keep your two rather large friends here company."

"See you later," I said, as Paul Kapulka led the delegation in our direction. He was a short, stocky Hawaiian with a full head of salt and pepper hair and a toothy grin. "Michael. You old dog," he called, his thick, pudgy hand outstretched. "Small world."

"You son-of-a-gun. How are you?"

The reunion evolved into a lengthy introduction of colleagues and staff. Directors first, scientists second. Paul did the honors.

Dr. Fritz Sanabria, Director of Manufacturing, Dr. Liang Liang, head of R&D's number one research team, and Dr. Amed Amezuca, team two's leader, joined us on a tour of laboratory facilities. The labs were state-of-the-art. No other description was appropriate. Electron microscopes, Perching lasers, spectrographs, gas chromatographs, climate-controlled incubators. The works. This was exactly what I was hoping to see. Skimping on lab equipment was no place to save money and invariably came back to haunt you.

Kym took the lead as we moved from one workstation to the next, detailing projects in their various stages of development. She was, however, also careful to allow her colleagues their rightful places in the conversation. This leadership skill was something else I was hoping to see. Lyn brought her marketing point-of-view into the discussion only when asked, respecting her sister's expertise in this arena and the delicate balance of personalities involved.

Slowly, the dialogue turned to the proprietary science that Dr. Chu Zhong Liu had developed over the years that allowed for the use of opium-based analgesics without the addictive side effects normally associated with the drug. I was fascinated. The CEO in me watched the participants in the discussion as closely as I listened to the scientific discourse. Team evaluation was as much art and feel as it was insight and fact, and I had learned to trust my instincts.

My instincts were telling me that Dr. Liang Liang was the weak link in the group despite his twenty-three years with Panda. They were telling me that Liang's agenda had a self-serving bent to it, that his lack of respect for Kym as Director of Research and Development was cancerous at best, and that he had not kept himself abreast of the technologies that were changing the face of health-related research at a breakneck rate. Dangerous trends.

Kym handled it beautifully, demonstrating a level of maturity well beyond her years. I, on the other hand, had never adhered to the philosophy of making the best of a bad situation. You didn't live with a cancer. You cleansed the body of it and moved on. I imagined that Dr. Chu Zhong Liu himself recognized Liang's falling stock and was just biding his time until someone else could see to Liang's removal. I would not ask Chu's blessing once I took the reins at Panda, but I would show him the respect he deserved by explaining my decision beforehand.

"Let's talk about the future, Dr. Chu," I said to Kym.

"With pleasure, Mr. King."

"Your research on molecular pain killers. The FL-47 in particular." I fell in next to Dr. Liang as we passed through an air locked door into a second hermetically sealed facility. He was, by my estimate, in his mid-fifties if the mottled complexion and the crow's feet around his eyes were any indication. "What are your thoughts on the direction this is taking, Dr. Liang? Worth pursuing?"

"I've been with the company over twenty years, Michael. I can call you Michael, I hope." He still spoke with a distinct Chinese accent. "A man of my age prefers a little less formality, you might imagine."

"Let's keep it formal for the moment, Dr. Liang," I said evenly.

"Certainly, Mr. King. Certainly," he said, his unctuous tone well practiced. "Dr. Chu. Dr. Chu Zhong Liu, that is, brought me into the company when it was first getting off the ground, and I have always put Panda first. If Dr. Chu..." Now he nodded in Kym's direction. "...believes we're on the right track with the molecular research, then I will do everything in my power to see it work."

"But you have concerns." It was not a question.

"Concerns? Research is a risky affair, Mr. King. You are as aware of this as any of us. But Panda is a progressive company. Progress requires a high degree of responsibility, and I have always held myself accountable to the well-being of the company."

While Lyn was shaking her head in disgust in the background, I was looking at the illusive nature of Liang's answer in a different light. He had been given an opportunity to champion his conservative position and had chosen instead the politically correct response. I was disappointed but not surprised.

"Very diplomatic, Dr. Liang," I said, as our tour led us to a huge water tank populated by schools of fugu fish and lionfish. Both fish, I thought, were a throwback to the early evolution of life underwater. The fugu, better known as the puffer fish, was a spotted creature with a bloated stomach. The fish scared its enemies off by inflating its body with water and displaying razor sharp quills much like a porcupine. If this false bravado didn't work, it resorted to poison, and the fugu was enormously poisonous.

"The liver and ovaries of the fugu contain a potent neurotoxin called tetrodotoxin. We call it TTX, for short, and it's at the heart of our research," Kym said. The lab facilities surrounding the tank – a dozen workstations – occupied seven technicians by my count, and they all wore protective suits that covered every inch of exposed skin. "We chose the fugu because its genome contains essentially the same genes and sequencing as the human genome."

"Yes," said Dr. Amezuca with growing enthusiasm. "But it carries those genes and regulatory sequences in approximately 400 million bases, as compared to the 3 billion in our DNA."

"What he's trying to say," Dr. Sanabria said with a smile, "is that the fugu has far less 'junk DNA' to sort through than we do."

"Exactly," Amezuca said. "Much more straightforward."

"The lionfish is different," Kym said. The lionfish had elongated dorsal fin spines, enlarged pectoral fins, and the patterned stripes of a zebra. Not the kind of fish you'd find in a person's aquarium back home. "It belongs to the Scorpion fish family. Its poison causes paralysis. But in a controlled setting, the poison has remarkable analgesic properties."

Dr. Amezuca said, "So what we're doing right now is reproducing the DNA sequence of the poison manufactured in the liver and ovaries of the fugu and cross-matching it with the poison from the secretion glands of the lionfish."

"Dr. Amezuca's team has stabilized the process over the last two months," Kym said. "It was a major breakthrough."

"Well done," I said to the young man from Bangladesh.

"It was a team effort, I assure you, Mr. King," he said.

"Should I be excited by your progress, or is it too soon for that?"

"If you're in research," he said, sharing a sheepish grin with Kym and Dr. Sanabria, "you can't help but be excited by the possibilities."

"Dr. Sanabria?"

"The potency factor of FL-47 is 10 squared in comparison with morphine. Which makes it a hundred times as potent. But the cost of production – and this is a best guess estimate – will only be a factor of 2."

"The profit potential is enormous," Lyn said.

"If we don't break the company trying to get it to market," Dr. Liang said under his breath.

"We're in Phase One trials here at the lab and with our animal test groups in Bangkok and back in the States," Kym informed me.

"And, as of yet, there have been no apparent side effects," Dr. Amezuca said, his enthusiasm unbridled.

Lyn was chuckling. "That's going under the assumption that the two-hour-long erections our male subjects have been running around with don't count as a side effect."

The young doctor was suitably embarrassed. "Yes, well, there is that to consider, I suppose."

"Not that I'm complaining," Lyn assured him.

"It sounds as if our marketing department sees some potential in this, as well," I said. "Perhaps on several fronts."

"Hell, yes, we do."

"What about the release profile?"

"Pain relief in five minutes guaranteed," Lyn announced.

"I think he was asking for a scientific evaluation," Kym said to her sister. "The release profile depends upon the dispensing method, Mr. King. But we think five minutes is a fair estimate, because the med is being designed for absorption through the skin."

"Increasing the risk of an overdose dramatically," Dr. Liang insisted. "And therefore putting our company at tremendous risk, Mr. King. I hope you can see that."

"Yes. Dosage is critical," Kym admitted.

"Yeah, well, we're not going to be selling it in the grocery aisle alongside the Bayer aspirin," Lyn said. "This will be a 'hospital only' product. Just like the rest of our lines."

"Addictive?" I asked.

"We're still a long way from crossing that bridge," Dr. Sanabria said.

"Right. So let's not think about it now. Let's keep throwing money at it," Dr. Liang said sarcastically.

"This is not the kind of medicine you turn your back on just because someone somewhere in the future might misuse it," Amezuca said, his voice rising. "You could say that about morphine. You could even say it about Ibuprofen."

"Apples to oranges," Liang argued. "Morphine is a be-be. FL-47 is a nuclear bomb."

I listened to the argument with interest knowing, like everyone in my industry, that the potential of overdosing and the possibility of lawsuits were inherent parts of the drug business. Truth was the best remedy. Make no bones about potential hazards. Overstate the dangers.

I was seeing the same potential as Lyn. A five billion dollar a year industry worldwide based upon FL-47 alone. That, of course, was contingent upon the US market, which was contingent upon FDA approval. But you did not back away from that kind of potential in any case.

I was excited. But this was neither the time nor the place to share that excitement. I looked at Kym and said, "What's next?"

"Follow me," she said.

One airtight lab led through a series of doors to another. I had never in my entire career seen such elaborate, sophisticated facilities. With the people to match, I thought, the competitive advantage was enormous. Kym was saying, "We've been experimenting with a blood clotting agent extracted from the venom of a Malayan Krait. It's a snake found exclusively in the jungles of Southeast Asia and Indonesia."

"Ungodly poisonous," Dr. Amezuca said softly. Four snakes the color of newly mowed grass and flecked with hints of brown looked out at us from behind a Plexiglas tank filled with tropical plants.

"Yes. It takes all of 1/14,000 of an ounce of its venom to kill a full grown human," Kym said.

"That's a powerful snake," I said.

"Yes. But it's not the power of its poison as much as it is the chemical composition that interests us."

We moved a dozen paces to a porcelain-covered workstation. Kym glanced at Dr. Sanabria for elaboration. He stepped forward and said, "We call it MK-119. The chemistry is very complicated indeed, but the result is a derivative that works instantaneously and with no ill side effects."

"We're far too early in the process to make that claim," Dr. Liang argued. "Let's not mislead Mr. King with false optimism."

"No ill side effects at this early stage and based upon experiments conducted so far," Kym said to me calmly.

"We've prepared a demonstration for your benefit, Mr. King," Sanabria said. And then, with a touch of cynicism, added, "With Dr. Liang's permission, of course."

"Someone has to be the voice of caution," Liang said.

"And I'll observe the demonstration with that word of caution in mind, Dr. Liang. I assure you," I said.

The experiment – performed at the expense of an innocent enough looking rat – was conducted by a lab assistant with bleached blonde hair and an English accent. She used a scalpel to remove the rat's tail. The flow of blood was instantaneous and heavy. She applied an FDA-approved clotting agent to the wound. Nothing happened. In the name of science, we all stood by and watched the rat slowly bleed to death. I seemed to be the only one who found this slightly inhumane, but, by then, the woman had removed the tail from a second rat. The experimental MK-119 had been converted to a lime green powder that she applied to the wound using an air syringe. I had never seen such instantaneous coagulation. The wound closed in less than a second, and the bleeding stopped an instant later. Except for the loss of its tail, the rat looked no worse for wear. Remarkable.

"Clearly, we are still in the discovery phase," Kym said to me. "But I'm sure you can see the potential for surgical care or catastrophic wounds."

"Considerable potential, yes," I said.

"In the marketing world, we call it a blockbuster," Lyn added. Her smile left no doubt, and no one seemed inclined to argue.

"I think I've seen enough for now, Dr. Chu," I said to Kym. "Thank you."

"Then I think I'll let these fine gentlemen get back to their teams." She turned to her three colleagues. "Thank you for your time."

I shook hands with all three scientists and said, "Very informative, gentlemen. I appreciate the insight." I had not formally taken the reins of Panda Pharmaceuticals, so there was still a very clear line separating our relationship today and the one that might exist in the near future. Crossing that line prematurely could have unsettling consequences, besides showing a lack of professionalism. However, keeping too great a distance from that line was equally as unwise. So I added, "The lab seems to be in good hands. Until next time."

"I'll be right with you, Mr. King," Kym said. "I need to collect a couple of samples. I'll only be a minute."

"We'll meet you outside," I said.

Lyn and I walked in silence to the exit. Outside, the air was heavy with the scent of rain, but the clouds overhead were parting, and a swatch of vivid blue appeared in the sky. "May I suggest lunch with a view, Mr. King?" Lyn asked.

"You may," I said.

"I hope I wasn't too aggressive in there," she said before her sister reappeared. "Sometimes I feel the need to say what I know my sister is only thinking. Which is crazy since I know she doesn't need me or anyone else to come to her rescue."

"No, she doesn't strike me as the kind who needs rescuing," I said. "But, on the other hand, sometimes the folks in Research and Development need to be reminded that we're in the business of selling products. Reminding them is part of your job."

"Diplomacy is not my strong suit, I'm afraid."

"Diplomacy is nothing more than nudging people toward your own way of thinking and making them believe it's their idea," I told her. "Giving ownership is the best motivator I know of."

"And if someone rejects ownership?"

"Then we don't need them," I said.

17

THE OPIUM FIELDS

*"Once the game is over,
the king and the pawn go back into the same box."*

A moment later, Kym emerged from the lab with two small sample bags in tow. I recognized the pale pink tablets in the first bag as prototypes of the fugu-lionfish analgesic. The lime green powder in the second bag looked very much like the blood clotting agent that had saved a rat's life not ten minutes earlier. She took note of my interest. "I want to take these to the university lab in Bangkok for independent testing. It's time for a second opinion."

"Excellent." I nodded and said, "Thank you for the tour."

"May I have your impressions?" she asked, as we followed a cobbled walk past the processing center.

"The research is promising," I said. "Your team is interesting."

"Define interesting, please," she said.

"There is friction. Friction can be a positive thing. I'm not questioning that. But when it's not, a remedy is necessary."

"Liang." Kym pursed her lips.

"You've earned your position, Dr. Chu Kym Dasao," I said formally. "It was not handed to you. A lack of respect on the part of a subordinate, a peer, or even a superior is not only bad form, it's a drag on productivity. And I'm not keen on either."

Kym stopped. We faced each other. She said, "My father…"

"Your father," I interrupted, "expects you to recognize your responsibility and exercise your authority. Nothing more, nothing less. And so do I, Dr. Chu."

Kym held my eye. I saw the muscles in her shoulders relax. Then she bowed. "Thank you, Mr. King."

After a moment, Lyn expelled a long sigh. "Good. Finally. Now that that's settled, can we eat?"

"My thought exactly," I said.

"Outstanding. Because here comes our ride."

The vehicle coming our way looked like a cross between a golf cart and a safari wagon. Teng Juewen was driving, Tom Palmer rode shotgun, and Ji Xiang sat on the first of three passenger benches. "I'm starved," Tom called, as we climbed aboard. "What took you so long?"

"I can't remember. Did you think to bring a lunch for Mr. Palmer, Sister?" Lyn said in a most sarcastic voice.

"It never entered my mind," Kym replied, equally mocking. "But then there's nothing more healing for a dispirited soul than a day without food."

"Okay, okay," Tom said. He held up his hands like a man surrendering. "I take it back."

"A wise decision," I joked, as Teng Juewen steered the cart away from the office park.

We curled up a macadam path and left a stretch of manicured gardens for a grove of coconut trees. The path wound through the forest for ten minutes, rising steadily. I heard the screech of monkeys and saw shadows moving through the trees. A bird with a yellow crest and yellow-tipped wings soared overhead followed by his mate and two babies. At the crest of the hill, the trees thinned. Blades of sunlight broke across the path. When the last tree fell away, we entered an oval park that looked as if it had been transplanted from a Japanese garden and put there just for our benefit.

Teng parked in the shadows. Ji Xiang carried a huge picnic basket and a cooler to a wooden table with an expansive view of the valley below.

Fields of bright orange poppies, like something out of Alice in Wonderland or the Wizard of Oz, stretched in both directions for as far as the eye could see.

"My goodness! Spectacular!" I stood there like a man captured in a Monet painting. "I would have never believed it."

"We came at the perfect time," Lyn said. "The flowers just opened."

"I wish Lauren and Hanna could see this," I said, knowing how much they would have appreciated the splendor. "Orange is Hanna's favorite color. Or, at least it was a week ago. Who knows what it is this week."

"The problem is," Tom said, his arm extended in the direction of the steel fences, barbed wire, and guard towers protecting the perimeter of the fields. "You would have to explain those to her, and I'm not sure she would understand why guys with machine guns were standing guard over a bunch of flowers."

"Thanks for ruining the moment," I said.

"Just doing my part," Tom said. He didn't sound overly chipper. But he also didn't sound as despondent as he had last night, and I took some solace in that.

Kym stepped up beside me. "You can't see them from here, but there is a womblike pod at the center of every flower." She made a fist with her hand to demonstrate the size. "Once the orange petals die back, the synthesis of a white sap occurs inside the pods. It's a phenomenon scientists have been trying in vain to figure out for the last hundred years."

"The sap is opium," Lyn said.

"This is Nakhon #1. It's the second largest legal opium field in the world, Mr. King," Kym informed me. "The largest is over the next rise. Nakhon #2."

"In the wrong hands," Lyn said, "there are enough of those pretty little flowers down there to keep the streets of the United States in heroin for a very long time."

"With enough left over to make a nice dent in the European market, too," Kym said.

"How sure are we that none of it gets smuggled out of here?" I asked. "By whatever means?"

"We police ourselves, as you can see," Kym said, casting an eye down to the fortifications surrounding the field. "And the Thai government polices us. It's a tight lid."

I knew what she was saying: smuggling and theft were facts of life in the drug business. To this end, I said, "But there are no guarantees."

"Kind of like life itself, if you ask me," Tom snarled.

"Can we eat before your happy-go-lucky friend here ruins my appetite?" Lyn said, as she and Ji Xiang set the table. They laid out a meal of fresh fish sandwiches, fruit salad, chopped vegetables, and helpings of seasoned brown rice and spring rolls. Enough food for ten people.

We sat around the table and served ourselves. My bodyguards did not eat despite an invitation from me and urging from the girls. They patrolled. Oddly enough, I was getting used to their presence and finding some comfort in it. Comfort against what or whom, I was not entirely sure. But among the six of us – Tom included – there was about 75 years of serious martial arts training, so anyone with ill-intent would find their hands pretty damn full.

It was just about the time this thought was finding a comfortable place in the back of my brain that I heard the sound of cars wending their way up the hill behind us. I don't know whether some degree of alarm showed on my face or whether it was Ji Xiang coming suddenly to attention, but Kym reached across the table and laid her hand on my arm. "It's alright," she said. "I've arranged for a couple of demonstrations while we eat. You mentioned Quality Control, and I thought it would be helpful to see how the opium is extracted from the poppy."

"Sure. Good idea," I agreed. She withdrew her hand. "You said a couple of demonstrations. What's the other?"

"What my sister calls a demonstration, most of the rest of us call entertainment," Lyn explained.

"Something less exotic, I presume, than what we saw last night at the PatPong," I said.

"You'll see." Lyn winked.

The cars came to a halt next to our cart. I heard two car doors open and close. Two lab technicians and a field hand – by the looks of his boots, blue jeans, and plaid shirt – emerged from the shadows carrying a lab kit, a portable incubator, a leather satchel filled with cutting tools, and a sealed bag with three newly harvested poppy plants inside. A canvas bag hung from the field hand's shoulder.

Kym greeted the men, but didn't formally introduce them. To me, she said, "The extraction process is simple, but very precise. Timing is crucial."

She nodded to the field hand and spoke a half-dozen Thai words that propelled him into action. The tool he lifted from his leather satchel was the length of a streak knife with a thick wooden handle, a short, curved blade, and a razor-sharp point.

The technician opened the sealed bag containing the poppies and passed the worker a four-foot-long tubular stem. The brownish pod at the head of the stem was the size of a baseball. "This is normally done in the fields after the poppy has flowered and the petals die back," the tech said. He cast an eye at the valley below. "We're still a couple of weeks away yet. Late October." Then he nodded at the field hand. "But this particular plant was greenhouse grown and is ready now."

The field worker tapped the pod with the handle of the knife to demonstrate its hardness, then scored the surface with a series of shallow, parallel incisions. White sap oozed from between the cuts and began congealing on the surface.

"One man cuts, two men collect," the tech said.

"Which suggests that all the harvesters are men," Lyn derided. "They're not. It's closer to half and half."

"Sorry," the tech said, glancing from me to Lyn and back again. "I didn't…"

"It's okay," I said. "How many harvesters?"

"A field like Nakhon #1…" The tech tossed his thumb toward the valley. "A thousand. Probably more."

"For how long?"

"Five to seven days. Twice a year."

"And then they're gone?"

The tech nodded. Interestingly enough, the field hand nodded, too.

"And they're well paid for their services, I assure you," the tech wanted me to know.

"We recruit as many of the same harvesters as we can from season to season," Kym said. "It's a controlled environment."

"At least as controlled as we can make it." The tech nodded with a certain excitement toward the pod and the congealing opium. He said, "Now watch."

I returned my attention to the poppy and saw the opium's pale color transforming into a brownish, black hue. The tech said, "That right there, that change in the color, tells us that the opium is ready for harvest."

Now the field hand drew a second tool from his satchel. It was a flat, dull-bladed knife apparently designed for scraping the thickening mass from the surface of the bulb, because that was exactly what the man did. He dropped the fruit of his harvest into the canvas bag.

"One man, or woman, collecting for twelve hours will fill three bags," the tech said. He caught my eye. "That, Sir, is a lot of opium."

"The opium is delivered to the processing plant in Panda City the same day to avoid contamination. Then the processing begins. A subject for another day," Kym said.

"Fascinating. Thank you for the demonstration," I said to the tech. I nodded to the field hand, but a part of me thought he understood what we were saying just fine. I don't know why this interested me, but it did.

The entertainment Lyn had spoken about consisted of the town's school choir, a very talented flutist, and two classical guitarists. I understood that the performance was Panda City's way of acknowledging my presence, and I tried my best to give the children my full attention. Admittedly, I was more entranced by the warmth of the sun on my weary body and could easily have closed my eyes and drifted off to sleep.

When the music ended, Kym and I clapped. Lyn whistled. Tom hooted. The kids tried to control their smiles and bowed politely. Inexplicably, something struck me as I watched them walk back to their bus, and I leaned across the table and caught the eyes of my two escorts. I said, "I'm curious about something, but I couldn't find an opportune time to ask your father about it."

"Then it is a question more appropriate to him than to us perhaps," Kym said in her most pragmatic voice.

"Perhaps. If so, please tell me," I said.

"Fire away," Lyn said.

"The missing pinky finger on his left hand? I noticed that Philip Chatzwirth shared the same...irregularity."

"And you're wondering the source? Or the meaning?" Kym suggested.

"We honestly don't know. The family does not speak of it."

"And we've learned not to ask," Lyn added.

"I do know that our father sees the missing finger as a source of internal strength." Kym shrugged. "More than that, I cannot say."

"That's fair," I said, putting the subject to rest for the time being. I stood up. "Ladies. It's been an enjoyable outing."

"Informative, I hope," Kym said.

"Informative in that the list of questions I now have will keep me awake for the next week. You've created a monster, and the monster has an insatiable appetite."

"That's a good thing, right?" Kym said to her sister with a wry smile.

"And I even think there was a compliment in there some place," Lyn said.

"All I know is that I've made two fine friends in less than 48 hours," I said with complete honesty. "And that I'm anticipating a productive and enjoyable working relationship with those two fine friends."

Kym acknowledged this rather personal statement with a silent bow. Her sister spoke for them both. "Why thank you, Mr. King. You're most generous."

"Let's head back, shall we?" I said. I was looking at Tom for signs of the guy who had tried to jump off my balcony last night.

"I'm ready," he said, a positive if not completely confident tone to his voice. "Time to face the music."

～

18

THE ROAD HOME

"All know the way, but few actually walk it."

I settled into my seat in the back of the Hummer and found myself admiring the jungle scenery with the right side of my brain, while the left side built a paradigm of Panda Pharmaceuticals' product pipeline, present and future. My first thought was that the company's five-year-strategic plan – a plan that had me salivating – had painted a particularly conservative picture of Panda's future. The upside, in my mind, far exceeded the plan's projections, and I found myself appreciating the fact that Dr. Chu and his fellow Board members had not tried to sweep me off my feet with pie-in-the-sky forecasts. We would meet the plan's goals in four years, perhaps even less. If we didn't, the Board should be asking for my resignation.

I was not trying to talk myself into the job. That was not necessary. I wanted it. Hell, yes, I wanted it.

We drove in silence until the steel gates of Panda City were behind us. I rolled down the window. The scent of rain had given way to the musky smells of a forest collecting itself for the cool monsoons to come. The crackle of the Hummer's tires played against the canorous tune of an unseen songbird. Tomorrow I would be on a plane for home. I could not wait to see my daughter and take Lauren in my arms. Sure, it had only been four days, but I missed them. I could not wait to sleep in my own bed again, with all due respect to the Presidential Suite at the Pearl Magnolia Hotel.

I was distracted from these very pleasing thoughts by a staccato ringing that grew louder as Kym drew her cell phone from the pocket of her blue jeans. She said "Hello" in Taiwanese, then in English, and then listened for twenty seconds with a grin tugging at the corners of her perfect mouth. She held the phone out to me and said, "For you, Mr. King. Karin Baxter. An urgent matter, she said, but I think she was being a little dramatic."

"Sounds like Karin to me." I took the phone and said, "Karin," realizing as I did so that this was not the female voice I really wanted to hear, not when I was on the verge of dropping my CEO veneer for a few minutes of well-deserved daydreaming. That said, Karin was acting on my behalf in the whole Panda negotiations and deserved an update. "How are you?"

"After the phone call I just hung up from, I would describe myself as exceptional," she gushed. "You did it, Michael. You flat out blew the Board away, and their reclusive Dr. Chu more than anyone. Congratulations."

"Thank you. But is this your opinion or one less biased?" I asked.

"That's the opinion of no less a source than Philip Chatzwirth," she replied.

"Well then. I guess congratulations are in order."

"Damn right, they are. They've got a 'sweetened' offer on the table, my friend, and all that's missing is your John Hancock. I told them they could have that the minute you stepped off the plane in Boulder."

Karin was fired up. And why not! For every 'sweetened' dollar Panda Pharmaceuticals anteed up, her slice of the pie grew a little bigger. I did not begrudge her that. Karin had worked her butt off getting into the big league of professional headhunting. Now she was reaping the rewards.

"You are on board, aren't you?" she said following an infinitesimally small pause. "Tell me you're on board, so I don't have to crawl through the phone and throttle you."

"I will tell you I can see the train pulling into the station," I said. "Close enough?"

"I'll take that as a 'yes.' A big, fat 'yes,'" she said. "Look for a contract on your desk next week. I'll call you tomorrow. In the meantime, don't let that plane crash no matter what happens."

She hung up. I handed the phone back to Kym and rolled my eyes. "Karin's been on the phone with Philip Chatzwirth. She gets a little excited."

"Join the crowd," Lyn said. "And why not. We're on the verge of something special here, Mr. King. A new era for Panda Pharmaceuticals."

"Very true," I said.

"How do you feel about being the CEO of the world's largest private pharmaceutical company, Mr. King?" Kym said. "I hope it's not too soon to ask such a bold question?"

There were two problems that caused me to hedge my bets. First of all, I had not signed a contract and no money had changed hands. One without the other hardly represented a done deal, and I was too much the skeptic to think otherwise. Second, I did not want to appear too anxious; it was bad luck. With that in mind, I said, "I'm honored that your father and Philip Chatzwirth would ask me to join the Panda family. It's a wonderful opportunity."

"Cut the crap, will you?" Tom said, disgusted. "Just say it feels great and get the hell on with it."

"It feels great. I admit it," I said. So much for hedging my bets! On the other hand, the smiles this admission brought to the faces of my two escorts made it all worthwhile.

The Hummer dropped into a narrow valley. A canopy of overhanging trees blackened the sky momentarily. A shadow fell across the backseat, and the temperature of the air plummeted as a cool breeze swept through the open window. It felt good after the humidity and heat of our afternoon vigil.

The Hummer caromed around a 45-degree turn, and the forest

deepened. My eyes glimpsed the fallen tree blocking the road an instant before Teng Juewen slammed on the brakes.

"Hold on!" I shouted.

The Hummer's brakes locked, but not before we rammed head-on into the tree's mammoth trunk. The force of the collision lifted the rear end of the truck into the air. It came down with a violent jolt.

"God damn! What the hell was that?" Lyn shouted.

"Is everyone all right?" I heard Teng Juewen call from the front seat. He glanced over his shoulder. "Mr. King?"

"We're fine, Teng," I said, but he was no longer looking at me. He was staring out the back window with eyes the size of silver dollars. "Teng? What is it?"

An instant later, another vehicle struck us from the rear. The impact drove us into the tree again and pinned us against the trunk. I twisted my head around. A band of soldiers was pouring from the back of a huge troop truck. They were dressed in combat gear. They were heavily armed and well coordinated in their movements. In a matter of seconds, we were completely surrounded. Two dozen automatic rifles were trained on the Hummer. I heard shouting, but it wasn't a language I understood.

"What's going on?" I said to Kym. "Who the hell are these guys? Army?"

"Not army," Kym shouted. "They probably belong to one of the drug lords."

"Oh, shit!" Tom was tugging at his seat belt. "This is bad. This is real bad."

"Stay calm," Lyn said in a level voice. "Just stay calm."

In the front seat, Teng and Ji Xiang had their weapons drawn, but it was too late. The butt-end of a rifle crashed against the driver side door shattering the glass.

One of the soldiers – a man with a full, black beard and a red beret – was shouting again. I saw my bodyguards lay their guns aside and was relieved. Another shout compelled Teng and Ji to open their doors. Two sets of hands dragged them from their seats and sent them sprawling to the ground. Before any of us could even think of coming to their defense, soldiers on either side of the Hummer drew pistols from their holsters, jammed the barrels against Teng and Ji's heads, and pulled the triggers. Blood flew in every direction, splattering the windows. The quaking bodies of my two bodyguards crumpled to the ground. Teng's legs jerked and then stopped.

"God almighty!" Tom uttered. "God all-fucking-mighty. We're all going to die."

"We're not going to die," Kym snapped. "This is no ambush."

"It's a kidnapping, Tom," Lyn said in a voice so chillingly calm that I was compelled to look at her face. The controlled fury was something I had only seen a few times in my life, and I was glad she was on my side. "Pull it together!"

"Let's just do what they say for now," I said. I was scared. Cold-blooded murder could do that to a man. I was also seething with anger as they pulled the four of us out of the Hummer.

A flurry of orders filled the air. The guttural, deep-throated voice belonged to the one man without a gun in his hands. He was a thick, squat man whose barrel-chest stretched the fibers of his army fatigues. He wore neither insignia nor markings of country or allegiance. I don't know what I was expecting. A tattooed tangle of vines grew along his arms and inside his shirt. He carried a two-foot-long machete, and the edge along the blade glistened from a recent sharpening. In his hands, the machete looked far more menacing than all the pistols and all the automatic rifles combined.

He used the point of the blade and a menacing grunt to guide Kym and Lyn toward an olive green panel truck. A similar gesture directed Tom and me toward the back of a canvas-covered troop truck.

"Forget that!" I shouted. "We go together!"

"Mr. King! No!" Kym called out, as I broke in her direction. I had not gone two strides before the nearest soldier gun-cocked me with the butt end of a rifle. The blow caught me just below the ear. A second blow – this from the handle of a Colt .45 pistol – struck me dead center of my solar plexus, but by then, the world was already turning black. I heard myself say, "Fuck," but I don't think the word ever even reached my lips, not that 25 Thai-speaking guerillas would have understood it anyway.

When I came to, I was lying facedown on the floor of one of the troop trucks. I was trussed head-to-foot like a pig. I opened my eyes and nearly passed out again from the pounding inside of my skull. When I tried filling my lungs with air, the pain spreading across my chest felt like a gun shot wound; I had never actually been shot, but it could not possibly have hurt any worse than this.

What made it worse was that I was being tossed around like a rag doll as the truck bounced along what had to be a dirt road, and my back and shoulders were bruised and beaten as a result. The stench that filled my nose – a nauseating mix of cigarette smoke, stale beer, and urine – was almost enough to make me forget my throbbing head. And then I coughed. My head and chest exploded with pain, and I felt my stomach turn over. I ordered myself not to be sick. Spare yourself that indignity at least, I thought.

My eyes opened long enough to see four soldiers seated toward the rear of the truck. They were tugging on cigarettes and laughing, probably at the plight of their captives. Guns that looked like Uzis or MAC-11s lay across their laps. They held bottles of beer in their hands. At their feet lay a dozen empties. Terrific.

"Michael," Tom whispered. "You okay, man?"

"Tom!" I twisted my head slowly around. Tom's legs, arms, and hands were bound with rope and secured with duct tape just like mine. "How long have I been out?"

"Two hours." The truck hit a deep rut and tossed us both in the air. "The last hour or so on a dirt road headed north, I think. Which means we're going deeper into the jungle."

"You okay?"

Tom grimaced. "I gotta pee real bad, man."

"Smells like someone beat you to it," I said between my teeth. "Where are the girls? Any idea?"

"In the truck ahead of us, I think. Shit, I don't know," Tom admitted. "Sorry about the beating you took, Michael. Shit, man, I had a gun in my ear before I could even think about moving."

"You're getting slow in your old age, my friend," I muttered.

Tom flashed a wicked smile. "Isn't this just great? Hell, buddy, I won't have to worry about going to jail after all. My wife can cash out my life insurance policy and spend the rest of her days sipping champagne with the Boston elite."

"Ain't life grand?" I deadpanned.

"I was going to say ironic. But then you've always had a bigger view of this fucking thing called life than I do." I could hear the fear in Tom's voice, but there was also a fighting edge there that reminded me of the guy I had known for half my life. "What the hell is going on here, Michael?"

"Don't know. But I'm sure as hell sorry I got you into this, Tom." I meant it.

"Horseshit. You didn't get me into this. I'd be splattered all over the pavement if it wasn't for you."

"Shhh!" Two heads turned our way. The laughing stopped. And then started again as one of the guards popped up and staggered our way. I prepared myself for the worst. The guard spat three unintelligible words at us and then smiled. Teeth the color of swamp water cracked open. His eyes moved independently of one another and made me think he was the kind of man who found pleasure in seeing pain inflicted but hesitated to inflict it himself. So when he held out the canvas water bag to me, I mistook his insincerity. I was too delirious and too thirsty to refuse, but the moment the liquid inside the bag touched my lips, I spit it back out and gagged until my empty stomach ached.

"Urine! You motherfucker!" I gagged again.

"Oh, Jesus!" Tom hissed.

Laughter rolled through the truck. My cross-eyed friend was suddenly a big hit with his buddies. He punctuated this moment of notoriety by driving the toe of his boot into Tom's ribcage. Tom held a grimace as tightly as he could between his clenched teeth, but the color drained from his face. His eyes watered.

When Tom's eyes closed, the soldier's smile disappeared. He drew an antiquated 9mm Luger from the holster on his belt. Something about the sheer lack of emotion in his face made me wonder if we weren't in for the same ignominious fate Teng and Ji Xiang had suffered. It made sense to me even as I tightened every muscle in my body. If this was a straight kidnapping as Lyn had suggested, then it was the daughters of Dr. Chu Zhong Liu who were of value here. These guerillas could not possibly know who I was, not unless word of my presence in Bangkok had somehow filtered down through the grapevine at the Pearl Magnolia or by way of Dr. Chu's servants or someone at the Panda City facilities. News like that spread even if a man of Chu's influence tried to prevent it.

The soldier waved the Luger in the air and listened to the laughter of his comrades. He drew back the hammer, put a foot on Tom's chest, and laid the gun against his temple.

"Michael." His voice quivered.

"Show him nothing, Tom. He doesn't have the guts," I said. "I can see it in his face. Show him nothing."

The man's uncertain gaze traveled from Tom to me. I looked back at him with the coldest eyes I could muster. It may have been that exchange that turned the tide, but it was probably the silence more than anything. Dead silence where seconds before there had been laughter. The man's resolve wavered. So did the gun in his hand.

One of his comrades called to him. Two quick, incisive words that made the soldier blink. And just like that, it was over. There would be no execution. Not yet anyway.

The guard holstered his Luger, spat on the bed of the truck next to my feet, and stomped back to his friends. They were already engaged in a new conversation, the fun over.

"I can't stop shaking," Tom confessed to me.

"Me either," I said, hoping that would help.

"Good. I'll stop when you stop." Tom grimaced, and then managed a grunt. "We're not walking away from this one, Pearl Man. Not without some serious luck. And I'm not feeling real lucky these days."

I closed my eyes and concentrated on taking one deep breath after another. An image of the twins filled my head, and I prayed their fate was no worse than ours. I tried not to imagine what 8 or 10 guys with a half a dozen beers under their belts might do with two women who looked like them. All I knew was that Lyn would die before she would let any harm come to her sister. And what Kym was capable of, I could only guess.

Tom and I lapsed into silence. Save your strength, I told myself. Think.

We crashed over broken road for another half hour if the clock in my head was anywhere near accurate. The first drop of rain struck the truck's canvas top sixty seconds later. Not thirty seconds after that, it sounded as if the god of rain had turned the full extent of his powers on our one truck. The shock of sound reminded me of a subway entering the Michigan Avenue station in Chicago. Our guards didn't raise an eyebrow – they had probably been through a thousand such storms – nor did the truck slow. The downpour ended as abruptly as it had begun, perfuming the air outside but doing little to cut through the stench trapped inside these canvas walls.

I spent the next half hour working through a dozen different scenarios that might explain what was happening to us. Kidnapping and ransom, sure. That made more sense than the Malayan slave trade, didn't it? And it made more sense than political blackmail. Well, maybe. I made the assumption that in the end it all came down to drugs. Wasn't that, after all, what life in this jungle world was all about?

I was bruised from head to foot by the time the convoy came to a halt. The back of the truck fell open. Tom and I were dragged from the truck and sent sprawling in the mud like unwanted sacks of potatoes. The first thing I noticed was an overwhelming chemical smell that permeated the air, but I couldn't put my finger on it. We lay there in the mud until the man with the machete came around and cut the rope bindings from our feet. He shouted something and gestured with the blade. I took him to mean, 'Stand up,' and that was what we did. I looked around.

We had been transported to a guerilla camp that had quite literally been carved from the heart of the jungle. Even at a glance, I was surprised by the size. There were six or seven bamboo shelters the rectangular shape of army barracks surrounding a huge central compound. Electric light formed a pale halo above the camp from a series of incandescent bulbs glowing atop strategically placed lampposts. Despite my confusion, I caught the hum of a generator.

Around the compound, oil fires swelled from the bellies of 50-gallon drums, and smoke spiraled in black plumes toward the night sky. The camp was a beehive of activity and seemingly home to at least 100 men, most of whom dressed in camouflage pants and black tank tops. The women I saw, most with their hands filled and moving nervously from one barrack to another, looked liked slaves, not comrades. Pigs, cows, chickens, and dogs scurried around the compound as if their days were numbered. A fleet of broken down troop trucks, army jeeps, and rusted out pickups was parked at the edge of the camp, and I saw men working under the hoods of a half dozen of these.

Next to them, I saw a sprawling tent-like structure built upon a frame of huge logs. The tent was clearly vented at the top and sides, and the chemical smell I had noticed rose from these vents. The last building enclosing the perimeter had a sophistication to it that was lost on the barracks and that was, apparently, unnecessary to the tent structure. It too was constructed from bamboo, but the door at the entrance was wood, the windows enclosing it were plastic, and the raised porch stretching across the front was furnished with four chairs and two side tables. Armed guards were posted at the door, further evidence of its importance. More than likely, I thought, the camp's headquarters.

Our arrival was greeted with considerable interest, but it was the Hummer they had captured that seemed to cause the greater stir until

Kym and Lyn were dragged from their escort vehicle. Catcalls and whistles rose on the air, and the hungry looks I saw on some of the soldiers' faces made me afraid for the twins.

As Tom and I were being shoved in the direction of a stone hovel, I caught Lyn's eye. She gave me the smallest of nods, and I tipped my head in return. I studied them. Their hands were tied with rope ligatures, and their arms were bound to their sides with the same gray tape that had been used on Tom and me. But their eyes and their postures, I told myself, were the key. Kym's eyes were probing the camp inch by inch, memorizing details, measuring distances, calculating the strength of the fortifications. Lyn's eyes seemed to be taking in the guerillas themselves, estimating their firepower, their commitment, even their moxie. Here I was, the erstwhile CEO, measuring the mettle of his now-unlikely employees. By the looks of them, the twins were not thinking about the mess they were in; they were making plans for getting out of the mess. Well, that made three of us. All I knew was that I couldn't let them die here. I may have been their responsibility before our capture, but they were mine now.

I felt a gun barrel jabbing me from behind, and I picked up my pace. The stone hut was the size of a windowless double car garage with a domed roof. A crudely designed grid of iron bars served as the door, and the rust on the bars told me we were probably not its first inhabitants. The door opened onto a black hole. Two hands shoved me inside, and Tom followed. The hut's ceiling was stone as well, but an iron grate looked out from the peek of the dome and shed a square of pale light on the hut floor.

The man with the machete followed us inside. He spoke. When we didn't answer, he held up his blade. There were two possibilities, I decided. One, he had chosen this black hole to slit our throats. Two, he was offering to cut our ligatures. I said a silent prayer for the latter and held out my hands. The machete split the rope like a fork through a noodle. Tom got the picture and allowed the man to cut his ropes, as well. He automatically said, "Thank you."

The man turned on his heel and stomped out. The door slammed shut. A deadbolt slid into place.

"Fuck!" Tom threw himself on the ground. "I actually told the bastard 'thank you.' What an idiot."

"Don't worry about it. He's probably the only guy here who is going to do us any favors tonight," I said. I didn't sit. I paced. I stopped for a moment beneath the ceiling grate and stared out at the night sky. I was calm enough to appreciate the swatch of stars shining down on me, and I took that as a good sign. For a brief, painful moment, an image of Lauren and Hanna, broken wrist and all, flashed through my head. I pushed it aside as quickly as it had come. Don't do that to yourself, I thought. Not now.

"We're dead. You know that, don't you?" Tom said. "The girls were the targets. Not us."

"Don't be so sure. We may have more value than you think. You're an executive with an American company well known throughout Southeast Asia for its plundering and pillaging. I'm an executive with an American drug company with a two-billion-dollar net worth and a huge cash surplus."

"And you think these thugs know that?"

"These thugs are running a pretty sophisticated operation here."

"Electric lights and a couple of vehicles with gas-powered engines is not a sign of sophistication, my friend."

"No, but that ambush was," I said. "Right down to the blind spot in the road."

"Come on, Michael," Tom protested. "Ransom or no ransom, we're dead meat, my good friend. We've got exactly one chance. And that's figuring out how to get our sorry asses out of here."

"Then let's get figuring," I said.

～

19

THE CAMP

"Fear and survival.
If you think you were born with anything else, think again."

Istood with my legs spread and my hands on the bars. I stared out at the camp.

I pressed my face against the bars and turned my head as far to the right as I could, but I could not quite glimpse the hut in which Kym and Lyn were being held. What I could see were two armed guards pacing in the shadows, and I could only imagine that they were stationed in front of their hut. I wondered what was going through their minds? I wondered if they had ever imagined such a thing as this happening to them? They may have been the strongest two women I had ever met, but no one was immune to fear, and I was not happy thinking about how frightened they might be.

Tom had always been the kind of guy who talked when he was strung out or hyped up, and he talked now, a voice in the dark filling the hut. I didn't discourage him. In fact, the sound of his voice was comforting.

"I know the jungle pretty well, Michael," he said. "At least I know the jungles of the peninsula. I've done three excursions along the Malaysian border over the last three years. Probably eight or ten weeks total. Open camping. Twenty-five pound packs. Walking or boating all the way. How different can this jungle be?"

I did not offer an answer. Tom's tone implied a distinct desire to hold up both ends of the conversation, and I wasn't going to deny him the pleasure. He went on about what it would take to cover the terrain from here back to civilization, on foot and with no supplies. Then he veered off into a discussion about fate and bad karma. When he said, "I suppose you reap what you sow," I stopped listening.

Instead, I took up my watch with renewed interest. The guerilla camp may have been a cesspool, but it was an active cesspool. I revised my estimate of their manpower to 200 men, most armed with the kind of weapons I was used to seeing on CNN's up close and personal reporting in Iraq, and most dressed in the regale of paramilitary soldiers. Motivation aside, they looked the part of a regular army.

Four vehicles – two canvas-covered troop trucks, a Humvee, and a Land Rover – came and went within the next half hour. The trucks may have been designed for the transportation of soldiers, but the long, narrow crates that came out of them could have contained anything from bananas to AK-47s.

"These are some busy folks," I whispered.

Tom didn't hear me because he was talking about the lack of drinking water in the Thai jungle. He wasn't trusting of the river water, he said, and two guys and two girls fleeing on foot were not going to have time to stop and collect rain water. It wasn't long after that, an army jeep pulled into camp with an escort of two rocket launchers, a 50-caliber machine gun, and a truck with guards positioned on the roof and hanging off the back. Their convoy included a smaller transport that looked almost like an armored car. Their arrival caused nearly as big a stir as ours had.

The bearded man in the passenger side of the jeep carried a leather satchel over his shoulder. He bounded up the stairs to camp headquarters. When he disappeared inside, I watched the armored car pull up beside the tent-like structure with the vented roof and walls, the source of the potent chemical odor that filled the air. Four soldiers piled out and formed a line from the rear of the truck to the entrance of the building. The last man in line pushed aside a stiff curtain exposing the interior. From where I stood,

I could see two huge electric fans pushing the air out the vents. At the heart of the room, four wood fires roared. It appeared as if oil drums filled with water were simmering above the flames. A man dressed from head to foot in white, with thick glasses framing a bald head, moved from one drum to the next with a long probe of some kind.

It wasn't until I saw the soldiers unloading canvas satchels exactly like the one the field worker back at Panda City had used to store the raw opium he had harvested that I knew what I was looking at: a jungle refinery.

"They're cooking heroin," I said in a low voice.

Tom jumped up. "What? They're what?"

"Cooking heroin."

"So that's what that god awful smell is."

Tom and I stood side by side and watched two-dozen bags pass from soldier to soldier into the refinery. "Any guesses where they're getting their opium?" I said in a tone dripping with irony.

"You had a pretty good idea just how vulnerable those poppy fields back at Nakhon might be to smuggling, didn't you?" Tom let out a sigh. "And damned if you weren't right on the fucking money."

"These are some seriously bad dudes, Tom. Seriously bad dudes." I stood there and shook my head as if I hadn't known it before.

"Drug running. Kidnapping. Murder. Fuck. Who in the hell knows what else they're into?" Tom replied.

We did not have to wait long for an answer, but Tom didn't stand around passing the time until we did. He began a tour of our hut, using his hands to study the walls inch-by-inch, hoping to find some flaw in the construction. Eventually, he turned his attention to the ceiling. He said, "Give me a boost, Michael. I want to check out these bars. You never know."

The domed roof was 11 or 12 feet at its highest point. The grate was a three-foot by three-foot square, and the iron bars were heavily rusted. I anchored my feet directly below the opening and used my hands to form a stirrup for Tom's foot. He put his hands on my shoulders and pushed off as I lifted him skyward. He caught hold of the iron bars and pulled. I stepped beneath him and guided his feet onto my shoulders. Tom weighed an easy 200 pounds and most of it was muscle despite his age. "Christ, dude. Maybe this little jungle excursion will give you a chance to drop a few pounds," I sneered.

"Quit your whining."

I could see him testing the strength of the grate one bar after another. I saw one move in his hand and heard him say, "Hey."

"What did you find?"

"We might be onto something," Tom said. He tugged at the bar. It gave another quarter of an inch.

Not five minutes later, the roar of several vehicles rumbling into the camp caught our attention, and I said, "Let's see what's happening. Give my shoulders a rest."

Tom dropped to the ground. We scrambled back to the doorway. The new arrivals were five in number. Three were troop trucks. Their escorts were army jeeps equipped with 50-caliber turret guns. Serious armament.

Twenty men converged on the troop trucks and threw back the flaps. The occupants inside, however, were not military. They were young girls. All Asian by the look on their terrified, tear-stained faces as they were herded out of the trucks and into one of the bamboo barracks.

"Jesus H. Christ! What in the hell?" Tom hissed. "Look at this. They can't be more than 13 or 14-years-old."

"You were wondering what was next," I said. "How does child prostitution sound to you? Sex slaves? Child pornography? You name it, these bastards are selling it."

"They're my daughter's age, Michael. They're Jessica's age, for God's sake." Tom had put on a good face up to this point, but the sight of these kids being forced into a world of terror and violence was enough to strike any man down a notch. "No one deserves to be that scared or that alone."

"No. No, they don't," I whispered, anger swelling deep in my chest. I was thinking about the men we were up against. I had wrongly assumed when we were first captured that they were a disorganized rabble dabbling in drugs and terror. My opinion had changed. Rabble they may have been. Terrorists, thugs, animals. But they were neither disorganized nor lacking in resources. And if the kidnapping of Dr. Chu Zhong Liu's daughters was any indication, they were not lacking in balls either.

We went back to work on the ceiling grate, taking turns on each other's shoulders, and finding the rock around the bars brittle enough to give us hope. After nearly two hours, one bar had broken free and a second was loose.

It had to be close to midnight when I heard the crescendo of footsteps hurrying across the compound, and by the sounds of it, they were coming our way. "We've got visitors," I said, jumping down from Tom's shoulders. "Shit. What now?"

I was brushing a layer of dust off my shirtfront when the bolt on the door was thrown. Two guards burst in. One held a flashlight. He moved the beam from Tom's face to mine. I saw a hint of recognition register in his eyes. "You!" he snapped. He grabbed my arm. "You come!"

"Hold the hell on," Tom protested.

Before the words were out of Tom's mouth, the second guard speared him in the chest with the barrel end of a cocked pistol and snarled. His English-speaking partner said, "Keep your mouth shut."

"What about food and water?" Tom said.

He glanced at his fellow guard. "If he speaks again, shoot him."

"It's okay, Tom. I'll be all right," I said.

I was out in the compound an instant later, a machine gun probing my back. I heard the clatter of the bolt being thrown on our cell door. I glanced over my shoulder. Tom was leaning helplessly against the bars. The air was thick with humidity. I heard the shrill call of cicadas in the distance.

"Your English is good," I said, glancing back at the English-speaking guard and hoping to get him talking. "Where are we going?"

He said nothing. His partner kept a safe distance, his weapon held ready in two hands and his eyes following my every step. It showed discipline. Discipline showed a line of command and organization. I may not have viewed this as favorable as far as our escape plans, but an organized team was often more open to discussion and negotiation than a splintered group with questionable leadership.

I was reaching with this rather dubious line of reasoning. I knew that. But this wasn't about logical and realistic expectations. I had to keep my mind active. This was about discovering a crack in the armor of our captors' defenses. This was about identifying even the smallest weakness and finding an opportunity to exploit it. But maybe even more than anything, it was about staving off panic. If I gave into panic, I might as well throw up the white flag. I was not ready to do that. I doubted I ever would be.

A subdued air had laid its hand on the camp by this hour – the refinery had shut down for the night, and there were few faces to be seen in the compound – but it could not silence the cries and whimpering that filtered out from the barrack holding the young girls who had been delivered earlier. The sounds caused a physical ache deep inside my chest. When my eyes drifted in that direction, the barrel of the machine gun burrowed further into my back. "Eyes forward," my escort ordered. He used the point of the gun to indicate the camp's headquarters. "There. Keep moving."

When we reached the far side of the compound, I climbed the steps to the raised porch fronting the building. Two armed guards blocked a thick wooden door. They followed procedure, exchanging words with my escort before opening the door. I was led inside. Two other guards protected the entryway. We walked through a room furnished with two unoccupied desks, a refrigerator with a poster of Steven Seagal taped to the door, and a broken down couch with an old newspaper spread across it. Two lazy window fans pushed air around the room. It didn't seem to be helping. The air inside was nearly as heavy and damp as it was outside, and my escorts' clothes were as soaked through with sweat as mine were.

We turned down a narrow hall. A wool blanket had been nailed across the threshold at the entrance to the room at the far end. One of the guards pushed the blanket aside. A hand in my back propelled me inside. A metal table and one chair had been arranged beneath a dim, flickering light.

"Sit," my escort ordered, and two pairs of hands helped me into the chair. "Hands flat on the table."

I did as I was told. The guards stationed themselves around the room. In my head, I paced off the distance from my chair to the nearest window. I measured the height of the sill from the floor. I watched the blades of the window fan as they turned and heard the labored squeaking of its motor. Three seconds, I estimated, to get out of my chair and kick the fan aside. Another two seconds to throw myself through the window, roll to my feet, and scale the porch railing. Ten seconds to cross the open space between the building and the jungle. Odds of making it to the jungle alive: 50-1. It was not the odds that dissuaded me. It was the fact that Kym and Lyn would probably pay the price for my actions.

By the time I got this far in my thinking, the curtain had been swept aside again. A diminutive, neatly groomed soldier in an impeccably pressed uniform swept into the room. I noticed the insignia of a Brigadier General clipped to his lapel and several medals I couldn't identify pinned to his chest. The man with the machete followed him in. The guards snapped to attention. Two of the four were dismissed.

"Welcome. You are Mr. Michael King. I am General SiSa Ket Paton, the leader of this small jungle nation," the newcomer said. His tone was not unfriendly, only untrustworthy. He circled the table taking in my bruised condition. I could tell from his clipped enunciation that English was a language he had long spoken, but not with any real pleasure. He stopped at the head of the table, patiently pulled off one leather glove after the other, and tossed them unceremoniously aside. Then he drummed the tabletop with a hint of contemplation. "Bring our guest some water. He looks thirsty. Are you thirsty, Mr. King?"

One of the guards had already stepped out to the room. I pictured him walking to the refrigerator. "I am," I said, controlling any impulse to say more. "Thanks."

"You're welcome," General SiSa Ket Paton replied, his tone implying something other than generosity.

The guard returned. He placed a metal cup on the table next to my hands. The water bottle, however, he handed to his superior. The General splashed a half-inch of water into the cup. Very generous. He raised an eyebrow as if negotiations had been opened. The corners of his mouth turned up. "Drink. Enjoy."

I filled my mouth with half the water, worked it in and around my gums, and swallowed slowly. I resisted drinking the rest in spite of my thirst, set the cup down, and nodded. I said, "Thank you," despite the fact that every fiber of my being wanted to shout something quite different. I waited.

Eventually, General Paton said, "You are the head of an American drug company of some note. The name eludes me." This was a lie, of course, but one designed to open the lines of communication between us. The first words were the most important ones in an interrogation, and he knew this.

I wanted to say, "If your information is that shoddy, maybe you should look for another line of work." I didn't. I said, "Peak Pharmaceuticals. We're based in Colorado and Arizona."

"Peak. Yes. Peak Pharmaceuticals. 500 million dollars in sales last year. Stock price as of yesterday $51.75, down a dollar. PE ratio of 8. Undervalued."

"On that we agree," I said.

"Yearly salary, $750,000 without serious stock considerations." General Paton grimaced. "Highly underpaid."

Dangerous ground, Michael, I heard a warning voice inside my head say as the General looked down on me, eyes expectant. Dangerous ground. I could think of several answers of varying degrees of wit and sarcasm, even several peppered with logic and business acumen. In the end, I reached for my cup and finished the water, using a nod to tell Paton how much more important fresh water was given my plight than my paltry financial compensation. I held onto the cup as the General filled it once again. He said, "Now you are in line to become the powerful, very powerful head of Panda Pharmaceuticals, a company with immense influence here in Southeast Asia. No?"

"Yes," I replied. Time to open a dialogue. "You are well informed, General Paton. I congratulate you."

"At a five-fold increase in salary, your wife Lauren must be thrilled at the prospect." Paton smiled. The smile said, 'You would be surprised at the pure tonnage of my knowledge.' For good measure, he then added, "Is she?"

Fuck, I thought. This is getting uglier by the minute. I glanced at the man with the machete. The blade dangled at his side. I said, "We're considering their offer."

"And the house in Virginia. I would imagine that you and Lauren are considering that, too," the General said. He leaned against the table. His eyes narrowed. "I think we can help each other, Mr. King."

"How's that, General Paton?"

"Our business interests are not really all that different," he said. "The thing is, like you, we fill a need, to be sure. But we also create new markets where we can."

"Let me see. Murder? Kidnapping? Gun running? Maybe my definition of similar enterprises just differs from yours, General. That must be the problem," I said. "Child prostitution? Sex slaves?"

"Child prostitution? Is that what you think we do? The slave trade? You're thinking about the delivery we took tonight." The General waved a finger at me and clicked his tongue. "We are thinking just slightly bigger than that, I must confess. And you're going to help us, Mr. Michael King. Actually, you already did when you delivered Dr. Chu Zhong Liu's daughters into our hands this afternoon. We mean them no harm. As soon as our demands are met, they will be released. As will you and your unfortunate friend."

"Oh. Extortion. I get it. Sorry I sold you short, General." My tongue was getting away from me, and I knew it.

"Extortion is a corporate term, Michael. You're familiar with it."

"What are your demands, General Paton?"

"Would you like more water, Michael?"

"I would like to go home, General."

He poured, this time filling the cup. "Have more water, Michael. It is a long drive back to Bangkok."

"No, thank you," I said evenly.

From the pocket of his perfectly pressed trousers, General SiSa Ket Paton produced a leather-bound notepad and a gold-plated ballpoint pen. He removed the cap on the pen but did not relinquish it. "Dr. Chu's lovely daughters will be freed once 50 million in American dollars have been deposited in an offshore account that has already been made known to him."

"I see."

"Your freedom and that of your American friend can be obtained in a matter of moments, however."

There was an ominous sound to this statement. I could feel a fresh trail of sweat rolling down my back. But this was different from the sweat of humidity or exertion. This was cold, cold enough to send a shiver along my spine. "How?"

"Quite simple." General Paton opened the notepad to a blank page. He laid it beside my cup. He held out the pen until I relieved him of it. "The synthesized DNA code for the fugu fish and lionfish analgesic. Please write down the formula in full, with all necessary footnotes. Once the model has been confirmed – and I have people standing by who are more than capable of that – you will be escorted back to the Pearl Magnolia Hotel in Bangkok. With luck, you will still make your plane for the United States."

I laid the pen down. I closed the notepad and pushed it across the table. I said, "You kidnapped the wrong man, General Paton. I can give you Einstein's formula for general relativity, though I don't have a clue what it means; something about the velocity of light in a vacuum, I think. I can recite a half dozen of Shakespeare's most romantic sonnets or give you the exact ingredients to the perfect gin martini. But I could no more tell you the DNA synthetic code of the fugu fish or the lionfish than I could the geological history of Mars. I'm a Chief Executive Officer, General Paton. A manager of people and ideas. I'm not a research scientist or a geneticist. Sorry about that."

"You are a liar, Mr. King." I could see the slightest change in General Paton's color. I could see an eye tic that had not been there moments before. "You value an unproven drug formula over your life. Is that it?"

"No, General. That is not it. I assure you."

"You value the secrets of a company who has yet to pay you a single dime over the life of your friend of twenty years?" He pressed hard against the table, and his voice rose in pitch and tenor.

"I don't have the knowledge you're seeking, General. That is the truth. I am not a scientist." I regretted saying that the moment it left my mouth, certain that Kym would be sitting in this chair shortly. I tried a different tact. "The information you're seeking is still in the developmental stage. That much I know."

By this time, two other guards had crowded into the room, alerted, I imagined, to the growing tension in our conversation. I said, "And what would you do with the formula if you did have it? It's worthless, General. Worthless at this stage."

"It's only worthless at this stage, Mr. King, because it has not been tested on anything other than rats," General Paton said confidently. "What would your company pay to have accelerated human testing? Complete and confidential human testing?"

I stared at him. Before I could work through the implications of what the leader of this 'small jungle nation' had just suggested, he was pushing the leather-bound notepad across the table at me again. "The formula, Mr. King. That, or face the consequences of your refusal. I will give you one last chance."

I pushed the pad away. I set the pen beside it. "I cannot write what I don't know. Sorry."

General Paton mouthed a single Thai word that propelled his guards into action. In less than a second, I was firmly in their grasp. One pair of hands took my right arm and bent it painfully behind my back. A second pair secured me in a well-practiced headlock, forcing my head and face down onto the table. A third took a fistful of my hair. A fourth pinned my left arm and hand to the tabletop. The man with the machete hovered over me. I closed my eyes and wasn't surprised that an image of Lauren and Hanna filled my head. I felt an emotion I couldn't afford at the moment welling up inside me and forced my eyes open.

The General paced. He did not look at me when he said, "Each night, I will again ask you to share the formula that you so foolishly protect. Each time you refuse, I will take a finger. If you continue to refuse, I will take your toes."

He blurted a second order, a Thai word I would hear in my dreams if ever I had another dream. Som!

Out of the corner of my eye, I could see the man with the machete step into the light. An instant later, I saw the steel blade moving in an arc through the air and flashing toward the tabletop. I saw the blade sever the little finger on my left hand, saw a fountain of red spurt from the open wound, and saw the finger carom across the table. I roared with pain. My eyes rolled to the back of my head, and I blacked out.

I was only vaguely aware of being dragged back across the compound. A part of me could feel the burning pain traveling through my left arm, but another part of me was responding to the trauma by shutting down. I had to fight it. I couldn't afford to go into shock. I didn't hear the bolt being thrown on the door of our stone cell, but I felt the jolt when I landed on my back on the rock-hard dirt floor.

I heard Tom say, "Jesus H. Christ, Michael!" Then I heard him stumble to the far side of the cell, fall on his knees, and throw up what was left of the meal we had eaten almost 12 hours before. I was shaking and couldn't stop myself. Suddenly, Tom was beside me. He stripped off his shirts. He used his polo shirt as a blanket to cover my chest and shoulders. He ripped his t-shirt into long, narrow strips.

"Oh, man. I'm so sorry," he kept saying, as he wrapped one strip after another around the hole where my finger had once been, causing me to cry out with pain from the pressure he was exerting. "We've got to get this bleeding under control, Michael. Shit, man. I'm so damn. Sorry."

I opened my mouth to speak. The words came out ragged and broken. "We're dead if we don't get out of here, Tom. We're dead."

20

JUNGLE RUN

"Our deepest fear is that we are powerful beyond measure."

"**F**orget it. You're in shock," Tom said, as I struggled to come to my feet.

"I'm fine." I wasn't fine, but I was focusing better than a man who had just seen his finger lopped off by a machete-wielding maniac should have been. I said, "Listen, Tom. The roof grate is our only hope. I can't help with the bars, not with this bandage, but I can still hold you on my shoulders." I paused a moment and thought about that. "I hope anyway."

Tom helped me to my feet. I steadied myself beneath the bars criss-crossing the ceiling. I tried lifting Tom using my right hand only, but I could not get enough leverage. He tried climbing up my back. It didn't work.

"I can't get enough lift," Tom said. "Goddamn it!"

"Let's try it one more time from the front. I need both hands."

This time, I made a stirrup using both hands. When Tom saw me cup my bandaged hand beneath my good hand, he shook his head. He said, "If you pass out from the pain, we're both fucked, you realize."

He was smiling. I tried smiling in return, but it came out a grimace. I did manage a meager-sounding joke, however. "The power of positive thinking. Is that what that is?"

"Just don't drop me," Tom replied. He gave me a pat on the shoulder.

The pain when he stepped into the sling formed by my hands was excruciating. I figured we were only going to get one chance at this, so I heaved with all my strength. He pushed off. I saw stars and then a scrim of black.

"You all right?" Tom called.

I think I nodded, but I couldn't be sure. Then I saw that Tom was dangling from the ceiling grate. "Shit. Hang on," I said and moved my feet until I was beneath him. He settled his feet on my shoulders. I staggered once, then found a reservoir of strength that had its source, I supposed, in a fear of dying. Maybe not a fear of dying exactly. More like this emancipating desire to live. I wanted that more than anything, I realized. Just to be alive when the sun came up. Just to know that the possibility existed of seeing my wife and daughter again. I drew a deep breath, gritted my teeth, and straightened my shoulders.

"Forget about me," I said to Tom, hoping it didn't sound too much like false bravado. "Get that thing open."

"How's this for a start?" A three-foot-length of corroded iron dangled from Tom's hand. "Watch your toes."

He dropped the bar, and it hit the dirt floor with a hollow thud. "Good work," I said as rivers of sweat rolled into my eyes and down my cheeks. I lost track of time. I heard the twisting and grinding of iron against stone and saw flecks of ground-up sandstone drifting down in the starlight like fairy dust.

"We're close," Tom said at some point. "We're damn close, buddy. How are you holding up down there?"

"Good. My legs are like Jello and my shoulders are numb, but other than that…" I didn't have the strength left to deliver the punch line nor the creative energy to come up with one in any case.

"Try thinking of something else," Tom suggested between grunts. "You know, like your last sexual encounter."

"Thanks for the advice."

"Mr. King!" It was a low whisper and didn't immediately register. I was not certain it registered with Tom, not until Kym's face suddenly appeared on the other side of the grate and scared the hell out of him.

"Oh, shit!" His left foot slipped off my shoulder, and he nearly lost his grip. He was on the verge of falling, and it took all my strength to hold my ground. A second later, he righted himself and looked up into Kym's magnificent green eyes. After a moment, he managed to say, "You got out. How?"

"Same way you are," she whispered. "How's Mr. King?"

"Not good."

"I'm fine," I grunted. I glanced up, but all I could see was the outline of her face. "Are you two all right? Where's Lyn?"

"They lopped off his finger," Tom said before Kym could answer. "We have to get him out of here."

I could hear them both working furiously to loosen the second bar. I honestly didn't know how much longer my legs were going to hold out. "Where's Lyn?" I asked again. I was gritting my teeth so tightly that I could hardly hear the question myself, but I heard Tom pass it on to Kym.

"Looking for water and guns. We'll need both." Kym's voice filtered down to me.

"What about the guards?" It was a silly question. Tom must have thought so too, because he didn't repeat it. If Kym was on the roof of our hut, and Lyn was looking for water and guns, the soldiers guarding their hut were dead. I was congratulating myself on the strength of my logic when the second bar broke free.

When the bar hit the hut floor, Tom jumped down. "Your turn, my friend," he said to me.

I glanced up and saw the slender gap that had been created in the grate. I saw Kym gazing down at me, and there was a surprising amount of hope in her eyes. "Grab the bar," she whispered. "I'll pull you up."

Tom took my right foot in his hands. I put my good hand on his shoulder. "On three," he said. "One, two, three."

I jumped, and Tom lifted. My outstretched hand took hold of the one remaining bar. Kym was waiting for me. She reached inside the cell and wrapped her arms around my shoulders. Tom pushed – I could feel his strength – and I was suddenly halfway out. I scrambled onto the roof. Kym was momentarily ecstatic, as if my safety far outweighed her own. She hugged me briefly, and then turned her attention to my hand. "I'll take care of this," she said without hesitation. "But let's get your friend out first."

This was a task easier said than done. I flattened myself on the roof and lowered my upper body back through the grate, arms first. I reached back into the hut with my good hand. Kym anchored her hands to my waist.

"Jump," I said, and Tom did. He latched onto me. I wrapped my arm around his shoulders and held on. I called out to Kym. "Go! Go! Go!"

Kym tugged on my waist while Tom scrambled up my back, eventually latching onto the bar.

Now it was just a matter of pulling him out, and the three of us were soaked in sweat by the time the job was done. Once Tom was out, we scrambled down to the backside of the hut. I could hardly move. The shock of my encounter with General Paton, the trauma of my amputated finger, and the energy I had expended over the last hours came together like a physical and emotional train wreck. Kym must have seen it. She did two things. Unlike Tom, she didn't apologize for the beatings or the change in our fortunes. She loosened her belt, unbuttoned her pants, and reached inside her underwear. Hidden there were the experimental drugs from the fugu and lionfish analgesic and the lime green powder from the Malayan Krait snake. She took two pink pills from the first bag and held them out. "You have to trust me," she said. "You trust me, don't you, Mr. King?"

"I trust you, Kym," I said simply.

She fed the pills one after another into my mouth, and I swallowed them. I remembered our discussion back in the lab about the rapid release profile. "Pain relief in five minutes guaranteed," Lyn had said. I could only hope.

Then Kym began unraveling Tom's makeshift field dressing. "What are you doing?" he said.

Kym ignored him. When she saw the bloody mess where two hours ago my little finger had been, she let out a low sigh and said, "Don't move."

She cracked the seal on the tiny bag containing the blood clotting agent extracted from the poison glands of one of the world's most poisonous snakes and very carefully removed an amount no bigger than a fingernail. She used the tail of her shirt to dab away the blood from the stump and then sprinkled it with the lime green powder. The powder changed hue almost immediately, shifting from green to pink and then to white. I heard a faint sizzling sound and saw air bubbles. By the time the bubbles had melted away, the bleeding had stopped. Seconds later, coagulation was complete.

"Holy shit!" Tom could hardly believe his eyes. "What is that stuff?"

Again, Kym acted as if she hadn't heard him. "The nerves have been traumatized," she said to me. "That's the pain you're feeling. The pills will help."

I reached out and touched her face. I was not sure how to put into words what I was feeling. It wasn't gratitude, though I was thankful. It wasn't wonder, even though I was as astounded as Tom was. It was kinship. When all was said and done, I settled for, "I'm glad you're safe. I missed you."

Her smile was genuine. So was her resolve. "We have to go."

I made a fist with my left hand. "Let's find your sister."

"Not necessary," Tom hissed. "She found us."

I heard a rustling noise coming from the edge of the jungle thirty yards away. A figure appeared in the shadows between two rubber trees. I could see the urgent wave of her hand, but only the outline of her lean, muscular body.

When the perimeter guards were out of sight and the compound was quiet, we crossed the open ground between the hut and trees in single file,

Kym, then Tom, then me. My legs were stronger than I expected. I wanted to attribute it to good conditioning instead of the fugu fish and lionfish pills, but it was probably a combination of both.

Lyn and her sister embraced for a split second before Kym asked, "What did you find?"

"Not as much as I hoped for, but as much as we can carry given where we're going." Lyn handed Tom a US-made MAC-11 machine gun, a Colt 45 pistol, and a water skin. Tom stared at the MAC-11. "American. Fucking American."

"Who do you think equips the Thai Army, Tom? Try the US or China. Take your choice. I prefer to shop American." Lyn gave us both a ten second operational lesson on the machine gun. "Slap in the magazine, hit the safety, and then hold on for dear life. Keep your bursts short. Otherwise, you're just wasting bullets, and we don't have that many to waste."

Lyn slapped a second machine gun, a pistol, and an ammunition belt into her sister's hands. The rocket launcher she gave to me was a handheld model with a minimum pack of three 75mm bombs. "Pull the pin, aim, shoot. Simple."

She stopped cold when she saw the missing finger on my left hand. She raised her head and our eyes met. I was not exactly sure what I saw in hers. Not sympathy, for certain, and I was glad about that. Maybe she was assessing my battle-worthiness; what I could handle. I suppose I was assessing her, as well. A moment later, she threw a second rocket launcher over her shoulder. Around her waist she strapped an ammo belt with a 9mm pistol holstered on one side and a six-inch blade sheathed on the other. She whispered, "The guards will be making their rounds again in 25 or 30 minutes, maybe less. When they find their dead comrades and our empty huts, all hell will break loose." She looked at each of us: Tom, Kym, and then me. "Until then, we run."

"Do we know where we're going?"

"Kym has the lead. Sister?"

"South and west," Kym said. She glanced at a sky so dense with stars that an astronomer would have thought he had died and gone to heaven.

"Best compass there is."

"Fine. Let's do it," I said.

We entered the jungle in single file – Kym, Tom, Lyn, and myself – and were immediately surrounded by towering rubber trees, banana and coconuts trees heavy with fruit, and stands of bamboo so thick that nothing larger than a lemur could penetrate them. I had never seen terrain like this, and for a time, we were only able to muster an unsteady gait over slippery ground.

A scent unlike anything I had ever smelled filled my nose. Pungent and strong, it was a mix of decay and wild growth battling heat, rain, and mystery. Kym stumbled upon a broken path that must have been a favorite of animals with sharp hooves and graceful steps. Kudos or elands, I guessed, though wild boars might have been closer. Whatever the source, it allowed us to quicken our pace to something halfway between a jog and a flat out run.

I had been running almost every day for the better part of my adult life. It had become a healthy addiction, as I called it. I craved exercise. I looked forward to the release and the freedom. I used the time to escape the pressures of work, to be sure, but I also found I did some of my best thinking when I was running. For now, one step after another, I was just happy for the conditioning. In the half-light of a gibbous moon and stars long since extinct, I looked at the jungle with unpracticed eyes and realized that a guerilla fighter could have been hiding behind a tree trunk not thirty yards away and I would not have been able to see him.

What the night enhanced, however, was the sense of hearing. A twig snapping, the breeze moving the canopy of branches overhead, a night hunter darting through the underbrush, even the sound of Tom's steady breathing. Tom was a fitness fanatic – he had competed in a dozen iron man competitions over the years; he ran a full marathon every spring – and he did not seem to be having much difficulty staying on Kym's heels.

Compared to Tom and me, the twins moved through the tangle of trees and vines like gazelles. I listened to their footfalls in contrast to that of a couple of ex-football players, and it sounded like a pair of wind instruments among overpowering tympanis. I glanced at Kym. Her stride, much like her mind, was swift and calculating. When I looked at Lyn, I saw a cheetah lurking inside. Loose and effortless, there was also an element of impatience.

What could they be thinking? Twelve hours ago, we had been celebrating a successful tour of Panda City and eating lunch in full view of poppy fields more precious and well guarded than the American Embassy. What had gone wrong? Did they know? Had their protection broken down or had we gotten lackadaisical? Had we been set up or sold out? The daughters of Dr. Chu Zhong Liu must have been wondering the same thing. I was their responsibility. And now the odds of Michael King taking the reins of Panda Pharmaceuticals seemed a pale second to our mere survival. I wanted to assure them that it was not their fault, but I imagined they would insist on shouldering every ounce of the blame no matter what I thought.

The truth was, I blamed myself. I had not fully understood the business landscape here in Thailand, and that was unforgivable. I should have known every inch of our tour, every curve, every potential danger spot. I should have known the enemy better than they knew themselves. I had come here expecting an interview much like a hundred interviews I had conducted – each with its own nuances and idiosyncrasies to be sure, but hardly unpredictable – and similar in most respects to the dozen or so interviews I had been the recipient of over the years.

Nothing about the process had fit my expectations, which surely made it the most enjoyable and challenging interview I had ever experienced. All well and good. Unfortunately, I had been so taken with Panda's pursuit of me and so enamored with the carrots they had been dangling in front of me that I had short sold my preparation. I had been so caught up in the personalities of Panda's esteemed Board that I had forgotten the dynamics of the company itself, the inner workings, and the pitfalls. Shame on me.

In my mind, Thailand was going to be just like Virginia: a love fest. I was Michael King, their sole candidate. It was me or nothing. They had put all their eggs in one basket, and I had a firm grip on the handle. I began to believe my own infallibility. The visit to Thailand and my meeting with Dr. Chu was an afterthought, a cakewalk, a formality. Right, my friend. And now here you are, running for your fucking life and banking on the skills of two 29-year-old women and a fallen friend with a death wish to get you back to civilization.

I heard the rushing water a full half minute before the jungle opened onto a precipitous ravine, a river thirty yards wide, and category 4 rapids based upon the rafting I had done back in Colorado. This was not a river you forged in your waders, but the path we were following merged with a rope bridge that looked about as unsteady as my friend Tom had been almost two nights ago. We came to a halt at the edge of a steep, rocky bank. I gazed down at the crashing water and the huge boulders.

"Look at this fucking thing," Tom groaned. He was not looking at the water or the rocks. He was shaking his head at the sight of the rope bridge.

"I don't know who built this, but it wasn't a 200-pound guy with a fear of heights."

"It's the only way." Kym missed the humor and ignored the irony. "We go one person at a time. Me first."

"Uh-uh." Lyn was already testing the strength of the rope and the tension of the hand lines. "You know this area better than I do. If I die, you still have a chance."

"That's very noble of you, Miss Chu," I said stepping up to the bridge and easing her aside. "But if it can't hold my weight, we're all in trouble."

"I don't follow your logic," Tom said, "But go ahead."

"Mr. King. I have to protest," Lyn said, but I was already inching along the bridge and out over the water. "Please be careful."

I was thinking about my chances if the rope broke. If I landed in the river, the fall would probably kill me. If I held onto the rope, the impact against the cliff face probably would. I was halfway across when I realized the strength of the bridge was not so much the problem as was the wind pushing it from side to side.

I started counting the steps. Four, three, two, one. Solid ground; I never knew it could feel so good.

By the time I turned around, Lyn had already started across, her step sure and steady, a rocket launcher dangling from her shoulder. She kept her eyes forward, something I had not been able to do, and I didn't see how tightly she was gripping the hand lines until she was nearly across. I reached out, took her arm, and helped her take that last dreadful step. The relief of having Mother Earth underfoot again was as much a shudder as a sigh, and I realized how scared she had been. "You all right?"

"I hate heights," she said with a weak smile.

Here was a touch of vulnerability I had not seen before, and it reminded me how much she and her sister meant to me. I drew her close for a moment and rubbed her arms and shoulders until the muscles began to relax.

"Thank you." Lyn averted her eyes. "I'm embarrassed."

"Not me," I said. "Hell, I don't know anyone who can't use a good hug once in a while."

Her eyes came up. "I guess that's true."

"Damn right," I said. "Let's get your sister and Tom across."

We need not have worried about Kym. She was halfway over and nearly running.

"That was fun," she said once she was across, but I could see she hadn't enjoyed it any more than Lyn or I had.

Tom was a full minute getting over and pouring with sweat when we finally hauled him onto dry ground. "That's one I'll leave to the locals, thank you," he said.

"Let's trash this bridge," I said, eyeing the blade Lyn had taken from one of the guards at the camp. "It might buy us some time."

Lyn slashed the hand lines with two quick strokes of the knife and left the bridge dangling. We set out and ran for ten more minutes before I felt the first drops of rain on my face. Two minutes later, Kym pulled up beneath the canopy of a broad-leafed acacia.

"Why are we stopping?" Lyn asked.

"I want to check Mr. King's hand," Kym answered.

"I'm fine," I said, even though blood was showing through the coagulated skin rising from the stump of my little finger. I was on the verge of mentioning the tingling sensation spreading through my hand and forearm, but thought better of it. Instead, I made a joke of it, saying, "At least now we can say that our first human test case was successful."

"Field tested," Tom added.

"Not so fast," Kym said. From her pocket, she took the pouch containing the blood-clotting agent and broke the seal.

"How well do you know this country?" I asked, as she extracted a tiny amount of the lime green powder.

"No one except the natives knows this jungle all that well," Kym admitted. She shook her head, but not at her lack of knowledge about the area. She was staring at my hand. "We've never had to reapply the KP-119 so soon after the initial application. I don't know what to expect. I'm sorry."

"Do it," I said. "You have my permission."

Kym sprinkled powder over the newly formed scab. The powder's color changed from green to pink and then to white, just as before. It burned, worse than before, and then evaporated. The show of blood vanished. Kym slipped me another pain pill. She said, "If we can make it across the Meko River…" She waved a hand in a southwesterly direction. "…We'll be in Chai Buri province and safe. The guerillas won't cross that line."

"The Meko!? Shit, that's nowhere near here, lady," Tom protested.

Kym looked at him with calm eyes. "Five or six hours," she admitted.

"Shit! Five or six hours?"

"Then we'd better stop talking about it and get moving," I said.

"Finally. A few words of wisdom," Lyn said.

In the distance, the echo of rifle shots rolled across the jungle, and the ominous sound sent a chill down my spine. "Our secret's out," I said.

"We've still got a 30-minute lead," Kym said. She swallowed a mouthful of water and suggested we all do the same. "Let's use it."

The tempo she set over the next hour led me to believe that Kym's knowledge of the area was more substantial than she had let on, but the rest of us managed to keep pace. I was high on human endorphins, an opiate made from two fish with enough poison running through their veins to paralyze a giant eel, and the aftereffects of a heretofore untested medicine extracted from the glands of the world's second most poisonous snake. I wouldn't have gone so far as to say I felt like Superman, but I sure wasn't feeling any pain.

Kym paused for the first time in forty minutes at the edge of a wide champaign. A pattern of tree stumps told me the area had been clear-cut. The density of the ground cover, however, told me it had been done some months ago. If someone had considered farming the land, they had changed their mind. I wondered why.

Overhead, the moon was still hidden behind a last breath of clouds, a bit of luck I felt we deserved.

Tom stepped to the edge of the clearing. "What's that sound?" he whispered.

Three seconds passed before I heard the faint hum that he was referring to, but I knew without thinking what it was. "Helicopter."

"You sure?"

"Any CEO worth his salt knows that sound," I said. I had ridden in a hundred choppers over the years and saved probably a thousand hours in commute time. "Best transportation known to man."

"They're north and east of us," Lyn said.

"Which mean they probably haven't found our tracks yet," her sister suggested.

"You can bet they'll have night goggles," Lyn said.

"True. But they won't be able to penetrate the jungle. Not from above."

"Don't be so sure," I said. "Let's get across this thing."

I led. Lyn and Kym followed. Tom brought up the rear. "Remind me to jump next time," I heard him grumble, but it was not the despondent man from two nights ago; this was the dark and sarcastic humor of my longtime friend. Good, I thought. He's back.

There were two discernable paths punching into the jungle once we navigated the clearing. The left fork showed less wear and tear and veered south and west. The right looked as if it led deeper into the mountains to the east. I looked over my shoulder at Kym. "Left?"

"Left."

I pushed as hard as I could, traversing low, sloping hillsides thick with vines and tangles of bracken. At times, the trees were so dense that the path we were following looked as if it were about to be swallowed up. Dozens of small streams pinched into the valley. Somewhere, I thought, they would feed a thirsty river I could only hope would be called the Meko. I was dreaming, of course, and I knew it. We were still hours away. But then, nothing sustained like hope, and if hope kept my feet moving, then so be it.

Eventually, the hills fell away. The plateau that replaced it was perfumed with tulip trees and mango. The moon broke free of the clouds and lit the jungle with shafts of white light. A poet would have had a field day describing the brush of heaven against the forest green. Sure, I thought, if only he hadn't been running for his life with a rocket launcher over his shoulder.

The only sounds were the pounding of my heart and the staccato beat of my companions' footsteps. As quickly and stealthy as we moved, however, I imagined that the echo of four scared and determined people running through the dead of night still carried on the breeze. I just wondered how far and who might be listening. Better to put such thoughts out of your mind, I told myself.

The clearing we came to at the heart of the plateau was not manmade.

Apparently, Mother Nature had seen it as a way of separating one forest from another, and the drug traffickers or the rebel Karen or some brilliant General in the Royal Thai Army had seen fit to turn the clearing into a minefield. Handwritten signs to that effect had been posted by farmers or hunters warning anyone who could read Thai, and Kym made sure I knew it.

She grabbed my shoulder. "Landmines," she hissed.

"Who in the hell puts a mine field out in the middle of fucking nowhere?" Tom could not resist asking.

"This is only the middle of nowhere in the world of Tom Palmer," Lyn reminded him unceremoniously.

"I knew you would say something like that."

"The signs are old," Kym said. "The field might have been cleared, but…"

"Yeah, that's an awfully big but," Tom said.

I studied the clearing. Wide, it was maybe two football fields. But lengthwise, it stretched beyond my sight. "Can we go around it?" I asked.

"I would advise against it, Mr. King," Kym said.

"We'll lose a good hour," Lyn estimated.

"Then we risk a crossing," I said.

Lyn unsheathed her knife. "I'll lead."

"You've done your share of leading. It's my turn." Tom stepped forward. He did a poor man's imitation of Groucho Marx: cigar, eyebrows, even the voice. "And since I have absolutely nothing in the world to live for, it would be an honor and a privilege to step on a landmine for two beautiful women and my old college roommate."

I had to give Tom credit. Here he was in the middle of the Thai jungle with a machine gun slung over his shoulder, running for his life and facing a degree of lawlessness neither he nor I could truly understand given our backgrounds. Men far more ruthless than any he had ever faced in his investment days were pursuing him with a single intent: to kill him. And for what? Because his good friend and savior, Mr. Michael King, had convinced him that a day trip with two lovely women would be good for his outlook. He was scared shitless and doing everything in his power to keep the fear down. I had to give him credit.

"Watch yourself," I said to him.

"That's some real salient advice, Pearl Man. Glad we brought you along." Tom stepped away from the relative safely of the jungle and onto the rocky, pitted terrain of the minefield. He set himself in a low crouch, Lyn's knife in one hand, and his eyes sweeping the ground at his feet. I heard him utter, "Just like the movies."

Lyn followed, placing her feet in Tom's footprints one after another and maintaining a distance of five or ten yards. "If they're out there, Tom, they're probably overgrown with weeds by now, so look for any unusual mounds or new growth."

"More good advice," Tom hissed. I saw him shake his head. "Keep it coming, people. Every little bit helps."

Kym used the template created by Tom and her sister. I was five yards behind, the last duck in the row. The spotlight of the moon created stark silhouettes of our slow-moving train and made us easy targets. I could only pray that the only living things tracking our progress were four-legged nocturnals, but I could not help the tendrils of fear creeping along my back and shoulders. The guerillas would spare none of their resources to recapture two women worth 50 million dollars to them or the man they thought held the key to…

I stopped dead in my tracks. Of course! Human drug testing. How stupid could I be? General Paton had practically spelled it out for me. I had accused him of using the girls we had seen in camp as child prostitutes and sex slaves. But it was a helluva lot more than that. How about using them as guinea pigs for the premature testing of drugs like the fugu fish and lionfish analgesic or the MK-119 blood clotting agent, for example. No wonder they were willing to take my fingers and toes to get the formula. But that couldn't be. Then they would have to have a buyer for the test results, and the only buyer…

"Mr. King!" Kym's voice filtered back to me. I looked up and realized she had put another 20 yards between us. "Are you all right, Mr. King?"

I nodded, took two steps, and heard Tom hiss, "Shit! Got one!"

"You sure?" Lyn whispered.

"Pretty damn sure."

"Find something to mark it with and keep moving."

"Your logic astounds me." Tom fished a white rock from the ground next to his feet and held it up, so we would all know it when we got there. Even from where I was standing, I could see beads of sweat pouring down his face and the scarlet hue of his complexion. "At least now I know what I'm looking for."

"Good. Get moving," I said. "We're like sitting ducks out here."

A series of three mines halfway across the field were less than ten feet apart, and Tom marked them without a word and pushed ahead. Every other step, I stopped long enough to study the dark shadows of the jungle looming along the clearing's foreboding perimeter. It was a dangerous game to play with myself. One part of my mind turned every flicker of light or gust of wind into a man with a gun. A more sensible voice accused my imagination of running away with me, but then nothing about this situation made sense.

We were thirty yards from the jungle when I finally started to relax. What seemed like an hour was probably only 20 minutes.

Tom jogged the last ten feet and collapsed against the trunk of the nearest tree. Lyn threw her arms around him. "We made it!"

Her sister joined them. "Wasn't that fun," Kym said facetiously.

"A million laughs," I said. I slapped Tom on the shoulder. "Well done."

I don't know what came first: the flash of orange I saw out of the corner of my eye or the brittle crack of a bullet leaving the barrel of a very accurate rifle. All I would ever remember was Lyn's chest exploding from the impact and the shower of blood spraying in every direction. She collapsed a split second later, and I shouted, "Gun shot! Get down!"

I threw Kym to the ground and covered her with my body.

Tom hadn't moved. He was staring down at Lyn's inert body and mumbling, "Oh God, oh God, oh God."

"Tom! Get down!" I rolled once, grabbed him by the waist, and dragged him down. A second and third shot missed the mark, but I could hear shouts echoing across the clearing. I helped Lyn onto her back and was almost sorry I had. Sorry for her sister. Blood was gushing from a two-inch wound and the color was draining from Lyn's face. With the last of her strength, she grabbed hold of Kym's arm, as if the connection might save her.

"Sister."

"Lyn. Hold on. Please! Hold on." Kym set to work trying to stem the flood of red, but Lyn stopped her.

"It's too late. Kym. Listen." Kym stopped what she was doing and took her sister's face tenderly in her hands. "Kym. My sister. You were my life. My pride. My hope."

"And you were mine," Kym whispered.

A weak smile was all Lyn had left to give. Then her eyes fell on me. "Take care of my sister," she whispered. "Take care of the family. It's yours now."

Her eyes closed, and her head lulled to one side.

"No!" It was such an impotent thing to say, but all of my emotions went into that one word. Pain, frustration, anger, futility. Yes, but also the respect, affection, and promise that had come so easily to our relationship. Gone.

I watched Kym kiss her sister softly on the forehead, then on the lips. "I love you, Sister. Your love will be with me always. In life and death." Then she removed the opal necklace from around Lyn's neck and placed it around mine. She curled her fingers around the stone and pressed it against my chest. She closed her eyes and bowed ever so slightly.

"I'm sorry, Kym," I said. "I'm so sorry."

"She lived well." Her eyes fell once more upon the lifeless body of her sister, but there were no tears. "She is in a better place now."

"They're coming," Tom said. I glanced up. A dozen soldiers had started across the minefield. They were running as if our capture was worth the risk of a landmine exploding at their feet. "The motherfuckers are …"

And then it happened. An explosion shook the earth, and a spire of dirt and body parts rose from the minefield. I could feel tremors rippling beneath me. "Jesus!" Tom shouted. "They tripped one of the mines."

He jumped to his feet. "They're pulling back. It looks like they're going around."

"Good. Let's go." Kym was on her feet. "They won't risk the minefield now. It should give us 20 or 30 minutes," she said with an icy calm.

"I've heard that before," Tom said, falling in behind Kym, as she looked for a suitable path through the jungle. "The helicopters will be all over us by dawn."

I wanted to say, "If we live that long," but I didn't. If Tom and Kym weren't thinking the same thing, they were thinking something pretty close. "How far is the river?" I shouted.

"Two hours. We'll make it by daybreak," Kym said. She hit upon a walking path that looked as if it had been maintained by hunters, trappers, or someone who passed this way on a regular basis. "This way," she called.

Kym didn't look back. I did. Leaving Lyn like that, alone and uncovered, was not something I could do. I wasn't made like that. I tossed aside my rocket launcher, stripped off my shirt, and laid it across her face and shoulders. I wanted to say something. I wanted to tell her how much the last two days had meant to me. I wanted to let her know that I would never forget our friendship or the sound of her laughter. I wanted her to know that she hadn't died in vain even though I didn't completely believe it.

When I realized that Lyn would have laughed at my sentimentality – in fact, I could almost hear the sound of her laughter – I said, "Goodbye, Lyn," threw the rocket launcher over my bare shoulder, and headed down the path.

~

21

THE SNAP

"Faith is the bird that sings when the dawn is still dark."

I could hear the echo of Tom's footsteps up ahead even if the jungle and the ebbing night hid them from my view.

I ran hard. I was emotionally smashed by what I had just seen, but I could not even begin to imagine what Kym was going through. They were more than sisters, more than best friends and soulmates. They were reflections of one another. Two hands working together. Two minds feeding off the same energy. Two hearts beating as one. Kym would carry on, because Lyn would have insisted that she carry on. She would run with the speed of a gazelle, because Lyn would be pushing her every step of the way. She would fight to the death, because Lyn would be urging her to live for them both. But eventually, the running and the fighting would end and all that would be left was living, grieving, and struggling just to get from one day to the next. I hoped I could be there for Kym when that happened. If we lived long enough. And it was a big if.

I felt a sudden slap of fear. It sent a shock wave down my spine and stole every ounce of air from my lungs. I would have stopped in my tracks had the fear not triggered a desperation that was at least as strong if not stronger. It was the fear of separation and loss, I supposed. I had found two people whose existence meant more to me than even life itself. Two people who had given meaning to this solitary being that was Michael

King. They were the bridge we all looked for; that was what Lauren and Hanna meant to me. As Lyn was to Kym. And now, running through the tangled jungle of an alien world, I could see the bridge fracturing. I could see my wife and daughter reaching out to me, and all I could muster were visions of the bridge between us crumbling, irrevocably. Fortunately, the desperation I felt proved to be a godsend. It got my legs pumping. It made me forget the oxygen deprivation and the cardiac overload.

When I caught up with Kym and Tom, they were hunched over a rambling stream, filling their water skins. "What happened to you? I thought we'd lost you." Tom's eyes narrowed. "Where the hell is your shirt?"

"Lyn," I said. "I didn't want her to be…"

They were both looking at me, but I didn't have the words to finish the thought. Tom nodded, as if finishing the thought wasn't necessary. He put a hand on my arm.

"Yeah. I know," he said and handed me the water skin. "Drink up, my friend."

Kym came to me and wrapped her arms around my shoulders briefly. "Lyn will watch over us. Just like she did when she was alive. I believe that, Mr. King."

"Me, too," I said.

"Take these," she said, putting two of the fugu fish and lionfish pills in my hand.

"Thanks." I washed down the pills. "I hurt all over."

"Give me your machine gun," Kym said. "I have an idea. Help me," she said to Tom.

"What do you have in mind?" Tom asked.

"You'll see."

I watched them prop three sticks into a tripod 18 inches high. They held the corners in place using river rocks. Kym secured the apex with a thin strip of cloth torn from her shirttail. She balanced the machine gun at the apex, released the safety, and jimmied the trigger with a twig. Then they used vines from a nearby bush to camouflage what they had built.

"I get it," Tom said. "Part booby trap, part early warning system."

"Exactly. It should give us an idea of how much of a lead we have," Kym replied.

"That's assuming we have any kind of a lead at all." Tom couldn't help himself.

Kym ignored him. "Our next stop is the Meko."

"They may already be at the river for all we know."

I had heard enough. "We have an hour before dawn," I said. "Let's use it."

"Take us home, Pearl Man," Tom said.

Kym nodded. "Let's run."

We picked up the path again on the other side of the stream. I set out at an easy lope, getting my bearings, and quickly increased our pace to something short of an outright sprint but considerably more than a jog. I didn't know how long I could maintain it. I could feel the remarkable analgesic coursing through my veins within minutes, and this helped.

The moon flashed in and out of the clouds, and beacons of white light pushed through the branches shielding us from the night sky. Twice I heard the distant hum of a helicopter. They had to know by now the course we had chosen, and logic must have told them we were headed for the river. A part of me wanted to take some type of evasive action. Another part told me to go full out for the river and hope for the best. My problem was that I had never been a 'hope for the best' kind of guy. My other problem, however, was that I was completely out of my element. We all were. The Thai jungle was more than just unknown terrain; in the dead of night, it was a whole new world.

By my watch, we had been on the run for 22 minutes when the distant echo of machine gun fire told us the guerillas pursuing us from behind had triggered Kym's booby trap. If our only adversaries were the relentless band we had encountered at the minefield, I thought, we might just make the river. But that was highly unlikely. Not with 50 million dollars in ransom and my fingers and toes on the line. The soldiers under General SiSa Ket Paton were motivated and better organized than that.

I tried to silence my thoughts and concentrate on running. I listened to the footsteps of my two remaining companions. Once, I peeked over my shoulder. Kym was ten paces behind. Her head was high, and her eyes were sweeping the jungle from all angles. If she was wearing down, I couldn't tell it. Tom was hunched over and laboring. His eyes were locked on the path ahead of him, and every ounce of his concentration was on the task of putting one foot in front of the other.

I did not believe in fate or predestination, so I couldn't blame our plight on providence. I did believe in luck, and sometimes bad luck was the order of the day. The beauty of luck was that you could turn it your way by working a little harder or reaching out a little more often. Running a half step faster didn't hurt either, so that was what I did. When I felt the ground rising beneath my feet, I told myself there was good news over the next hill.

The path swept upward through the trees. I heard water tumbling down the hill beside us. The wind blew across our path. Leaves quaked, and branches high above us swayed. The sweat cooled on my skin for the first time all night. The result was a burst of energy that carried me to the top of a thinly forested hilltop. I pulled up, more because I was suddenly aware of dawn's first surprising breath than from exhaustion. A hint of orange light burnished the eastern horizon, but the moon still dominated the night sky, mixing a soft gray hue against the black.

Kym drew up beside me. While I was looking to the heavens, she was stretching a hand out across a wide valley painted orange with poppies in full bloom. They ran for miles in either direction and, by my reckoning, a half-mile or more across. Four-foot-high stalks moved in gentle waves on the dawn breeze. Moonlight struck the huge orange pedals, setting them aglow, like a field of rare gems.

"One of Panda's fields?" I asked.

"No. One of the drug lord's," Kym answered.

"Where are we?" Tom said. "Are we close?"

Kym raised her hand. "Across the field. See it?"

"See what?" Tom asked.

"There," I said. Beyond the field, a band of mist rose above the ground: by my eye, part fog, part spindrift. But I knew you didn't get spindrift like that from a slow-moving, gentle body of water. "The Meko."

"We're going to make it!" Tom grasped his machine gun in two hands and started down the hill to the poppy field. I slung the rocket launcher over my left shoulder and took the Colt .45 from the holster on my waist. I nodded to Kym, and we set out after him.

We ran side by side, she with her finger on the trigger of her machine gun. The rocket launcher dangling across her back looked like a small tree. Tom's words kept ringing in my ear as we slid beneath the barbed wire fence protecting the poppies. "We're going to make it." I wished to God he hadn't said it. I wanted the hope I was feeling as we ran through the tall stalks to push aside the fear, but the fear was too overpowering. The fear, however, was like a catalyst pushing me on. I could also see the desperation in Tom's long stride and the wild swinging of his arms as he willed himself to the other side of field. In another lifetime, Kym would have been Dorothy running beside the Tin Man and the Scarecrow, the land of Oz calling to them in the distance. We would be laughing instead of gasping for air and drowning in our own sweat. There would be flying monkeys pursuing us instead of army troops. And the only sound I would be hearing in the distance would be the voice of the wicked witch instead of the roar of a helicopter to the east and the crack of gunfire behind us.

"Keep moving," I shouted. "Keep moving."

Tom reached the far side of the field three seconds ahead of Kym and me, and we discovered a fifty-foot drop to the blue and white rapids of the Meko River. The mist was thick along the cliff face, and the roar of the water was like thunder rolling across the sky.

Even against the backdrop of the river, I could hear the crush of soldiers pressing toward us from across the poppy field. Platoon-sized groups were moving in from two directions. An attack helicopter charged toward us from the east, and the poppies bent over under the downdraft of its spinning rotor.

"Now what?" Tom was staring down into the rapids. "We're fucked."

"Now we jump," Kym shouted.

"You're crazy."

"It's the only way."

"Let's buy ourselves some time," I said. I threw off my rocket launcher, and Kym did the same. I settled myself on one knee and balanced the gun on my shoulder. When Kym was ready, I said, "This is for Lyn."

"The chopper is mine," Kym replied, her eye to the sight.

When I had the soldiers racing through the heart of the field in the crosshairs of my sight, I called, "Ready? Fire!"

The rockets shot from the launchers with incredible force, and tails of fire drove them toward their targets. Mine exploded at the feet of 25 or 30 onrushing soldiers, lifting a dozen of them into the air and producing a fountain of body parts and poppies ripped from the earth. An instant later, Kym's rocket blew apart the fuselage of the helicopter and put the remains of the craft into a languishing tailspin. The chopper hit the earth with enough force to shake the ground beneath our feet. A combination of gasoline and ammunition burst into flames, and fire mushroomed skyward.

We looped the launchers over our shoulders, turned, and sprinted toward the cliff. Gunfire erupted all around us. I heard a whizzing sound in my ear – like fireflies on a hot summer night – and the pit in my stomach told me it was the sound of bullets ripping past my head, death just inches away.

We threw ourselves off the cliff and out over the raging waters of the Meko River. The fall stole every ounce of air from my lungs; I was that frightened. I entered the water between two boulders. I came down hard, but my feet took the brunt of the fall. I was underwater and breathless. I felt my lungs collapsing. With a panicked surge, I kicked my legs and reached with my arms and hands for the surface. I broke through the water, desperately gasping for air. There was an instant of relief so palpable that I wondered if I hadn't actually glimpsed death.

A split second of disorientation passed. I tried treading water as the current pushed me through the rapids. I thought I caught a glimpse of Tom tumbling through the white water ahead of me, but I couldn't see Kym.

I rode the current through a stretch of fast moving chutes, cracked my elbow and back against a protruding rock, and landed feet-first in a deep, wide pool at the base of the rapids. I came up for air and saw a sandy beach on the far side of the river. Tom was swimming toward it, his stroke labored and his legs heavy.

I turned and saw Kym floating in my direction. She was face down in the water, and her arms were stretched out at her sides. Something was wrong.

"Kym! Kym!" I called.

I started swimming. My first thought was that she had cracked her head on a rock and was unconscious. As I reached out for her, I saw a red film on the water. Oh, God. No!

I grabbed her arm and turned her onto her back. I cradled her head. A show of red drifted up from her chest, and her eyes were closed. I tried to rouse her again. If she was breathing, I couldn't tell. I held her in my arms and side-kicked toward shore.

Out of the corner of my eye, I saw soldiers gathering along the cliff further up river. I looked back toward shore and saw Tom lying face down in the sand. I called his name. "Tom!"

His head came up. "Michael. Goddamn!"

He struggled to his feet and clamored into the water. He took hold of my arm and dragged us toward shore. I collapsed on the sand with Kym's limp body beside me. The rocket launcher was still looped over my shoulder. Could anything be more ironic?

274 ~ King Hurley

"Is she…?" Tom didn't finish his question. He just stared. The hole in Kym's chest was an exit wound. A bullet must have caught her in the back as we were jumping from the cliff. There was no other explanation. "Not Kym."

"The bastards killed her. They killed her," I said. I took Kym in my arms and cradled her on my lap. Tears flooded my eyes. I heard the churning blades of a huge helicopter and the roar of its engines as it dropped into the canyon. I didn't even look up. The fight had gone out of me. But not Tom.

He lunged for the rocket launcher and screamed, "You motherfuckers!"

He dropped to his knee and anchored the weapon across his shoulder. He took aim. A spate of orange fire erupted from the turret gun of the helicopter an instant before Tom was able to pull the trigger. The bullets tore through his chest and drove him onto his back. Blood splattered over the sand and pricked my skin. The rocket launcher fell impotently at his side.

"Tom!" I laid Kym's head gently on the sand and crawled across the beach. Tom's insides were pouring from his chest and stomach, and I was hopeless to stop it. A team of the world's best surgeons could not have saved him.

"Tom." I said his name again, but there was no plea of urgency in the word, only inevitability and total sadness. "Oh, man. I'm so sorry."

Tiny slits appeared where his eyes were, but the life was fading fast from them. "No," he said in low whisper. He gripped my hand. "No, Michael, no. Don't be sorry. You gave me back my life. My dignity. I thank you. I…"

His grip loosened, and his hand dropped to his side. His eyes fell silent.

I laid my head in my hands and rocked forward in the sand. The roar of the helicopter's huge engine and the flutter of front and rear rotors echoed off the canyon walls and vibrated across the water. I heard the chopper setting down in the clearing next to the beach. I wasn't frightened. After seeing Lyn, Kym, and Tom die before my eyes, brave and unafraid, the least I could do was face death with the same dignity.

I stood up and drew myself to my full height. Dust and sand filled the air, and I shielded my eyes with my hand. The helicopter settled in the clearing like a battleship dropping anchor in a calm sea. It was huge. This was not a gunship or an attack chopper. This had all the heft and polish of a presidential escort or a corporate transport. Twin rotors churned to a slow halt above a glistening white fuselage with the words Panda Pharmaceuticals stenciled across the side.

When the rotors fell silent, a sliding door was thrown open along the face of the cabin. A stair ramp dropped down to the ground, and the sound of applause filtered out from within. I heard someone shout, "Bravo, Mr. King. Bravo."

I could hardly have been more shocked when I saw Dr. Chu Zhong Liu, his slender, lean figure silhouetted against the dark interior, emerge from the cabin and step gracefully down the ramp. He was smiling broadly, his head nodding with approval, and his slender hands clapping softly. This did not strike me as a man whose daughter lay dead in the sand at my feet.

Before I could even begin to collect my thoughts, Dr. Philip Chatzwirth and his wife Celia followed Chu down the ramp, she holding his elbow as if they were parading through the lobby of a theater opening, and he in a perfectly tailored suit, his hawkish features and inquisitive eyes gleaming with pleasure. "Bravo, Mr. King." It was his voice I had heard a moment ago, and he repeated the words as if an encore performance was in the offing.

What the hell is going on?

The parade of Panda Board members continued one after another. Judith Susanne Claymore, petite and elegant, gazed at me as if a part of her was surprised at the sight of a living, breathing human being here on this riverbank, and another part was amazed to find that I was the living, breathing human being she had come upon.

Former Virginia State Governor Willy Kellerman, on the other hand, was almost beside himself with joy. He shook his head and chuckled. "I knew it," he called to me enthusiastically. "I just knew it."

Patrick Truit, former Navy Seal and erstwhile CIA Director, fell in next to the Governor. His eyes took in the carnage on the beach and in the water as if this was what the world was all about, and now I was one of its survivors. He gave me a thumb's up and a nod of camaraderie. "Michael," he said.

Last and least enthusiastic was Sir Adrian Glass, molecular biologist and research guru extraordinaire. He was stroking his salt and pepper beard with laconic irascibility, as if his time was more precious than a trip to the Thai jungle could ever be, even if it involved the highest order of Panda Pharmaceuticals' business. Ironically, the smile that touched the corners of his mouth was more like that of a man running into an old friend and wondering at the coincidence.

I didn't feel quite that way. I was more angry than bewildered at this point, because by now I knew that my interview was only now officially concluded. They came toward me with a flush of excitement, like parents and grandparents thrilled with the performance of a child they weren't quite convinced had it in him. If there were two dead people bleeding in the sand next to me, well, it wasn't their mess to worry about.

"Michael. Congratulations, Sir," Dr. Chu said, his arms held open. "You passed our final test. And you did so with flying colors, as they say in America."

Philip Chatzwirth took my right hand and pumped it like a man who knew I would never disappoint him. "Proud of you, son. Proud of you."

I wanted to shout, 'What in the fuck are you talking about? Proud of me? Passed your final test? Are you people crazy?' But all I could manage in the end was, "What are you doing here?" And that sounded foolish even to me. I knew what they were doing here.

"The interview, Michael," Dr. Chu said. "You've completed it to our satisfaction. We've found our new CEO. I know we misled you to a degree, but we felt it was necessary. We felt we had to challenge your mettle in the most difficult of situations. Now we're certain. Now we know what you're truly capable of."

He held up his left hand and made a proud display of the missing pinky finger. Philip Chatzwirth did the same. "You're one of us now," Chu continued. "You proved your inner strength, and you proved it beyond doubt. Most importantly, you proved to us that our family will be safe and secure in your hands."

"To no one's surprise," Governor Kellerman proclaimed. He embraced me like a child embraces a favorite doll, and it took all my will power not to push him aside.

"Did you know we had been kidnapped?" I said, staring at Chu. "Are you saying that whole ordeal was part of some insane interview process?"

Chu gestured toward the helicopter with an open palm. "You're probably starving, aren't you? Let's eat something. You deserve to know the whole story, and we're eager to tell it to you."

"Indeed we are, Sir," Patrick Truit agreed. "Indeed we are."

I didn't move. "That's your daughter lying there dead," I said to Chu, the blood racing through my veins. "I left your other daughter up on that mountain with a bullet hole in her chest. Dead! Your flesh and blood! And now you tell me congratulations? Well done? Let's have a meal and talk about it?"

Dr. Chu was unfazed. "Their deaths served a greater good, Michael. The well-being of the family is more important by far than the lives of any one person. My daughters. Myself. Philip. You. Kym and Lyn knew that. Their deaths were the ultimate sacrifice."

The words rolled off his tongue with surprising ease and with a lack of emotion that made me realize how little my own life meant to them. Kym and Lyn, two of the most vibrant, vital human beings I had ever met, were mere tools. They had served a purpose, dying in a scheme they had no knowledge of. Or had they?

"Did they…?"

Chu must have seen the question on my face even before I began to articulate it. "Did they know? Of course not," he said incredulously. "That would have compromised their participation in the interview process, and their participation was essential."

"Yes, of course. I understand." I pointed at Tom, a friend, comrade, confidante, and unsuspecting dupe. "And Tom Palmer?"

"Come, Mr. King. Let's talk inside," Philip Chatzwirth said. He and his wife stepped forward and took my arms, she gently, and he like a great uncle with at least some affection for a lesser relative.

"We'll put a call into your wife after you've eaten something," Celia promised. "She is a remarkable woman, Lauren is. So is that little daughter of yours. A prize. An absolute prize."

Why did her words send a shiver down my spine? Why had that sounded almost like a threat? I didn't know exactly. I knew I was walking toward the helicopter, and that the Board seemed eager to have me away from my fallen comrades.

"Are Lauren and Hanna back home?" I asked.

"Safe and sound," Celia assured me. "Your daughter is quite proud of that cast on her wrist, by the way. You should have seen how brave she was!"

"We've notified your wife about the slight delay in your travel plans," Patrick Truit said, glancing over his shoulder. "She's anxious to hear from you."

As we approached the loading ramp, my eye fell on the helicopter cockpit. The smiling face looking back at me from the co-pilot's seat belonged to the drunken Australian from Shabu's, the entertainment bar in the PatPong. Lauren was right; they had planned it down to the last detail.

I climbed aboard the helicopter. A crewmember offered me a dry shirt, a towel, and a moment alone in a private stall with running water, a sink, and hand soap. No, I thought as I stared at the reflection in the mirror.

Not private. Nothing – not Shabu's, not the Hummer, not my hotel suite, not my phone conversation with Lauren, not the balcony scene with Tom Palmer – not one thing had been private.

I was still staring at my reflection when the color suddenly drained from my face. No, I thought, that couldn't be! Not Tom.

I stepped out of the stall and found the Board gathered at a table laid out with all the accoutrements of a four-star restaurant, right down to the folded napkins and the polished silver. A place at the head of the table had been reserved for me.

"Join us, Michael," Dr. Chu said graciously.

"Yes, join us, Mr. King," Sir Adrian Glass said with a well-designed smirk. "Time to get your hands dirty. Time to dig into things."

"You can start with Tom Palmer," I said, dropping into my seat and placing my hands carefully on the table. The interview, I told myself, had not ended on that riverbank no matter what Dr. Chu may have said. Play it out, Michael. Play it out. "Hard to plan for a loose end like that, I imagine. I'm talking about Tom's unexpected problems with American Financial and the Feds."

"We had to scramble a bit when we heard you and he were meeting that first morning," Patrick Truit said. "But we looked at it as an opportunity."

"You know the press. Especially here in Bangkok," Judith Claymore added. "They can turn a rumor into a fact faster than anyone in the world."

"All we had to do was plant the seed," Truit said.

Oh, my God, I thought, feeling lightheaded and homicidal at the same moment. "You set it up, didn't you? The whole thing. The fraud charges, the indictment, the headlines." I glanced around the table. "Nicely done. Poor Tom didn't know what hit him."

"It really wasn't that big of a stretch, Michael," Judith assured me. "AmFin had been playing both ends against the middle for a long time. Your friend Tom wasn't unaware of that."

"All you did was give the investment scandal a little shove," I said.

"You handled it well," Philip Chatzwirth said plainly. "Your friend didn't."

"His death wasn't part of the plan," Willy Kellerman assured me.

"I'm sure it wasn't, Willy," I said thickly. I could feel a twitch in my hand as I reached for the water glass. I used the act of drinking to compose myself. "I am curious about a couple of things."

"Ask away," Philip said.

I held up my left hand and drew their attention to the stump where my finger had once been. "General Paton's army."

"Ah, yes. The General and his army," Dr. Chu said. "The army is part of our off-balance-sheet-ventures. Mr. Truit will acquaint you with those ventures over the next few weeks."

Truit shrugged. He gestured toward a metal suitcase resting near the end of the table. He laid his arm across it and drummed the surface of the case with his fingers. "We offered the General a million dollar bonus if he succeeded in killing all four of you."

Truit held my eye. Every muscle in my body was yearning to lunge across the table and wrap my hands around his throat. "We're rather glad he failed," Truit said matter-of-factly. "Rather glad."

"I'm rather glad myself," I said.

"Now the money is yours," Philip Chatzwirth said. "Call it an added bonus."

"Thank you. But what about this?" I displayed my missing finger again. "Why were the General and his men so eager for the fugu fish and lionfish formula?"

"They really weren't," Sir Glass answered. "That was really more a test of your loyalty to the company."

"That makes sense," I said. "They don't perform the human-testing for the drug as General Paton suggested. How stupid of me. They just supply the candidates. It's brilliant. Why should we wait 5 or 10 years to get a product to that stage when we can start testing it on human subjects today? Complete and confidential was how the General put it. After all, life is cheap in Thailand, isn't it?"

"It's not quite as morbid as all that," Sir Glass tried to assure me. "It's purely voluntary."

"Is this before or after they volunteer to be part of the General's child prostitution ring?" I was surprised at how calmly the question had come out.

"The subjects are treated well, Mr. King. I assure you," Patrick Truit said. "We pay them handsomely. We compensate their families."

Sir Glass said, "If we can get a drug on the market even a year ahead of the ridiculous schedules that the various governments around the world set for us, we can save thousands of lives and reduce who knows how much suffering."

"And if it costs a 14-year-old girl her life in the process, well, it was worth it," I said. I could feel my upper lip quiver. Play it out, I told myself. "I admit it. That is one I'll have to get used to."

"Panda Thai bases its operations on practices standard to Thailand, and they are sometimes incongruent with US practices. That's the nature of the international drug community. We all know that. We adjust to it. We have to," Philip Chatzwirth said calmly.

"Life in Thailand is not the same as it is in the States, and life in Bangkok is a far cry from life in New York, Denver, or Charlottesville, Mr. King. For better or worse," his wife offered.

"Celia is right. Life and death are viewed differently here. We can be naïve about it. Or, we can try and understand it."

"An interesting point of view," I admitted. And extremely convenient, I thought. I looked in Philip Chatzwirth's eyes and knew my fate had already been determined. Any hint that I might refuse their offer after the information they had shared with me over the last 40 minutes would lead to consequences I didn't even want to think about. If the lives of Dr. Chu's twin daughters – two women who had given their hearts and souls to the family – could be wiped from the face of the

earth with as little compunction or regret as even their father demonstrated, think of how little my death and the death of my wife and
daughter would mean. How had I gotten myself into this mess? And
how was I going to get myself out?

"If the human testing practice doesn't work for you, Michael," Dr. Chu
assured me, "we'll find an alternative."

Be careful, I thought. Be very careful. "I appreciate the consideration,
Dr. Chu," I told him. I put on my CEO face and looked at Patrick Truit.
"How much opium does General Paton 'steal' from us, Mr. Truit?" I asked
with absolute seriousness. A hush filled the inside of the helicopter, and
I let it settle for a moment. "How much?" I asked again.

"Tell him," Chu said.

"We use less than 60% of our current opium crop on Panda products,"
Truit said to me. "Our storage capabilities account for 10 to 15 percent
more."

"But our facilities are near capacity even with new construction,"
Judith said.

"And the rest?" I asked.

"Our options are limited," Truit admitted.

"For God's sake, Patrick. Just tell him," Sir Glass snapped. He rolled
his eyes in my direction. "The markup of raw opium harvested from our
fields here in Thailand compared to its street value once the refined
heroin is sold in London, New York, or Toronto is 1000 to 1, Mr. King.
The heroin is going to come from somewhere. We can't stop that. And
someone is going to reap the profits."

"And it might as well be us," I said. I even smiled. I pictured Kym lying
out on the riverbank with a bullet hole in her back and wondered how
much she knew about Panda's extracurricular activities. I could not imagine her complicity. Family or not. Which, now that I thought about it, may
have made her expendable. In fact, it may have made her a target. "And
General Paton is a perfect conduit. It's brilliant."

"The money is well spent, Michael," Dr. Chu said. "It funds activities we could never afford without it. It has also made the members of our Board some of the wealthiest men and women in the free world. That wealth opens doors for us we would never have access to otherwise. It gives us the wherewithal to influence policies at all levels of government and allows us to fund the kind of social and educational programs that you and I talked about earlier. And it allows us to live the kind of lives that were once reserved only for royalty. Not a bad perk," he couldn't resist adding.

I nodded. "No, not a bad perk at all." My eyes fell upon his left hand and the missing pinky finger. The scar tissue was purple and knurled. "Guerillas?" I asked. "Drug runners? Mercenaries?"

"Koreans," Chu answered. "Philip and I served together in the war. We were in the same POW camp."

Something told me he was lying. Something told me it was a lie he hated to tell. But whatever was behind it, something told me that it was the beginning of his slide into a world where honor and integrity took a backseat to manipulation and rationalization. He would eventually tell Panda's new CEO the truth. He would have to. It would eat away at him until he did. I may have thought all this, but what I said was, "I don't suppose you had the benefit of MK-119 back then."

"The blood clotting agent!" Chu looked at my hand. He was ecstatic. "It worked."

"Like a charm," I said. I glanced around the table. They were not nearly as surprised as they should have been. "Your daughter was proud of how well it worked. She couldn't wait to tell you. Pleasing you meant more to her than anything."

"She was like that," Chu admitted.

"Does her mother know? Jiang Li? Does she know?"

"She will understand," Chu assured me. "Jiang Li felt very strongly that you were the right man for the CEO position. She'll be happy to know you survived the final test."

"Enough talk," Philip Chatzwirth said with a sudden burst of energy.

"Champagne," he called to one of the attendants. "It's time for a toast."

"A toast," Celia agreed. The attendant materialized a moment later with Dom Perignon on ice. He uncorked the bottle, foam spilled out, and everyone cheered. "Well done!"

Glasses were filled, and everyone looked to Dr. Chu Zhong Liu for the complimentary toast. He raised his glass. "To continuity, progress, and sacrifice." How appropriate, I thought. And what about deception, manipulation, and crime? Well, another time perhaps. Chu's eyes traveled around the table and came to rest on me. "To Mr. Michael King. The new President and CEO of Panda Pharmaceuticals."

The table erupted, and glassed clinked.

Celia Chatzwirth said, "Hear, hear," and Judith Claymore said, "To the future."

I touched the glass to my lips and stared at the men and women who had recruited me, courted me, and tested my resolve like it had never been tested before. How had they come to this place? And how had they determined that I would take my place among them?

"To our new leader's first decision," Philip said with a glass newly topped with champagne. "May it prove insightful and illuminating, as we all know it will."

"What will it be?" Judith asked when the toast had been celebrated.

"I'd like to know that myself," Willy Kellerman said. "What will it be, Michael? That first decision?"

"I'll have to think about it," I admitted. I set my champagne glass aside. It was still full.

"Well, I am afraid you'll have to think about it once we're airborne," Dr. Chu said. "We're all expected at the Prime Minister's palace for dinner. He's eager for an introduction to our new man."

"Don't take off without me," I said. "I left something on the beach. I'll be right back."

"What is it?"

"A gift," I said. "From your daughter."

I stepped down from the helicopter and felt the eyes of seven curious people on me. I wondered if they could feel the fury scorching through my veins. I wondered if they knew, like I did, that the interview would never be over. There would always be a new test, a new question, a new challenge. They lived for it. And, at this point in the game, turning down the position wasn't an option. Neither was walking away from the position in a year or five years or even ten years. These people played for keeps. My life didn't mean a thing to them. And neither did Lauren's nor Hanna's. I was totally fucked.

I crossed the clearing to the riverbank and the stretch of sand where the bodies of Kym and Tom lay undisturbed and unattended. I knelt down at Kym's side. The color had been bleached from her skin, and the bleeding had long since stopped. I pushed a strand of black hair off her forehead and touched her eyelids. I maneuvered the clasp on her opal necklace and removed it from her neck. I put it on alongside Lyn's. "Be at peace, Kym," I whispered.

I glanced over at Tom and thought of his final words. 'You gave me back my life.' I didn't believe it. He deserved to live a lot longer than he had. He deserved to see his kids grow up and maybe even hold a couple of grandkids on his lap. How was I going to explain to his kids that he had died on a beach in some jungle in Thailand with a rocket launcher at his side? I stared at the weapon and thought: What kind of legacy is that?

I stood up and looked back at the helicopter. Seven pairs of eyes watched me. "We have to go, Michael," Philip Chatzwirth called to me. "It's time."

"But I've made my first decision as Panda's new CEO," I replied.

"Excellent! What is it?"

"I've decided we need a new Board of Directors."

I could have predicted their reactions. Chu would be dismissive. Chatzwirth would be impatient. Truit and Sir Glass would be incredulous. Judith and Celia would be angered and hurt. Willy Kellerman would be confused.

"That's not funny, Mr. King," he called.

"I'm not being funny." I bent down and picked up the rocket launcher. The safety was already off. I balanced it on my shoulder. I saw disbelief and fear on all their faces. All except Chu's. On his, I saw a smile of what looked like approval, some sign that I was ridding the earth of an evil he regretted ever creating and, deep down inside, no longer wanted any part of. I pulled the trigger. The rocket shot from the launcher, a stream of fire and smoke in its wake.

It struck the outer shell of the helicopter a split second later. The explosion shook the ground. A ball of fire mushroomed skyward, and trees burst into flames. The chopper blew apart like an egg shattering from the inside out. Fiery fragments of steel and glass rocketed in a thousand directions and fell like the wrath of God all around me. I never moved. The Panda Pharmaceuticals' Board of Directors died instantly. They had no time to be remorseful, but then these were the kind of people who had long since forgotten the meaning of the word. Thank God I wasn't one of them.

I turned toward the river and heaved the rocket launcher into the water. I spent nearly an hour digging a shallow grave for Kym and Tom, knowing their spirits had long since departed the bodies they had once inhabited. Maybe they were in a better place. I could only hope. I used the river to wash the sweat and ash from my body and realized I would probably find my way back to civilization if I just followed its winding course. I was preparing to leave when I saw the glistening silver suitcase reflecting the sun at the edge of the wreckage. I walked toward it. Somehow, the suitcase containing the million-dollar bonus had survived the explosion.

I grabbed it by the handle and set out. The river coursed in a southerly direction, and I could only hope it eventually emptied into the Gulf of Thailand. Midmorning, I spotted a fisherman steering a skiff along the far bank and waved him down. I yelled, "Bangkok," and his eyes widened.

He steered his boat closer. He stared at my suitcase. "Bangkok?"

I nodded and said, "Please," doubting the word meant anything to him.

He shrugged his shoulders as if to say he couldn't very well leave a fool and his suitcase stranded on the banks of the Meko River and eased his boat up to the bank. I leapt onto a deck littered with fishing tackle and two barrels stinking of fish. I bowed with all the dignity I could muster and said, "Thank you."

What he said in return I wasn't sure, but the smile that creased his pinched and wrinkled face was genuine. I found a place off the bow and sat down next to the suitcase. I stared out at the passing water and a jungle that seemed to go on forever.

The skiff had been fitted out with a tiny outboard motor, and it pushed us down the river only slightly faster than the current itself. It didn't matter. I was numb and just grateful to be moving.

We passed a dozen other fishing boats, and my pilot seemed to know them all by name. The first sign of civilization was a village with two dozen bamboo huts set at the confluence of the Meko and another nameless river. The hills diminished. The jungle began to thin. Rice fields appeared on either shore, and the skyscrapers of downtown Bangkok peeked above the horizon. The fisherman pointed, and I nodded.

The farms of rural Bangkok stretched for miles; I thought they would never end. On the outskirts of the city's industrial district, marked by factories, warehouses, and tall chimneys belching smoke into the air, the Meko merged with the Chao Phraya River. The traffic on the river increased dramatically, but the old fisherman was unfazed. I could see that he had spent many hours scurrying between barges, freighters, and houseboats. When I called out, "Soi 34," he seemed to know exactly what I was talking about and responded with a grunt and a nod.

I recognized the Harum Mosque first and then the pier where Kym and Lyn's speedboat had been docked that first day. The sight of it only made me sad. The fisherman docked his tiny craft at the pier and bowed as if the honor of our voyage had been his. I bowed in return.

Before stepping ashore, I handed him the silver suitcase, bowed again, and said, "Thank you."

He looked at me with a hint of confusion, and I used hand signals to indicate that the case was a gift from me to him. I was halfway to Charoen Krung Road when I glanced back over my shoulder and saw him peeking at the money inside.

"Spend it wisely," I whispered and trudged up the road to the Pearl Magnolia Hotel. I was shirtless and bloody, and the look on the face of Mr. Somporn Devakulu, the hotel's general manager, made me wonder if news of Dr. Chu's death had already reached him.

His first words told me different. "Mr. King! What happened, Sir?" he asked, keeping his distance.

"There's been an accident," I said. "You'd better call the authorities."

"What kind of accident?"

"A bad one," I said. "I need to clean up, Mr. Devakulu. Are my clothes still in the suite upstairs?"

"But of course."

"Let me know when the police arrive. And call the American Embassy for me. I think I'll be needing them."

The Thai police arrived long before I had a chance to shower. An attaché from the Embassy wasn't far behind them. I told them the story from the time we left the hotel for the Panda Thai lab near Nakhon until the time the fisherman dropped me off at the dock. I told them where they could find the remains of the helicopter and blamed General Paton's army for shooting it down. I repeated my story four times to four different arms of the Thai government. I was confined to the Presidential Suite for 24 hours while my story was confirmed.

The attaché from the American Embassy demanded an apology for the trauma I had suffered and insisted upon my immediate release. I think the Thai government was glad to see me go.

∾

22

THE CHOICE

*"If you can just observe what you are and move with it,
then you will find that it is possible to go infinitely far."*

T he crystal clear water of the Snake River in Wyoming looked nothing like the muddy water of the Meko in Thailand. The Snake was a blue so vibrant that it made me think the sky and the water had somehow come together in the perfect marriage. The river coursed along the valley floor at the foot of the Teton Mountains, a view almost too spectacular for words.

It was the ideal setting for my fly-fishing operation. I called it Opal Ventures. I ran my business out of a storefront in Jackson Hole. Lauren had hung up her shingle in an upstairs office across the street: Attorney-at-Law. Hanna's pre-school was located in a converted two-story house a block away, and I walked her to school each day with her warm hand embraced in mine. We were in the process of building a cabin at the confluence of the Snake and Heart Rivers where the cutthroat trout regularly grew 15 to 18 inches long and the occasional rainbow weighed in at three pounds. My specialty was packing in five or six avid fisherman on horseback into the best fishing holes the river had to offer.

Twelve months had passed since my interview. I had resigned from Peak Pharmaceuticals my first day back in Boulder. My new enterprise had already booked three excursions. I had six more planned for next spring. I had grossed almost $15,000 since opening my doors. I continue to wear

Kym and Lyn's opal necklaces as a reminder of their vitality and their love of life. Lauren, Hanna, and I are the happiest we have ever been, and I awake each day with a renewed energy. I have no stockholders, no Board of Directors, and no interviews to worry about.

THE END

Following is a list of quotes used in *The Interview* and their attributions, with thanks from the author.

CHAPTER 1 - The Call
"It was the best of times, it was the worst of times."
– Charles Dickens

CHAPTER 2 - The Offer
"Rejoice! Rejoice! You have no other choice."
– Stephen Stills

CHAPTER 3 - The Board
"To know one's self, one should assert one's self."
– Albert Camus

CHAPTER 4 – The Show
"He not busy being born is busy dying."
– Bob Dylan

CHAPTER 5 – The Perk
"It is our light, not our darkness, that most frightens us."
– Marianne Williamson

CHAPTER 6 - The Offer
"If you try sometimes, you might find you get what you need."
– Mick Jagger

CHAPTER 7 - The Final Step
"Granted that I must die, how should I live?"
– Michael Novak

CHAPTER 8 – The Journey
*"I may not have gone where I intended to go,
but I think I have ended up where I needed to be."*
– Hermann Hesse

CHAPTER 9 - The Escorts
*"If it is thought that men are made by nature unequal,
then where do we turn for understanding?"*
– Seneca

CHAPTER 10 - The Estate
*"The wild geese do not intend to cast their reflection;
the water has no mind to receive their image."*
– Zenrin poem

CHAPTER 11 - The Palace Dinner
"In the great future, you cannot forget your past."
– Bob Marley

CHAPTER 12 - The Dance
*"Do not dwell in the past, do not dream of the future,
concentrate the mind on the present moment."*
– Buddha

CHAPTER 13 - The Dojo
*"Remember, we all stumble, every one of us.
That's why it's a comfort to go hand in hand."*
– Emily Kimbrough

CHAPTER 14 - The PatPong
"Do not wait for the last judgment. It takes place every day."
– Albert Camus

CHAPTER 15 - A Friend in Need
"Adversity introduces a man to himself."
– Anonymous

CHAPTER 16 - The Lab
"Everything has beauty, but not everyone sees it."
– Confucius

CHAPTER 17 - The Opium Fields
"Once the game is over, the king and the pawn go back into the same box."
– Italian Proverb

CHAPTER 18 - The Road Home
"All know the way, but few actually walk it."
– Boddhidharma

CHAPTER 19 – The Camp
"Fear and survival. If you think you were born with anything else, think again."
– Steve Shiver

CHAPTER 20 - Jungle Run
"Our deepest fear is that we are powerful beyond measure."
– Marianne Williamson

CHAPTER 21 - The Snap
"Faith is the bird that sings when the dawn is still dark."
– Rabindranath Tagore

CHAPTER 22 - The Choice
"If you can just observe what you are and move with it, then you will find that it is possible to go infinitely far."
– J. Krishnamurti

ACKNOWLEDGEMENTS

To Mark Graham, thank you for helping make The Interview a reality. It was a miracle to find an individual that was a perfect artistic partner and a wise sage. Thank you also for introducing me to Nick (the amazing artist who created the cover), and to Nobuko, the beautiful heart that helps inspire your ideas.

To Hazel, for your endless love that you have given me since I was born on your birthday. You have shown me what true love is between a mother and a son. Your hugs have inspired me to make it through the toughest days and your unquestionable love has given me the courage to share my love without boundaries.

To Michael, your memory is with me every single day. Your quiet strength and love for music and gardens has helped me look at the world with kind eyes.

To Carole, thank you for being my rock in the most turbulent waters and my closest friend who never stops loving and caring. You have given me the strength, the support and the love to be forever excited about the future.

To Emma, thank you for igniting my senses with the love and sweetness found between a father and daughter. You amaze me every single day with your love. I am excited to see you grow into a dynamic, loving and beautifully spirited woman.

To all my dear friends and family, thank you for all your love and support. It has given me the strength to always look at the world with hope and courage.

∽